DAVID

SORRENTINO

*

BACK TO

THE GARDEN

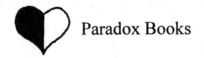
Paradox Books

For Thomas Sorrentino

1952 - 1972

Sell the kids for food
Weather changes moods
Spring is here again
Reproductive glands. . .
We can have some more
Nature is a whore
Bruises on the fruit
Tender age in bloom

—Kurt Cobain, 1991

All that's sacred comes from youth

—Eddie Vedder, 1994

Back to the Garden

PROLOGUE

I first met Tommy Redivo in the fall of '91. At the time, my car was in the shop with transmission problems, so I placed an ad in the Cahill State University paper hoping to find another student living in or around Oakwood that I could bum a ride to school from. Tom called me up a couple days after the paper came out; a Monday night to be precise (I remember 'cause I was watching *Monday Night Football* while we were talking). He told me he lived with his family in town— a stone's throw away, actually— and that it would be no trouble giving me a lift.

"I'll pay you for gas and for your trouble," I told him. "But, uh, I can't afford alot."

"Forget about it," he answered. "I mean, it's not like I'm going out of my way or anything."

The next morning, he pulled up in his black '85 Camaro about fifteen minutes later than scheduled.

"You're Will Flaherty?" he asked as he pushed open the passenger door.

"That's me," I said as I slid in. He was listening to Nirvana on the car stereo that morning— it was the first time I'd ever heard them. He wore a beat up, black Rolling Stones concert T-shirt, blue-jeans, and black Reebok sneakers. . . Being a life-long geek, my cool guy radar went crazy.

"Nice car," I remember telling him.

"Thanks," he replied.

It gets kind of foggy, the rest of that conversation. . . As I recall, there were the few obvious questions about my car troubles to go along with the obligatory guy-talk about sports, but outside of that, I guess we didn't say much. What can I say? My parents trained me really well in my anti-social skills.

Seriously though, things were really falling apart for me back then, and I guess I just wasn't in the mood to try and make casual conversation with some guy I had just judged as your typical pseudo-rebel— the same kinda guy who had snubbed me and generally made my life miserable all through high school.

You see, in addition to the car, I was also having a bitch of a time with this introductory course on philosophy— a course I never meant to sign up for in the first place except that by the time I got my ass in gear with registration, it was one of the few courses left open; so I had no choice but to take it if I wanted a full schedule. And by the time I realized there was no way to keep from flunking, it was too late to get a full tuition refund, which meant I'd have to go to my parents on hands and knees, begging for extra money for the following semester— like we really needed something else to argue about. . . Plus, it was a real bad allergy season and my sinuses were killing me. And of course, the Giants were having their usual post-championship season of shit football. Oh yeah, and the week before I had accidentally washed my red shirt with my whites; leaving me with a collection of all-pink underwear.

But the worst of it was with my girlfriend, Jen. I guess you'd call her an average-looking girl; certainly not gorgeous. Come to think of it, she didn't have much in the way of personality, either. But at the time, I didn't realize any of this because I was so overwhelmed that *any* member of the opposite gender would find *me* attractive, it blinded me. All that mattered was that I had a girl. Any girl. It made no difference who.

Anyway, two weeks after the semester started, she had suddenly informed me, via the U.S. mail, that she was seeing another guy she had met in her chemistry class. I was crushed, though I can't say I hadn't seen it coming— she had gone to school in Connecticut, while I had stayed in Jersey, so it was only natural that we'd drift apart. Still. . . *two weeks?*

In retrospect though, maybe what was really bugging me was that I had always imagined I would be the first to find someone else and she would be the one wondering how she was supposed to go on. Talking about it now, it's kind of embarrassing, but we were each others first and only, and I guess I thought I was in love. Anyway, the bottom line was that I had been dumped.

Getting dumped sucks.

So after telling you all this, you can imagine how difficult I was to get along with at the time. And things remained real uneasy between Tom and me those first couple of days. . . up until Friday. When he picked me up that morning, he was listening to Howard Stern on the radio, and I remember I found it kinda strange that he hadn't listened to him on any of the three days before. Anyway, Howard was really on fire that particular morning; screaming at Gary, Stuttering John and all the interns. And every time Fred would play that stupid cart of "Baba Booie, Baba Booie," I would have to stifle a laugh.

"You a Howard fan?" he asked me as I tried to surpress my laughter for what had to be like the hundredth time in ten minutes.

"Yeah, actually," I said. "I am."

"You must be. This is the first time I've seen you smile." I wasn't sure whether or not he was taking a shot at me, but the remark did make me feel a tad uncomfortable.

"His show is probably the only thing that makes me laugh out loud," I said, trying to ignore his last comment. "How come you never put him on before?"

"Well, y'know, Howard says alot of off-color things and I wasn't sure if you were one of those politically correct types who might get offended."

"So what made you decide to put him on today?"

"I don't know," he said. "I just figured that since you were acting like such a stuck-up asshole anyway, why should I care if you get offended?"

Ouch.

"You think I'm a stuck-up asshole?" I asked him, more than a little stunned.

"You're sure acting like one," he said with a semi-shrug. "But you tell me: are you an asshole?"

Of course, looking back on it, he was a hundred percent right. Still, right or not, maybe you think stuff like that to yourself, or maybe you say it when you're really pissed and you've had all you can take, but you don't just spit it out like nothing; like he just did, to people you don't even really know. It was an incredible thing. I mean, there was zero anger in his voice. His tone was totally flat, totally matter-of-fact. It was weird, but at the same time, he laid it all on the line and I had to respect that.

Plus, I couldn't tell if he might just snap and kick the shit out of me.

"I like to think I'm not," I answered meekly.

"So what's with the Helen Keller impression the last three days?" he asked me. "Something's definitely *up* with you, man. What is it? Problems at home? Your parents?"

I shook my head no.

"Come on. I always say there are two types of parents: the kind that are divorced and the kind that should be. Which type you got?"

"The latter," I said, cracking a smile. "But they're not the real problem at the moment. Usually, but not this time."

"Then it's a girl." I offered no verbal confirmation, but he knew he had hit the nail on the head. "So what's her name?"

I don't know what made me decide to spill my guts. Maybe since he was being so up-front with me, I felt compelled to be up-front in return. Or maybe I just needed to get all that shit out. But whatever the case, I told him all about Jen. And when I finished talking, he got real quiet. I remember really regretting opening my mouth in the first place and being sure that he thought I was the world's biggest dork— shit, I would've rather he had still thought of me as an asshole.

6

Then, without a word, he pulled over and parked the car. This is it, I thought. He's gonna really kill me now. He's decided I'm too much of a pussy to live and he's gonna kill me.

"Have you ever thought about what this means, Will?" he asked at last, pinching the crucifix he wore around his neck.

"Not. . . deeply," I said. It felt like a trick question.

"You know what it means to me?"

I shook my head no.

"It means that nothing ever ends."

. . .

"Huh?" I cogently offered.

"I mean, to see things in terms of beginnings and endings is a mistake. Nothing ends. Life doesn't even end in death. That's what this tells us."

Now, usually, when people start talking Jesus and I zone right out. But this was different, somehow.

"We perceive things in a linear form," he continued, "but that's not the way things really are. It's the classic juxtaposition of the eastern and western mind. It's like looking at a beautiful diamond one facet at a time instead of seeing the entire jewel. If what you had with this girl was beautiful, it doesn't cease to be beautiful just because it's over. What you shared isn't erased."

Incredibly enough, I heard him. Really heard him— in a way that a cynical, smart-aleck eighteen year old isn't supposed to hear anyone. I remembered some of the times I had with Jen again, only this time I remembered how things felt at the time, rather than how they felt in the context of having lost her. And in that brief moment, they became happy memories for me once more.

"I guess you've been through it before, huh?"

"We've all got the same story," he told me in an almost bored tone. "Sometimes the style is Hemingway; sometimes Chandler; sometimes it might even be Joyce. But the plot doesn't really change: boy meets girl, boy loses girl. . . boy gets really depressed and consumes copious amounts of alcohol."

"Is that *your* story?"

"Well. . . More or less."

"So, that's it? Doesn't anybody get a happy ending?"

"Of course not. Most of us end up marrying someone we don't really love out of fear of being alone. . . Then we decide to have kids we don't really want because we can't figure out any other way to lend meaning to our pathetic, little lives."

I actually laughed at this. Recounting it now though, it sounds sad— not funny at all. Maybe you had to be there.

"Y'know, I really don't feel like sittin' through classes today. . . Whaddaya say we blow off school?"

The suggestion caught me a little off-guard.

"Uh, sure," I said, "why not?"

So we hit this coffee shop about a mile off campus. Quaint, little place with hand-painted pictures of Disney characters hanging on the walls— a little surreal sitting there with a guy wearing a black shirt that said "fuck parental guidance" in white lettering on the front. There were two waitresses; both knew Tom by name. He ordered a cup of tea (two sugars) and a corn muffin. I had a cup of coffee, black, and a cheese Danish.

"How did you get into this religious stuff?" I asked him right after we were served. "Are you, like, born again or something?"

"Ah, no."

"But you believe in God, right?" I don't know what made me decide to ask that particular question. It just seemed like the next logical step in the conversation.

"I believe a God exists, yes. Assuming we both mean the same thing by the word 'God.' " He smiled. "I do know that God's existence wouldn't matter if I didn't believe it, first."

"Um, yeah. But how did you come up with that stuff about beginnings and endings and Jesus and all?" This had to be the first serious discussion about theology I had ever had with anyone and I wanted to keep it going.

"It's a little bit of zen and a little bit of Kierkegaard— there's this great line from his journals about how the stone at the entrance to Christ's tomb was the philosopher's stone, 'cause after it was rolled back, it gave all the philosophers so much to think about. When I first read that, I had this real epiphany about where things begin and end." He stopped a moment to blow softly at his tea. "The diamond analogy though, I swiped that from 'The Watchmen.' "

"The comic, you mean?"

"By Alan Moore, yeah."

"You're kidding." I was more than a little surprised. "I knew it sounded familiar! I loved that series! You collect?"

"I used to. The problem is that since I've moved around alot, most of my old comics got conveniently lost in transit by my mother."

"I know how you feel— my parents are constantly bugging me to quit wasting my money on it." I took a bite of my Danish. "What are your favorites?"

"I prefer the old Marvels from the 70s. Y'know, like *Howard the Duck*, *Master of Kung-Fu*, *Warlock*, *Omega*, *Killraven* . . ."

"No shit!" It was too much. A minute before, he was the Maharishi and I was one of the Beatles; now he was suddenly one of my old nerd-buddies from the junior high school comic book club. "Me and this guy I know once played this game, *Gamma World*, and we based all the characters we created on the cast of *Killraven*."

"You game, too?" he asked, putting his tea cup back just as he was about to take a sip.

"Yeah," I said, rather astonished. "What do you play?"

"Everything. *Gamma World*, D & D. . ."

"D & D? What setting?" I asked.

"*Greyhawk*," he answered. "That was the only setting they had when I got started."

"Oh, man," I said, slouching back in my seat.

"See? All this time you've been giving me the silent treatment, we could've been swapping monster stats."

"I know. I'm such a jerk."

"Just out of curiosity," he said, getting back to that postponed sip of tea, "who played Killraven?"

"I did. For the most part. We'd swap off, now and then. My buddy preferred being the GM, most of the time."

"Did you save all the character stats?"

"Oh, sure."

"We've definitely got to play together," he said. "As long as I'm Killraven, of course."

"Oh no. I'm Killraven, you're M'Shulla."

9

"Come on, mud brother." Killraven and M'Shulla always referred to one another as "mud brother"— a reference that maybe six other people on the planet would've caught. "You can be M'Shulla *and* Old Skull."

"I'll tell you what," I said with a laugh, "you can be K.R. and I'll be M'Shulla if you help me out with this one thing. . ."

"Shoot," he said, with a mouthful of corn muffin.

"It has to do with philosophy. Since you've obviously taken some courses, do you think maybe you could help me out with Intro to Philosophy? I'm gonna flunk if I don't turn things around in a hurry."

"I'd be happy to help you," he said. "But studying philosophy is no walk in the park— you can't sleepwalk through your course work like the business majors do. You sure you're up to it?"

"Um. . . I think so."

"Knowledge is like food, you know— man needs it to sustain himself. They say give a man a fish, he'll eat for a day; teach him how to fish, he'll feed himself forever." He took a dramatic pause, holding that still-steaming cup of tea before his mouth. "I intend to make a fisherman of you, William."

We both went silent for a minute, but this time it was a comfortable silence. And as I sat across that table from Thomas Peter Redivo, the future voice of my generation (and Lord, would he ever strangle me if he heard me refer to him that way!), I remember thinking how I couldn't have possibly read him more wrong with my first impression. I realized then that getting to know this guy would be a challenge. An adventure. And I looked forward to it.

That night, my father told me I'd be getting my car back Monday. He had decided that rather than overhaul the transmission, the mechanic was just going to shut off the overdrive. All that meant was that the car might be a little slow to accelerate on the highway and that it might eat up more gas— other than that, there were no problems with me driving it. So just like that, I had my car back again.

Of course, I didn't bother to tell Tom until about a month later.

Y'know, it's funny. I just realized that I described my first impression of him as "typical pseudo-rebel." But "typical" would be the last word I'd ever use to describe him now. He was something else. A species unto himself.

CHAPTER I

I'm in shock because Meredith Trembly has answered the door. Could I have taken down the wrong address?

"Yes?" she asks, standing in the doorway. I can hear the television, inside.

"Uh . . . Hi. I was looking for Tommy Redivo's house?"

"Don't worry." She motions for me to come in. "You've got the right place."

I'm not surprised that she doesn't recognize me. Almost no one I went to high school with would. But I certainly remember her. I only took that one class with her— trig, our junior year— but it was enough. I sat behind her every day and would watch her as she crossed and uncrossed her long legs. Watch her, as she would toy with her long, light-brown locks. Watch, as she would nibble, seductively, on the eraser at the end of her pencil.

"He's upstairs," she says as she closes the door. "Follow me."

"Thanks."

I stop for the briefest moment as we pass by the hallway mirror to check myself. If I had only known I'd be seeing Meredith Trembly today, I would've taken a little more care in choosing my clothes instead of just throwing on this sweatshirt and these jeans. My hair looks awful, too. Thin, stick-straight, brown hair. And I absolutely hate my eyes. Totally ordinary, blank, brown eyes. Unlike Tom's, they bespeak no mystery, no hidden torment, nor any of that secret suffering that never fails to hypnotize all the girls back on campus.

"The emperor is in his room," Meredith tells me. "He probably didn't hear the doorbell."

"No prob."

I watch with hunger as she walks up the stairs ahead of me in her long-sleeved tunic top, smooth knit pants and beautifully naked feet. Her hair is cut a bit shorter than she had it in that math class two years back, but if anything she's even hotter now. Less a girl and more a woman. She must be Tom's girlfriend (that son of a bitch), but what am I supposed to say? Should I just ask her what she's doing here? I keep hoping she'll explain it herself, but she just continues up the stairway without a word.

Upstairs, the air is an indistinct mixture of shampoo, conditioner, moisturizing lotion, nail polish remover, and several other fragrances I don't recognize. Kinda like what I've always fantasized a sorority house would smell like.

"In there," she says, pointing to the door to my immediate left. Then she goes down the hall and disappears. Weird. Where is she going? I should've tried to make some conversation with her. A little late now. Christ, I am *such* a ballless wonder. Finally, I rap on the door.

"Will?" Tom asks as he opens the door. He's in a T-shirt and sweat pants, looking like he just rolled out of bed. "I'm sorry. I didn't even hear the bell ring. C'mon in."

Tom sits down in front of his stereo and begins sifting through a stack of CDs. The room's a beautiful mess: scattered on the floor are various books, some old copies of *Rebel, Seventeen, YM, Sassy, Teen*; a bunch of audio cassettes, a few register receipts, scraps of notebook paper and, propped against the stereo cabinet, a *Golden Crisp* cereal box. He has some cool posters up— Hendrix, Joplin, Lennon... An old movie poster of *Enter the Dragon*, with Bruce Lee prominently displayed. Above the head of his bed though, he has this huge poster of. . . himself? Bizarre. I almost ask about it, but than think better.

"Cool digs."

"What's that?"

"Your house. It's nice."

"Thanks." He begins leafing through some CDs. "Any requests, mud brother?"

"Ah, not really." His sweat pants have holes in the knees and the logo on his t-shirt is so faded I can't read it. He's neither showered nor shaved yet.

"You look like you've been camped out here for a month. Next, you'll be letting your nails grow and obsessing about microscopic germs."

"Well, I haven't started *Ice Station Zebra* yet. . ." He puts in a disc of the Clash. I pause a moment before asking the obvious question.

"So, uh. . . how do you know Meredith?"

"Meredith? She's my sister."

"Your sister?"

"Half-sister, technically," he says, crawling across the floor, back to his bed. "Hey, that's right— I guess you two graduated from Oakwood together."

"Yeah. Took one class together, actually. I don't think she knew me, though. When she answered the door, I mean." Tom wriggles under the covers and buries his head under the pillows.

"Aaaargh. What day is it, again?"

"It's Saturday. Two days after Thanksgiving. 1991. . . A.D. Um, did I wake you, just now?"

"No, of course not," Tom replies. "Well, maybe."

"Late night last night, huh buddy?"

"Early morning's more like it," he says with an evil grin. "You shoulda come along, Will. It was real."

"I'm not really the stay-out-til-dawn type."

"Will, Will, Will. . . I'm tryin' to help you break out of that shell of yours, but you've gotta work with me, man."

"Yeah, yeah. I know."

Before now, the only other friend I ever really had was Arnie Fletcher. He and I grew up together. We bought our comics together. Played with our *G.I. Joe* action figures together. Watched *He-Man* every afternoon after school at four o'clock on channel five together. We saw our first movie without our parents together (it was *Ghostbusters* back in June of 1984, when we were eleven years old). And, in later years, we'd play D&D together. Our junior year, we even talked about going to the same college, joining a frat together and nailing a different girl every night of the week. Of course, we were both losers, so we could only talk about getting laid— neither one of us could imagine it actually happening.

But then in our senior year, the impossible happened: this girl— Jenny Dole— demonstrated a spontaneous interest in me. I couldn't believe it. Of course, I immediately blew off Arnie and spent all my free time with her. My every waking thought was consumed with trying to schedule time alone with her, in either her house or mine, so we could make out. It didn't take long for Arnie to get pissed off and give up on me. Near the end of senior year, we stopped bothering to even say "hello" when we'd pass in the halls.

I had a feeling at the time that the day would come when I'd regret not having Arnie for a friend and, sure enough, after Jen broke up with me, it was like I was a leper. I was left without a friend in the world, not a one. Just over a month ago, I could so easily see myself growing old and dying alone.

Then I met my mud-brother.

Tom is like the first legitimately cool person to ever even acknowledge my existence, let alone call me his friend. But he's more than just cool— it's like he's so cool, he actually spits in the face of coolness. He reads comic books, plays D&D, even spends time with a nobody like me and he's *still* cool. It's like he rewrites the definition of cool every day. That's why he's my hero.

"So," I say, "I guess you're not up for goin' out anywhere today, huh?"

"Not really. You don't mind if we just hang at the house, do you?"

"Hey, I don't mind. It's cool for me."

15

"Let me give you fair warning though, William: next time I go out to light up the town, I'm takin' you with me. Even if I gotta drag you kickin' and screaming." He shoots me a serious look.

"Alright, alright, I gotcha."

Suddenly, through the crack of the door bursts this gray blur, flying into the room and darting under Tom's bed. Caught wholly off-guard, I stumble back a step. A collie-mutt follows into the room quickly after, stabbing its head in the dusty darkness beneath Tom's mattress. The dog barks in wild frustration, unable to fit completely under the bed frame.

"What *is* this?" Tom seems to ask no one in particular. He looks down and sees the dog still has a leash attached to her collar. "Tempest— did you lose Tiffany again?"

A little blonde girl, can't be more than eight or nine, comes tripping through the doorway. "I held on to her the whole time we were out! Honest!" It takes her a moment to notice me there.

"Oh, hi!" she says.

"Hi."

"William," Tom says, reaching down and unlatching the dog's leash, "this is my sister, Tiffany. And my dog, Tempest." She smiles and waves at me with an eloquent roll of her fingers, like British royalty. Tom snaps his fingers and the dog jumps up on the bed and lays down next to him. "Cowering beneath the bed is Fido the cat."

"His name is not Fido!" Tiffany loudly corrects, stroking her long hair away from her face. "It's Sigmund!"

"Sigmund?" I ask, as Tiffany gets down under the bed to retrieve the cat.

"Meredith named him after her personal hero, Sigmund Freud," Tom explains. Tiffany emerges from beneath the bed, cradling the cat. "I wanted to name him 'Fido.' Wouldn't that be a cool name for a cat? 'Fido'?"

"You are so weird," Tiffany states as she leaves the room with Sigmund/Fido. Tom scratches Tempest behind her ear and the dog cocks her head toward him, emitting a mumbled kind of growl that sounds as if she's trying to spit a word out.

"So," I say. "You have any more sisters?" Tom looks up at me.

"Do you really wanna go there? Do you really wanna hear my whole sordid family history?"

"Well, yeah," I answer with a shrug.

"Let's head down to the kitchen and I'll make us some popcorn. This might take awhile."

He leads me back downstairs, back through the front hall, through the living room— the room that I heard the television in, before. There's a girl on the couch who. . . well, she has to be Tiffany's twin sister, as they look exactly alike, except she's got her hair cut a little bit shorter.

"Will, this is my sister, Samantha. Sam, this is Will."

"Hi," I say.

"Hi," she responds, softly. She's wrapped in a quilt, resting her head on a pillow. She's wearing a black Champion sweatshirt that I recognize as Tom's. Her hands only make it halfway through the sleeves.

"She and Tiffany are twins," Tom says. "Obviously."

"Well, duh."

"Wise ass," Tom mutters. I follow him into the kitchen.

"I'll try and trim as much fat outta the story as I can," he says. "Gonna tell it in less than three minutes. A new record." After he puts a bag of popcorn in the microwave, the two of us sit down at the kitchen table.

"Y'know," he sighs, "if this were a sitcom, we would be in the awkward pilot episode now."

"Come again?"

"You know— the pilot episode? The premiere show where all the action and dialogue is so transparently contrived just to introduce the principal characters to the audience?"

"Right, right. You're gonna give me the principals."

"Exactly," he starts. "We'll begin with our dashing hero: moi." I laugh. "I was born in '69. At the time, my mother was 17 years old and still in high school."

"You're parents are divorced, I guess?"

"They never got the chance to get divorced. Or married, for that matter," Tom says. "My father died in a car accident three months before I was born."

17

"I'm sorry, man." Jeez. I wish I could think of something more to say.

"Don't sweat it. It's something I worked through a long time ago. For the most part." For a moment, I can feel that veneer of his almost begin to crack. Almost. "He was a hell of a character, my old man. I've heard alot of stories about him; got alot of pictures, too. You saw the one on the wall, in my room."

"That was your father? Damn! I woulda swore that was a picture of you!"

"Everybody says that," A big smile comes over his face. "Do I really come off like that big an egomaniac? Like I'd put up a giant, poster-size picture of myself on my own bedroom wall?"

"What do I know, man?" I answer, feeling a little stupid, now. "Different strokes for different folks." You *know* I'm at a loss for words when I start tossing out the clichés like this. The timer on the microwave goes off. Tom reaches over and takes out the popcorn.

"So, anyway," Tom continues as he opens up the popcorn, "a couple years after I was born, Lisa hooked up with this guy. . ."

"Who's Lisa?"

"That's my mother," Tom answers, shoveling a handful of popcorn in his mouth. "So she hooks up with this guy she met. . ."

"Meredith's father."

"Right," Tom answers, offering the bag to me. I reach in and take a handful. "They got married in '72 and we moved from Northdale to Riverview. After they split up in '76, we moved back to Northdale. Lisa dated a couple of real losers for awhile, then ended up getting married again in '77."

"To the twins' father."

"No, no. To Frankie's father."

"Now who's Frankie?"

"She's my other sister. She slept over a friend's house last night. She'll probably be back this afternoon. But back up a minute, I'm getting ahead here. . ." He gets up and grabs two cans of *Yoo-hoo* from the refrigerator, putting one can on the table for me.

"So my mom got married and we moved to Maple Grove. Then my sister Frankie was born in '78. Lisa and Mike were together 'til, when was it? 1980, I guess? Yeah, 1980. But we lived in Maple Grove until '82."

"Then what?" I ask, a little dizzy. We both shake up our *Yoo-hoos* before opening them.

"Then we ended up moving to Carver," Tom answers as he takes a quick swig, "because Lisa got hitched again. And the twins were born in '83."

"This is getting hard to follow."

"Be thankful, pal: like I told you, you're getting the severely abridged version." He takes another handful of popcorn. "But anyway, that marriage lasted 'til around Thanksgiving, 1984. Six months later, Lisa got a temp job, and that's where she met her current sugar daddy, George McMullen. They got married just after I graduated high school— which would be July of '87. That's when we moved to Oakwood.

"And that's it. The severely abridged version."

"Five kids in the family, huh?" I observe with my usual grasp of the obvious. "That's alot."

"Yeah. We're one kid away from being the *Brady Bunch*. Scary."

"Two," I say. "You forgot Oliver."

"Right. I should've known better than to forget him."

"Poor little guy. Everybody forgets lil' Ollie."

"What are you talkin' about?" Tiffany asks as she saunters in like Miss Junior Runway Model.

"We're talkin' about you, termite," Tom tells her.

"You tellin' him about our family?" Tom looks at me, then looks back at her.

"You weren't eavesdropping just now, were you?"

"Did you tell him why me and Sam are twins?" she asks, ignoring the question.

"Now why would I wanna bore him with that stupid story?"

"We were born on Mom's birthday," Tiffany tells me, pretending Tom isn't there. "And in our family, um. . ."

"It's a stupid coincidence," Tom interrupts.

"Any time someone is born on their parents' birthdays, they're twins!"

19

"Lisa has two uncles who were born on her grandfather's birthday who are twins," Tom explains. "Tiffany thinks it's like, magic or something."

"It *is* magic," she insists. Tom smiles.

"You're *too* adorable," He says, cupping her face in his hand.

"Cut it out!" she orders, pushing his hand away.

"You wanna do me a favor, my beautiful baby sister?"

"What?" she questions, cautiously.

"You wanna keep my friend here entertained while I hop in the shower?"

"Okay!" she answers without hesitation.

"Do you mind, Will?"

"No, of course not."

"I won't be long," Tom tells me as he starts back upstairs. Meanwhile, Tiffany grabs me by the sleeve and drags me back into the living room. She's got quite a ferocious grip for such a little thing. Samantha's still there, lying on the couch.

"What do you want to watch?" Tiffany asks me as she picks up the remote.

"Hey!" Samantha yells.

"It's alright," I say. "Whatever your sister is watching is fine." Then I notice she's watching one of those nature programs on PBS where the insects are always eating each other and my heart quickly sinks.

"Sam always watches this creepy junk."

"S'not junk."

Tiffany puts the remote back down and crawls over to the television cabinet.

"You wanna watch a video?"

"No, it's fine."

"Oooooh, you wanna see pictures of us?" Tiffany asks hopefully as she pulls out a big photo album.

"Um, okay." I lie down on the floor next to her, negotiating a space between the coffee table and this giant potted plant. She flips right to the back of the album and I immediately recognize the first set of pictures.

"Hey, Cranden Field," I say. "I guess these are from Meredith's graduation, huh?" It was only five months ago, but I'm already feeling nostalgic.

"Yeah," Tiffany responds in a semi-bored tone. She flips through a few more pages. "Oooh, here's some good ones!" She points to some pictures marked July, 1989. They are on the beach, all of them: Tom, Meredith, the twins, and another girl who I assume to be Frankie.

"That was at the shore, two years ago," Tiffany informs me. Samantha shifts on the couch and looks at the album over my shoulder. Tiffany keeps on flipping.

"This was my first day of school," she says, as she points to a photo of herself and Samantha standing in front of a school bus.

"*Our* first day of school," Samantha corrects.

"I was *such* a beautiful child," Tiffany observes.

"Oh, *Gawd*," Samantha says with a roll of her eyes. Tiffany ignores her and continues with the photo tour.

And through all the birthday parties, the Christmases, the graduations, the communions and the Easters, the one thing I can't get over is how beautiful all the faces are— unlike my own family album, which more closely resmbles a combined Ernest Borgnine/Sandra Bernhard look-alike convention. I mean, these people are nothing short of *gorgeous*. The Mom, the sisters, the cousins. . . They're not a family, they're a friggin' pantheon.

The dog is barking now. I hear the back door open and close, followed by what sounds like several shopping bags being piled on the kitchen table. A moment later, Tom's mother enters the living room— I recognize her from the photos.

"Hello," she says, as she takes off her jacket. God, she looks so young. Even younger than in her pictures. It's hard to believe she could even be the twins' mother, let alone Tom and Meredith's.

"Hi, Mom," the twins respond.

"And you are. . ." Her voice is too sexy to belong to someone's mother. . . It distracts me, momentarily.

"I'm Will," I say, after a brief hesitation. "I don't know if Tom told you about me. . ."

"Oh, you're the one he's been driving to school! It's good to finally meet you!"

"Good to meet you, too."

"And who's this?" George McMullen asks as he enters the room. I recognize him from the photo album, also.

"Honey, this is Will— the one Tom has been driving to school."

"Pleased to meet you," he says, extending his hand. The grip of his handshake is uncomfortably firm. Unlike Lisa, he looks slightly older in person . . . His thin, blonde hair nearly recedes to the back of his head and the dark slacks he wears don't quite reach his ankles. "So where is Tom, anyway?"

"Oh, he just hopped in the shower real quick," I answer.

"Will you be joining us for dinner, Will?" Lisa asks.

"Uh, I dunno. Tom didn't actually ask me. . ."

"That's alright," Lisa says, "we'd all love to have you. Sweetie, will you get the big pot of gravy out of the refrigerator in the basement while I get the macaroni started?"

"Okay." George gives her a quick peck and she giggles like a little girl as they both exit.

The two of them make quite an. . . odd couple. No pun intended.

"Well, you don't have any more pictures, do you?" I ask Tiffany. "Like maybe some old ones of Tom?" It just hit me that if I could find some really embarrassing pictures of him it would be great ball-busting material I could really put to use, later.

"I don't think so," Tiffany answers, "but lemme check. . ." She looks back in the television cabinet. "Here," she says, dragging out another album.

I take it and start looking through; this time from the beginning. The first photo— of Tom popping out of a cardboard box with a cowboy hat on— is marked 1972. Tom was already, what, three? The following picture— of Tom posing with a chocolate Labrador— is also marked '72. Now that I think of it, I don't notice any baby pictures of him on the walls to go along with those of his sisters, either.

"What gives? Don't you have any pictures of Tom as a baby?"

"I dunno," Tiffany says. I shrug it off and keep leafing through.

22

None of the photos reveal any secrets. There's a photo of the whole family when Meredith was just a baby. Tom's got these ridiculous plaid pants. Lisa's gorgeous, with that really long, hippie-hair— Ah-oo-ga! Reminds me of Barbara Hershey in *The Baby-maker*. I guess the guy with the wild sideburns is Meredith's Dad. . . Here's one from Halloween, 1974, with Tom in a Lone Ranger costume. Another shot has Tom and Meredith lounging on a bed with the same chocolate lab from before, surrounded by stuffed *Sesame Street* toys. Still another pic shows Tom at about eight, holding a basketball, wearing a checkered shirt, jeans, and green and yellow "zip" sneakers that I recognize from the ads on the back of some old comics I have.

"What are you doing?" Tom asks as he enters the living room, cleaned up and shaven, with a glass of water in his hand.

"Tiffany was just showing me some old pictures."

"Tiff— I'm sure Will's not interested."

"Yes he is."

"I really am," I add, reassuring him. He stoops down to water the plant on the floor next to me.

"What's this?" I ask, returning my attention back to the album.

"Oh," Tom says, clearing his throat, "that's me and Meredith dressed up for Halloween in 1978. I'm Luke Skywalker and she's Princess Leia."

"What's that thing you're holding?" Tom leaves the empty glass on the coffee table and sits down on the floor with us to get a closer look.

"That's Frankie," he says with a laugh. "We wrapped her in this brown towel and tried to make her up like a jawa."

Again, the dog is barking. Again, I hear the back door quickly open and slam shut. Hurried footsteps clamor down the short corridor between the kitchen and the living room. "Speak of the devil," says Tom.

"Tom!" shouts a girl who has to be Tom's sister, Frankie. "You've gotta talk to Mom for me!" She practically jumps on top of him.

"Frankie, this is Will," Tom says. "Will, Frankie."

"Hi," I say.

23

"Oh. Hi." She stares at me for the longest moment.

"So what's this big thing I have to talk to Mom about?"

"Um, well, Jill's father told her he could help me get my name changed and all we'd have to pay for is the legal notice they put in the newspaper. Which is like, nothing."

"Aren't we past this yet?" Tom sighs, running his hand over her long, black hair.

"No!" she says, forcefully. "I hate my name!"

"Frankie, you have a beautiful name. You were named after your father's mother. You don't want a different name, believe me."

" 'Francesca' is such a geeky name."

"Good— it fits," Samantha jokes. Tiffany laughs. Frankie reaches over and punches Sam in the leg.

"Ow!"

Then Meredith enters the room and lets out a horrified gasp when she sees Frankie. Time briefly stands still.

"My sweater!" she hisses. "I've been looking for that! Get it off NOW, you little TOAD!"

"Watch it, cookie," Tom warns her. "Don't make me hafta sit on you. . ." Frankie bolts out of the room and Tom grabs hold of Meredith's ankle just as she's about to pursue her.

"Leggo!" Meredith screams. Tom pulls her down on the floor and pins back her arms.

"Free shots, girls!" he announces. The twins jump on top of the two of them and all four wrap themselves up in one big Chinese knot. They wrestle on the floor; the twins laughing while Meredith screams. Finally, she manages to wriggle free of that cartoonish dust cloud.

"You-you-you," she sputters, pointing down at Tom. "I'll get you for this, mister!"

Lord, she is *so* sexy when she's pissed.

"Are things always this exciting around here?" I wonder aloud.

"Actually, you caught us on a slow day," Tom informs me. "Stick around, maybe things'll pick up."

By the time dinner's on the table it's after six and I'm like *starving* 'cause my family almost never eats later than five. Once we sit down, George begins peppering me with questions like it's a job

24

interview or something. I suppose it's one of those old people-things where it would be somehow impolite not to engage a dinner guest in conversation every single minute.

"So what was the problem with your car, son?" he asks, as the interview drags on.

"Transmission glitch," I explain. "It was stalling every time it shifted out of overdrive."

"So what did you do?"

"My father just had the mechanic turn off the automatic overdrive. That doesn't mean the car can't shift into overdrive— it just has to happen manually. Occasionally, it'll have trouble kickin' into high gear, but what can you do, right?"

"Your father's a smart man," George replies. "Saved himself a bundle. Trust me— it would've cost him a small fortune if he tried to overhaul the transmission." I catch Tom giving a look.

"Frankie, punched me before, Mom," Samantha announces out of the clear blue.

"She called me a geek, Mom," Frankie says in her defense. "And Tiffany laughed." Lisa groans, refusing to acknowledge either of them; hoping, I imagine, that they'll eventually stop if she just ignores them.

"It was funny," Tiffany says. Frankie just simmers.

"Did you know you two were originally Siamese twins?" she says.

"Cut it *out*," Samantha whines.

"You were joined at the head," Frankie continues, "and you only had one brain between the two of you. So when the doctors separated you, you both only got half a brain."

"Mom!" Tiffany yells.

"All three of you mutants shut up," Meredith commands.

"Hey, don't call my sisters mutants," Tom tells her as he flicks her on the forehead.

"Oww!" She rubs her forehead, wincing. "If that bruises, I swear. . ."

"Everybody stop it!" George orders. "Right now! We have a guest here, for God's sake!" Tom is grinning from ear to ear and I'm trying real hard not to.

25

"You better cut it out," Lisa tells them, "all of you."

Everybody goes quiet as George and Lisa run their icy stares over everyone. Then, as their attention returns to their plates, Frankie quickly sticks out her tongue at Meredith. The twins and I continue holding back our laughter. Meredith, in turn, stares back at Frankie wide-eyed with her lips curled back in mock disgust; pressing her finger against the side of her nose at the identical spot where Frankie has a tiny zit just blossoming.

Immediately, Frankie throws her hands over her face. Tom lets out a burst of breath in a kind of half-gasp, half-laugh. Then, we're all laughing.

In the back of my mind, I'm already concocting excuses for stopping by and eating over again, tomorrow.

CHAPTER II

I'm waiting in the mall, just outside of Sears, giddy with anticipation. It's Martin Luther King Day— January 20, 1992— and Tom
and his sisters will be arriving any minute to get their picture taken
at Sears. It's a 40th birthday present for their mother, Lisa. And as
far as I'm concerned, the only thing cooler than hanging out with
Tommy Redivo is hanging out with Tommy Redivo and his family.

There were some days this past semester when my last class got
out earlier than Tom's, so I'd go over to the house and wait for him
to get home. Somedays, I'd listen to Lisa tell Tommy-stories. Other
days, I'd just sit on the den couch and watch the twins wrestle over
the remote control. Frankie would always ask me for homework
advice. Then, out of the blue, Tom would come bounding in,
shouting "Noogie patrol! Noogie patrol!" and the girls would all run,
screaming. And all I could think when I saw all this was how
awesome it must be, having younger siblings to torture.

At long last, I spot them. Tom's wearing a black suit with this
maroon-kinda tie. Frankie and the twins are wearing floral patterned
dresses with frilly trim. And Meredith. . . Meredith is wearing a
cherry red dress with a sweetheart neckline that takes my breath

away. All together, they make for a stunning sight to behold— like the Kennedy children or something.

"Hey, mud brother." The suit makes Tom sound strangely adult. "You're late."

"One house, two bathrooms, four sisters. Need I elaborate further?"

"And what is *he* doing here?" Meredith asks.

"I asked him to be here," Tom tells her. "You didn't expect me to spend the entire afternoon with my four sisters without someone else there as a buffer, did you?" He starts into Sears with his sisters behind him and me pulling up the rear.

"Well, maybe *I* need a buffer," Meredith declares. "What do you think, that you're some dream to live with?"

"Please— I'm a saint! You don't know how good you've got it, having me for a brother."

"Yeah," Frankie says, throwing her arms around his waist as they walk. "Tom is the best big brother there is!"

"Forget it, kid," Tom says with a smile, "I'm not carrying any extra cash on me today." Frankie groans and releases Tom from her grasp.

"What's the matter, little sister?" Meredith asks as she opens her purse and takes out a handful of money. "You need some of this?" She dangled the wad of bills under Frankie's nose.

"Oh, Meredith," Frankie cries dramatically, just as we're passing through the television section, where thirty screens are playing the daily episode of *Days of Our Lives*. "Have I ever told you how much I love you?" She can't even keep a straight face.

"How much do you love me?"

"This much!" Frankie proclaims as she throws out her arms.

"Enough to be my slave?"

"Well. . . How much would you give me?"

"What the hell do you need money for?" Tom asks.

"Lots of things!" Frankie says emphatically, as if deeply offended by the question.

"I'll tell you what," Meredith says as we're all getting on the escalator, "you be my slave for, oh, six months, and I'll give you twenty bucks."

"Make it."

"You drive a hard bargain. . . Alright, thirty."

"Yes!" Frankie rejoices.

"Wait a minute," Tiffany says. "*I'll* be your slave for twenty."

"Mind your business, butthead," Frankie says as we file off on to the second floor.

"Don't you tell her to mind her business— she has a right to make a bid," Meredith says. I'm loving every second of this.

"All of you, cut it out," Tom tells them as we walk past the store's vast selection of towels. "Nobody's getting sold into slavery on my watch."

"Why not?" Meredith asks. "You've bought, bribed and black-mailed me into shitty chores plenty of times."

"That was different, cookie," Tom says, smiling again. "That was always for your own good; it was never exploitive."

"Pleeeeeease," Meredith sighs.

We continue through the bath section, to the back of the store where the photo studio is. The photographer comes out as we arrive, all smiles.

"May I help you?"

"Yes. We're here for a group portrait. The name's Redivo."

"Ah, yes. . ."

The photographer and Tom begin going over the specifics of what they want one last time. A problem develops as they're discussing the background: Tom had originally asked for a black background, but Meredith is balking.

"It's impractical," she says. "Mom'll be windexing it every five minutes. Get the light blue background— the dust won't show as much." I'm in total awe, seeing her brilliant mind at work. Tom grudgingly concedes to her judgment.

With all the details ironed out, the photographer leads us still further in back, to the room where the portrait is to be shot. Frankie, Tiffany and Samantha all sit on small stools in front of Tom and Meredith, who remain standing. I stand in back, well behind the camera, watching.

"Alright, everybody," the photographer says, almost singing, "smile, now." They all smile, save Samantha.

29

"C'mon everybody," he repeats, "big, big smiles, now."

Samantha's still straight faced. Finally, the photographer comes out from behind the camera.

"What's the matter little girl?" he asks, melodically. "Does the camera make you scared?"

"No," Sam replies, plainly.

"Then why won't you smile for me?"

"I *am* smiling," she insists.

"Can we take a break for a minute?" Tom requests. For a brief second, the photographer's face betrays slight annoyance. We all take a step to the side as Tom begins to talk to Sam.

"What's the matter, Sam?" I hear him ask her.

"Nothing," she sighs.

"Why won't you smile?"

"How am I supposed to smile?" she asks. "I hate getting dressed up like this and I hate posing for pictures."

"Come on, Sam. I've seen you smile before, so I know you can do it. . ."

"That's only when I'm not *trying*. I can't make myself smile the same way on *purpose*. I'll look *stupid*."

"You think that if you try to smile on purpose you'll look stupid?"

"Well, won't I?"

He stops for a moment, apparently taking what he's about to say into careful consideration.

"You're a very sensitive girl, you know that Sam?"

"What does that mean?"

"It means you think alot about things. But that's okay, 'cause I can be the same way alot of the time."

"Yeah?"

"Yup. See, I think about these same things, too— like what people might think of me if they see me smile or laugh or cry. . ."

"Exactly!" Sam exclaims.

". . .But I've learned some very important things about sensitive people like us."

"Like what?" she wonders.

"Like most people aren't like you an' me. Most people don't think much about what other people are *really* thinking or feeling. People like you and me might think about these things, but we're special."

Sam looks down and starts to smile, just a little.

"This isn't *funny*," she warns.

"I'm not being funny," he assures. "I'm being totally honest with you, like grown-ups, 'cause I know you're not a baby, right?"

"Right," she agrees in a near-whisper.

"So don't worry about what anyone else might think about your smile. Just smile as best you can, okay? Pretend you're at the dentist and you're showing him your teeth. Can you do that? Pretty-please?"

"I dunno. I still think I'll look *stupid*." He reaches out and touches her shoulder.

"You should always be true to yourself and what you feel inside, Sam— but there are better times and better ways to show it, y'know?" Sam says nothing. "This picture is gonna be a present for Mom— you don't want her to see you looking all sad, do ya?"

"No," she mumbles.

"Here," he says, turning up the corners of her mouth with his fingers, "just hold your face like this."

"Stop!" She swats his hand away.

". . .Or I can just tickle you, like this," he says, reaching for her armpits.

"Stop!" she repeats, laughing and reining in her arms tight so he can't get to the ticklish spots.

"I know," he says, lowering his voice. He lifts her chin, forcing her to look him directly in the eye. "When the cameraman says 'cheese,' I want you to think about how much your big brother loves you, okay?"

Her eyes narrow and the corners of her mouth tremble ever so slightly.

"You're such a jerk," she tells him, her face breaking into a smile despite her efforts to resist.

"So are you ready to try and smile now?"

"Yeah," she submits at lasts. He kisses her forehead and she blushes just a little.

31

Tom motions to the photographer and everyone reassumes their positions. This time, they all smile and the pictures are snapped without a problem. Tom stops to talk with the photographer briefly before we leave.

"Alright," he says as we exit Sears onto the second floor of the mall. "We've got about forty-five minutes to play with. Let's meet up at the pizza place on the first floor at a quarter after two. . . have you got the twins, Mer?"

"Yeah," Meredith sighs.

"Alright then." The girls scatter. "And don't let anything happen to your good clothes!"

"Just where is Lisa, anyway?" I ask as we begin walking.

"I set things up with her friend Kathy to keep her occupied all day. They're runnin' around north Jersey somewhere, far from here."

"What was up with Sam back there?" I ask, feigning ignorance.

"Ahh, she was just a little camera shy, is all."

"Hey," I say, as we're briefly separated by a group of people walking in the opposite direction, "back in my car, I've got this totally gross episode of *Ren & Stimpy* I taped off of MTV, Saturday. You'll love it."

"Every time I turn on MTV lately, all I see is *Ren & Stimpy*. Do they even play videos anymore?"

"You know, I was surprised you didn't dress the twins in the same outfit for the picture." Tom stops dead in his tracks and gives me a look.

"I have introduced you to the twins, haven't I?"

"They wouldn't appreciate wearing the same outfit, I take it?"

"They don't appreciate wearing the same *skin*," Tom says, as we start forward again. "Well, I shouldn't say 'they.' It's more Sam than Tiffany."

"Is it really that bad?"

"Are you kidding?" Tom asks, loosening his tie. "When Tiffany was taking her first steps, Sam grabbed her by the diaper and yanked her back down to the floor." I laugh.

"Have you ever known twins before?" Tom quizzes. "Identical ones, I mean?"

"No, actually."

"Well, I've known a couple myself, and I've developed a few theories. . ."

"Of course," I rib.

"Well, just one theory, really, and that is that one twin is always crazy and maladjusted while the other is always totally happy, sane and super well-adjusted."

"I can tell you've done alot of research on this."

"Come on. Doesn't it make sense when you think about it? Imagine how you'd feel if there was this other version of you walking around. Not just someone who looks exactly like you, but someone who, at least genetically speaking, *is* you."

"Gee. I think it would be kind of cool. Guess I'm warped or something."

"Trust me," Tom scolds, "if it was something you had to live with every day of your life since birth, you'd feel differently. That's what Sam's starting to go through, now: she's trying to establish an identity of her own, and she feels she can only do that by being the exact opposite of Tiffany." Tom starts to turn toward the escalator. We both hop on.

"Where did you wanna go?" I ask, as we slowly descend back to the first floor of the mall.

"To Alwilk. Greg played me this song over the phone last night and I wanna see if I can find it on CD."

"Greg?"

"Yeah, you know— the editor of the Sentinel?"

"Oh, him." Tom was referring to the editor of the school paper. He introduced us just over a month ago. I found him a bit on the creepy side, with that bizarre Greg Brady-perm and the voice like Bullwinkle J. Moose. "Who's the band?"

"They're called 'Live.' "

" 'Live'?"

"Yeah, I know, it's a fucked up name," Tom says as we enter Alwilk.

"So what does 'Live' sound like?" I ask. "Anybody?"

"I dunno. It's hard to describe. Greg was telling me that their album was produced by one of the guys from Talking Heads and that he thought they sounded alot like them, but I don't buy it."

"Shit. You'd have jumped out the window if they sounded like Talking Heads." Tom's pretty open minded when it comes to music, but Talking Heads is the one band he absolutely can't stand. Sort of his musical kryptonite.

"Yeah. They've got a much more commercial sound, in my opinion. Kinda like a cross between R.E.M. and Kiss."

"Oh, Jesus! This I gotta hear!" Tom begins sifting through the "L" section. After he finds what he's looking for, we shop around the store a little bit more. I come across a new CD I've been looking for, but only have five bucks on me.

"I'll get it for you," Tom tells me. "Just spot me the five so I have enough for pizza."

"So I'll owe you what, ten?" He shoots me a look of bemused disbelief.

"What are you, with the I.R.S.? Forget about it. What's ten bucks between friends?" He takes the CDs up to the register and pays for them with his Visa card.

After we leave Alwilk, we bum around the mall, girl-watching until 2:15. When we get to the pizza place, all his sisters are there except Frankie, who shows about ten minutes later. Then Tom orders two pies that we can all share as a late lunch. Once they're ready, we exit the mall. Much to my disappointment, Meredith goes with Tom and the twins in his car while Frankie rides with me on the short trip back to their house on Shepherd Terrace.

After getting back from the mall and tearing themselves free of the confines of their dress clothes, the girls swarm the kitchen, devour their pizza and descend on the living room. Frankie stakes a claim to the spot on the couch next to me, putting her feet up over my left knee as she lies back. Sam is sprawled over George McMullen's chair while Tiffany spins through the room, practicing dance steps. Tom and Meredith remain in the kitchen, cleaning up.

"Turn on the television," Frankie demands, suddenly.

"Oh, Will is sick of watching t.v.," Tiffany says. "I'll bet he'd much rather listen to the stereo, wouldn't you, Will?" Before I can answer her, Tiffany has opened the stereo cabinet and turned on the CD player.

"Put the t.v. on, dork!" Frankie reiterates. The sounds of Earth, Wind & Fire's "September" begins churning out of the speakers set on the floor. Tiffany resumes her dancing.

"You dance like a reject," Sam says, as she gets up off of my lap. She kicks her feet out and back again expertly, like one of the fly girls on *In Living Color*. Frankie watches them both, smiling.

"I think you're *both* rejects," she says, as she finally gets up and joins them. I marvel at how well she moves. She may be only thirteen years old, but she can shakes and grinds her hips like the most seasoned lap-dancer. You can tell she's spent alot of hours in front of the television, studying those MTV dance shows.

"So who's the best dancer, Will?" Frankie asks me.

"Uhhh," I stammer. Luckily, Tom comes strutting into the room just as Chic's "Good Times" begins to play.

"*These-are-the-good-times!*" he sings, pointing his finger up at the ceiling and thrusting his ass back. Meredith enters the room, shielding her face from her siblings.

"I'm not related to these people," she says, as she flops down on the couch next to me. Her knee brushes against mine and I just about choke on my own breath.

My groin screams at my brain to say something. Anything.

"You guys are really into disco, huh?" I ask, clearing my throat. It's amazing how hot she is, even in those baggy sweat clothes.

"It's not like we had a choice," Meredith answers. "It's practically all we listened to, growing up."

"Really? I would never have figured it." I'm doing it! I'm talking to her!

"Yeah, well, don't buy that crap about Lisa being a hippie. She's 100% disco queen, believe me." Her attention remains partly divided between me and her siblings, who continue dancing.

"Hey, I hear you're majoring in psych," I say, gaining slightly in confidence.

"Yes. And before you ask why, just take a look— as you can see, my family is in desperate need of help."

I'm already out of conversation ideas. Come on, Will, think of something. . .

"Can you believe how cold it was outside, today?"

"Uh, yeah. It's been pretty cold the last few days," she responds, looking at me like I just grew a third eye. I can already feel myself sinking fast as the opening bass line and keyboard tones of the Little River Band's "Reminiscing" begins to play.

"Come on, Cookie," Tom says, grabbing Meredith by the hand, "they're playing our song!"

"Oh, no," Meredith pleads, with one of those deer-in-the-head-lights expressions.

"Oh, come on! Don't be such a stick in the mud!"

"Don't bother fighting it," I advise her— I'm actually relieved that I've lost the opportunity to further embarrass myself.

"No, no, no!" she persists. The twins, both laughing uncontrollably, come over and begin pushing her off the couch. Tom grabs hold of her other hand and pulls her up. He tries to slow dance with her, but she lets her whole body go limp. Tom's basically holding her up by himself, but he doesn't seem to mind.

"*Friday night, it was late, I was walkin' you home, we got down to the gate and I was dreaming of the night,*" Tom sings, like Bill Murray doing "Star Wars." Meredith slowly cracks a grudging smile. "*Would it turn out right?*"

"You are *so* retarded," Meredith says, laughing, "I swear to God!" All the same, she begins to pick up her feet, take hold of his hand and dance along with him. The girls watch them and laugh; likewise swaying in time with the music.

"*How to tell you, girl?*" Tom continues. "Sing it, Mer!" he cajoles.

"*I wanna build my world around you,*" they sing in unison, "*tell you that it's true. . . I wanna make you understand I'm talkin' about a lifetime plan. . .*

"*That's the way it began, we were hand-in-hand, Glen Miller's band was better than before. . . We yelled and screamed for more. . .*"

Frankie grabs Samantha and begins to slow dance with her. Then Tiffany cuts in on both of them and soon all three are slow dancing, together. They all sing (or try to, anyway).

BACK TO THE GARDEN

"And as the years roll on, each time we hear our favorite song, memories come along. . . Olden times we're missing, spending the hours reminiscing."

The girls all laugh as the song ends. I'm still laying back on the couch, enjoying it all. Apparently, insanity is contagious around here 'cause I'm beginning to wonder if I should get up and join them. Tom goes over to the CD player and begins to search for a song. "Here it is," he declares, "our theme song!" Sister Sledge's "We Are Family" begins to play. Again, they all sing together.

"We are family! I got all my sisters with me! We are family! Get up everybody, sing!"

"Take it!" Tom directs.

"Everyone can see we're together," Samantha sings, *"as we walk on by."*

"And we flock just like birds of a feather," sings Tiffany, *"I won't tell no lie!"*

"All of the people around us they say," Meredith hams it up, *" 'can they be that close?' "*

"Just let me state for the record," Frankie jumps in, *"we're givin' lovin' a family doh-oh-ose!"*

"We are family," they all sing together.

"I got all my sisters with me!" Tom shouts.

"We are family. . . Get up everybody, sing!"

Tom gives Samantha the bump and sends her munchkin-behind spinning to the floor. He bumps Tiffany and she does likewise. Frankie steps up to take a shot, but her skinny ass proves no match for the buns of steel, either, as she falls on top of the twins. Meredith is the last to go, as she ends up tumbling backward, over the ottoman and into the loveseat. By now, we're all laughing so hysterically that none of us can breathe.

"What is going on here?" Lisa asks, as she enters the room. We all keep right on laughing without answering her.

I end up staying for dinner, of course— we're at the point now where no one even has to invite me. Lisa makes pot roast and pota-toes. As usual, Tom's sisters tease and bicker throughout the meal.

So much for giving lovin' a family dose.

Afterward, I go with Tom upstairs to his room to watch that tape of *Ren & Stimpy* and listen to the CDs we bought. Tom's room is in even worse shape than usual; apparently, he hasn't done any cleaning all winter break. After we finish watching the tape, he asks me if I'd mind helping him clean up 'cause he figures if he doesn't get something done now, it's gonna be impossible, what with the spring semester starting tomorrow. Naturally, I happily agree to help.

"Your sister Meredith is so hot," I observe as we're getting started.

"Here we go again, folks." This is not the first time we've had this conversation, in case you couldn't tell.

"Back in high school," I go on, wholly obsessed, "she used to remind of that girl from *My Two Dads*. You know— the one who's on *Step By Step*, now?"

"Staci Keanan," he says, sorting through a stack of books on top of his dresser. . . How does he know all this shit, anyway?

"Yeah, her. But you know who she reminds me of now?"

"I don't know, Will. If I begged ya, would you tell me?"

"Bridget Fonda," I say, with a mixture of lust and awe. "You remember her in that last *Godfather* movie? When she was in bed with Andy Garcia?"

"You know what the sickest thing is? I can tell you've deliberated over this for like *hours*."

"You're right. I'm a sick man."

"You are." We laugh.

"Seriously though," I beg, "aren't you ever gonna put in a good word for me?"

"Well, there is one thing you can do," he says. Immediately, my ears perk up. "Stop calling her by her full name. She hates that."

"That's what you and the girls all call her, though. . ."

"Yeah, but we're bustin' her chops."

"Really? What am I supposed to call her, then?"

"Call her 'Merry.'"

"'*Merry*'? Are you puttin me on?"

"No, really. That's what she prefers. It's what her Grandma Trembly calls her. Seriously."

"I'll have to keep that in mind," I say, still sifting through the same pile of periodicals. "For a minute there, I thought you were gonna tell me to call her 'cookie.'"

"Ha!"

"What's the story behind that, anyway?"

"Aw, it's no fun tellin' ya now. . . Remind to tell ya sometime when she's around so I can really embarrass her."

"What the fuck is up with these teen-girl magazines, anyway?" I ask as I resume gathering them up off the floor.

"Most of them are Frankie's. . . don't knock 'em, they're a great read. Check out those 'most embarrassing moments' that get sent in. There's one in there, somewhere, that's a real killer— this girl talks about the time she's at cheerleading tryouts and she goes to do a split and her tampon pops out!"

"Hey, check out how old this sports page is," I say, picking up some old newspapers. "It's dated December 2nd!"

"Waitaminnit," Tom responds, noticing something on the back page, "check *this* out."

"What?"

"This," he says, as he stands up and grabs the paper out of my hands. He flips it around so I can see what's caught his eye.

"'*Marczewski among 5 from Westfair on All-County,*'" I say, reading the headline aloud.

"Forget that. I'm talking about *her*." He points to one of the head shots that runs alongside the main story.

"Whoa." Courtney Erikson is her name. With long, blonde hair sweeping down the right side of her face, wide, bright eyes and the most adorable, cherubic cheeks.

"I swear I'm in love," Tom says as he sits down on his bed. "Let's see what it says here about my sweet little Viking Princess. . ."

"You're too much."

"Just look at her— the picture of Aryan perfection. She could be a Valkyrie, fer Chrissake!" I laugh.

"Courtney Erikson," he reads, still mesmerized by the photo, "from Overbrook High."

"Even her name is hot," I observe.

39

"Oh, man! This is the all-county list for field hockey!"

"Field hockey?"

"Yeah! You ever see field hockey girls, before? In those uniforms, with the short skirts and the cute little clubs they carry around? They're the hottest!"

"I must confess, I never noticed before."

"*'Courtney Erikson,'* " Tom continues, "*'the offensive catalyst for Overbrook (10-5-2), finished fourth in the county with 35 points on 15 goals and 5 assists. The senior right inner displayed...'*"

"What's a right inner?" I interrupt.

"Who cares?" Tom answers. "Whatever it is, she *'displayed excellent stick work...'*"

"Hi-oh!"

"*'...crisp drives, and a selfless work ethic on the front line.'*" Tom refuses to take his eyes off her picture. "Damn! Homegirl is foy-ine! Don'tcha think?"

"Absolutely. You plan on framin' that or what?"

"I'll do better than that." He picks up the phone and dials.

"What are you doing?" I ask.

"Yes. Do you have a listing for an Erikson in Overbrook? That's E-r-i-"

"Are you insane?"

"...k-s-o-n." Tom reaches over and pulls out the top drawer of his night table. He takes out a pencil and a piece of paper. "Three? Alright. Can you give me all of them?"

"Tell me you're pullin' my chain." Tom starts writing down numbers on the paper. "Oh my God, you're *serious?*"

"Thank you," Tom says. He laughs once he gets off the line.

"You're really going to call this girl?"

"Hell, yeah! Lemme see... Which number should I try first?"

"What do you plan on saying to her?"

"I'll figure that out when I get her on the phone." He begins dialing again.

"I can't believe this."

"Yes, hello. I'm looking for Courtney Erikson?" Tom looks at me and gives me the Belushi eyebrow. I've gotta hold my hand over my mouth to hold in my laughter. "Well, I'm calling on behalf of the

40

admissions department of Cahill State University. You see, we're canvassing for potential students and... Yes, thank you." Tom puts his hand over the receiver and we laugh, together. "Can you believe it? I got her on the first try!"

"You *are* insane!"

"Hello," Tom says as he takes his hand away from the receiver, "Courtney? Hi! My name's Tom Redivo. How are you doing, this evening? Oh, that's good."

"So how is she doing?" I ask. Tom looks at me sternly and gives the "cut" sign.

"Well," he continues, "I'm a student at Cahill State University and I work in the admissions office part-time. I'm calling to see if you might be interested in enrolling at our fine institution."

"You're spinnin' your wheels, man."

"Well, we were very impressed with your school record. Come again? Well, all your activities, including field hockey... Your record would seem to indicate that you'd make a fine addition to our campus community."

"*'Campus community'?*" I repeat in disbelief.

"How familiar are you with our university? I see. Have you considered what you want to major in? Oh, okay. No, it's alright. Look— why don't I send you our undergraduate catalog? Great... No, actually, the application deadline isn't until March, so you still have time... Can I just double-check your mailing address?"

I watch Tom operate in starry-eyed disbelief. I try to picture myself doing what Tom's doing right now, but I can't. I'm trying, but I keep envisioning myself stuttering, mumbling, with the voice cracking, and just generally making an ass of myself. It's pathetic. Even my fantasies can't measure up to Tommy Redivo's reality.

"Alright, very good," Tom continues. "I'll tell you what— why don't I call back in a week or two, after you've had a chance to look over the catalog, and perhaps we can set up a time when I can give you the grand tour of our facilities... You'd like that?" Tom offers me a wide-eyed look. "Alright, then! Of course. No, it's no trouble at all, believe me. Really, I enjoy it, it's one of the perks of the job— I love meeting new people. Sure. Yes, I know. Well, we certainly do things our own way here, it's true. Alright. I guess I'll be speaking to you again, soon? Okay. Buh-bye, now." He hangs up the phone, and laughs.

"She goes, 'I never heard of a college calling up people like this.' "

"What about the catalog, smart guy?" I ask.

"William, you disappoint me. That's the easy part— I'll just stop by the registrar's office tomorrow and request one with her name and address."

I just can't get over it.

"You're seriously gonna go through with this?"

"Well, let us take a moment to examine my options, here. On the one hand, I could sit around this house all day and night, watching the hair on my palms grow. On the other hand, I could seduce this Norse goddess and make mad, passionate love to her. . . Monty, I believe I'll take door number two."

"Alright," I concede. "But still— you gotta figure she has a boy-friend. A girl like that is born with one."

"Big deal," Tom tells me. "Any girl worth pursuing is gonna al-ready have a boyfriend, ninety-nine time out of a hundred. Shit, if I gave up every time a girl told me she had a boyfriend, I woulda shaved my head and joined a monastery years ago."

All I can do is look back at him in awe.

"You are my God, man."

CHAPTER III

"Will they cancel this show if it rains?" Mom asks me.

"Ma," I say, adjusting the collar of my shirt, "for the gazillionth time, they will not cancel the show. It says so on the front of the ticket: 'U2, Giants Stadium, August 13, 1992, *rain or shine*.' See?"

"Who's going, again?"

"It's me, Tom, Tom's girlfriend, and a few other guys from school," I tell her. "Willya get off my back already?"

"Fine," Mom replies as she exits the doorway of my room. Five minutes after she's gone downstairs to finish the laundry, I'm on the phone to Tom because, try as I might, I can't get that stupid voice of hers out of my head.

"Hey Tom," I whisper, "is everything still on?"

"Why wouldn't it be?" he responds, laughing.

"Well, um, I was just thinking that with the weather and all. . ."

"Will. . . you're too much. Just be in lot four in an hour, okay?"

"Are Keith and Tamara coming with us?" I never really hung out with any of the few black guys I went to school with— then again, I barely hung out with *anybody* of *any* color. Still, though it shames

43

me to admit it, I feel even more self-conscious than usual when either of them are around.

"I don't *know*," Tom says. "Look, I've gotta go pick up Courtney, now. Why don't you have a bite to eat, read the paper, maybe lie down for twenty minutes and when we hook up at school we'll iron it all out."

"O-*kay*. I'll see you in an hour."

Upon hanging up, I begin to wonder whether or not my endless worrying is giving away the truth; the truth being that I've never been to a live rock concert before. It's quite humiliating, actually— Nineteen years old and never been to a rock concert. Could I be a bigger dweeb?

I try my best to follow Tom's advice, but can't resist spending the next half-hour pacing in circles around my bedroom and changing my clothes three more times. At last, I settle on my white and blue striped, short-sleeved collared shirt to go along with my jeans and moccasins.

"I'm going, Ma," I holler as I'm going out the back door.

"Wait a minute," she yells from the kitchen. "Your father wanted me to tell you something," she says as she pokes her head into the back hall.

"What is it?"

"First of all, are you taking your car to the stadium?"

"I don't know— why? What's the difference?"

"Well, your father told me to tell you to be careful with the car."

I groan. What does she want me to do— hire a friggin' security guard to stand watch over the stupid car while I'm at the concert?

"Alright," I say, humoring her, "I'll be careful with the car."

"Alright. Don't stay out too late, now!"

The ride to school seems to take forever. God, I'm sweating like a madman here, and it's not even hot out. At every red light, at every stop sign, I primp myself in the rearview mirror, but it's hopeless. My hair's all over the place, I'm all sweaty... Christ, I'm a mess. Part of me wants to just turn this heap around and go home.

...Okay, so it's more than just the concert. See, there's this girl that Tom's setting me up with and I'm a nervous wreck over it. Originally, I was supposed to meet her at his "Midsummer's Eve" party back at the beginning of May, but unfortunately, she came down with tonsillitis. Then, Tom tried to get us hooked up when they went to Lollapalooza just a few weeks ago, but I didn't go because I. . . Well, I pussied out. Anyway, I've been kicking myself ever since. So I promised myself that tonight I was gonna see this through come Hell or high water. Her name is Kate Green, an English major entering her senior year, a five foot-something brunette with green eyes.

"She's just what you need," Tom told me. "Someone who'll take charge and whip you into shape." I'm still not quite sure what he meant by that.

When I pull into student parking lot #4 at Cahill State University, Tom and Courtney are already there.

"Will!" Courtney shouts. I park beside them and, as I get out of my car, she steps up and gives me a hug. Though I first met her at that "Midsummer's Eve" bash over three months ago, I still can't get over the fact that it's *her*— that same goddess that Tom picked out of the back of the sports section that afternoon in late January.

"How've you been?" she asks. "I haven't seen you around lately."

"Yeah, uh, well, I've been busy with different things."

The truth is that in the last couple of weeks, I was beginning to feel like a fifth wheel. Back in May, when she and Tom were still in that platonic gray-area, it was different. We would get together, the three of us, hang out at Tom's and it was all cool. But by July, you could see things between her and Tom shift into high gear. All of a sudden, the two of them couldn't stand within ten feet of each other without some kind of physical contact— hand holding, waist hugging, neck nuzzling. . . you get the picture. A short while after that, once they started throwing around the "hons," the "sweeties," and the "babes," I knew the three of us had suddenly become a crowd.

"Come on, Will," Tom chides. "Where's the excitement in the voice? The spring in the step? C'mon, get psyched! In just a few short hours, you'll be nose-to-nose with Bono and Edge!"

"I *am* excited," I whine.

"There's Keith!" Courtney shouts, as the familiar brown Malibu of Keith Simmons rolls into the lot. She runs over to it, with Tom and me behind her, and hugs both Keith and his girlfriend, Tamara,

45

as they get out of the car. I marvel enviously at the ease with which Courtney manages to establish such social intimacy with people she's only just met. I can't remember the last time I hugged my own mother or father the way she hugs Keith and Tam. Tom likewise greets the two of them.

"Hey, William," Keith says as he extends his hand.

"Hey," I say, as we shake. "Hi Tam."

"Hey, Will," Tamara answers.

Then *she* steps out of the back of the car. A brunette vision in strategically torn blue jeans, and a loose-fitting, striped tee.

"Deev!" she exclaims as she embraces Tom.

"Hey Kay," Tom replies. "Will, this is Kate. Kate, Will."

"Glad to finally meet you!"

"Hello," I say, somehow managing to avoid stammering.

"You didn't lie, Tom, he *is* cute!" she teases as we shake hands. Looking into her green eyes, I try to think of something witty and charming to say, but the most I can bring myself to do is clear my throat.

"So," Tom says to Keith, "are you guys comin' with us?"

"Get out. You can't squeeze six people in your car."

"Why not?"

"Look, we're sitting in different sections anyway, so why don't we just meet someplace *after* the concert?"

"I don't know," Courtney says. "Tom and me have been out every night this week. I don't know if I'm up for another all-nighter."

"Let's compromise, then," Kate suggests. "After the show's over, we'll just go for coffee."

"This is my first night off in awhile, though," Tamara explains. She's got a job working behind the counter in a video store just off campus.

"What are we doin', then?" Tom asks. I'd throw in my two cents, but I seem to have lost the power of speech at the moment. . . Kate is just so *gorgeous*, I keep thinking there must be a catch, somewhere. Why would Tom set me up with such a babe rather than keep her for himself? Then again, he's got Courtney, so I guess he can afford to be generous.

46

"Well, who says we have to do everything together?" Keith asks. "Why don't we just go our own way for tonight?"

"Are you trying to tell me that you guys are capable of havin' fun without me?"

"Aw, we still love you, Tom," Tamara says as she playfully wraps her arms around him.

"Hey Key, you notice how she always finds an excuse to put her hands on me?" Tom squeezes her tight and she laughs.

"Watch it, son," Keith warns, kiddingly.

"Alright you two, break it up," Courtney says, getting between Tamara and Tom. She hugs Tom's torso and buries her head in his chest, staking out her territory.

"Are you positive you guys don't want to meet later?" Kate asks.

"You heard my lady— she's the boss," Keith answers as Tamara leans back against him and smiles. Guess they're not coming with us. I feel slightly relieved. Then I feel slightly guilty for feeling slightly relieved.

"Call you tomorrow, then?" Tom asks.

"Whatever."

So Keith and Tamara get back into his Malibu while Tom, Courtney, Kate and me pile into Tom's Camaro. Our two cars drive off the lot, one after the other, into the gray evening. I remain closed-mouthed in the back seat with Kate, while Tom spends a good ten minutes trying to find a decent song on the radio.

"Why don't you just play a tape, babe?" Courtney finally asks.

"Ah, I've played 'em all to death."

"Here," she says, reaching into her purse, "I've got the *Singles* soundtrack on cassette."

"Oh, sweet! Have you heard this yet, Will? Westerberg's actually got some solo cuts on here."

"No," I say, finally summoning up the nerve to speak. We all go quiet again as the eerie sounds of Alice In Chains begins to fill the car.

"So," Kate pipes up, "how was the show Monday?"

"Great," Tom says. Meredith and her boyfriend Matt (ugh) took Tom and Courtney to the show on Monday— it was an early birthday present for Tom, who was born on the 17th. Then on Tuesday,

47

DAVID SORRENTINO

Tom and Courtney saw Bruce Springsteen in the arena. So it has indeed been a busy week for the two of them. "I've gotta warn you, though: no cuts from any album before *Joshua Tree*."

"No?" I say. "Nothing from *War*? Nothing from *Boy*?"

"They did play 'Pride,' hon," Courtney reminds him.

"Ah, yes," he says. "I stand corrected."

"It still doesn't sound promising," Kate says.

"Oh, don't worry," Courtney reassures us, ever the bundle of sunshine, "it's a great show! You're gonna love it!"

"Guess who showed up to jam with the band?"

"Ooooh, you'll never get this!"

"Lou Reed," says Kate.

"How did you know?"

"She cheated," says Tom. "Who told you?"

"I heard it on MTV."

"What'd they play together?" I ask.

" 'Satellite of Love,' " Tom replies.

"Tom flipped out," Courtney interjects. "I wish you could've seen him."

"Well, I thought they might play a couple of Velvets' tunes. 'Sweet Jane,' at least. Maybe 'White Light/White Heat.'"

"I swear," Kate says, "I can just see you, Deev: 'give us 'Heroin,' Lou!' "

"Where does 'Deev' come from, anyway?" I ask.

"'Divo' was my father's nickname," Tom offers. "I think Lisa was talking about it one time, when I had a bunch of friends over, and they all picked it up and ran with it."

"Hey," Courtney says, playfully, "maybe I should start calling you 'Deev,' babe."

"When did you guys first meet?" I ask Kate.

"When was it, Deev? The fall of '90?"

"I guess. . . Yeah, it had to be."

"Ask 'em about the class that they took together," Courtney says, turning to face the back seat.

"Please don't."

"It was a course on ethics," Kate tells me, as she begins to crack a smile. "I caught up with him after class one day to correct him

48

about something. That's how we 'introduced' ourselves, I guess you'd say."

"Some introduction. You friggin' ambushed me."

"Oh, stop it," Kate says. "We just had a little disagreement about Nietzsche. How was I supposed to know you wanted to have the guy's baby?"

"What is it, Kay? You think 'cause you're one-eighth Jewish or whatever that you're required to hate Nietzsche? Have you ever even bothered to read him?"

"First of all, I'm half-Jewish; second of all, the point I was trying to make was that the things he wrote were used in Nazi propaganda— you can't dispute that."

"And it doesn't matter how much those words were twisted around and taken out of context?"

"He would still be responsible for writing those words that were so easily twisted around, Deev."

"I thought we put this argument to bed a couple weeks ago— what happened?"

"We're not arguing. I'm just explaining to Will, here, how we met. You're the one who's making it an argument." Courtney is visibly shaking from trying to hold in her laughter.

"Did you ever read that copy of *Beyond Good and Evil* I gave you?" Tom asks. Kate's smile widens as she remains silent. "Did you or didn't you?"

"I read it some," she answers, sheepishly.

"Liar, liar, pants on *fire*," Tom scolds as Kate breaks down, laughing.

"You still haven't refuted Nietzsche's contribution to Nazism," she persists. I have to admire her stick-to-itiveness.

"Well, if you had ever read him, you'd know that Hitler's superman is a total perversion of Nietzsche. The literal translation of 'übermensch' is 'overman,' not 'superman'— it's a theme that Nietzsche makes alot, juxtaposing the 'over with the 'under.' That's what Nietzschean philosophy is all about: *over*coming and overcoming oneself, specifically. It never had anything to do with racial superiority or any such crap. And if you want to judge works of literature based on how they're interpreted or misinterpreted, then what book has caused more war and murder than the Bible?"

"You may as well forget it, Kate," I advise. "You can't win an argument with Tom Redivo when the subject is Nietzsche."

"Right," Kate sighs. "Or Martin Scorsese movies."

"Or punk music," Courtney adds.

"Or mythology," I say. "Or. . ."

"Alright, alright," Tom warns. "Knock it off."

We turn off at the exit on route 3 and join the long train of cars waiting to pull into the Giants Stadium parking lot. When we reach the actual entrance to the lot, Tom pays the seven dollar parking fee himself, above our protests. We pull in while all around us, the tailgate parties are already in full swing. I look up at the sky as I get out of the car and moan.

"What's the matter?" Kate asks me.

"There's gonna be a monsoon," I tell her.

The four of us walk through the lot, absorbing the sounds of U2 emanating from the seemingly endless number of car trunks and vans. Before finding going insides, we stop to buy t-shirts. I get the white one with the band outlined in multiple colors on the front and the satellite dish on the back, while Kate gets the one with Bono's face taking up the entire front. Tom and Courtney are already wearing matching shirts that they bought three nights earlier: black (of course), with Bono silhouetted in white and "U2" in purple lettering just above him.

"How would you rate Monday's show?" Kate asks as we pass through the entrance to the stadium floor. "Better than Lollapalooza?"

"I wouldn't go *that* far," Tom says. We show our ticket stubs to one of the ushers who, in turn, directs us up several rows.

"Oh, come on," I say, my excitement building as the stage grows bigger and bigger in my sight. "This is U2 we're talkin' about."

"Yeah, but the Lollapalooza line-up kicked ass, man," Tom responds. "Pearl Jam, Soundgarden. . ."

"Don't forget the Chili Peppers," says Courtney.

"The Chili Peppers are alright," I concede, "but I'm not into Soundgarden."

"What about Pearl Jam?" Kate asks me. "You don't think 'Jeremy' is an awesome song?"

"That black-and-white video they show on MTV all the time? Yeah, that one's cool," I say, worried that I'm beginning to sound dangerously unhip.

"Have you heard 'Black' yet?" Tom asks.

"No, I haven't."

"Listen: I *order* you to listen to that Pearl Jam tape I made you, first thing when you get home."

"You were right, Tom," Kate says. "He is adorably square."

"Ain't he though?" I laugh and pretend to be a good sport about their ribbing.

"You should've heard the covers the Peppers sang," Courtney interjects. "They did Hendrix, Dylan, Stevie Wonder, Neil Young. . ."

"Yeah," Tom says just as we reach our seats. "Kiedis sang 'The Needle and the Damage Done,' A Cappella."

"Whoa," I say as I'm sitting down. "We are *close* to the stage, man." I can't believe I'm sitting in the middle of the Giants Stadium field. Shit, in a couple weeks, I'll be watching L.T. and Phil playin' on this very field.

"Toldja they were kick-ass seats." We sit silent for a good minute, all of us just soaking it in.

"This is gonna be great!" Kate squeals, unexpectedly grabbing hold of my arm.

"Yeah," I agree, as my heart rises into my throat. I'm not sure what significance there is— if any— to the contact.

We sit and watch the opening acts of Primus and Hiphopcrisy as the first few tiny drops of rain begin to fall. Then, a DJ comes out and spins some records and tosses out condoms to the crowd as the drops begin to fall more steadily.

"Do you think there's a chance they might cut down their set if the weather gets bad?" I ask.

"Nah," Tom responds.

After the DJ leaves, the crowd begins to grow restless. The rain continues falling and the anticipation swells. Finally, the lights suddenly go out, and Giants Stadium lets out a collective screech.

DAVID SORRENTINO

Now, I'm not worried or even thinking about the rain.

President Bush appears on the giant twin television screens, poised on opposite sides of the stage— and everyone begins to boo. Then, this all-too familiar drum beat starts up underneath the Presidents words as he speaks:

"We will, we will, rock you."

Mass hysteria.

Then, somewhere in the darkness, the Edge hits the opening strings of "Zoo Station."

Worse mass hysteria.

"Aaaaaaaaaaaa-owwwww!" Tom screams, cupping his hands around his mouth. And now this wave of energy washes over me— running over my shoulders, tingling up the back of my neck and through my brain. Against one of the screens, I can make out Bono's silhouette, head down, taking a puff of a cigarette. Then the lights go up and I hear his voice, like thunder in my face:

"I'm ready. . . I'm ready for the laughing gas. . ."

Total chaos. Everyone in the floor section is standing up on the seats of their chairs. Everyone is screaming, but none of us can even hear ourselves— the exploding guitars and drums of U2 drown us all out.

"Hello, New Jersey," Bono says upon finishing the song. He holds out his hand and feels the falling rain that the rest of us are now numb to. "Feels like home," he says with a smile, just as the band launches into "The Fly."

They pass around a hand-held camera and show pictures of themselves on the big screens as they play "Even Better Than the Real Thing." A belly dancer takes to the stage as they play "Mysterious Ways." Between songs, Larry Mullen playfully reminds Bono that he was the one who gave him "his first job in rock-n-roll."

"This is so fuckin' awesome!" I yell in Tom's direction. Tom holds his hand to his ear, Hulk Hogan-like, smiles and shrugs his shoulders.

"One," is their first slow number of the night and as Bono sings, the entire stadium sings along with him. Kate looks at me and I look back at her; holding my gaze just long enough to intrigue her. As

52

she smiles back at me, my blood races fast and hot as my imagination indulges in fantasies over what the night may yet hold in store.

As they begin to play "Tryin' to Throw Your Arms Around the World," Bono takes a girl from the audience by her hand. She's wearing a nap sack on her back, along with hiking boots, and looks like she walked all the way from Alaska just to make it to this show. Bono hugs her, then sings to her. He gives her a bottle of champagne and together they spray it over the audience. Then, he gives her the camera and she films the band as they finish the song.

After that, the stadium lights go up as Bono and the Edge move out to center stage with their guitars, where they're about fifty feet away from us. I can actually distinguish their features; their faces no longer a blur to me. They begin to play "Running to Stand Still," and as Bono hits the line referring to the "drivin' rain," I see him offer a wink to the crowd, I swear. I look over at Kate and we both grin.

The Edge leaves Bono alone as he begins a solo acoustic version of "I Sill Haven't Found What I'm Looking For." It's my favorite U2 song, and Bono sings it beautifully. Perfectly. All around me, in the mass of faces, I begin to feel a kinship— the rain is only adding to all of it, now. As the song ends, someone throws an Irish flag at Bono's feet. He picks it up and holds it above his head as the we all roar.

They go on to play all my favorites— songs Tom and Courtney said they didn't play two nights ago, songs they weren't supposed to. They play "New Year's Day." They play "Sunday, Bloody Sunday." They play "Pride," with the image of Martin Luther King filling the twin screens, proclaiming that "We, as a people, will get to the promised land!"

U2 finishes the show with a rousing rendition of "Where the Streets Have No Name." They come out for their first encore with "With Or Without You." For their second encore, Bono emerges on stage in a shining, silver cowboy outfit as the band ends the night with "Desire." It's only after they've finished playing that all of us in the floor section realize we've been standing on our chairs through the whole show.

"Lemme give you a hand," I say, as I help Kate off her chair.

"Ow!" she exclaims. "My ankles are killing me!"

Courtney giggles as Tom grabs around her waist while helping her down. Then all of a sudden, the two of them are sucking face like he just got back from the War. Kate and I start to look at each other but then quickly look away, embarrassed. Uncomfortable looking at each other, and not wanting to stare at Courtney and Tom, we both just look down at the ground. Their embrace continues for a full ten seconds more— which feels like an eternity, considering all Kate and me can do is stand around and wait for them to finish.

"Quite a show, eh?" Tom asks casually, as he takes Courtney by the hand and starts to make his way to the main aisle.

"Mm, quite," Kate says as she follows them both, with me behind her.

As we exit the stadium, Courtney takes hold of Tom's wrist and drapes his arm over her shoulders. Then Kate, without warning, takes hold of my own hand. For the first time in a long time, I'm achieving an erection from actual human contact. We walk through the parking lot, breathing in the strange mixture of pot and beer that for some reason the rain has failed to wash away, and try to recall where our car is.

"Did they live up to expectations?" Kate asks. I'm not sure if she's putting on a sexier voice now or if it's just my imagination.

"Oh yeah. They were awesome." I squeeze her hand a little more tightly as I answer her. "It was weird, but the rain seemed to add to it. It was like we were at Woodstock or something."

"Well, Tom would know about *that*."

"What do you mean?"

"He was born at Woodstock. Didn't you know?"

"Right!" I exclaim. Courtney and I both laugh out loud. Kate remains straight faced and Tom is saying nothing.

"I'm serious," Kate says.

"Get out," Courtney says with a look of disbelief. We all stop for a moment to allow a few cars to pass.

"You seriously didn't tell them, Tom?" Kate asks, as we again press forward.

"Y'know you've got a big mouth, Kay?" Tom says, smiling.

"Oh, come on! Why do you make it such a big deal?"

"I don't believe it," I observe. "Tom— you were born at Wood-stock?"

"While Hendrix was playing *The Star-Spangled Banner*... Or so legend has it." Now that I stop and think about it, he *was* born in 1969. And his birthday *is* the 17th— which, I'm pretty sure, is about the same time as that historic weekend...

"Why didn't you ever tell me, hon?" Courtney interjects. "This is so cool!"

"Please. It's so humiliating, why would I wanna talk about it?"

"When did he tell you, Kate?"

"A year, year and a half ago. I figured you both knew."

"I can't believe it," I go on. "How did it happen?"

"The short of it is that my mother was supposed to give me up for adoption," Tom says, "but decided she couldn't go through with it. So she ran away."

"But how'd she end up at Woodstock?"

"Because she wanted to go," Tom answers with a laugh. "Her defense is that I was two weeks premature. But I say when you're due in two weeks, you don't go running off to rock festivals to party with half a million people."

"I still think it's cool," says Courtney.

"But wait," I say, making little effort to disguise my fascination, "I still don't get how it happened, exactly."

"How it happened?" Tom repeats, just as we reach the car. He checks underneath for beer bottles before unlocking the door. "Mom and Dad never toldja about the birds and the bees, Will?"

"I mean, you were born *at* Woodstock, in the middle of the con-cert an' all?"

"Well, it's not like I remember firsthand, but that's what they tell me, yeah," he answers, holding the door for me and Kate, then Courtney. "During Sha Na Na's set, my mother started to go into labor," he continues as he gets in and starts the car. "Somebody yelled for a doctor, and there was this pre-med student who helped deliver me. Took about two hours for me to be born. Quickest de-livery Lisa's ever had."

"Wow," is all I can say.

"We're just going for coffee, right?" he asks as he pulls out.

"Sure," says Kate.

We all agree on a nearby diner that Kate and Tom both know well. During the brief ride over, Tom reminisces about last time he saw U2 here, in '87. Meanwhile, I barely speak a word, still trying to absorb the Woodstock revelation.

"So, were they better than three nights ago?" I ask, after the waitress leaves with our orders. Apparently, this diner isn't a very well-kept secret— it seems half the concert-goers are here.

"Oh, yeah," Tom answers.

"Definitely better than the other night," Courtney adds.

"I can tell you're walking on cloud nine, Will," Tom observes. "I'd almost think you'd never been to a live concert before." He flashes that patented cheshire-smile.

"Yeah, well, U2 is like my dream show, y'know?" I respond, trying to play cool. "I've been dreamin' of seeing them for forever."

"What would your dream concert be, Deev?" Kate asks.

"The Mats, natch. But only with Bob back on guitar."

"Besides them," I say.

"Hm. I wouldn't mind seeing Nirvana again."

"Again? When did you see 'em the first time?"

"Well, that's the whole thing— they weren't even really Nirvana yet when I saw 'em."

"He never told you that story?" Courtney asks. "About the time he met Kurt Cobain?"

"You met Kurt Cobain?!? Shit! Did you know this, Kate?"

"It's news to me!"

"Calm down guys," Tom instructs us. "This was back in '89. I went with some friends to this club in Hoboken 'cause there was a hot rumor that Sonic Youth was gonna play this unannounced gig. Nirvana was actually playing there that night, but none of us even knew or cared about them back then; we all just wanted to hear Thurston and Kim do 'Teenage Riot.' I'm not even sure Kurt and company had released *Bleach*, yet. Youth never did show up, either. . ."

"But when did you meet Kurt?"

"I saw him in the parking lot afterward loadin' up some equipment and I said 'hi' to him. That's all. End of story."

"Holy shit!" I say, astonished. "What other revelations have you got planned tonight?" Things go quiet for a moment as me and Kate let this sink in. The possibility of Tom telling a tall tale never enters my mind. That's one thing about Tom: he doesn't lie about this kind of shit— he doesn't need to. But I can't get past the picture in my head: Tom standing there, with Kurt Cobain, in some parking lot somewhere in Hoboken, making small talk. Damn!

"You guys are too easily impressed," Tom says. "It was no big thing, really. I mean it's not like we hung out all night."

"I've gotta tell ya," I say, backtracking, "I'm still disappointed you never told me about the Woodstock thing, before."

"Yeah, hon," Courtney chimes in.

"Oh come on. It's so damn stupid, why would I wanna tell anyone? I would've never told Kate if I wasn't shit-faced at the time."

"I can't believe you didn't go public a couple years back when *Rebel* was conducting that big search," I observe, referring to the music magazine's quest to find the Woodstock baby in 1989— the concert's twentieth anniversary year.

"Believe me, being born at Woodstock is *not* something I wanna be famous for."

The conversation stalls briefly. The rest of us still have a ton of questions— about Woodstock, about Kurt— but Tom is obviously getting tired of discussing it all. Eventually, we resume talking, centering our attention on the upcoming school semester. It'll be Courtney's first year at Cahill and the rest of us all have advice to share. . . which professors are cool, which courses are gimme's, why you should always buy the used copies of books from the bookstore (aside from the savings, there are always useful notes in the margins, left behind by the books previous owner), what time you should arrive at the parking lot on any particular day if you want a decent spot, which cafeteria foods to steer clear of if you want to avoid a slow, lingering death. . . By the time we decide to call it a night, it's almost twelve-thirty. Anyone who hasn't finished their order has long since lost their appetite.

"You don't mind giving me a ride home, do you, Will?" Kate whispers to me in the backseat of Tom's car as we're on our way back to CSU.

"Oh, I don't mind. It's no trouble at all." Actually, I was agonizing over how we would work out the driving arrangements all night. I wasn't sure whether or not I was supposed to say something or if it would be cooler to not bring it up and just *expect* to be the one to take her home. Anyway, it's a relief to be let off the hook. Then I suddenly realize something.

"Um, where *do* you live, exactly?" Kate just smiles back at me.

"So hey," Tom says as he drops us off back at the lot, "great time tonight, huh?"

"Yeah," Kate and I respond in unison.

"We've got to do it again, soon," Courtney says as Tom begins to pull away. He honks his horn as they exit the lot.

I silently walk over to the passenger side of my '83 LeBaron with Kate. I unlock the door and hold it open for her as she gets in.

"So," Kate says as I sit down in the drivers seat.

"So," I repeat. "Here we are."

"So was I what you were expecting?" she asks.

"Well," I say with a half-laugh, "you lived up to your billing, let's put it that way."

"Why? What did Tom tell you about me?"

"He told me you. . . were hot." I can't believe I just said that. I look away, out the drivers side window, out on the deserted lot. U2 is playing in my head: "*Isolation, desolation. . .*"

"You *are* shy," Kate remarks.

"Is that what Tom told you?" I turn to face her again.

"He said were a shy, sweet guy," she tells me. "He was right."

"That Tom's a hell of a guy," I observe.

"Yeah, he is," Kate agrees. We both go quiet.

"Dating in the 90s kinda sucks, huh?" she says from out of nowhere.

"How so?"

"Well, there are no real 'dates' anymore. Like twenty years ago, we would've called this a 'blind date'; but today we just say we're hangin' out, like we're afraid to attach too much meaning to it. We're probably both wondering right now if this is a date or not."

"So is it?"

"I don't know— is it?"

"I asked you first." She smiles at me.

"I don't know if I can answer that. It takes two to make a date, right?"

"Oh, you're *good*." Now she laughs.

"Tell me what you think, then I'll tell you what I think."

I inhale deeply, mustering all my courage.

"It's a date," I say as I finally exhale again.

"Good," she says, appearing pleased. "Then it's a date."

I begin to relax. I look up, admiring the moon.

"I just can't get over it," I say.

"Over what?"

"Tom. I can't believe he was actually born at Woodstock, y'know?"

"Will," Kate purrs, "are we gonna spend all night talking about Tom?" She draws her face so near to mine that I can feel her breathing. Looking into her eyes, I take a moment to silently thank God for my ridiculous fortune.

"No," I reply softly.

CHAPTER IV

I'm sitting in my living room, on the couch, alongside my parents.

"Come on, Ed," my mother nags, "*Wheel of Fortune* is about to start!"

"Not for five more minutes yet!" my father snaps back, clinging to the remote.

All of a sudden, out of the clear blue, Kate walks in, wearing Daisy Dukes and a bikini top, and goes over and stands in front of the t.v.

"Kate," I say, rising to my feet, stupefied, "what are you doing here?!?"

"I had to see you," she says with oh-so sexy breathlessness. On the small of my back I feel this invisible hand, pushing me toward her.

"I need you," she says as we wrap our arms around one another. Both my parents' jaws are on the floor. "I need you *now*."

"But Kate, my parents. . ."

"I can't help it, Will. You're the only man who can satisfy me and I don't give a damn who knows it! Kiss me, my darling!" Her wide-open, starving mouth meets mine and I taste that exquisite tongue.

"Oh Will," Kate moans as our lips part, "what a man you are! I never dreamed it could be like this— you're the only man who could ever satisfy me! I'm so in love with you!"

"I love you too, baby," I tell her, as I run my hands over her perfect, heart-shaped ass. She drops to her knees and, with her hands still clenching at my shirt, pulls me down with her. Now we're kissing again, with a passion hot enough to set the whole damn world on fire. We're going to fuck right here on the floor, with both my parents there on the couch, in catatonic shock.

I swear this is happening. It's real— I know it is. Yet the cool breeze I'm feeling on my face is telling me that I'm not in my living room. . . I'm outside, somewhere. Around me I hear voices. And they're growing stronger.

"Where's Tom?" It's Courtney.

"Still in the water," I hear Tamara answer.

"The boy's got gills," says Keith.

My eyes flutter open and I remember I'm at the community pool in Maple Grove. Maple Grove was where Tom lived with Lisa and husband number two— Frankie's father, Michael Torretti— between 1978 and 1982. Torretti's one of the few husbands of Lisa's that Tom actually likes, and vice-versa. So the guy happily renews Tom's pool pass every year despite the fact that Tom hasn't lived here for ten years. Since Torretti works for the township (for the water department), getting the pass was easy. From there, all Tom had to do was present his valid pool badge at the local community center to get guest passes for the rest of us.

"Are we gonna check out a movie tonight or not?" Courtney asks.

"We have to wait for your boyfriend to come up for air before we can decide," Tamara says. I roll over and look at Kate, lying down alongside me on my giant beach towel. Her eyes are closed, so I can't tell if she's asleep. I stare at her face, admiring the sexy crop of her nose.

"You can quit worrying," says Keith. "Here comes Aquaman, now."

"Well tell him to get a move on," Kate says, startling me. Her eyes remain closed. "We've got to grab something to eat, then get home, shower and change if we're going out tonight."

"How many laps you do?" Courtney asks Tom as he collapses on the grass next to her.

"Wasn't counting."

"Jesus, man," Keith says, "you're like Dan *and* Dave combined."

"A one man Dream Team," Courtney adds, massaging his back.

"So you feel like a movie tonight or what?" Tam asks.

"Yeah, yeah," Tom says, toweling himself off, quickly. "Sorry, guys— I didn't realize the time."

"It's no biggie," I say. "We can still stop for something to eat if we're going to a later screening."

"Alright, we better get a move-on then, 'cause I really do wanna grab a bite." We all gather up our stuff and exit the pool.

"You have any place in particular in mind?" Keith asks in the parking lot.

"Yes, actually," Tom answers. "I've got a real craving for a turkey sub from SubStop."

"Where at?"

"You know the one in Carver? It's only ten minutes out of our way."

"We've been there before, Key," Tam reminds him.

"Oh yeah."

"Well, I don't know it," Kate pipes up.

"You know Carver at all?" Tom asks.

"A little."

"You know where Carver High School is?"

"Yeah, I think so."

"I know it," I say.

"Well, the Sub Stop's the block right before. You can't miss it, really."

"Okay, man."

"You sure you can find it? Or would you rather follow one of us?"

"Don't worry," I assure him, "we'll find it."

Kate and I hop into her car. She starts it up and I pop in that Pearl Jam tape Tom made for me. (The day after the U2 show, I listened to it from beginning to end and ended up falling in love with the band.) The traffic is unusually heavy, for whatever reason, and it takes us twenty minutes to get to Carver. We find the SubStop, standing in the shadow of Tom's old high school, no problem. A tall, thin blonde woman, late twenties I'd say, who knows Tom by name, works the register.

"Who's that?" I ask as we find a table.

"That's Penelope Jansen. We were neighbors back when I lived here."

"Hey, hear the latest about Woody?" Keith asks.

"Oh, God," says Kate. "Please— I don't think I can take any more."

"They say he used to pick up Soon Yi from school in a hearse so he could do her in the back."

"That's gotta be the stupidest the thing I've ever heard," Tom observes. Leaning forward to take a sip of his soda, you can see the white shadow of his crucifix burned into his chest by the sun. "He's got his own apartment— why wouldn't he just take her there?"

"Did he really have his own apartment?" Courtney asks.

"Sure. He and Mia have always kept separate homes. Or so I've read."

"Anybody know when that new movie of his new comes out?" Keith asks.

"I think another week or two."

"Eee-yew!" Kate exclaims. "You would put money in that perv's pocket by going to see his movie?"

"How many film directors are perverts and we just don't know it, Kay?"

"That's the whole point, isn't it, Deev? We don't know about anyone else but we know about Woody."

"I thought the point was that you didn't want to put money in the pocket of a pervert; and I'm sayin' you probably can't spend a dollar in this world without some pervert, somewhere, getting a piece of it."

"I would feel like a voyeur watching it," Tam confesses.

"Well, Woody's says it's not autobiographical," I offer.

"Oh, puh-*leeeze*," says Kate. We all laugh.

"Can we possibly change the subject?" Courtney asks.

"How 'bout politics— is that safe?"

"I would imagine so. Is there anyone here even considering voting for Bush?"

"Lisa's absolutely in love with Clinton," Tom chimes in. "I think she wants to have his baby."

"You guys have a softball game tomorrow?" Tamara asks.

"No," Tom answers. "Our season's over."

"Thank God. And I'm tellin' you right now, there's no way you're gettin' me to play again next year."

"Please, Keith— do we have to go through this every year?"

"So what are you doin' tomorrow?" Kate asks.

"Rehearsing with Shag."

"I'm the test audience," Tamara says.

"How's it coming along?"

"We're strictly a guitar and drums operation right now. I'll happily move to bass though, if we can ever get our boy, here, to sign on."

"That'll happen," Tom says. He has a guitar, but I've never seen him play, myself. He's very good, from what Keith says.

"Shag swears he can line up gigs," Keith insists.

"I can't believe Labor Day's almost here," I say.

"Our last week of freedom before the fall semester starts," Tam observes. "Better enjoy it."

"Is this really your last semester, Tom?"

"Should be," he says, knocking on the table top.

Tom's taken an extra year and a half to graduate because he's rarely taken on a full courseload in any semester, as he's always held some part-time job in addition to school. (One semester his freshman year he tried taking on a fifteen credit schedule in addition to working a twenty-five hours a week, but his grades really took a nose-dive. Ask him about that semester now and he'll groan like somebody just kicked him in the stomach.) There was even one semester— spring of '89, I think he said— when he dropped out completely so he could save up money for tuition. In fact, in the time

I've known him, this upcoming semester will be the first one in which he won't be working in addition to taking classes. Up until a week ago, he held a job at Grunnings' Ice Cream Parlor with Courtney; occasionally, he'd also fill in at Dominic's Pizza Place right here in Carver, making deliveries an odd night here and there. As for the rest of us, Keith works at High Notes (a musical instrument store), Tamara at Video Matinee, and Kate at the Gap. I also just quit my summer job at Shades, the sunglasses place at the mall, two weeks ago.

"So what are we gonna see tonight?" Tam asks.

"Just a sec," Tom says, getting up. "I'm sure somebody's got a paper in back." He goes back up to the counter and talks to blondie. She ducks away for a second, then returns with a paper for him.

"Alright now, let's see. . ." He flips to the leisure section. "Well, *Bob Roberts* just opened Friday."

"What's that about?" I ask.

"It's about a crooked politician, I think."

"Crooked politician?" asks Keith. "Isn't that redundant?"

"I heard it's real good," says Kate. "Got Tim Robbins in it."

"Oooh, did you see *The Player*?" Courtney asks.

"That was *so* good," says Tam.

"Maybe we should see *Bob Roberts*, then."

"I dunno," Tom says. "I'm readin' the review here and it sounds like a snooze-fest."

"Keep in mind," Tam warns, "this is coming from a guy who thinks *Heathers* is the pinnacle of American Filmmaking."

"Hey— it *is* the pinnacle of American Filmmaking."

"I think you like it for the Mats references," I observe.

"That helps. But even without 'em, it would still be my favorite."

"Well keep going," Kate commands. "What else?"

"*Diggstown*?"

"What's that?"

"It's about boxing or something. With Louis Gossett Jr."

"Next."

"*Johnny Suede*?"

"Oh, that's the Brad Pitt one! I didn't know it was still playing. . ."

65

"He's gay, y'know."

"Please. Every good looking movie star is gay, according to you."

"They are," I agree.

"What is it?" Tam asks. "You guys insecure about your own looks?"

"Thank you, Tam!" Kate exalts. "These guys froth over other women night and day, but the second they here a woman talk about some guy that way, they totally lose it."

"You do the same thing," Keith throws in. "You always tearin' down famous women for havin' boob jobs or liposuction or whatever. . ."

"Excuse me? I *never* do that!"

"You do so!" Tom says with a laugh.

"Please guys," Courtney interjects, "can we just pick a movie?"

"Alright, what about *Mistress*?" I ask. "I heard Robert Wuhl talking it up on Howard last week. Supposed to have a great cast, including DeNiro."

"Nah," Tom says. "That's one of those art-house films only playing in select theaters. We'd probably have to go into the city for it."

"Oh, let me see," Kate says, taking the paper out of Tom's hands. "Oooh! Here's one!"

"What?"

"*Single White Female.*"

"Is that the new one with Bridget Fonda?"

". . .And Jennifer Jason Leigh, yeah."

"Bridget Fonda?" I ask, intrigued.

"Oh, the commercials looked scary!"

"Sweet! Let's see it!"

"*Single White Female*?" Tom questions. "Come on. That's standard, formula pap-crap. I don't wanna see that. Hey, here's something!" He points to an ad on the back of the page. "*Batman Returns* is still playin' in Maplewood!"

"Everyone here's seen it already!"

"So? Let's see it again. It was good."

"Oh, bullshit! What do you say, Key?" Tam asks.

"Sorry, honey. I'm with Tom on this one."

"Well then, young Will," Tom says, turning to me. "Loyal friend. Buddy. Pal. Looks like you could be the swing vote— what's it gonna be?" The whole table goes silent as everyone hangs on my decision. . .

"Bridget Fonda," Tom spits out in disgust as we exit the restaurant ahead of the others.

"Oh, come on. It'll be good!"

"Traitor!" He accuses, but with a smile. "Benedict Arnold!" I laugh.

"So look, I wanted to ask you what you had on tap for tomorrow?" Kate's taking a ride out to Long Island with her brother to spend the day with their Dad. Courtney, I know, has her sister's baby shower, and Keith and Tamara already have their plans.

"I'm was gonna visit my grandmother. You wanna tag along?"

"Gee, would she mind?"

"Nah, you kiddin'? Nanna loves company; the more the merrier."

"How long do you think you'll be there?"

"Not long. I wanna get home with enough time to eat some dinner before *Parker Lewis Can't Lose*— I hear tomorrow's the one where he finally loses." He's kidding, of course— *Parker* isn't on Sunday night anymore. It's a shame, 'cause Sundays used to be the best t.v. night too, with that and *Flying Blind*. I think Tom was damn near ready to start a new religion centered around the worship of Tea Leoni. Ah, well. We still got *Living Color* and *Married with Children*, at least.

"Still stewin'?" Keith playfully asks, patting Tom on the back as he and the girls come out after us. Tom snarls at him and he laughs. "It'll be okay, Tom— ya can't win 'em all. There is some good news: I know somebody who works at one of the theaters it's playin' at. . . I think I can get us in for free."

"That's the spirit, Keith," I say. "Stick it to Uncle Charlie." Suddenly, everyone is breaking up.

"Uh, I think you mean 'Mister Charlie,' Will." I feel my face go red.

"Oh." Christ, I wish I could crawl into a hole, somewhere.

"No, no— he's talking about *My Three Sons*, Keith," Tom teases. "You know what an s.o.b. that Uncle Charlie was. Now, William Frawley— there was an uncle, dammit!"

Everyone finishes having a good laugh at my expense. God, the humiliation. I promise myself that I will *not* be opening my mouth again, tonight. Hell, maybe not ever.

The next afternoon, I arrive at Tom's about 1:30 and discover him watching the Yankee game on channel 11. (He was right about *Single White Female*, by the way— it really blew, despite Bridget.) I watch the game with him through the bottom of the first, then we depart for his grandmother's in Northdale.

"So you and Kate look like you're really hittin' it off," he observes as we pull onto Route 19.

"Yeah," I answer.

"Havin' fun, huh pal?"

"Nothin' but." I'm getting worried. Sounds as if there's something important on his mind. Some dark revelation about Kate that he's trying to decide how to cushion.

"What about Jen?" he asks. I actually have to stop and think for a second.

"Oh, her? Yeah, well. . . It's weird, y'know? But in light of what I have with Kate, it's like that was never even real."

"Come again?"

"I mean, it was more of a crush than it was love. Just a childish kinda thing. What Kate and I have is so *adult*, y'know?"

"Mm-hmm." Why do I get the feeling I'm being humored?

"I know it's just been over a week, but. . . I'm tellin' ya, I'm just, I just. . . I'm in love. I know this is the real thing this time. I know it's real."

"Well, just be careful," he tells me after a thoughtful pause. "It's one thing to love someone and it's another thing to be afraid that you'll never find anyone else." By now, Tom's brutal honesty should no longer stun me, but it does.

"Jesus, where'd that come from?" I ask.

"It's just that from the way you've been talking lately, it's like you're. . . I dunno, shopping for china patterns already."

"I. . . No, of course not!" Have I really been that bad?

68

"Alright, take it easy. I was just a little concerned."

"Don't worry. I've got things in perspective." At least I thought I did.

"Just enjoy it, y'know? I mean, I set you up with her because she's bright and funny and she's gorgeous, obviously. Just enjoy each other. That's all I'm trying to say."

"I gotcha. Look, I'm not naive. I'm obviously not as experienced as you, but. . ."

"*Not as experienced as me?* Who the hell am I— Wilt Chamberlain?" We laugh. "Hey Will, I'm just lookin' out for you is all. You're like the little brother I never had."

"Little mud brother."

"Exactly. I didn't mean to pry or anything."

"It's cool. Really. It's all cool." He fiddles around with the radio for a bit.

"So. . . This is your father's mother we're visiting, right?"

"Yeah. It's probably close to three weeks now since I saw her last. I've really gotta do a better job of making time for her."

"Sounds like the two of you are pretty close. I don't think I see either one of my grandmothers more than three times a year."

"You could say that we're close. When you think about it, she is the closest connection to my father that I have, really."

"How does Lisa get along with her?"

"They used to be real close back when Lisa and Dad were first dating. And even after I was born, they were close. But then when Lisa got married she moved us away and I think that pissed Gram off a bit. . . Did I ever tell you about when she tried to sue for custody of me?"

"What? You mean she took Lisa to court?"

"Well, not quite. It never did get that far."

"Jesus! What the hell happened?"

"This was back in '76. I was six, goin' on seven years old. Lisa was divorced from her first husband and she was dating alot of guys. The 70s, right?" He winks at me and clicks his tongue. "Anyway, Gram was worried about some of the guys she was hanging out with— and rightly so. Lisa could pick some real winners back then, lemme tell ya."

69

DAVID SORRENTINO

"Oh yeah?" I say. Tom groans.

"Just thinking about the parade of losers she used to bring home. . ." He shakes his head and starts to smile. "Whenever she'd go out bar-hopping with Kathy— which was just about every other night, in those days— she was a magnet for every one of those guys with the gold chains, the hairy chest and the shirt buttoned down to his navel. Most of them were harmless, but there was one guy who wasn't. He got a little free with his hands a couple times, with Mom and me, both."

"Jeez."

"Yeah. . . So anyway, Nanna got pretty upset over it and decided I'd be better off living with her."

"So how'd it end up?"

"When Lisa told me about it, I hopped on my bike and rode over to her house and talked her out of it."

"You talked her out of it?" Jesus, was Tom born twenty-three years old?

"Yeah. I just told her how sad I would be if she took me away from my mother and sister."

"Now, I assume your grandfather died, when, a few years before all this?"

"He died when my father was like ten years old. Kind of ironic: my father lost his old man and then I lose him."

"And you don't have any other family on your father's side?"

"Some. My father had two sisters; both older. Much older in fact. One of them lives there, still, with her husband. The age differences can get a little extreme, 'cause my grandparents were both in their forties when my father was born."

"Their *forties*?"

"Grandpa definitely was. Maybe Grandma was still in her late thirties. Anyway, it was definitely an unexpected surprise when she found out she was pregnant. But a very pleasant surprise. From what Nanna tells me, grandpa really wanted a son, bad."

"What'd your grandfather do? For a living?"

"He ran his own construction business with his younger brother. I told you about my Uncle Angelo, didn't I?"

70

"Y'know, my parents weren't exactly spring chickens when they had me, either."

"My uncle and my cousins still run the business, in fact."

"I don't know if they really consider me a pleasant surprise, though."

"Hey, we're just about there." Tom turns right off Northdale Avenue, then makes the next left onto Deo Street. His grandmother's house is just a couple houses down, number thirteen. Tom turns into the driveway and parks in the back.

"This is it," he says as he gets out of the car.

"Nice." It is, too. A middle-class homeowners dream. The back door of the house opens.

"Tommy?" Gotta be Nanna.

"Nanna?" She holds open her arms and Tom goes over and hugs her. "How you been?"

"Fine!" She squeezes his face in her hand. "And where have you been keeping yourself?"

"Well, I've been busy, y'know, workin' an' stuff." I step over, closer toward them. "Nanna, this is Will, my friend from school."

"Hi," I say.

"Good to meet you, William." I shake her hand, gingerly.

"So how's the back wall of the garage?" Tom asks.

"Still falling apart, I'm afraid."

"Didn't you tell me Uncle Angie called the exterminator for you?"

"Oh sure. The termites are gone, but the damage still needs to be fixed up."

"I'm sorry, Nanna— I really should take care of it myself, I guess. . ."

"Oh, don't you worry about that, now. Come on inside."

She shows us in the door, past a short staircase going up to the first floor, and leads us into this cozy little basement-converted apartment. There's a kitchenette with a table & chairs overlapping with a small living room set-up.

"Have a seat," she tells us. "Gimme a minute— I'm just going to run upstairs and see if Luisa has any cake or pie." Tom and I watch her move slowly up the stairway.

71

"Wait," Tom says as I'm about to sit down. "Wanna see something spooky?"

"Sure." He opens the door into this room right off to the side of the little kitchen set-up and enters. I follow him in.

"Voila," he says as he flicks the lights on. It's a bedroom.

"Yeah? What's so spooky?"

"It's my father's room," he tells me with a little drama in his voice. I take a good look around. "My grandmother cleans this room religiously, everyday, but she hasn't moved a thing, not one piece of furniture, since he died."

"Damn." He ain't kidding. Tacked to the wall alongside the bed, there are yellowed newspaper clippings about the Northdale High School football team, circa 1968. Above the door, a crumbling Northdale High pennant. "It's like we stepped into the way-back machine, dude."

"After Grandpa died, my Aunt Luisa moved back in with her family, upstairs, while Dad and Nanna moved down here." He sits down on the bed. "Y'know, she's got this perfectly good bed here, but she won't sleep in it. She still sleeps on the pull-out couch, out there."

"Wow."

"Here," he says, abruptly getting up and going over to the closet. He slides open the door and drags out this milk crate with some old record albums in it. I kneel down on the floor alongside him to get a better look. "These were his."

There's a wide variety of stuff here: "Wheels of Fire," some Who, the Stones' "Aftermath" and "Beggars Banquet"; but also "Highway 61," "Blonde on Blonde" and Joan Baez's "Baptism." Even a couple Zappas.

"Pretty eclectic tastes."

"Boys?" his grandmother calls from outside. We exit the room together.

"I was just showing Will around Dad's room."

"Oh. Well, I hope you like crumb cake, William," she says. "I know Tommy likes it."

"I love crumb cake, Mrs. Redivo. That'll be fine."

"Do you take coffee or tea?" I notice she has the kettle on.

"I'll take tea."

"He actually prefers coffee, Nanna."

"No, that's okay."

"I'll put the coffee on for you," she insists.

"No, please don't bother— tea is fine."

"Are you sure, dear?"

"Yes, yes, really." We all sit down.

"I'm sorry I didn't think to ask before I put the water on," she apologizes. "Just force of habit, 'cause I know that's what Sonny always. . . Oh! I mean, Tommy!"

"That's alright, Nanna."

"Sometimes I look right into your face and you look so much like your father, I just say it without even thinking."

"It's okay," he says, laughing a little. "It doesn't bother me."

"So, what were you doing in your Dad's old room?" she asks. "Were you telling your friend, here, any of those old stories about your father?"

"Actually, I figured I'd save that for you, Nanna. You tell 'em better than me, anyway."

"Which one would you like me to start with? The streaking incident?" You can actually see her cringe at the thought of this story.

"How about 'borrowing' the police car that time when he was thirteen?" Tom requests. "That's my favorite."

Nanna smiles brightly as she removes her glasses and wipes the lenses against her sun dress. With faraway eyes, she begins to regale me with this tale of Tom's father, and about halfway through, I look over at Tom and I wonder to myself what it must be like for him when he hears all of this. I know he's enjoying it on one level, but I imagine it must be kinda sad for him too, no? I mean, how rough is that, having no firsthand experiences, no memories, of your own father?

Then again, this is Tommy Redivo. He still has his Mom and his sisters, not to mention Nanna, here. I suppose having them more than makes up for what he missed out on with his Dad. I know I can only dream of getting along with my own family so well, so effortlessly, as he does.

CHAPTER V

Tommy Redivo is driving the twins home after their soccer game with Lisa in the passenger seat, beside him.

"Did you talk to the head of the English department?" she asks him.

"Yeah."

"Well, what did he say?"

"Just what I told you he'd say: I've gotta take one more course in comparative lit to fulfill the requirements of the major. So it looks like you're stuck with me one more semester after this." Lisa stares straight ahead, without reaction. "Hey, I had the course scheduled for this semester— it's not my fault the professor died on me."

"Did I say anything?"

"Yeah, but it's the *way* you didn't say anything." The girls remain stone silent in the back seat. They're fighting again.

"They're throwing a 30th birthday party for George's son, Jack. Would you be interested in going?"

"Hell, no."

"And why not?"

"Why not? I barely know the guy. Why would I go?" He begins to turn up the volume on the radio.

"Keep it down," his mother says, lowering it.

"Hey!" He turns it up again, defiantly.

"Well, at least put on a decent station, then." She tunes to another station. Then he to another. Then she, again.

"There! Is this one good enough for you?"

He doesn't answer. She hesitates a moment before letting herself slump back in her seat. She begins her old meditation ritual: closes her eyes, finds her center. Draws in her breath, through her nose, through her lungs, through her abdomen.

. . .Exhale.

There. She feels more relaxed already. The Elton John song that's playing seems to have calmed Tommy down, as well. He even begins singing along with the words.

"*Baby— so they give you anything. . . Darlin'— all the joy money can bring. . . Baby— do they bring you happiness? Darlin'— you're no different from the rest.*"

It's funny that she doesn't know this song, because she considers herself a big Elton John fan. Still, it's a nice song.

"*Can't you see that it's love you really need? Take my hand. . . and I'll show you what a love could be. . . before it's too late. . .*

"*Mama don't want you, Daddy don't want you. . . Give it up baby, baby. . . Mama can't buy you love. . .*"

She opens her eyes to see him smiling back at her. And he goes right on singing:

"*Mama don't want you, Daddy don't need you. . .*"

"Why do you feel it necessary to start a fight every time we spend more than five minutes together?"

"What? I'm just singing. You're the one who picked the station." She clicks the radio off, angrily. "I beg your pardon! I was lis-tening to that, thank-you-very-much!"

"Stop it, okay? Stop being a smartass!"

"Why don't you punish him, Mom?" Samantha asks. "Like you do us?"

"Yeah!" Tiffany agrees excitedly.

"You two just be quiet back there."

"Yeah, Mom, go ahead— waste me."

She does not respond. In fact, she does not utter another word the rest of the ride home. After pulling in the driveway, she exits the car and enters the house, ahead of the others. The twins begin to fight over who gets out of the car first; Tommy has to break them up. Inside, they find Frankie in the living room along with Stacy from next door.

"Hi, Tom," Stacy greets, practically singing. Sam doesn't bother to stop, continuing straight through to the kitchen.

"Hey, Stace."

"That's, um, a nice shirt," she remarks, biting her lower lip.

"Why thank you, dear! May I say you look positively ravishing, as well?" She squirms in her seat and looks down, swallowing hard.

"Thanks," she says, blushing.

"So did you guys win?" Frankie asks.

"We lost 'cause Sam wouldn't pass me the stupid ball," Tiffany informs her.

"I think somebody needs to get a cool drink and simmer down," Tommy counsels. He gently nudges her along, out of the living room and into the kitchen.

"How was the game?" Meredith asks as they enter. "This one's not talking," she says, referring to Samantha, sitting at the table.

"Jeez, aren't you ever in Pennsylvania?" Tommy asks. He's being sarcastic, of course, but the question reminds her of just why she isn't in Pennsylvania right now: her break-up with Matt, only a week ago.

"We lost," Tiffany says, "because Samantha's a ball hog."

"I am not a ball hog!" Sam yells, standing up.

"So why didn't you pass me the ball, stupid?!?"

"You weren't even open!"

"Enough." Tommy gives them a double-barrel flicking.

"Owww-*uh!* That hurt!"

"God!" They both rub their foreheads.

"No more yelling or name calling." He takes two juice boxes from the refrigerator. "The games over; let it go."

"Tom got into a fight with Mom in the car," Samantha informs Meredith as she punches in her straw. "But she wouldn't punish him or ground him or *anything*."

"What else is new?" Meredith's eyes burn a hole in him. He's surprised by the sudden anger in her voice— he has no idea of the nerve he struck, before.

"Why don't you take your juice into the living room and watch t.v. with Frankie?" he suggests to the girls. They hesitate a moment. "Go ahead."

Slowly, they shuffle out; Samantha looking back a second before going.

"You got a bug up your ass about something?" he asks, once he and Meredith are alone. "What's your problem?"

"Nothing," she says, casually putting her feet up on the chair next to her. "So you and Mom were at it again, huh?"

"What of it?"

"I just think it's silly. . ."

"*What* is silly?"

"The way you can't resist getting into these petty little wars with Mom— all because of an unresolved Oedipus complex."

"God, how I rue the day I bought you that Freud book." She was always saying how everyone in the house was nuts, how they all needed a psychiatrist, so he got her that beat-up copy of Freud's *The Interpretation of Dreams* from the used bookstore and gave it to her for Christmas back in '87. It was supposed to be a joke. Sometimes he thinks she adopted it as her Bible just to spite him.

"It just pisses you off that I've got you so pegged. Watch— I bet after Courtney, your next girlfriend is a much older woman."

After Courtney. The word echoes in his head.

"Yeah. Absolutely right, Mer. You've got me all figured out. Now, do I get a chance to analyze you?"

"Go ahead. I can't wait to hear this." The volume of both their voices begins to rise.

"Let's start with why *you* can't maintain a long-term relationship. Could it be that you're acting out Mom's pattern of dating losers?"

"*I* can't maintain a relationship? Look who's talking!"

"Or maybe you just bring home these jerks as a way of aggravating her, huh? Getting back at her for divorcing Joe? Or maybe it's Joe's attention you've been shooting for all along, huh?"

"Oh, Fuck off."

"What's wrong, Mer? Truth hurt?"

"SHUT THE HELL UP!"

"THEN DON'T FUCKIN' START WITH ME!"

"What is going on here?" Lisa asks as she comes running in. "I can hear you two all the way upstairs!"

Tommy and Meredith lock on each other, with anger.

"I'll be up in my room," Tommy states, finally. "Call me when dinner's ready."

That night, dinner passes in near-complete silence. George cracks wise about whether or not he's eating in the right house. No one laughs. One by one, as each of them has finishes eating, they excuse themselves and retreat to the sanctuaries of their respective rooms.

After a short while, Meredith takes it upon herself to be the first one to break the ice.

"Yes?" Tommy responds to the knock at his door.

"It's me."

"Come in." Meredith enters and slowly closes the door behind her. Tommy's at work, writing something in his notebook as he sits in his bed.

"I think we should talk."

"Okay. Talk." She can't tell if his being short is designed to annoy her. She decides to ignore it. She really doesn't want to get angry all over again. At least she's trying not to.

"I guess I just wanted to tell you that I didn't mean those things I said before." It takes great effort to get the words out. Her pride weighs down each syllable. "I'm. . . sorry."

"Don't be ridiculous," he counters. "You meant every word you said and so did I. How are we supposed to effectively hurt each other with anything less than the truth?"

She snaps.

"You haven't changed since you were ten, you know that? You're the most obstinate, most childish person I've ever known.

78

There's never any apologizing with you, no olive branches, no white flags, nothing."

She expects him to lash back but he doesn't. He just looks at her, betraying no emotion.

"You love me, cookie?" he asks at last, closing his notebook.

"Ye-eesss," she concedes. "You're my brother; of course I love you."

"And you know I love *you*, right?"

". . .Yes."

"Okay, then. Don't you think our relationship is strong enough to survive a little tiff now and then?"

"Well, yeah, but. . ."

"Then no apologies are necessary," he tells her. He moves to the edge of the bed and pats the mattress. "Sit." She walks over and sits down next to him.

"Now. . . what got you so pissed off, before?"

"It was no big deal. It's silly, actually."

"Mer, it's me. C'mon— spill."

"It's just. . . When you asked me about why I wasn't in Pennsylvania, it reminded me of Matt. . ."

"I see. I guess I should've realized that."

"No, it's alright."

"Why don't you call him, then?"

"I don't know." They both fall silent.

"Do you really think I'm drawn to losers?" she asks him. He laughs a laugh of relief.

"Maybe I just hold your boyfriends to impossible standards. Maybe I feel like no man can ever be good enough for my favorite sister."

"Yeah right," she says. "You *sure* there's no sibling rivalry going on here?"

"Don't start with the psychoanalysis again."

"Really," she persists. "Maybe you run down the guys I date as a means of belittling *me*, and therefore make *yourself* look better in the process."

"Now see? I try to pay you a compliment, try to let you know I care, and you go right back to this. . . Maybe all your over-analyzing is a way to keep from expressing you real feelings, huh? Ever consider *that?*"

"Hey asshole, didn't I just say 'I love you' a minute ago?" He laughs again. She gazes down at the floor and smiles.

"So you think I'll ever find somebody?" she playfully asks.

"Ah, you will," he assures her. "Don't be so quick to write off Matt, either."

"I don't know. I'm nineteen years old and I've never been in love. Is that normal?"

"Oh, come on— I've seen you head-over-heels before. Lotsa times."

"Not really, no. I mean, I've liked different guys, sure, but I've never seriously fallen for anyone before. Like I remember the first time you brought Sheila home, how cow-eyed you both were... I wanna feel that way about someone, someday."

He takes a heavy breath. That name caught him off-guard.

"I'm not so sure that you do," he tells her.

"What do you mean?"

"I..." He hesitates. "I would just hope it works out better for you than it did for me."

A fresh knock falls upon the door.

"It's Mom. Can I come in?"

Tommy glances back at Meredith. She nods, letting him know it's okay; that she has nothing else to discuss with him.

"Yeah." Lisa opens the door.

"You two are talking again?" she asks, surprised.

"Yes," Meredith tells her.

"Well, that's good." She leans forward, holding the bed frame. "Could I possibly have a minute to talk to your brother, alone?" Now it's Meredith looking to Tommy, who in turn nods. She gets up and leaves, closing the door behind her.

"I don't suppose you're here to discuss our little brawl in the car, earlier?"

"No," she answers matter-of-factly. Her answer doesn't surprise him. There are two basic courses of action to take when trying to make up with someone after a fight: talk it out or pretend it never happened. Lisa and Meredith are exact opposites in this regard. "Actually, I wanted to talk to you about Samantha."

"Sam? What about her?"

"Well you saw what happened at the game, today."

"Yeah, so?"

"So? So she's constantly fighting with Tiffany. And when she's not, she's depressed."

"Mm-hm. I guess George is tired of watching her mope around the house, right?" She doesn't answer him. She never answers him when he's right. "Alright, so you want someone to talk to her. Why me?"

"You know why. She listens to you." He rubs his chin and taps at his notebook.

"You think I'm just going to talk to her and make everything right, just like that?"

"She's nine years-old, Tommy. Whatever it is that's bothering her, how serious could it be?"

"Yes, how foolish of me. I forgot that nine year-olds don't have real problems. They never ask serious questions or have serious thoughts."

"I think she's just looking for some special attention right now. And she won't open up to me."

"Look," he concedes, "I'll talk to her. . ."

"Thank you."

"But," he adds sternly, "I can't guarantee results."

"I know." She smiles back at him as she leaves the room.

He sits there a moment, thinking. Then, deciding on a course of action, he exits his room and moves quickly toward the stairs. But before he begins to descend, he hears something disturbing coming from Frankie's room: the sound of Paul Westerberg's voice butchering the lyrics to Black Sabbath's "Iron Man." He vacillates briefly before abruptly turning back around.

"Is that my 'Mats tape?" he asks, barging into Frankie's room. "Do you know I've been goin' nuts looking for this?"

"You said I could listen to any of your tapes," Frankie says in her defense. She sits up in her bed, where numerous text books and loose-leaf paper are strewn about.

"I said you could listen to them, I didn't say you could hoard 'em! How long have you had this, anyway?"

"God, I don't know!"

"Oboy," he says, noticing his softcover edition of *The Complete Love and Rockets*, Volume 7, on top of her stereo. "And this. . . I don't think Mom would appreciate you reading this."

"I wanted to ask you about that."

"What about?" he asks cautiously.

"Are Maggie and Hopey supposed to be lesbians?"

"Interesting question." He begins to squirm. It takes alot to make him squirm.

"Well are they or not?"

"It's complicated," he says, sitting next to her on the bed after clearing away some of the debris. "Do you know what a bisexual is?"

"Of *course* I know what bisexual is."

"What is it, then?"

"It's someone who swings both ways."

"Uh, yeah. Well that's kinda what they are."

"But are they like a *couple?*"

"Well, that's the whole mystique of the strip— I wouldn't want to spoil it for you. Don't worry though, you'll figure it out."

"I don't know," she tells him. "And I don't get what happened to Speedy, either."

"What don't you get?"

"I mean, what happened? Did he kill himself? Or did those gang-guys get him?"

"No, no. He killed himself. The gang-bangers figured they got Speedy when they shot 'Litos' eye out. So they wouldn't even be looking for him at that point."

"I guess not," she says, unsure. "I just felt so sad for him when Maggie was yelling at him in the hospital."

"Yeah. It was pretty sad." They both stop for a moment to appreciate the sounds of the Replacements coming over her speakers.

"Can I ask you something?" Frankie inquires.

"Sure, sweetie. Shoot."

"Why do you like Courtney?" He takes a second, reflecting on the question.

"Why ask me that? You're not trying to set me up with Stacy again, are you?"

"*No*," she answers, annoyed that he hasn't figured out what she's getting at. "There's this really cute guy in my biology class and I need some advice."

"I see. And you want *my* advice?"

"Who else am I gonna talk to about it?"

True enough. Meredith would tease her endlessly and she certainly isn't going to talk to the twins. And all the siblings she has in the world live under this roof— something she and Tommy have in common. Meredith has a younger brother, Dan, that lives with her father up in Massachusetts; while the twins have an older sister, Veronica, from their father Steve's first marriage. (Tommy actually had quite a crush on her when Steve and Lisa were first dating, but that's another story.) Meredith and Dan probably haven't seen each other more than a half-dozen times in their lives, and the twins see Ronnie only slightly more often than that. Still, it must be nice knowing they're there, at least.

"I don't know, Frankie. Aren't you a little young to start worryin' about guys?"

"Excuse me, but I happen to be in high school now in case you didn't realize it. And besides, I've had other boyfriends before."

"Excuse *me*. If you've had other boyfriends, then what do you need my lousy advice for?"

"Because this one's different. He's a sophomore."

"Oh, an older man. I could see where this one would be a little tricky for you, then."

"Yeah!" she exclaims; excited that someone else finally seems to understand her.

"I know I'm going out on a bit of a limb here, but maybe you should try talking to him."

"Talk to him? You make it sound so easy."

"It is. You see how Stacy was charming me, before? The way she said she liked my shirt? Guys eat that stuff up."

"Really?"

"Yeah, you kiddin'? She had me wrapped around her little finger."

"What else do I tell him? After I say he has a nice shirt? Or whatever?" She sits transfixed, waiting on his answer.

"Whatever's topical, Frankie. Talk to him about whatever's going on in biology class."

"I could. . . tell him I need help with my homework?"

"Frankie. . . don't ever dumb yourself down just to make some guy feel smart."

"What am I supposed to do, then?"

"Ask him to. . . I dunno, be your study partner. Quiz each other with those dopey questions they have in the back of the texbooks."

"You mean the chapter reviews?"

"Yeah, those. At least that way, neither one of you is made to feel smarter than the other."

"Okay," she says, twisting her long hair between her fingers. "I'll think about it."

"What's to think about?"

"I'm just gonna think about it!" she tells him with a grin.

"Stop playing with your hair," he tells her as he smooths over her lush locks. He takes a minute just to look at her.

"*You*," he declares, "are my favorite sister."

"I know," she says, proudly. Smiling at her, he gets up to leave.

"Just remember to put my stuff back whenever you're done using it, okay?"

"I will. I promise."

Tommy moves rapidly downstairs to the first floor. To Samantha's room.

"Hey."

"What?" Samantha asks, opening her door.

"I was just going to take Tempest for a walk," he says. "Wanna come?"

"Okay!" She goes and retrieves the leash while he calls for Tempest. They converge at the front door.

"I get to put it on!" she says as she attaches the leash to Tempest's collar.

"Alright, but let me hold it. At least until she calms down, a little." Samantha opens the door and Tempest charges out, violently pulling Tommy with her.

"Can I hold her now?"

"Jeez! You see how she is— give her a minute."

They're about to start up the block when his attention is captured by something on the sidewalk. Just as he's reaching down to pick it up, Samantha snatches it away.

"Ha! Got it!"

"Hey, you!"

"See a penny pick it up an' all the day you'll have good luck," she recites. Tempest stops to smell the trunk of her favorite tree.

"Here, smarty," he says, offering the dog's leash. Tempest does her business and the walk resumes.

"If I ask you a question," he says as they turn the corner at the top of the block, "will you promise not to get mad?"

"What?"

"You promise?"

"Yeah, I promise."

"Why didn't you pass Tiffany the ball, today?"

"Because she wasn't open," Samantha insists. Tommy puts his hands in his pockets and looks out on the setting sun.

"Okay. . . Let me put it this way: would you have passed her the ball even if she was open?" Samantha doesn't immediately answer him.

"No," she finally confesses.

"Why not, Sam?"

"Because she. . ." She struggles for the words, but he will not interrupt her. "She's already so popular, everybody loves her. . . Why can't I get a chance to score the goal?"

"And nobody loves *you?*"

"Not like *her.*"

"Come on, Sam."

"It's true! And besides, I was the one who wanted join the soccer league *first*. Does Tiffany have to do *everything* I do?"

"Sam, nobody's out to get you."

"Yes you are. Everybody always takes her side."

"You're wrong."

"No, I'm not."

"How am I supposed to convince you?"

"You can't! It's the truth!"

"Fine," he sighs. "I won't waste my time trying, then." He continues walking, not offering anything further. They go by a couple more houses before Samantha's curiosity overwhelms her.

"What were you going to say?" she asks him.

"About what?"

"To convince me, stupid!"

"Oh, that!" he says. "I was just going to ask you if you thought *I* loved Tiffany more than you. Is that what you think?"

"Maybe not *you*," she concedes.

"What about Meredith?"

"I dunno."

"Really? You don't know, huh?"

"Maybe not."

"Frankie, of course, can't stand either one of you... Do you think Mom loves Tiffany more than you?"

"I know she loves *you* more than any of us!"

"Ha!"

"She does! She never punishes you for anything, she barely yells at you..."

"Sam, it's because Mom *does* love you that she yells at you and punishes you. If she didn't love you, she wouldn't pay any attention to you at all." Tempest stops momentarily to sniff a fire hydrant.

"So... You don't think Mom loves you? 'Cause she won't punish you?"

"No... Mom loves me. The two of us just need to work on some things." Tempest finishes smelling the hydrant and proceeds onward. "Kinda like you and Tiffany."

"What do you mean?"

"I mean you two need to work on things, too." Sam makes one of her classic faces at him. "You need to figure out how to get along and not fight so much."

"God! I'll try, okay?" They're at the bottom of their street now, having completed their circle around the block.

"You can unlatch her now— she'll go right home from here." Samantha reaches down and releases the dog's leash.

"Can I ask *you* something now?" she inquires as Tempest walks just ahead of them.

"Sure," he tells her.

"Why do you love me?"

"Why do I love you?"

"You said you love me as much as Tiffany," she says with an impish grin. "I wanna know what you love about me."

"Well," he begins, "for starters, you're the only other person in the house who likes to eat that white-cheddar popcorn with me."

"Be serious!"

"I am," he assures. "And I love playing Nintendo with you. . ."

"What else?"

"Oh, tons of things. I love you for those pictures you give me that you draw in school, I love jumping rope with you, walking the dog with you. . ." Sam looks down at the sidewalk, embarrassed yet pleased. "You're my favorite sister, y'know."

"Cut it out!" she orders. They walk on a little further.

"Close your eyes," she commands, just as they're just reaching home.

"You think I'm stupid?"

"I'm not gonna do anything!"

"Right!"

"I'm not!" she insists. Finally, he complies.

"Alright, now hold out your hand." He does. "There!"

He opens his eyes and there's the penny, right in the center of his palm. He looks up and watches Sam race Tempest into the house.

"Lil' stinker," he mutters to himself, smiling.

Back inside, he's about to head upstairs when he hears Tiffany moving around in her room, right across from Sam's. He takes a good minute, just thinking to himself, then raps on her door.

"C'mon in."

"Hey, sis." She's playing with her dolls.

"Tommy? What's up?"

"Nothing really. Just figured we haven't hung out for awhile. Thought we could use a little big brother-baby sister time."

"I am *not* a baby," she retorts, predictably.

"I know, I know," he says with a roll of his eyes. "So is there anything special you'd like to do?"

"I dunno."

"Go ahead. Whatever you wanna do."

"We could play a game I guess. . . Oh! I know!"

"What?"

"You could French-braid my hair!!"

"Oh, no! Meredith's home— you can get her to do that."

"But I want *you* to do it. You're better at it than she is."

"Come *on*," Tommy begs in his best high-pitched whine.

"You *said* whatever I *wanted*. . ."

It's a lost cause. He's being out-whined.

"Oh, alright! But you're gonna have to wash your hair now if you wanna wear it to school tomorrow."

"*Yes!*" she rejoices.

Tiffany takes a quick bath (quick by Tiffany-standards, at least), after which Tommy blow dries her hair. The two then retreat upstairs to his room to watch *Beverly Hills 90210* on his t.v.

"What am I doin' here?" Tommy questions as he brushes her head. "A fishtail? A twistie? Or just a straight braid?" Growing up in a house full of girls, he has become a connoisseur of hairstyles and feminine hygiene products.

"Can you gimme a ring?" she requests.

"You mean a halo? Aw, honey, be reasonable— I don't wanna be here all night with this. . ."

"*Alright*. Gimme a regular braid, then."

"Inside kind or outside?"

"*Inside*," she responds like it's the stupidest question ever asked in history. The conversation suddenly halts as the show starts.

"Brenda is such a *skank*." Tiffany declares at the first commercial break.

"A what?"

"Y'know— a skank. Damaged goods."

"Where did you get that word from?"

"From you. From when you were shooting baskets outside with Keith last night." He groans.

"Don't let Mom or George catch you using that word."

"Why? I betcha they don't know what it means, even."

"Let's keep it that way." The two fall silent again as the program resumes.

"Do you think I'll have big boobs?" she asks at the next break.

"I doubt it, kid."

"Why do you say that?"

"Because Mom is flat as a board. So are Frankie and Meredith. It runs in the family." He pauses. "Why are boobs so important?"

"Because that's what guys like, isn't it?"

"Mm. The wrong type of guy." The show comes back on and they go quiet again.

"Will you give me away at my wedding?" she queries once the program breaks again.

"I can't. That's your father's job."

"Who says?"

"That's just the way they always do it."

"You don't like weddings much, do you?"

"No, actually, I don't."

"How come?"

"Because they're all the same. The ceremony's always the same, they play the same songs at the reception, do the same dances. . ."

"I like the chicken dance." Again, the talk abruptly halts as the show comes back on.

"There," Tommy declares— finishing his sister's hair just as the final credits begin to roll. "Now just try and sleep on your tummy tonight so it stays perfect."

"Thanks!"

"Aw, you're welcome, sweetie. . . Don'tcha know you're my favorite sister?"

CHAPTER VI

I'm standing at first base, Shaggy's at second, and someone whose name escapes me is at third. Top of the ninth, two outs, down three. The pressure is all on the batter's shoulders.

Tom's shoulders.

"No battah, no battah! Suh-wing battah!"

Damn, could the second baseman shut up already? Over in the stands, Courtney and Kate are in the stands, doing a two-woman wave and laughing their asses off. . . God, how I wish I was up there with them. As simple a task as running the bases may appear, trust me, it's terrifying. What if I trip? Can you imagine the humiliation? How did I ever let Tom talk me into this in the first place? I suck! The only reason I'm even on base right now is 'cause the pitcher hit me, fer Chrissake!

The wind-up. The pitch.

"Ooooh," everyone moans as Tom drops on his ass, brushed back.

We came into the inning down five runs. Keith led off with a hit, then the guy after him got a hit and then the next guy walked. Then Shag came up and got a hit, plating two runs, and the deficit was three. After I got hit by a pitch, the lead-off guy struck out and the number two hitter popped up to short. Now, it's up to Tom.

The wind-up. The pitch.

Bang.

"Aw, fuck!" the pitcher curses. I almost get whiplash trying to keep up with the ball— Tom's absolutely destroyed it, his second dinger of the game. Shit, you'd swear it was a hardball the way it's carrying. It finally lands in the brook, a good four-hundred feet away, no lie.

Best part is I don't have to worry about running the bases.

"Alright everybody, calm down," Tom tells us all, after crossing the plate and accepting the hi-fives. "We've still gotta finish this off."

The next guy up grounds weakly to third to end the inning, and we all run out to assume our positions: Shag's pitchin', Keith's in left, Tom center and I'm in right.

"C'mon Shag," Tom shouts, "three up, three down!"

The first guy up flies out to Keith, in left. Then the next guy grounds it right back to Shag for a quick two outs. You can feel the anticipation running through the whole team now— our first victory, we can taste it. But then the third guy up hits a laser down the left field line and by the time Keith can get it back into the infield, the guy's standing on third.

It's never easy, is it?

The next guy up takes Shag's first two pitches for balls. He fouls off the next two, but you can tell he was definitely on 'em— a hair higher or lower, and we'd be on our way home on the losing end. Again. Shaggy enters his wind up and all I can do is pray it isn't hit to me. Dear Lord, please, anything but that.

He hits it, a high pop up, right to Tom— praise be to God. I can see Keith already has his hands in the air, celebrating. Suddenly though, Tom tosses his mitt aside.

"Shit!" Keith bellows. Tom casually removes his cap and catches the ball in it. We all mob him.

"Motherfucker," Keith swears, "if you ever dropped that ball. . ."

"Take a pill willya? I had it all the way."

We go through the game ending ritual of lining up to shake hands with the opposing team— a little easier to stomach today, having finally won one. Then the friends and well-wishers come over from the stands. Courtney throws her arms around Tom.

"Awesome!" she exclaims.

"You were great, honey," Kate tells me.

"Thanks babe." I know she's only stroking me but still, I appreciate it.

"Pepperoni pies all around!" Tom cries as we all burst into Dom's. "On the house!"

"On the house?" Dom questions from behind the counter. "You won?!?"

"That's right, old timer! That'll be two at this table!" Tom holds up two fingers. "Doo-ay! Doo-ay!"

"How'd you manage it?" Dom asks, sliding a fresh pie into the oven.

"Sheer luck— what else?"

"Fuck that," Keith says. "We earned every bit of this one."

"You shoulda seen the last one Tommy hit, boss," Shag says. "Into the friggin' *brook*."

"Please," Tom says. "On the third bounce maybe."

"Like hell," I jump in.

"You should take your bows while you can, Tommaso," Dom advises as he brings over a pie. "Before you know it, you'll be an old man, and you can't even bend over to tie your shoes."

"Ah, I ain't living that long, Dom." We all begin to dig in.

"You know you're on tomorrow, Seymour?" Dom asks as he returns with the second pie.

"Yeah, yeah," Shaggy answers. "Y'know, Dom could use some extra help around here. . ."

"I *know* you ain't talkin' to me," Tom says.

"Aw, c'mon. . . it'll be like the old days."

"That's what I'm afraid of! Especially with summer comin' up— the place gets like a mad house. . . and with the ovens firing day and night, you sweat your ass off."

"Don't you ever give up, Shag?" Courtney asks. "You've been trying to coax him back here the whole time I've known you."

"Ah, they all come back. It's like that old gag from *Taxi*: 'the only guy who ever made it outta here was James Caan. . . and he'll be back!' "

Shaggy graduated Cahill with a degree in history two years ago, but still works here. In fact, he's been here almost eight years, starting when he was a junior at Carver High back in '85. He helped get Tom a job here the following year, and the two convinced Dom to get involved in the local softball league in '87.

"Think you'll make the playoffs this year?" Kate asks.

"You kiddin'?" Keith says. "We're cruisin' in the left lane, with the top down and our feet up on the dash."

"Will you listen to this?" Tom says. "You've gotta be the most up-and-down guy I know. When we win, we're major league material, and when we lose I've gotta talk you in off the ledge."

"We turned a corner today, I can feel it."

"We're still one and three!"

"Anyone here decide who they're gonna be for the party on Friday?" Courtney asks. Tom's Midsummers Eve party has a 70s theme this year and everyone is supposed to come dressed accordingly.

"Don't you wanna be surprised, Court?" Tom asks her.

"I've got some ideas," Kate admits, "but I don't wanna give it away yet."

"You guys aren't seriously getting dressed up in cheesy 70s clothes, are you?" Shaggy asks.

"Of course!" Courtney answers. "I can't wait for the rest of you guys to see me and Tom!"

"You're *all* fucked."

"I've gotta go pick up Tamara at work," Keith says as he finishes off his first slice. "You want me to call you?" he asks Tom.

"Sure, whatever. If I don't hear from you, we'll catch up whenever." Keith takes two more slices to eat in the car as he's leaving. The rest of us stay and finish off what's left. After we're done, Shag stays to talk to Dom about something while the rest of us are filing out.

"You play Saturday or Sunday next week?" Kate asks in the parking lot.

"Sunday."

"That's good. You'd probably be too hung over to play Saturday."

Tom's Camaro screeches to an abrupt stop right in front of us.

"Jesus!" I swear.

"Are you guys coming back to my place or not?" he asks, revving the engine.

"Yeah," we tell him. Giving us the thumbs-up sign, he drives off in his black chariot with Courtney in the passenger seat; like dark Hades carrying off bright, shining Persephone to the underworld.

"Gonna be one of those nights," I predict. Kate just smiles at me and says nothing.

Sunday morning. Sweet, lightless oblivion is interrupted by the sound of my mother's screeching voice.

"Will, pick up the phone!" I pick up the extension in my room.

"What the fuck?"

"Rise and shine, mud brother!"

"What time is it?" I rub my eyes and look at my clock. "Shit!" It's 11:30!

"Hey, do me a favor, willya?" Tom asks. "When you come over, stop at the Spring Street Deli and get me some crumb cake. You know the kind I like, right?"

I hang up on him, laughing.

I grab a quick shower before running over to Tom's, stopping at the deli along the way. When I get there, he's in bed looking as ragged and decrepit— and happy— as I've ever seen him. The proverbial pig in shit.

"What took you so long?" he asks.

We watch Bret "Hitman" Hart (Tom's favorite wrestler) bitch-slap Shawn Michaels like he owes him money on channel five with the volume turned down and the stereo blaring out some mix tape of 7" punk singles Tom's made. Frankie happily comes in to serve him his customary Sunday tea to go with the crumb cake I brought. Once the wrestling's over, Tom goes to take a shower while I hang out in his room, reading the latest issue of *Eightball* that I've discovered on his night stand.

Every weekend for the last ten months has been like this. I swear, I never even used to have dreams that were as good as my

94

reality is now: staying out 'til dawn, laughing, partying, drinking, fucking. . . sharing hours at a time of those eyes-locked, souls-bared discussions that make me feel like an actual member of the human race. Every moment is fun and rollicking and profound and thought-provoking and life-affirming. Just as it should be when you're young and alive.

"Shoot some hoops?" Tom asks me upon his return from the shower.

"Sure!"

He scoops up his basketball and we storm down the back stairs with Tempest in tow. Five steps out the back door, he takes a quick shot and sinks it. As he's retrieving the ball, he whips off his T-shirt.

"What are you doing? It's not that hot."

"I know. But every now and then I like giving Stacy a thrill."

"Stacy?" I start to turn around.

"No, don't!" Tom orders, and I quickly stop myself. "You'll scare her off! She's at her window. . . Just wait a second, then try not to be too obvious about it."

I wait a good minute. Then, casual as I can, I begin to turn. On my initial 180-degree sweep I catch nothing. The second time around, I catch a glimpse of her, peeking through (I assume) her bedroom window.

"You see her?" Tom asks.

"Yeah," I answer, my back to her house, again. "How'd you spot her so quick?"

"I just assumed she'd be there. She almost always is."

"Really?"

"Yup. I guess she hears the ball bouncing."

What's it like, I wonder, to know you can make a girl act like that? Feel like that?

After awhile, once we notice Stacy has left, Tom puts his shirt back on and we finally get down to some serious shooting.

"I love that sound," he tells me.

"What sound?" He takes a shot, all net.

"Ffffft— that sound. When I put it right through the center of the hoop, nothing but net. Oh, is it sweet." The ball bounces into my hands. "Courtesy?" I bounce it back his way. He sinks it again.

"Damn! How do you do it?"

"Ah, there is no technique to it, grasshopper," he enlightens. "Technique must be transcended so that action is rendered effortless."

Fffffft— he hits again.

"You see, even if the human mind were capable of occupying one-tenth of all infinity, it would still be absent in the other nine-tenths. Only when the mind is nowhere. . . is it everywhere."

Fffft.

"All that shit goes right over my head, man."

"Don't try to understand it," he says as he walks toward me, spinning the ball on his finger. "It's simply a device for opening the mind. Just try to feel without thinking."

"Uh, right." Sometimes I just go along with whatever he says so as not to betray how stupid I really am.

"Here— give it a try."

"It'll never work."

"Oh, just try. Use the force, Luke."

I hold the ball up and try to let my mind go blank. I release it; trying to shoot without shooting. It hits the hoop, then bounces off the backboard and rolls around the rim once before falling off.

"Damn," I spit. That was *so* close.

"Tempest!" Tom screams. Turning around, I find he's no longer behind me, but hurdling the fence into the neighbors' yard after Tempest, who's two houses up.

What the fuck?

I break for the back fence because I can see that's the direction Temp is headed. Now I'm running through some stranger's front yard the next block over behind Tom's house, still not stopping to figure out what the hell is happening, exactly. I'm booking up the street at warp five, figuring I'll head Tempest off at the pass, when I notice that she's already on the other side of the street and motoring in the opposite direction with Tom on her heels. I do a quick about-face and follow them.

Oh shit. They're headed right toward Parker Street. I freeze a moment, averting my gaze. I hear the sounds of car horns honking and brakes squealing. I feel my face go pale. I look back up and immediately start to run again... But upon reaching the end of the block, I spot— much to my relief— the top of Tom's head, running down the other side of the Parker.

I begin running in the same direction on my side of the street. I last about another hundred yards before I absolutely have to stop and catch my breath. I've long since lost sight of Tom and I can feel a cramp coming on in my stomach. I'm not sure if it's from the running or the nervousness or both. I continue on, walking.

Jesus, I gotta get in shape.

It's dawning on me now, after facing the prospect of seeing her pancaked by a bus, just how much Tempest means to me. Like every other boy, I would've loved to have had a dog, but my mother's supposedly allergic to all forms of pet life— even goldfish— so I've never had any kind of pet of my own before. Tempest is probably the closest I'll ever come to having my own dog. I'm picturing the way she and the cat fight with each other like Abbott & Costello. The way she swallows without chewing, every time I break off a piece of my chocolate chip cookie and toss it to her. The way she sits in the middle of the friggin' doorway when you try to enter the room, never moving, refusing even to acknowledge your existence, until you practically step on her— at which point she grudgingly gets up and out of your way, shooting you (I swear) a dirty look as you pass.

She's gotta be the coolest dog who's ever lived... Dear God, don't let anything happen to her.

Finally, I see them. And hallelujah, I think she's alright— Tom's carrying her in his arms back up the block, toward me.

"Is she ok?"

"Yeah, she's fine," he says, not even winded.

"What the fuck happened?"

"She was chasing that stray dog that's been nosing around the block the last couple of days— didn'tcha see it?"

"Jesus, no, I missed it."

"Yeah, well, I guess it wandered into the yard next door."

"How'd she clear the fence?"

"She managed to hop up on the picnic table, then over. The little fink." Tempest moans. She always knows when you're talking about her. "God, are you ever gonna get it once I get you home!"

The first thing Tom does back at the house is move the picnic table away from the fence and place it alongside the garage. Then he goes inside to grab us something to drink out of the basement fridge. He comes back out with two Yoo-hoos and a bag of Doritos. We sit at the table together, catching our collective breath.

"Y'know," I say, taking a swig of my Yoo-hoo, "when I first heard you yell, I think my heart stopped!"

"I lost my head there, I know." He takes a couple healthy gulps of his own. Then he starts to open up the Doritos when Tempest looks up at him and offers the most heart-breaking whine she can muster. Tom looks down at her with disbelief. The ears go back and her eyes seem to grow bigger as she whines again. She can tell he's pissed at her.

He flips her a chip, then reaches down and pets her head.

"She's the coolest dog," I tell him.

"Dogs *rule*. If anyone ever asks you what's so great about dogs, just remember this face," he says, cupping her face in his two hands. "When I look into this face, I know this sweet creature has never felt malice or hate or selfishness in her life. At the same time, I know there hasn't been a single minute of my own life that I haven't felt all those things."

"She's a special one."

"I've been real lucky with both my dogs. . . I've told you about Cocoa, right?"

"Not really. I mean, I've seen a couple of pictures of her, with the deep brown coat. . ."

"And the blue eyes, yeah. Well, she was originally my father's dog— he got her a year before he died. Then, when Mom moved us out of Northfield the first time, Nanna let me take her with us. It was like having a piece of my father, still alive, with me."

"When did you get Tempest?"

"Temp I got in '85— my girlfriend went to the local pound in Carver with me and helped me pick her out. Well, she wasn't officially my girlfriend at that point. . ." He seems to grow a bit uncomfortable, momentarily; like he's grasping for words.

"You remember I told you about that guy Lisa dated for awhile back in '76? The one who slapped me around?"

"Yeah. What about him?"

"Well, the day it happened, he was supposed to be baby-sitting me and Meredith for the afternoon. . . Lisa was out working while his lazy, unemployed ass was *home* with *us*. Anyhow, he got mad at me over something stupid, I don't even remember what, and he started draggin' me around when Cocoa went right after him; bit him on the leg."

"Ha! Like super-dog!"

"Yeah. Only then, Lou gave her a nasty kick in the ribs. I'll never forget the sound she made, that yelp, as long as I live."

"Jeez. . ." It's strange how different it feels hearing Tom go into detail about this. It never really sank in, what it must've been like, when he first told me about it going to his grandmother's that time. "What finally stopped him?"

"After he kicked Cocoa, he dragged me out in the hall and pushed me down the staircase. Meredith was cryin' like crazy, the dog was barking. . . it was nuts. Then Kathy— who was renting the house along with Lisa at the time— happened to walk in, and that's when tough-guy beat a hasty retreat out the back door."

"How bad were you hurt?"

"Oh, I wasn't really hurt. Just shaken up."

"And what happened to this Lou-dude?"

"Ended up in jail."

"For what he did to you?"

"No. . . Kathy was naggin' Lisa to press charges, but before anything even came of it, we found out he got busted in some bar a couple towns over, two nights after the thing at the house. Heard he took a swing at an off-duty cop and when they took him in he was carryin' a couple grams of coke, supposedly."

"Shit." I can't even imagine what it must've been like, livin' with all this as a kid. "That's fucked up."

"Anyway, the point I was trying to make was that Cocoa knew I needed her. That dog woulda given up her life for me, I know it.

Dogs are empathic; they sense what we feel. They have hearts. They have souls."

"What about cats?" I wonder aloud.

"Ah, cats have souls, but not hearts. Not like dog-hearts, anyway. Don't get me wrong— I love Sigmund, he's great, but that cat would never jump on any grenades for me like Cocoa would. Or Temp."

"So whatcha gonna do with this one? You said she was gonna get it, remember?"

Tom looks at me. Then at Tempest.

Then he leans down and kisses her on her head.

* * *

It's the middle of the week by the time Kate and I finally get around to hitting the local thrift shop to patch together our clothing ensembles for Friday night. Kate's set on Barbara Streisand, circa *A Star Is Born*— she even came up with this gigantic perm-wig from God only knows where. Naturally, she's been pushing for me to go as Kris Kristofferson, but I can't grow any semblance of a beard and refuse to wear a false one.

Of course, Kate does alot of pissing and moaning about me being difficult. So to appease her, I agree to let her pick out whatever clothes for me she wants as long as she gives up the beard-thing. She ends up picking out this really loud shirt, decorated with all variety of multi-colored, tropical vegetation; along with these hip-huggers that feel three sizes too small.

"That's the way they're *supposed* to fit," she insists.

She's really enjoying this, I know.

Friday night, April 30, 1993. The Midsummers Eve party. . . the last big party before we all buckle down for the upcoming final exams. Kate and I arrive around twenty to eight— just a little early— and we still can't find a place to park on the same block. We end up on the next street over, where we can still hear the gentle sound of Andy Gibb's voice wafting on the spring breeze. We get out of the car and follow the bizarre procession of pilgrims to Tom's house: ahead of us stride Elton John, Linda Ronstadt and Leif Garret;

bringing up the rear are Shaft and Superfly, along with Gene Simmons and Ace Frehley in full make-up.

I imagine this is what being at Mardi Gras must feel like.

"Hey, were you guys here last year?" Gene Simmons asks, catching up to us.

"I was. She wasn't."

"Year before last, I was though."

"I knew you guys looked familiar! This our third one."

"Cool." I wait for them to get a little further ahead of us. "You recognize them?" I whisper.

"No. . . under that make-up, I guess it could be almost anyone."

The first of these parties took place at Tom's old house in Carver back in '87; although it wasn't christened the Midsummers Eve party until the following year. The first party Lisa would allow Meredith to attend was the year after that, 1989. That was also the first party with a theme— a 60s theme, in honor of the twentieth anniversary of Woodstock— totally Merry's idea. This year being Frankie's first, Tom let her pick a theme and she chose the 70s. Merry's slightly annoyed because she feels it's a rip-off of her 60s idea. She's also pissed because Frankie's a year younger than she was when she was first allowed to attend.

"Hi, Will!" Frankie greets us as Kate and me are halfway up the driveway of the house. She's got Stacy-from-next-door with her. "Guess who we are!"

"Uh. . . Laverne & Shirley?"

"Right! How'd you guess?"

"Well, the 'L' stiched on your sweater is kind-of a giveaway."

"Oh, yeah! Hey, you guys look really cool!"

"Ha!" Kate laughs. "Thanks!"

"So. . . you guys are early, huh?"

"Well, a little," I say. "But everybody's early."

"Yeah, I know," she says. Stacy just stands there, fidgeting. "Well. . . I'll see ya, I guess?"

"Right. Later."

"Okay," the two of them respond in unison as they depart.

"Weren't Laverne & Shirley supposed to be in the 50s?" I ask.

"Yeah, the show was set in the 50s; but it aired during the 70s."

"Hmm. She didn't sound *too* excited, huh?"

"Oh, don't make fun," Kate reprimands. "It's so adorable, how excited she is. You know, I think she may have a little crush on you. . ."

"You think so?" I glance behind me, giving her another look.

"You are such a perv!" Kate slaps at my shoulder. "She's fifteen for God's sake!"

"Oh jeez, look— there's Barb an' Shag!" I say, deflecting.

"Buenos noches," Kate salutes. Barb is wearing a baggy, orange sweater, skirt and big granny-glasses. Shag is. . . well, I'm not sure what Shag's supposed to be 'cause he's dressed the way he always is.

"Hi!" I say.

"Hey!" Shag greets. "Keys?" He holds open a pillow case and I drop in my car keys.

"And you are?" Kate asks.

"Who else?" Barb responds. "I'm Velma!"

Ah, now I get it.

"Gee," Kate drips sarcastically, "then I guess that would make you. . ."

"Shaggy is Shaggy," Keith says as he and Tamara sneak up from behind us. "He's already a 70s character."

"Hey!" I greet.

"Don't tell me, Keith," Kate orders. "Lemme guess. . ."

"I am the dude who's outta sight, the one they call KID DY-NO-MITE!!" The goofy hat was a dead giveaway.

"And who are you, Tamara?" I ask. She's got a wig too; hers is long and brunette.

"*Ahhh. . . Love to love ya, bay-beh. . .*"

"The Queen of Disco, herself," Shag reveals.

"What about you, Will?" Barb asks.

"Oh, nobody special. . . Just your standard 70s-whiteboy."

"C'mon," Kate says, tugging at my arm. "I'm dying to see what Tom and Courtney look like!"

"Wait'll you see them!" Shag warns.

"Don't! Don't tell us!"

Penetrating deeper into the backyard, we spot Meredith at the picnic table against the house. She's dressed up in a collared shirt, tie and vest, just like Diane Keaton from *Annie Hall.*

"Well, la-di-da," she greets. "Look at you!" The androgynous get-up is really getting me hot. But who am I kidding? She could be wrapped in a potato sack and I'd be hot. "You both look great!"

"So do you. . . Oh, hi." Matt, Meredith's recently reconciled-with-boyfriend, is behind her— and not dressed for the occasion.

"Hey, Phil. Kate."

"Hi."

"Uh, that's 'Will.' " You jerk.

"Oh, sorry."

"So which of you brave souls is gonna be the first to sample our kamikaze punch?" Meredith asks.

"What's in it?"

"What's not in it would be the better question! Tom basically mixed a couple bowls of Kool-Aid and dumped in whatever was left in George and Lisa's liquor cabinet. . ."

"Hit me," I say, stepping forward and grabbing a cup. She does. I drink.

"Shit! That is absolutely vile! Gimme a double." They laugh.

So at least my first lame joke of the evening went over.

"Where is the master of ceremonies, anyway?" Kate asks.

"Over yonder," Meredith informs us, directing our attention toward the garage, where Tom and Courtney are slow dancing. Tom is John Travolta, complete with white leisure suit and gold chains, and Courtney is Farrah Fawcett-Majors, with the feathered hairdo and everything. We wave to them and they come over.

"Where the hell did you dig up that outfit?" I ask Tom.

"It's Mike Torretti's— a little snug, but it gets the job done."

"Oh, Courtney, the hair!" Kate gushes.

"God, I love yours, too!"

"Thanks— you can borrow it anytime," Kate quips. She takes a step back and looks her over once more. "I can't get over how *great* you look!"

"Meredith's the one who deserves all the credit. She was working on it with me practically all morning."

"It's not like she didn't have lots of practice," says Tom. "Didn't you used to have that old Farrah-head-toy-thing with the hair, Mer?"

"It may actually be up in the attic, somewhere."

"So where are the twins tonight?" I ask.

"The twins are with their father. And George and Lisa went to Atlantic City for the weekend."

"*Bad girl, bad girl,*" Tamara sings as she and Keith come over— she is *really* into this.

"How's it look so far, J.J.?" Tom asks.

"Looks like another winner, Tony," Keith answers. "You remain the undisputed party-master General." Suddenly, "Boogie Wonderland" dramatically strikes up.

"C'mon, Key," Tam says.

"Yeah, hon," Courtney cajoles.

We all dance— even yours truly. Tom starts out voguing, then segues into the robot, funky chicken, & cabbage patch— all at once, seemingly— and everybody eats it up, laughing like mad. I've come to the conclusion that that's what defines coolness: as long as you never care whether or not you make an ass of yourself, you never will. That's coolness in a nutshell.

And that's why I'm not cool. I stick to the standard heterosexual-low energy-two-step; with the eyes down, making sure I don't step on anyone else's feet. When I eventually do glance upward, I'm shocked by what I see.

"What?" Kate asks, reading my expression. I motion with my head for her to look over her shoulder, where Gene Simmons and Ace Frehley are dancing with each other. And I mean *grinding*.

"Don't worry, Will," Kate says, leaning in and whispering right into my ear. "I'm pretty sure 'Ace' is a girl."

She smiles. I cringe. And there we have the first foot-in-mouth moment of the evening. Not the last, either, I'm sure.

"C'mon," she tells me after a couple songs. "I'm thirsty."

There's another table set up with a punch bowl, along with a keg and some snacks aside the garage. Kate and I worm our way there through the crowd and pour ourselves another cup of the dreaded punch of the damned. I imagine we'll be spending the better part of the evening dancing our way from one punch table to the other.

We've barely wet our whistles though, when a commotion rumbles up from the opposite end of the yard.

"This is bullshit, man!" someone's yelling.

Kate and I quickly make our way over to see what's up. We find this tall, flannel-wearing, goateed guy with a pierced right eyebrow giving Tom a hard time.

"*Disco*, man? This whole party is *bogus!* What a total hypocrite you are!"

"Nobody's holdin' you hostage, Igor," Tom replies with a smile. "You can get to steppin' any time."

"I will!" And the guy stomps off.

"Who was that?" Meredith asks.

"Igor," somebody in the crowd answers. All laugh. The rubber-neckers begin to break up and get back to dancing and drinking.

"I have no clue who that was," Tom says, still smiling. "Never saw him before in my life."

"Looked like he was on a tryout for Soundgarden," Keith observes.

"I always get a kick outta guys like that," Tom continues. "Guys who think everything in life has to be this big test of integrity. Even when you throw a stupid party, it has to reflect your values, somehow. Nothing can ever just be for a goof."

"How many of these people *do* you know, bro?" Meredith asks.

"Jeez. . . I dunno." He looks around. "Maybe half. Maybe."

"How can you know only half the people here? When did these parties get so out of hand?"

"I know Greg ran an announcement in the Sentinel for one of the parties two or three years back," Shag says.

"That hump!" Tom declares. "Where the fuck is he, anyway?"

"Haw! Probably still sleeping off last year's party!"

"Tom?" asks a hopeful, feminine voice from behind us. Turning around, I see this painfully beautiful girl. Tom seems to go a little pale at the sight of her.

"Nina? My God, how've you been?"

"Pretty good," she says, hugging him. It takes him a moment to hug her back. "And what about you?"

"Good, good."

"Ex-girlfriend," Kate whispers to me. She has long, curly, light-brown hair, big brown eyes, that olive-type skin (which Tom always goes ape for, I know), and an absolutely killer body.

"Kate, Meredith. . . my God!" she exclaims. "Keith, Tamara! How are you guys?" They all offer her greetings.

"Nina," Tom begins, "this is Will, this is Meredith's boyfriend Matt. . . and my girl, Courtney."

"Good to meet you," Courtney offers coolly. Matt and I also exchange pleasantries with her.

"Nina!" Frankie shouts as she comes running over, Stacy slowly behind her.

"Frankie!" Nina gives her a big hug. "Stace! Look at you two!" I glance over at Courtney, who appears a little less than thrilled at the moment.

"Come on," Kate says, gently tugging at my shirt. "I think they're playing our song." She drags me away, back into the sea of polyester, platforms and halter tops, where we begin slow dancing.

"That wasn't too uncomfortable, now was it?"

"It wasn't that bad," I say. "So was that *the* girl?"

"*The* girl?"

"Yeah. Tom's great lost-love." Kate takes a moment to ponder.

"I don't think it comes down to just one girl. I think it's more an accumulation of several. . ."

"Really?" That wasn't the impression I got at all.

"Look, maybe we should save this discussion for another day, okay?"

We complete our dance without another word on the subject. Then it's back to the punch bowl. Along the way, we exchange sunny hellos with everyone we bump into— from Luke Skywalker to the Fonz to Donny & Marie. It would seem that all of us being dressed in these stupid clothes together somehow makes up for being total strangers; like it automatically grants us permission to be as warm and as personable as if we really knew each other. Wouldn't it be great if we could always feel this way? There really is this sense of brotherhood, a camaraderie, between everyone who's dressed up here, tonight. It truly breaks down walls.

That and the punch.

"Watch this," Courtney's voice shouts out just as Kate and me are draining our cups.

In the center of the black-topped yard, Tom and Meredith clear away a spot in the middle of the crowd. The two of them then proceed to do just about every variation of the hustle there is: New York, Latin, tango. . . plus some moves I can't recognize. They end their little number with a flourish; spinning in a circle while holding on to each other's hands— á la Tony and Stephanie— until they both end up falling on their asses. The crowd laughs and roars as they get up. Kate and I hurry over to them.

"You messed it up, stupid!" Meredith says, playfully slapping at the back of Tom's head. "And after all that practice, too!"

"Watch the hair!" Everyone breaks up, laughing. "Y'know, I work real hard on my hair, an' 'den ya hit it."

"Jeez, how many times you guys see that movie?" a voice asks.

"Only about a million," Meredith responds.

"My favorite line," Tom elaborates, "is the one Stephanie gives Tony in the diner, the one about him bein' a cliche. That line is fucking *killer*."

"Oh no," Keith disagrees. "The best one is where Travolta goes 'fuck the future,' then his boss goes 'no, the future fucks you.'"

"You guys are crazy," Meredith says. "Everybody knows the best line is when he brings his brother, the priest, to the disco. . . and he dances with that girl, remember? And he tells her, 'y'know, if you're as good in bed as you are on the dance floor, you must be lousy in bed!' "

"Yeah," Tom breaks in, "then she says to him 'why do they always send me flowers the next day, then?' And Travolta goes. . ."

"*'Maybe they think you're dead!'*" nearly everyone around shouts in unison.

"Speaking of lousy on the dance floor," Shag remarks, "you guys really did look pitiful out there."

"Aw, don't say that," Courtney says. "You were good, guys, really. I mean, you weren't terrible."

"I'm shocked you knew as many steps as you did," I say. "Where'd you pick it up?"

107

"Lisa used to make us practice all those stupid disco steps with her, back in the day," Meredith answers. "We had enough practice—we shouldn't have been *that* bad. . ."

"I know what the problem was," Tom says. "I had the wrong partner." He takes Frankie by the hand as "Native New Yorker" begins to play and yanks her out into the dance crowd.

"Come on," a smiling Meredith commands, grabbing hold of Matt. Keith, Tam, Barb and Shag all follow. Tom dances in the same ridiculous, over-the-top style; but Frankie almost makes him look good out there. I notice Stacy watching the two of them, wistfully. They come back over to the rest of us just as "Misty Blue" starts up.

"How were we?" Tom asks.

"Definitely an improvement," Kate tells them. "Maybe you just needed to get warmed up."

"Hey, why don't you give Stacy a dance, Tom?" Courtney asks. Stacy's jaw drops.

"Uh, sure! You game, Stace?" Stacy nods an almost terrified yes. Tom takes her out into the center of the crowd. He puts his arms around her and she looks about ready to melt.

"Isn't that sweet?" Courtney asks.

I tell you, Courtney's alot more secure and mature than I would've given her credit for. I mean, it's not like Stacy's ten or twelve— she's fifteen, and not a kid. Not a kid as far as her body goes, I mean. . .

Hey, I'm just observin' the Charmin, Mr. Whipple, I ain't squeezin' it!

"That was *so* cool," Frankie declares as the song ends. "Thanks, Court!" Tom gives Stacy a peck on the forehead and she just about floats away.

"Oh, it's alright," Courtney tells us. "I remember my first real crush. It was my sister Heather's first boyfriend. . . Not too awkward, right?"

"Well, it's a good thing you're in a charitable mood tonight, Court," Kate says, looking over in Tom's direction. He's dancing with Nina now, as "Turn the Beat Around" plays, and the two of them appear to be really enjoying themselves.

BACK TO THE GARDEN

Quickly and purposefully— and without wasting any time excusing herself from us— Courtney marches over, literally jumps right between the two of them and begins dancing with Tom, herself. Kate and I look at each other and laugh. We finish our latest cups of punch, then join them.

"Switch!" Tom shouts, just as he and Courtney are dancing next to us. He grabs Kate while Courtney grabs me and the four of us continue dancing with each other's partner. When the next song starts up, he shouts "switch," again— next thing I know, I'm swept up in Tom's arms. Kate and Courtney squeal with delight at this and the crowd really eats it up.

With the next song, Tom and Courtney re-start the whole swapping process with Keith and Tamara, while Kate and me take a break.

"You look totally hot tonight," I tell her as we fall back against the wall of the house. The punch is really starting to work it's magic now.

"You ain't lookin' half-bad yourself," she retorts, tickling my behind. "You really make these pants work."

I glance left and right, quickly. Then I take Kate's hand in mine and we slip into the house, giggling like grade-schoolers. Inside, I lock the back door and pin her against the wall in the hallway. We start to kiss. . . That wig of hers is a *major* turn-on, I don't know particularly why. We neck and dry hump for a while— not long enough— until someone starts bangin' at the door.

"Gotta use the john," Fred "Rerun" Berry informs us as we let him in. I lean back against the opposite wall while Kate adjusts her wig.

"Am I red?" she asks me. I reach out and gently stroke the side of her face.

"You're perfect," I tell her. She smiles. Taking my hand in hers, she leads me back outside.

"We lucked out this year," Tam says as Kate and I rejoin the group. "The actual date fell on the weekend."

"The date of what?" I ask in drunken ignorance.

"Midsummers Eve," Courtney tells me.

109

"What is Midsummers Eve supposed to be, anyway?" someone asks.

"The eve of May 1st is when all the fairies come out and the magical forces reach their zenith of power," Tom edifies. "When all things are possible!"

"Yeah, but why the party?"

"Who cares about why?" Keith asks. "I say we start celebratin' *all* those under-appreciated holidays; like Groundhog Day, Presidents' Day, Arbor Day. . ."

"Arbor Day!" Shag repeats. "Haw!"

I stop a moment and look up at the night sky while the laughter of the others fades into background noise. I swear, there really *is* something special about this night— I only wish I could properly articulate it. I just don't have that feeling now, that feeling of wanting something and not knowing what. . . That feeling that's been there ever since the day I realized I was too old to still be playing with toys, too old to still be trick-or-treating on Halloween. It's been there every day since, every night since. Until tonight.

I smile as the disco pulse of the Bee Gees' "Night Fever" begins to play.

"Shit, this is it!" Tom shouts as his eyes light up. "This is the song!" He runs out and begins taking over the dance floor.

"C'mon!" he exhorts.

Courtney, Frankie & Meredith all run out to join him. Matt remains standing, next to me and Kate— Jesus, why'd he even bother coming tonight? I tell ya, the guy's got all the personality of wet cardboard.

"What are they doing?" he asks.

"Guess we'll find out," Kate says.

Tom and the girls begin line dancing. After one or two missteps in the beginning, they get in synch. Three steps forward, three steps back, spin left, clap, spin back right, point up in the air, then down at the ground a couple times and start over again.

They go through the routine one or two times when Keith and Tamara join in. Then Shaggy, Barb, Kate and I jump in, too. Before long, just about everybody's doing it. Three steps forward, three steps back, spin left, clap, spin back right, point up in the air, then down at the ground a couple times and start over again. . .

By 11:30, Tom switches off the external speakers and turns up the volume in the house as the party begins to move indoors. Everyone, it seems, is pitching in moving shit inside and rearranging furniture in the living room so there's more room to dance. It's past midnight by the time the party has moved completely inside the house, and I'd say there are probably less than half as many people here as when Kate and I arrived. I think I recognize almost everyone now. Dancing and mingling goes on for awhile, until Shaggy suddenly calls for everyone to quiet down.

"Listen up everybody," he commands. "It's toastin' time!" Everyone packs into the living room, with some small spill-over into the adjoining hallways.

"Now, as most of you probably already know," he begins, "several of us— including our gracious host— are set to graduate in a couple weeks. And, like myself, they will be joining the ranks of the misemployed in the adult world."

"Sell-outs!" somebody shouts from in back. The room breaks up, laughing.

"Anyway," Shag continues, "I was thinkin' alot these past couple of days about what to say; and in the end, I figured I'd just go with my heart and say it as simple as I can. So to Tom, Keith, Kate. . . and everyone else takin' the plunge: best wishes and God bless." Shag raises his cup, as do we all, and drinks. Tom approaches Shag, and the two hug, playfully. Then Tom covers Shag's mouth and gives the back of his own hand a big wet kiss. And everyone applauds.

As if to celebrate, Tom breaks out the *Twister* mat and forces us to play. A fresh batch of punch is whipped up; a little popcorn-throwing rebellion starts up and is quickly quelled. . . The singing and dancing and drinking goes on, and before you know it, I turn around and it's 3 a.m.

Where has the night has gone?

"I think little sister has had it, bro," Meredith says, glancing over at the couch as she's re-loading the CD player with some fresh discs. Frankie is sleeping there, with Tempest asleep on the opposite end.

"Stacy go home?" Tom asks as he sits down between his sister and his dog.

"Hours ago."

"Did she have any of the punch, you notice?"

"I never caught her, but I imagine she had to be sneaking a little." Having reloaded the CD player, Meredith starts it up again at a more modest volume. Nobody's dancing, though— everybody's either sitting on the floor or propped against a wall.

"C'mon Tempest," Courtney exhorts, "c'mon girl. . ." Tempest looks back at her, letting out a low growl. "Tommy! Aren't you going to reprimand her?"

"For what? For loving her Daddy?" Courtney makes a face at him. "What can I tell you, she can't stand being away from me." He whistles and Temp hops down off the couch.

"God!" Courtney says, sitting down in the dog's former place on the couch. "She's so fucking possessive!" Tom gingerly strokes Frankie's hair away from her face.

"The kid's dead to the world," he observes.

"Boy," Meredith says, laughing, "is she ever gonna be sorry in the morning!"

"Don't laugh— you're the one who's gonna be holding her head over the toilet, tomorrow."

Yeesh. Now there's a picture.

"Right. That'll happen."

"It's tradition, cookie— I did it for you at your first party, now you've gotta do it for her."

"Does that mean Frankie's gonna be holding both the twins' heads in a couple years?"

"That's the luck of the genetic draw. . . Guess I should get her into bed, huh?" He gently begins to scoop Frankie up. "Be right back."

He carries her limp form out through the hall and up the stairs. Everyone left finds a spot in the living room and sits. Looking around, there are about a dozen of us still here, including Gene and Ace.

"So much for the 70s," Keith says, finally taking off that stupid hat. Kate and Tamara peel off their wigs.

"A shame it has to come to an end," Meredith remarks. "Y'know, there's this one nugget from the 70s I was looking for all week and I really wanted to share it with you guys. . . Wish I coulda found it."

"What was it?"

"It was this 45 record Tom made when he was about five. He made it in one of those old recording booths they used to have on the boardwalk at Ortley beach."

"What's he do on it?" Kate inquires.

"He sings 'Crystal Blue Persuasion.' And part of the theme from *The Partridge Family*."

"Oooh," Courtney gushes, "Are you sure you looked everywhere?"

"I wish I had it to play for you. . . he sounds like Mickey Mouse with a lungful of helium."

"Ha!" Keith laughs.

"Cut the guy some slack," Shag interrupts. "What did you say he was? Five?" Sometimes it's hard to tell which of us is more gay for Tom: Shag or me.

"That's okay, guys," Tom speaks from behind us. "Keep on talkin' about me like I'm not even here."

"Ah, the alpha-male returns," Meredith observes.

"Maybe if we ask nice enough," Keith suggests, "he'll perform unplugged for us right here, tonight."

"You know I'm not the performing type. I'm much too shy."

I've still never heard Tom play guitar, but he has started sharing his short stories with me over the past six months or so— some good stuff, in my own humble opinion.

"*The Partridge Family* song, Tom?" Keith asks. "Say it ain't so!" He exhales slowly, a beaten man.

"You had to tell 'em, didn't you Mer?" Meredith smirks, proudly. "Now what humiliation can I heap upon you in retaliation?"

"How about where 'cookie' comes from?"

"Ah, good one, Will."

"Oh God," Meredith moans.

"Aw, come now. It's cute, really."

"Just get it over with."

"Well, it's not like there's alot to tell," Tom starts. "I'd watch *Sesame Street* with her when she was real little, and she used to flip whenever Cookie Monster was on. Y'know how he'd yell 'cookie' every time he saw a cookie? Well, Meredith would do the same thing. She'd run around the house yelling 'cookie' all day and night."

"*Awwwww,*" everyone coos collectively. Meredith offers a sarcastic smile.

"I pray you all die slow, painful deaths," she tells us. We laugh. Shaggy tosses a a handful of popcorn at her.

"That wasn't too bad, Merry," I say. She gives me a dirty look.

"Come on, Mer, give us a little of your Cookie Monster," Tom goads. "Oh, if only I had caught it on film. . . You should've seen the way she'd jump around, yelling 'cookie, cookie!' "

"You better watch it, pal! I haven't even scratched the surface with you, yet!"

"You got more, Mer?" Kate asks.

"She's fulla shit," Tom says. "Her holster's empty, trust me."

"Oh, yeah? You want me to tell 'em about the time when cousin Johnny got you to strip down to your underwear and tossed you into the Passaic River?"

"Oh shit!" I say. "When was this?"

"Go right ahead, cookie," Tom dares. "Tell 'em."

"Well. . . it's no fun if you're not going to be embarrassed by it!"

"Actually, we weren't cousins," Tom informs us. "His mother, Beth, was Lisa's cousin. So technically, that would've made him our second cousin. Or is Beth our second cousin?"

"Wouldn't that make him Lisa's second cousin?" Courtney asks.

"I've never gotten how that works," Gene Simmons observes, kicking back in George McMullen's recliner.

"Whatever," Tom proceeds. "Anyhow, the thing is he was the guy who introduced me to punk music. He had his own band and everything."

"Really?" Barb asks.

"Yeah. First time I met him was around '79, when I went over his Mom's house with Lisa and he was rehearsing in the garage."

"Did he ever get anywhere with it?" Keith asks. "Would any of us know his stuff?"

"Oh no," Tom responds, smiling. "He had almost no musical talent. . . but he was still too *cool*, man! Upon his counsel, I went home that night and immediately dumped all my old records."

"Yeah," Meredith interrupts, "right into my room!"

"How'd you get into the Passaic River, though?" Tam asks.

"I'll field that one," Meredith says. "This was in '81— I don't think Tom was twelve yet. Anyway, Tom was always buggin' Johnny about wanting to hang out with him and the band. So Johnny finally told him that to be a real punk, he'd have to be initiated. And the initiation required stripping to your underwear and getting tossed into the river."

"You *didn't*," Keith gasps. We all laugh.

"You guys yuk it up all you want. . . but that stunt got me into Max's to see the Feelies play."

"Whatever happened to Johnny?" I ask.

"He. . . died. Got into it with this guy over some girl. Ended up stabbed in the throat."

Meredith looks down and traces her finger in the carpet. No one is saying anything.

"Damn," Kate says at last. "Let's get stoned."

"Alright," Tom agrees. "You got the shit?"

"Right here," Shag answers as he reaches down into that ubiquitous napsack of his and pulls out this whopping bag of pot, along with two small bowls.

"I'm tellin' ya, after last year's debacle, this better be the shit, too."

"Christ! Are you ever gonna let me live that down?"

"What happened last year?" Kate asks.

"Last year I told Shag to score some grass for the party and I think he brought back actual lawn clippings." Keith is absolutely hysterical over this line.

"Oh shut the fuck up already, willya? One time I get took with low-grade. . . One time and I never hear the end of it."

"I don't know why you don't just raid your Mom's stash, asshole— she's always got the good stuff."

"Fuck man, Mom stopped harvesting her own weed ages ago. I'm the one supplyin' her these days."

DAVID SORRENTINO

"Alright, alright— enough ballbusting. Seymour, prepare the libation!"

"Ya mon!" Keith seconds. We all form a circle on the floor as Cheryl Lynn's "Got to be Real" begins to play. Shaggy packs a small bowl and passes it on to Tom. Shag lights it for him.

"Mmmm." He passes it along to Courtney

"How is it?" Meredith asks, excitedly. Shag is already working on a second bowl.

"Shit!" Tom says. "Give it a minute or two, willya?"

After Courtney, it goes Keith, Tam, Meredith, Matt, and Kate. When it gets to be my turn, I try and hold it in my lungs as long as possible, playing it like the super-cool, veteran burner. Finally, I exhale and pass it on to Gene Simmons, sitting to my left.

"Ooooh, I think you got the good stuff this time, Shag," Kate says. "I swear, I feel it already."

"Toldja," Shag boasts.

"Great hay," Tom says as he takes a fresh hit.

"Essex County gold," Keith concurs.

After my second hit, I can start to feel it, too. Usually, I'm not even that into grass, but I have to admit I've got a pretty good buzz goin'. Beginning to relax, I let my head fall back. "Cisco Kid" begins to play as time slows down. Looking up, the ceiling seems to slowly advance down on me, then rises slowly back up, a hundred miles overhead. I begin to notice patterns in its tiles that I never saw before.

"Oh!" Matt exclaims suddenly.

"What?" Meredith asks.

"I was just. . ." He breaks up for no reason. "I forget!"

"Haw!" Shag laughs in that patented cackle of his.

"What's so funny?" I ask. "What are you guys laughing at?" Kate grabs at my arm and laughs right in my face.

"You always get paranoid when you smoke grass!" she says. She throws herself on top of me and we begin to kiss. It feels like our whole bodies are kissing, not just our mouths. She laughs. I laugh. Everybody laughs. We're all laughing at anything and everything at this point. "Moonlight Feels Right" strikes up just as everybody seems to have gotten completely stoned.

116

BACK TO THE GARDEN

"The wind blew some luck in my direction. . . I caught it in my hands today. . . I finally made a tricky French connection. . . You winked and gave me your okay. . ."

I swear I can feel the music flowing over me like water. Shag and Barb are dancing while everyone else remains loafing around them. I grab a handful of that white-cheddar popcorn Tom loves so much from a bowl on the coffee table and shovel it in my mouth. I normally don't even like it the shit, but I'm hungry all of a sudden. Hungry for anything.

"What a fucking party," Ace slurs. She 's got a fantastic smile; all teeth.

As "Afternoon Delight" kicks in over the speakers, Meredith gets up on the coffee table and begins a mock striptease. She slithers out of that vest while the rest of us all howl our approval. I go on munching popcorn while everyone else shuffles around me; some dance, some eat, some drink. Darkness begins slowly creeping in from the corners as I barely feel myself drift away. . .

"Hey you," Kate tells me as she gently shakes me awake. I open my eyes only to shut them again, instantly— the light is almost physically painful. Guess the sun is up.

"What time is it?"

"Mmm. Seven."

I let my eyes flutter open again, cautiously. The place is a disaster area. I don't see Tom. Or Courtney. Meredith, Matt, gone. Gene Simmons is spread out on the floor.

"Where is everybody?"

"Shag and Barb are passed out in the basement. Keith and Tam are in Tiffany's room. . . and you an' me got dibs on Sam's room. C'mon."

She helps me to my feet as "Wildfire" plays softly over the stereo. Hobbling through the front hall, we come across Ace sitting on the floor by the front door, back propped against the wall. For the first time all night, she isn't wearing that smile.

"Whatcha down about?" I ask.

"What else?" she sighs. "The party's over."

CHAPTER VII

I can hear the sounds of the Stooges in the distance. Tom and Courtney can't be more than a block away.

"She'll be comin' round the mountain any minute."

"Hey, don't be so sure," Kate remarks. "That could be almost anyone blasting 'Funhouse.' "

The two of us wait eagerly in front of Kate's house for the sight of Tom's car turning down the top of the block. But instead of the familiar Camaro, he pulls up in George McMullen's Lincoln.

"Where's your car?" I ask as I'm sliding in the back seat with Kate.

"In my backyard," Tom responds.

"Why?" Kate asks as he's pulling back out of the driveway.

"Because George wanted him to take his car," Courtney says. "Something about testing the tires."

"What the fuck?" I ask, half-laughing.

"George had his sister and her husband over," Tom elaborates. "I don't know if he was trying to impress them or what, but he was really pushin' the car on me, hard. And I kept telling him 'no,' like a hundred times. Then he starts tellin' me about how the car hasn't

118

been feelin' right to him lately since he got these new tires put on and that I'd really be doing him a big favor if I took it out and let him know how I thought it felt; if it felt right. So finally I was just like 'fuck it,' and took the stupid car."

"But wait a minute. How are you supposed to know whether or not the car feels 'right' when you never drive it?"

"Oh please, Will. Like it's even about the car."

"What's it about, then?"

"The guy loves doing me favors because he likes the idea that I'm indebted to him, somehow. . . that I owe him something. It's like a subtle way of trying to control me, almost."

"You're pretty hard on him, Deev," Kate observes. "I don't know that any human being could be as sinister as you make George out to be."

"Yeah, well. . . maybe I'm reading too much into it, I dunno. Maybe he was just looking to impress his family with the fact that he owns this nice car; that he can afford to get new tires put on; that he's so magnanimous toward me, his 'step-son'. . ." Tom all but chokes on "step-son."

"Is he still on his early retirement-jag?" I ask.

"Yeah. . . I ever tell you about this, Kay?"

"Does this have anything to do with the thing about him renting out the second floor?"

"No, that was something else."

"He wanted to rent out the second floor?" I ask.

"That one was a couple years back— his plan was to get me out of the house, get Meredith settled permanently in Pennsylvania, and move the twins into one room on the first floor with Frankie in the other. That flopped 'cause I wasn't going anywhere and it became obvious the twins would never be happy sharin' a room."

"So what's this about early retirement, now?" Kate questions.

"In the last year or two, he's come up with this early retirement plan. . . he wants to retire early, sell the house altogether and move to one of those cheap little bungalows in Ocean County that cost practically nothing to buy and almost zilch in property taxes."

"And when does he wanna retire?"

DAVID SORRENTINO

"At sixty-two," Courtney answers. Obviously, she's heard this rap before.

"How old is he now?"

"He'll be sixty next year," Tom tells her.

"So three years, huh? What about Frankie and the twins?"

"That's why it's perfect for him. Frankie should be starting college in the fall of '96, so once she's set up at school. . ."

"Who's to say you and Meredith'll even be out of the house by then? Does he have any idea what today's job market is like?"

"How do you retire at sixty-two, anyway?" I ask. "I thought you hadda be sixty-five."

"I don't know how," Kate answers, "but you can do it. I know people in my family who have."

"I don't think Lisa would seriously go along with it, though," Courtney says.

"I don't know about that," Tom says warily. "She's balking now, but I could see him browbeating her into it in three years. He'd live to regret it though, 'cause if he thinks Lisa's gonna be happy living in some retirement community at forty-something years old, he's out of his fucking mind."

"Man," I say. "He's got it all planned out."

"And lemme tell ya, after livin' with the guy all these years, I got a pretty good idea of his finances— and he's gotta be sittin' on a half a mil, *easy*. A couple more years and he'll be cashin' a social security check he doesn't even *need* while you an' me are *starvin'*."

"Alright," Kate laughs, "so maybe he *is* that sinister!"

"You know what the thing is, though?" Tom goes on. "It's just the principle of movin' my sisters out of *that* house. When we moved to Oakwood six years ago, I got down on my hands and knees and swore an oath to my Lord, Jesus Christ, in Heaven, that my sisters were never, ever gonna be forced to move again. I swore that the twins would never have to go through what I went through; that they'd go through one school system, they'd never have to say goodbye to every friend they have, and that they'd never have to learn to call any other place 'home.' "

"There's one thing I still don't get," I say. "What's the big deal if he sells the house in three years or ten?"

"You have to think like a money-obsessed lunatic, Will. See, he wants to sell a.s.a.p. because everyday that goes by is a day he's losing interest on the money he'd get from the sale."

"You just said he's sittin' on half a mil."

"Not enough, William."

"Oh, come *on*."

"Seriously, Will— it's a generational thing. Anyone born around the Depression era is money crazy; they never have enough of it, they can never save enough. If you're a baby boomer and you've got one dollar in the bank, then you're a dollar ahead. But if you're from the depression era and you have less than $800,000 in the bank, you're behind."

"It's true," Kate backs him up, "he's not exaggerating— my grandfather's the same way."

"God," Tom sighs.

"What, hon?" Courtney asks.

"Lisa's husband and Kate's grandfather are from the same generation. It's depressing." The rest of us laugh.

"Hey, I know— I'll blow the fucker's engine out! That'll teach him!" Tom slams down on the gas and the car bursts forward, the abrupt shift in momentum pushing us back in our seats as we laugh some more.

"Where are we going, again?" I ask.

"To this club I know out in Munson: 'The Wasteland.' "

"What's the place like?"

"It's hard to describe it. You'll see when we get there."

Tom's taken us club-hopping alot over the last year and he always seems to know where the hottest spots are. Most of them are in the city of course; usually, they're the basement club variety— y'know, with the exposed plumbing, stale air, and way too many bodies per square inch. Generally speaking, the dingier it seems, the hipper it actually is. My personal fave was CBGBs— not for any aesthetic reasons (the place has a really awkward layout; you can't even see the band playing unless you're way up in front), but just for the history there. . . just the idea that the Ramones debuted there; that Television and Patti Smith played there. CBs is like the Yankee Stadium of punk.

Anyway, this 'Wasteland' is located (appropriately enough) in the middle of nowhere; nestled between 66 north and south in Munson, without any other sign of life in sight. The place is totally unremarkable— there's not even a sign, blinking neon or otherwise, to tell you what it is. If I were to pass by during the day, I'd probably figure it for a Teflon processing plant or something.

"Is this some kind of redneck bar or something?" I ask, wondering if maybe Tom's putting us on.

"Don't be ridiculous," he tells me.

We park behind the club and Tom leads us to the service entrance door. There's a cute little sign pasted there: "abandon all hope ye who enter here." Tom slams his fist against it several times, hard. After a minute, this big bouncer-type sticks his head out.

"What the Hell?" he asks.

"April is the cruelest month," Tom recites, "breeding lilacs out of the dead land, mixing memory and desire, stirring dull roots with spring rain."

"Say *what?*"

"Oh, just tell Gil to get his boney ass out here, already. We're expected."

"You're Tom, I take it?" Tom nods, affirmatively. "Oh. Follow me, then."

The guy leads us through the back, behind the bar. The handful of employees present all stop and stare— I feel like we're Pesci and Liotta with their molls in *Goodfellas*, entering the Copacabana.

"Gilberto!" Tom shouts at some guy by the doorway.

"Thomas!" The guy is pale and emaciated, wearing all black, with a shaved head and goatee. "How the hell have you been?"

"I'm hangin' in there."

"Oh, my— and which of these is yours?" He asks, referring to the girls.

"*Excuse me?*" Kate pipes up.

"Ahem! Gil, this is my girlfriend, Courtney." Gil gives her the once over.

"Thomas. . . your taste just keeps improving, doesn't it?" He kisses Courtney's hand. "Lady, you are an absolute vision!"

"Why, thank you!"

122

". . .And these are my friends, Will, and Kate."

"A pleasure," he says, nodding in my general direction. His hand reaches for Kate's to kiss it, but she abruptly grasps it in a firm handshake, instead.

"Nice meeting you." (That's my girl!)

"So are the rumors true?" Gil asks. "Did you finally get around to graduating?"

"Yes, unfortunately."

"That's fantastic! Now you can finally take me up on my offer to co-host the place!"

"Ah, well, I don't think so, Gil. . ."

"Come on," Gil drips, "it's like throwing a party every night! All this could be yours. . ." He holds open the door to the club's interior, allowing us a glimpse inside. All I can make out are these semi-human silhouettes cast by a ghostly light that slowly changes from red, to pink, to violet, to plum; all of them moving in time to the sounds of the Fall.

"Uh, no thanks, Gil. I'm looking for a career that'll satisfy some of my higher, artistic urges. . . in addition to some of the baser, more hedonistic ones. Man cannot live by bread alone an' all that."

"Your life, homey." He calls over a waitress. "Camille? Will you show these people to the best table in the house? And see that they're well taken care of."

"Wait— ain'tcha gonna stamp our hands?" Gil responds with a playful shove to Tom's back. Camille leads us into the colored darkness.

"What did I tell ya, hah?" Tom asks. "Does this place have ambiance or what?"

I gotta admit, the place has got atmosphere in spades. It's not a basement, more like a cavern— the kind I've adventured through in my mind countless times while playing D&D. I half expect to find the dreaded vampire-queen here, with her horde of evil hobgoblin henchmen, lying in wait to ambush me and steal my +3 flaming sword. There's a dance-pit in the center of the place, along with a booth for the DJ, and a large platform just adjacent to it— sorta caddie-corner— for live entertainment, I suppose. Small tables surround the outside of the pit, with booths up against the wall. Camille shows us into one of the booths.

"What would you like?" she asks.

"Just beer," Kate says. "Lite."

"Wait," I interrupt. "Who's driving tonight?"

"You volunteering, Will?" Tom asks.

"I second the volunteering!" Courtney quickly adds.

"I third!"

"Et tu, Kate?" I ask as they're all laughing. "God, you guys *suck*, y'know that?"

"You may as well bring us a pitcher," Tom tells Camille. "Then some water for our teetotaler friend and a bottle of tequila for me."

"Damn, man!" I say, as Camilles jots it down and leaves. "What's with you tonight?"

"Yeah hon," Courtney says. "I thought you were straight edge, except on Midsummers Eve."

"I just got the itch. I'm jumpin' off the wagon tonight."

"So how'd you meet this Gilbert-guy?" Kate asks. "He's a serious piece of work."

"He was a grad student at Cahill. I met him sophomore year, when I took this course, 'Religious Dimensions of the Poetry of T.S. Eliot.' "

"You took a *grad* course your second year?" Kate asks.

"I talked to the professor and he said he couldn't be sure when it would be offered again. So I had to jump on it."

"Shit!" I say. "How'd you do?"

"Ended up getting a 'B.' I remember the prof telling me there was no way he could give an undergrad an 'A' for that course, just on principle. Plus, he was afraid the other grad students would lynch us both."

"And that didn't piss you off?" Courtney asks.

"Sweetheart, sweetheart," he scolds. "It's not about grades. . . it's about self-fulfillment."

"I guess you're an Aristotelian, then?" Kate asks with a smirk.

"Let's not start with the philosophy, okay?" I request.

"So how does Gil go from being a grad student to owning his own club?"

"He comes from this super rich family. His father is a big-time coffee magnate from Colombia or somewhere 'round there. Grad school, this club. . . they're all like indulgences of his— he doesn't need any of it. I don't know that he takes any of it very seriously."

"It's a good thing you're his friend," Kate says just as Camille arrives with the alcohol. "Otherwise I would've plucked out that goatee a hair at a time."

"Hey, you remember that Norman-guy?" I ask, after everyone's poured their first drink. "I ran into him at the mall last week." Norman is this forty-something guy who's going to Cahill. Tom introduced him to us back around March, when he sat down and ate lunch with the four of us in the caf.

"Ah, Will, you're really lookin' to get me started again?" I can't help smiling. I know I shouldn't have brought it up 'cause Tom's already gone off once tonight, but I can't help it— I love listening to him rant.

"I know," I say. "I'm a bad boy."

"Norman?" Courtney asks. "The guy who ate with us that time? What about him?"

"Will's just lookin' to get me goin' hon."

"What's your problem with him?"

"What's my problem? It just pisses me off, these old guys who have to have it all," Tom says, knocking back his first tequila shot. "They can't grow old gracefully; they've gotta infect everything like a friggin' disease. Check it out, I'm sure there are a few of 'em here tonight. . . I swear, there isn't a single sanctuary left for us."

"What?" Kate asks. "You're not allowed to go back to college after you're forty?"

"Do you honestly think he's the least bit interested in learning anything or bettering himself in any way, Kay?"

"And what *do* you think he's interested in?"

"Some young poon!" Tom barks. "Geishish! What else?" Kate groans in disgust.

"Why are you so hard on him?" Courtney asks. "I feel really sorry for the guy— he just got divorced, he's trying to rebuild his life. . ."

125

"See what I mean? I guess you bought that whole thing then, huh Court? Back me up, Will: was the guy on the make or what?"

"Totally," I agree.

"Oh for God's sake!" Kate exclaims. "Just because the two of you are constantly on the make doesn't mean every other guy is, too."

"Yes it does," Tom informs her.

"Absolutely," I agree once again.

"Well, *I* think he was sweet," Courtney says.

"I still can't get over the way he tried to act so cute. . . Remember that remark he made about seeing me with a notebook?" One of the many campus legends regarding Tom is that he doesn't take notes in class. Totally true, by the way. Not because he's apathetic or lazy— he just doesn't need them.

"You're the one who introduced him to us, y'know."

"I was just being civil! The guy was standing there; what was I supposed to do?!?"

"Besides, Court," I add, "I don't know that 'hey Norm, you don't wanna eat with us, do ya?' constitutes a legitimate invitation."

"Can we *please* change the subject, already?" Kate pleads.

"Okay, I got one for ya," I say. "See if you can guess what really obscure, old cartoon I happened to catch on the tube recently."

"That's not exactly the direction I was hoping to go. . ."

"Oh, television trivia are all these generation x-ers know or discuss," Tom says in his best game show host-voice. "If you'd really prefer the conversation take a more high-minded turn, we could always go back to debating the tenets of Nietzschean philosophy. . ."

"No!" Courtney and I shout in unison.

"Alright, Will— give us a hint."

"Um," I think, "okay. . . he had that voice like Curly from the Three Stooges."

"Oh," Tom says, the glint of recognition in his eye. "Jabberjaw!"

"Jabberjaw?" Court asks.

"Yeah, isn't that it?"

"No, man. . . I've never even heard of Jabberjaw."

"Sure you have," Kate says. "He hung out with that teen band called 'The Neptunes.' "

"Yeah, that's the one," Tom says. "Jabberjaw was the big fat shark who talked like Curly."

"Whatever. . . it wasn't Jabberjaw, okay?"

"Y'know what old, old cartoon I loved when I was real little? This one called 'Goober.' "

"Which one was that?" Kate asks.

"This is all before my time," Courtney throws in. "I can't remember any cartoon, pre-Smurfs."

"Goober was this blue-haired dog," Tom explains, "that had the power to turn invisible. . . Only he was always wearing this stupid ski hat; so even though the rest of him was invisible, you could always tell where he was 'cause of the dumb-ass hat!"

"What was the cartoon about?" Courtney asks. "What did the dog do? I mean, how come he could turn invisible?"

"I can't remember it ever being explained. As far as what he did, he was basically the pet of this group of bungling teenagers who went around solving mysteries."

"A Scooby knock-off," Kate says.

"Pretty much, yeah."

"He-*looo*-oh?" I say. "You still haven't guessed *my* cartoon!"

"As far as I know, Jabberjaw's the only cartoon that sounded like Curly, Will. And I'm an accredited expert in this field."

"We give up, hon," Kate concedes. "What was it?"

"Funky Phantom! I can't believe you guys!"

"Funky Phantom?"

"Yeah! Funky Phantom was the revolutionary ghost with the pet ghost-cat who would snicker like Muttley. . . remember?"

"He didn't sound like Curly though," Tom informs me. "He sounded more like Stinky from the old *Abbott & Costello Show*. Basically the same voice they used for Snagglepuss."

"Who was Snagglepuss?" Courtney asks.

"*Who was Snagglepuss?*" Tom repeats in shock.

"I told you guys I don't know any cartoons pre-Smurfs!"

"Oh, come on, Court— you know Snagglepuss!" Kate exhorts. " 'Heavens to mergatroid? Exit stage left?' "

127

"Anybody else beside me think Snagglepuss might've been gay?"

"Please," Tom responds. "He was flaming, *eee-vin*!"

"You guys are awful," Kate scolds.

"You know what made me think of Goober, before? I used to think that if Will was a cartoon character, he'd be Goober."

"Excuse me?"

"Yeah, when I first met you, that's what I thought— I got the feeling that you'd like to make yourself invisible because you were like. . . omniphobic."

"He used to be real shy, yeah. He's come a long way, though," Kate says as she pinches my cheek.

"Gee, thanks."

"See, now Kate would be Rocky the flying squirrel," Tom goes on.

"Excuse me?" Kate retorts.

"Yeah, 'cause he's a bit of an agitator, like you are."

"An agitator??"

"I can see that," Courtney adds.

"Courtney!" Kate exclaims as her jaw drops.

"I mean, you like to stir things up! Debate an' stuff!"

"Start fights, you mean," Tom clarifies. Courtney and I both laugh.

"And who would you be, wiseguy?" Kate asks.

"Oh, I dunno. Batman; maybe Spider-Man." We all break up. "You know who I could be? Space Ghost. Y'know, the mysterious cosmic avenger-type."

"Space Ghost!" Kate repeats with a guffaw. "Oh, listen to you!"

"What would you say, then?"

"I think Goofy would be alot more accurate." We all laugh some more. "You'd be Goofy, I could be Mickey. . ."

"And what would that make Will? Minnie?"

"No," I cut in, "Tom is Donald Duck, Courtney is Daisy and George is Uncle Scrooge." We all break up again.

"Good one, babe," Kate congratulates me.

"Seriously, hon," Courtney interjects, "which cartoon character do you see *me* as?"

"Awww," Tom purrs, "you'd be my Wonder Woman and I'd be your Superman, baby!" He kisses her on the cheek and she grins.

"Can you explain something?" Kate asks. "How did Superman go around using his x-ray vision without giving everybody cancer?"

"He wasn't actually projecting x-rays," Tom explains. "I think he actually used his microscopic vision to focus between the molecules of solid objects."

"I don't think so," I say. "Remember Lex Luthor always lined his hideouts with lead so Superman couldn't see him? I think Kate got it right, I think he does project x-rays."

"Did you know Superman wasn't really super-strong?"

"Now how do you say that?"

"Because you know how he lifts buildings sometimes? Or moves whole planets? That should be impossible, 'cause the buildings should collapse under their own weight. And he would just burrow through the surface of a planet."

"What's your explanation, then?"

"Actually, what he does is control gravitational fields, see? It's not really muscle power at all. In reality, the Hulk is the strongest super-hero."

"This conversation is so stupid!" Kate declares. We all share another good laugh, just as the Cure's "Just Like Heaven" strikes up.

"Oh God!" Courtney says. "This song takes me back to junior high!"

"Hmmm. . . What grade were *you* in when this song came out, Deev?" Kate asks.

"Just two grades ahead of you girl, so watch it!"

"C'mon hon!"

"Oh, *alright*," Tom offers in a sarcastic whine.

"Whaddaya say there, cowboy?" Kate asks me.

"Come on."

We all hit the floor, moving. We dance straight through "Just Like Heaven," then "Hold My Life," "Mirror in the Bathroom," and Prince's "Private Joy." Then, having broken a sufficient sweat, we all scurry back to our booth as Sonic Youth's "Titanium Expose" begins to play.

129

"This place *rawks!*" Courtney declares as we sit back down. Over Thurston's guitar noise, the DJ reminds us about the live performance coming up at midnight.

"You ain't findin' a playlist like this anywhere else," Tom adds.

"Too true, unfortunately," I say, just as Camille reappears.

"You guys need anything else?" she asks.

"Aren't you the eager beaver?" Tom observes. She seems to shrink slightly at this.

"Well, Gil did tell me to take special care of you. . ."

"We're still nursing the same pitcher, thanks," he says, sweetly. "But there is one favor you can do for me— can you can ask the DJ for something a little slow?"

"No problem," she answers with somewhat-greater-than-friendly inflection.

"What was that about?" Courtney asks after she's left.

"What?"

"I dunno. . . you don't think your tone with her wasn't a little overly cozy, there?"

"Sure. That's how you get good service, Court."

"The service is good enough, thankyouverymuch!" Kate and I laugh at the two of them.

"Well, here we are." It feels strange being at such an in-spot, mingling with the beautiful crowd. I feel compelled to say something witty and charming. "It's so great, bein' out, the four of us, uh. . . together, that is."

The girls are just smiling back at me now, with their indulgent, what-are-we-to-do-with-our-silly-Willie smiles. . . Honestly, I knew what I wanted to say when I first opened my mouth; I swear I did. It sounded so nice in my head. Really. Somewhere between my brain and my mouth though, I just lost it. And I can't even blame it on alcohol.

"Will is trying to say something, ladies, but he doesn't know quite how to broach the subject," Tom says, trying to throw me a life preserver. "He just means that since we've all grown so close, maybe it's time we took the next logical step in our relationship. Collectively speaking."

"Which would be?" Courtney asks.

"I mean we've been hangin' out together, the four of us, almost a year now; so Will and I were just discussing where we all might be heading together. What new horizons we could explore."

"Oh, boy," Kate predicts. "I can see where this is going!"

"What?" Courtney asks, intrigued. I have no clue where he's going with this, either.

"Lemme guess: you wanna swap, or something?"

"No, nothing so gauche."

"What then?"

"Well. . . Just hear me out on this now. . ."

"Go on," Kate pushes, "spit it out already!"

"Well, William and I were wondering if the you two ladies might consider experimenting in a little lesbianism for our viewing pleasure."

"What?!?"

"Ha! There you go— thanks Tom!" Good save, mud brother.

"Oh, God! *You guys are disgusting!*"

"Come on— just kiss for us."

"Ee-yew! I can't be-*lieve* you two!"

"Oh please, Kay— you're telling me you never dabbled in it before? Never practiced kissing with any of your sixth grade girl-friends?"

"Get the fuck *out!*"

"You're both sick," Courtney tells us, cracking a smile.

"Come on, Court— it's all the rage these days!"

"Don'tcha wanna be chic?" I add, following mud brother's lead. "You can at least kiss for us, can'tcha?"

"Really. . . The way you two are always hugging each other hello and goodbye, you're saying you never get aroused? Not even a little?"

"Now you're getting *really* ridiculous," Kate responds.

"What kind of kiss?" Courtney asks. "Would there have to be tongue?"

"*Court!*" Kate gasps.

We all revel in our silliness. After a short while, the lights turn from warm, light-orange to dark blue, just as the Smashing Pumpkins' "Crush" begins to play.

"Sounds like the DJ got the message," Tom says. He takes Courtney's hand. "C'mon, love."

Kate and I follow them back down to the floor, where we all slow dance. We continue slow dancing through R.E.M.'s "Find the River," then return to the table to wet our whistles Then we dance some more. Then back to the drinking. This routine persists a couple hours, until around eleven o'clock, when the crowd begins an almost lycanthropic transformation from middle class college kids to hardcore punks. By eleven-thirty, the workboots and shaved heads are ubiquitous.

"Let's slam!" Tom commands, knocking back another swig of tequila just as the DJ begins to spin some vintage Minor Threat.

"Ah, no thanks," I say. "That crowd looks like it might be a little too rough for my tastes."

"I'll have to sit this one out, too," Kate seconds.

"Me three," Courtney says.

"Chickens," he brands us.

Starting toward the pit, Tom's just about to jump in when this baby-faced skinhead who's on his way out gets up in his face. Tom just smiles at him, grabs him and flings him backward like a toy. With that, he plunges in and begins mounting a one-man hostile takeover of the pit.

How would I describe a pit to someone who's never experienced it firsthand? Well, just imagine being in the middle of an earthquake, a hurricane, a typhoon and an inferno, simultaneously. That's a good start. Once one starts up, it's like there's this irresistible, invisible force pushing everyone outward from the pit's center; you're pummeled by human bodies, none of them in control of where they're going. It's chaos, pure chaos, but of a glorious kind. To be in the middle of one is both liberating and terrifying, all at once.

And I can't imagine another human being more at home in the middle of a pit than Tom. Looking in now, from slightly above and outside, I feel like a Roman citizen watching as the Christians are getting thrown to the lions. And Tom's the biggest lion.

"He's a madman tonight," Courtney states matter-of-factly.

"Tell me about it." In no time at all, Tom's got 'em whipped into shape; doing the circle moon-stomp, pumping their fists and shouting "oi!" in unison.

"I've never seen him more happy than right now," Kate observes.

At almost midnight precisely, a live act calling themselves "Simian Intercourse" takes the stage to the delight of the crowd. After several quick— *really* quick— numbers, the lead singer announces the beginning of the "karaoke" segment of the show. And to our collective shock, he pulls Tom up out of the crowd.

"Are you kiddin'?" I say.

"This I gotta see!" Kate says. The three of us go over to the edge of the pit to get a better view.

"*Twenty-twenty-twenty fo' hours ah-go-oooo,*" Tom sings, "*I wanna be sedated. . .*"

"Oh, *gawd!*" Courtney says with a smile.

"He's good!" Kate says. And he actually is.

"You know he's gotta be *really* drunk to do this, though!"

"*I wanna be sedate-eeeed,*" Tom finishes singing as he falls on top of the crowd. Everyone applauds. Several minutes later, he seeps out of the mass of people, back to us.

"How was I?" he asks.

"You were great, hon!" Courtney tells him just as the band's pulled someone else out of the crowd and they begin to butcher "God Save the Queen." She hugs him like the proud parent. From out of the shadows, Gil emerges like some pallid ghost.

"That was great!" he declares, shaking Tom's hand. "Can I start booking you on a regular basis?"

"Thanks, but no." Tom takes out a ten-spot. "I think we're about ready to jam, Gil. . . Can you pass this along to Camille for us?"

"Certainly. I'll just put the drinks on your tab," he says with a wink.

"Thanks for havin' us, man."

"Thomas. William. Ladies. A pleasure meeting you."

"You too," the girls say,

"G'night," I add as he melts back into the darkness.

"So how was it in the pit?" Kate questions as Tom leads us out.

"Oh, it was cool. Most of the guys are really, really cool."

"I dunno, man," I say. "It looked like there were some serious bad-asses out there."

"Nah, they were alright. All of the skinheads were of the kosher variety— no nazis. And the pit etiquette was exemplary." He fumbles around momentarily for the car keys as we're walking out the front door.

"Maestro," he says, handing them over to me.

"I'll be gentle with her, sir." We walk around to the back of the club, where the car is parked. Kate gets in the front with me while Tom gets in the back with Courtney.

"So what did that one guy say to you?" Kate asks as she turns to face the back seat.

"Which guy?"

"The junior-skinhead. The one who said something to you on your way in the pit."

"Oh, he just made some smartass remark about my clothes, my look."

"Typical," Courtney sighs.

"That's the shitty thing about the scene: everybody's constantly judging you; your integrity, your dedication. And they're always making these judgments on the most superficial levels."

"What he call you?" I ask. "A sell-out?"

"No, he didn't— though that's usually the favorite phrase. . . There are alot of guys who just can't enjoy the scene unless they get to make martyrs of themselves in the process. They have to prove they're the only ones with integrity, that everyone else is a phony."

"You hear alot of that, I know."

"Sell-out is just a term used by insecure people to make themselves feel morally superior. There are no 'sell-outs.' People are what they are, what they choose to be. Some are assholes, others aren't, some are both at various times."

"You're saying the basic character of a person never changes?" Kate questions.

"What I'm saying is that people don't trade in their values for money or fame or sex or. . . whatever. If they appear to, then that means they never really held those values at all. 'Cause if they really did, they couldn't have been bought off in the first place, right?"

"Which makes anyone who ever put any faith in them a sucker?" Courtney adds, rhetorically.

"That's why I don't believe in heroes, babe— I put my faith in me! You can never be sure what's in someone else's heart, but you always know what's in yours. Or you should, anyway."

"That's no way to live," I say. "You gotta be able to trust *some* people in life, just practically speaking. No man is an island, dude."

"Oh, of course. I'm just talking about making idols of people, here."

"Even so, isn't there *anybody* you look up to?"

"I guess I see my father as a hero. . . But he's dead, so I know he can't disappoint me."

For the next half-hour, the four of us drive around looking for some place where we can buy beer. Finally, we come across a 7-11 and buy a six-pack of Coors and a Snapple iced tea for me. Then we go find a place to guzzle 'em down.

"Check it out," Tom tells Courtney as we sit in the vacant parking lot of some bank in the middle of a town we don't know the name of. "It's the big dipper."

"Really?"

"Yup. And there's Orion. . . and there's the scorpion, right behind him."

"And there's Ursa Major," I add.

"Where? Show me! I can't see 'em!"

"They're bustin' on you again, Court," Kate sighs. Courtney looks back at us and we laugh.

"I *hate* you guys!" she says, slapping Tom on the leg.

"I was just trying to start some conversation, honey," he says.

"Don't be mad, Court," I add with a smile.

"I'll tell you what," Tom offers her. "We'll let you decide the next topic of conversation."

"Okay. . . Let's talk about sex," she says mischievously.

"We haven't talked that subject to death yet?" Tom asks as he stretches out across the hood of the car.

"Nah," I say. "It never gets old."

"Who would be your ideal woman, Tom?" Kate asks.

"I know who Tom would go for: Tea Leoni, right?"

135

"Nah. . . I bet it's Linda Fiorentino. Y'know, that Brett Ashley-character from *The Moderns*."

"Nope," Courtney says. "You're both wrong. It's Laura San Giacomo— the slutty sister from *Sex, Lies, and Videotape*."

"You're *all* wrong," Tom tells us. "Although those were some excellent choices."

"Who then?" Kate asks.

"Well, we know she's Italian, whoever she is," Courtney says.

"Yeah, right!" I concur. "That's a given."

"You don't get insecure about that, Court?" Kate asks. "That you're not Italian, I mean?"

"Nah. I know I'm just his shikse fantasy— I've come to accept it." We laugh. Kate, especially, seems to get a kick out of her use of the term "shikse."

"Alright, then who?" I ask. Tom hesitates theatrically, keeping us on the edge of our seats a moment.

"Jennifer Capriati," he reveals at last.

"*Jennifer Capriati?*" I ask.

"Well, she *is* Italian. . . in fact, the name 'Capriati' signifies that her family originates from or around the isle of Capri, which would be the same general area my ancestors are from. Then, keep in mind she is a very talented athlete, so we'd probably have strong, athletic children. . ."

"You sound like a dog breeder!" Kate observes.

"One has to consider these things, Kay. Throw in the fact that she's already quite wealthy, and her earning potential for the future is great, so she could easily finance my publishing ventures. . ."

"That's like my grandmother: 'remember Katie, it's just as easy to love a doctor as anyone else.' " We laugh some more.

". . .Plus I would get to travel and see the world while she's going to all these various tournaments. And yes William, I do believe she possesses many of those other qualities that the superficial man might appreciate. . ."

"For real?" I question.

"Sure! She's cute!"

"I can't believe you," Kate tells him.

"Well, it's an odd question, Kay. You're asking this very rational question regarding something that's usually governed by emotion and sheer chance. . ."

"The *one* time I wasn't looking for any big, cerebral answer," Kate responds with a roll of her eyes.

"Alright then, who would you take?"

"Brad Pitt," she answers before anyone can blink.

"Holy Shit! You can take a *little* time, Kay; at least *pretend* you need two seconds to think about it!" We're all breaking up. "You catch that, Will?"

"I caught it." We take a second to calm back down.

"Who would you go for, Court?" Tom wonders.

"You know you're the only man I dream about," she answers, hugging him.

"Oh, come on."

"Really!" she insists.

"She's so fulla shit," Kate says with a grin.

"What about you, Will?" Courtney asks.

"Uh. . . Bridget Fonda," I say, off the top of my head.

"Why her?" Courtney wants to know.

"Why? She's totally hot!"

"Didn't you once tell me that Meredith reminded you of Bridget Fonda?" Tom asks (already damn well knowing the answer).

"Oooooo-*ooooh*!" Courtney moans, painfully. Kate smiles, but her eyes are shooting daggers at me.

"Thanks, Tom." He grins.

"As long as we're talking about sex," Kate says, steering the conversation away from that last flaming wreck, "I had something kinda weird happen to me a week or two ago."

"What?" Tom asks.

"I caught my brother David on the couch, face-sucking with this girl. I got totally weirded out by it."

"I know where you're coming from," Tom commiserates. "The last couple of months, I've had a million different boys calling the house, asking for Frankie. It feels weird— I still think of her as this little baby."

"You guys are so lucky to have brothers and sisters," I say.

"Why didn't your parents have more kids, Will?" Courtney is probably the only human being on earth truly sweet enough to ask the question without it sounding like an insult. "I mean, couldn't they?"

"Are you kidding? I don't even think they meant to have *me*. When they first got married, nothing was happening in that department, and they ended up thinking that they couldn't have kids. . . The old man was probably relieved to hear it. Anyway, Mom always told me I was this big blessing when I was little. But it's obvious they never set out to have me. Lately I've been feeling like I was their biggest mistake— like maybe they would've just divorced a long time ago, but stuck it out for my sake."

"You're not alone, Will," Tom says. "We're all mistakes; everybody. No parent can ever really know what they're getting. It's not like you can draw up blueprints beforehand. They all end up disappointed to one degree or another."

"When your parents actually are divorced though, you can't help but think that," Kate adds. "You start to ask yourself, 'if they could go back and do it all over, would they still get married and have me?' Let's face it: probably not."

"Can any of you picture your parents *doing* it?" Courtney asks.

"I sure can't. My mother grew up going to Catholic School. Everything she knew about sex she learned from nuns."

"Pfffff!" Tom chaffs. "What does a nun know about sex?"

"What's more comfortable: three fingers or four."

"Ooooh. . . Good one, Will," Tom says. "That was actually sick enough to have come from my own mouth."

"Thanks." I take that as the highest compliment. My second commendation of the evening— I'm on a roll.

"Remind me again what we see in these two, Court," Kate requests.

"Right now, I couldn't even tell ya."

We all take a moment to sip our beverages. An awkward silence persists for several long seconds.

"I have a question for everybody," Tom announces, breaking the ice.

"What?" I say. He pauses, dramatically.

"Where do dead squirrels go?" he asks, finally. The girls and I look at each other, wholly perplexed.

"Huh?" I ask.

"Y'know, the squirrels. What happens to 'em when they die? How come you never come across a squirrel, lying on the ground, feet in the air, dead of a heart attack? I mean, they can't *all* get hit by cars. . ."

"Maybe they go where those missing socks go," Courtney offers. "You know, the ones that seem to vanish in the dryer?"

"Maybe there's a squirrel's graveyard," I say. "Y'know, like the elephant's graveyard?"

"Could be," Tom says. "I just find it so incredible, the way God designed nature. I mean, the way the natural world seems to clean up after itself."

"I'll never understand how you can believe in God, Tom. That's the one inconsistent thing about you."

"How so, Kay?"

"I mean, you're so logical in your approach to everything else. What makes you believe in God?"

Here we go— Kate is shoving her bullshit atheism down our throats again. Even Courtney looks to be tired of it at this point. Hey, I love her, but every time she gets on this, she just comes off so phony.

"Oh, stop it, hon." I tell her. "You know in your heart of hearts, you believe in God, too."

"You think she's frontin', huh Will?"

"Definitely."

"Oh, bullshit. You know I'm right on this one, Tom. It's like Hume— the way he never carried his skepticism to its logical and obvious conclusion, which would have been atheism. You're the same way."

"Come on. That's the same kinda logic behind that poseur in his Doc Martens an' suspenders back at the club, thinkin' I wasn't a real punk just 'cause I didn't dress like he did. Isn't punk supposed to be about non-conformity, fer chrissake? I can choose my beliefs for whatever reason I like."

"You read Hume, Will?" Courtney asks.

139

"Yeah," I answer.

"What did you think of him?"

"I didn't like him, really. I kinda thought he came off like. . . I dunno, a naysayer."

"Yeah. Like he disagrees with everything just for the sake of disagreeing."

"But even you have to concede," Kate goes on, "that there is no scientific evidence that supports the existence of a supreme being."

"If one is going to accept that God is truly omnipotent, Kay, you also have to accept that he/she/it has the power to change or break any rule it wants— so science no longer applies."

"How do you dismiss science?" Kate asks, insistently. This has been happening more and more lately— Tom and Kate start having these super highbrow debates, and it's like Courtney and me aren't brilliant enough to be invited to participate.

"Don't you find it conspicuous how there's no evidence at all to support God's existence? You'd think you could find *some* evidence to make a case for it; whether God did exist or not, there would still be some incidental evidence. It's as if God has presented humanity with this wonderful opportunity: to choose to believe in the face of absolutely no physical evidence. And those that do gain the greatest gift of all: faith."

Is it just me, or is Tom actually more coherent when he's drunk?

"I don't buy it," Kate persists. "The reason no scientific evidence exists is because *there is no God!*"

"That's the beauty of it though, Kay: there can be no arguing about it. It's faith— you either have it or you don't."

"You have faith in God but you're a total cynic in regard to everything else, though!"

"That's right: I have total faith in God, just none in mankind. The two issues are mutually exclusive in my mind."

"It's amazing to me how the logical mind can rationalize the most ridiculous notions just to comfort itself."

"What's more comforting, Kay? A world that contains unsolvable, unknowable mysteries, or a world where science provides a pat answer for every question?"

"How do you vote, Court?" I ask.

"Let's see. . . In Intro to Philosophy, there were three basic theories, correct? There was Aquinas, Anselm, and the third one— the watch analogy."

"Paley. The teleological argument."

"Right. . . that was the best argument, I thought. You would assume the watch was created by someone, so why wouldn't I assume the world was created by someone?"

"You've got taste, love," Tom tells her. "That's a favorite of mine, too. And you, Will?"

"Which one was the prime mover-theory?" I ask.

"That was Aquinas. The cosmological"

"Yeah, I like Aquinas. He seemed the most logical to me; like every action has a reaction, y'know? So the universe, by its very existence, suggests some force behind it's creation."

"What was Anselm's argument, again?" Courtney asks.

"I don't remember, exactly. I do remember that I liked his least, though."

"Yeah. That was the more metaphysical one. 'That which is understood, exists in the understanding.' "

"Right. Read more like a sermon than genuine philosophy, too."

"Yeah well, you guys are making the case for something," Kate says, "but that something isn't necessarily God." We all we begin to protest together at this.

"Help me," she cries, "I'm surrounded by zealots!"

"She's one tough nut to crack, huh Will?" Tom remarks. "You wanna see me shut her up?"

"Please. By all means." Tom hops down off the car.

"Do you believe science could answer any question, Kay?" he asks. "Or is there an ultimate limit to reason?"

"I don't know that there is or there isn't."

"Ah-ha!" Tom exclaims. "You don't know! That, itself, is a limit! So you will concede that there are certain truths that yet elude us?"

"Alright, I'll concede that much."

"There are things that remain unknown to us, right?"

"Yes! I thought I just admitted that!"

"And you'd concede that just because science hasn't discovered these things, that doesn't mean they don't exist, right?"

"Well. . ." she responds, growing a bit uneasy. "But that doesn't prove they do or don't."

"As Kierkegaard put it, 'I reason *from* existence, not toward it.' When two lawyers plead their cases at a trial, they don't argue over whether the accused *exists*, they argue over whether he's guilty or innocent."

"Alright. . . but that still doesn't prove God exists. All you've done is fight me to a stalemate: I can't prove he doesn't exist and you can't prove he does."

"But I've rendered the very question irrelevant. Even if science could prove anything one way or another, might not some other evidence be discovered at a later time that might refute it?" Kate is tight-lipped. "Truth is ultimately subjective, Kay— so it'll always come back to whether one chooses to believe. . . Faith, faith, faith!"

He jumps back up on the hood of the car.

"*Da-na-na-na*," he sings, "*can't touch this!*" Courtney and I laugh; Kate casts a grudging smile.

"Still the Champ!" he boasts. "Even drunk on my ass, I can't be beat! This is cause for celebration!"

"What did you have in mind?" I ask.

"I dunno. . . What can we do to celebrate?" None of us have any suggestions for him.

"How 'bout some mailbox baseball?" he asks, hopping down off the car.

"What the hell is that?"

"My father and his football buddies used to play it in high school," Tom explains. "It's when you drive around smashing people's mailboxes with a bat."

"You're crazy," I say.

"Loosen up! It'll be fun!" He holds out his hand to me. "Gimme the keys, Will— I've got the softball equipment right here in the trunk."

"No *way!*"

"Come on, Will," Kate says. "Every now and then you gotta say 'what the fuck.' "

"What is this? Am I the only sane one here? Court? You wanna back me up, please?"

"Aw, how can you say no to this face?" she asks me, squeezing Tom's face in her hands. "Give him the keys, Will. Let him have his fun."

I take a minute, looking back and forth between the two girls, searching for a voice of reason somewhere. Eventually I realize I'm not going to find one. Reluctantly, I toss Tom the keys. He opens the trunk and stops for several seconds, just staring inside. Then he starts to laugh.

"Oh, shit!" he says. "I'm so drunk I forgot this isn't my car! All I've got here are George's golf equipment! Damn— I must really be loaded to the gills!"

"So much for mailbox baseball," I say with no small amount of relief.

"Titleist," he says, picking up a couple of golf balls. "Aren't these really expensive?"

"I think so," Kate says.

"Oh, wait. . . This is even better." Uh oh. I don't like that look on Tom's face. "You ever play golf before, guys?"

"No," we all answer.

"Well, I don't know about you, but I'm dyin' to learn. . ."

We all pile back in the car, where Tom immediately directs me to Dutch Plains, where he claims to know of a golf course we can use. Why am I doing this, one might wonder? I only wish I knew. It's almost 4:00 in the morning and Tom's got one of his mix tapes in the cassette deck, playing the Modern Lovers' "Roadrunner." The girls sing along with the "radio on" chorus while Tom bellows out the verses.

"*Got the car, got the a.m., got the. . .*"

"*Radio on!*"

"*Got the car from Massachusetts, got the. . .*"

"*Radio on!*"

"*Got the road, got the turnpike, got the. . .*"

"*Radio on!*"

We park on a little side street, just off one of the main roads in town. Getting out, Tom leads us across to where this course lies. It's surrounded by a simple, chest high chain link fence— almost too simple, I think. I spy a little yellow sign, the size of a car license plate, reading "no trespassing under penalty of the law."

"Uh, guys? Check out the sign?"

"Aw, stop bein' a party pooper, Will!" Tom chastises. He puts his hands on the fence and I half-expect him to get an electric shock, but no. He hops over it with ease, then helps hoist each of the girls over. I hand George's golf bag to him, then go over, myself.

"God, how are we supposed to get through this?" It's pitch black and there's about twenty feet of trees and brush between us and the rest of the course.

"Here," Tom says, extending a hand to Courtney. We form a human chain with Tom leading us through.

"I can't believe you're going along with this," I mutter to Kate.

"It's healthy to pull a stupid, drunken prank like this every once in a while, Will. Besides, I always wanted to try and play."

"William, my nine-iron if you please?" Tom requests once we're out of the woods— literally, not figuratively.

"What's a nine-iron?"

"Damned if I know." The girls laugh. I hand him a random club.

"Any tees in there?"

"I don't think so."

"Ah well— fuggit." He lets a ball fall to the ground, carelessly. "Fore!" he shouts, cocking back with the club and then letting it fly. In the darkness, I can't tell how far it goes.

"Shit," Tom curses. "I guess I gotta go find it now?"

"Now me!" Kate exhorts. "Now me!" I give her a club, too. Tom rolls her a ball. She swings at it several times, unsuccessfully. Both she and Courtney are giggling more uncontrollably with each miss.

You know, it is *so* not fun being the only sober person in a group of otherwise fun-loving drunks.

"Fore!" Kate yells, finally making contact. The ball dribbles off about ten feet. "Gee, was that as bad as it looked?"

"Much worse, actually," Tom informs her. "You go, Court. With your field hockey skills, I bet you're a natural."

"Oh, God," says Courtney. She grabs a club out of the bag and Tom tosses a ball down in front of her.

"Just remember to keep your eye on the ball," he coaches. She rears back and smacks one. Further than Kate, for sure, but not nearly as far as Tom.

"Come on," Tom says. "Time to practice our putting." We start for the nearest green. Along the way, the girls stop briefly to play in a sand trap. Tom and I eventually drag them out.

"You wanna putt at least, Will?" Tom asks.

"No, man. I just wanna get outta here. . . really. Can we, please?"

"Lemme just putt one here," he persists. "You got a putter in there for me?"

"Does this qualify?" I ask, handing him a new club.

"Whatever," he tells me. He drops a fresh ball, then takes a minute to size up the shot.

"Just be careful," I tell him. "Don't tear up the green or anything."

"Do you know what this green represents?" he asks. "I'll tell you: animal-killing pesticides, deforestation, wasted water. . . not to mention homeless people, who could be living in low-cost housing on the land wasted by this stupid-ass course. Do you know how much it costs to build and maintain a course green? Like, over $20,000— no shit. We should all piss on it!"

"Putt on it, piss on it. . . Just make it quick, alright?" Tom reassumes his putting stance. He taps at the ball, gently rolling it in.

"Hoo-*hah!*" he exclaims, pumping his fist.

"Let me go now," Kate insists. She takes a different club out of the bag as Tom drops a ball for her. She takes a few practice swings.

"Are you practicing or actually trying to hit the ball?" Tom asks. Kate and Courtney both laugh.

"I'm practicing, asshole!" She takes a couple more practice swings, then starts breaking up again for some reason.

"What?" I ask.

"I was actually trying to hit it on that last one!"

Now we're all dying, including me.

Eventually, Kate manages to compose herself, and gives it another go. She hits it, only too hard. It just about rolls off the opposite end of the green. She goes over to hit it again, only too softly this time, and it barely moves.

"Don't take this the wrong way, Kay," Tom says, "but you really suck at this." Again, we're all laughing. Suddenly, we hear someone behind us.

"What do you kids think you're doing?" the cop asks, shining a flashlight in our faces. The question hangs in the air forever; like the punchline to a really bad joke. Me and the girls practically wet ourselves.

"We're playing golf," Tom finally answers non-chalantly.

"Yeah, well. . . round's over, pal."

Back at the Dutch Plains Police Station, we're sitting down on a bench alongside the front desk, where there's this ugly, mean-looking desk sergeant. The four of us remain there, dead silent, for the longest time.

"Can I take my one phone call now?" Tom asks at last.

"No," the desk sergeant tells him.

"I thought I was allowed one phone call."

"Wrong. You're allowed one phone call if we charge you. Right now, you haven't been charged."

"Are we going to be?" Kate asks. "Charged, I mean?"

"You in a hurry young lady? You got some place to go?" None of us say a word. "Just sit tight. When we figure out what we're doing with you, you'll be the first to know."

Again, we sit quiet for awhile. Again, it's Tom who breaks the silence.

"Can you tell me if officer Burnham is still on the force?"

"Officer Burnham?" the sergeant repeats, wide-eyed.

"Yeah, is he still on the force?"

"He's on the force, alright," the sergeant says.

"I was kinda hoping you could call him, maybe?" The sarge looks back at Tom like he's trying to stare him down. Tom doesn't blink.

"You sure you know him, now?" he asks. "Because if I call him at this hour. . ."

"I swear, he's an old friend of the family," Tom insists. Sarge looks down at his paperwork and sucks his teeth.

"What's his wife's name, then?"

"Joanne," Tom answers immediately. "And he has two daughters: Rebecca and Ashley. Rebecca's gotta be in high school by now; don't ask me how old Ashley is. . ."

The sergeant looks surprised. He turns and picks up the phone on his desk.

"Who should I tell him is calling?" he asks.

". . .Just tell him it's Tommy's son."

Less than a half an hour later, this forty-something guy bursts in wearing slacks and a pajama shirt.

"Tommy?" he asks.

"Hey, Mick," Tom responds. "What took you so long?" The guy starts to give him a killer dirty look, then cracks a smile.

"You wanna handle this yourself?" the desk sergeant asks him.

"Yeah," he sighs. "I'll take care of it. . . C'mon kids." He motions for us to get up and follow him. Tom stops to retrieve George's golf bag from behind the front desk.

"I can't believe you," this Burnham-guy tells Tom outside the station. "You might actually have bigger balls than your old man, you know that? Get in the car."

"Aren't we takin' a squad car?" Tom asks. "Come on! I wanna run the siren!"

"Get the fuck outta here!" We all get into his car. "These your friends?" he asks, starting the engine.

"Just some people I met on the course, tonight."

"Christ, what a smartass!" he laughs. "I'm Mick Burnham," he introduces. "I was good friends with Tom's father."

"Hi," we all say, sheepishly.

"Y'know, I'm real impressed, Mick," Tom says. "The way you just walked us out of there, you've really got major stroke."

"I should hope so, Tom; I'm the friggin' chief, after all!"

"The chief of police?" Tom asks, his mouth dropping open. "How the fuck did that happen? When?"

"Whaddaya mean, how? The last chief retired, and I was the guy with the most service and the highest score on the chief's exam. Happened like two years ago."

"I thought there had to be more to it than *that*."

"Not really," he says. "I was the youngest guy to make captain in the history of the force, y'know."

"You sound proud."

"Well, sure."

"Shit. . . What do you think my father would say if he could see you now? Northdale's most infamous juvenile delinquent, now the chief of police in Dutch Plains?"

"Second most infamous," he corrects. "Your old man was the most infamous. By far."

"I don't know, Mick. I've heard Gus tell some stories about those days. . ."

"Oh, Gus was drunk through half of high school and hung over the other half. He doesn't know what he's talking about. . . You're parked near the country club, I take it?"

"Yeah," Tom says. "Right off Pierson."

"So how's your Grandma been?" he asks.

"She's good."

"God, I used to stop by and see her every Christmas. All the guys on the team used to. I've gotten lazy these past couple years, though."

"Chief of police," Tom says, still in shock, apparently. "I can't get over it."

"You're damn lucky I am!" he responds with a laugh. "Where would you be now, otherwise?"

"Ah, they weren't gonna do anything to us. They were just gonna make us cool our heels 'til morning, then call our parents to pick us up."

"True," Burnham concurs. "But I spared you that indignity, at least."

"We're here," I say, motioning to the street where we're parked. He pulls in alongside our car and lets us out.

"One of you is fit to drive, I would hope?" he asks, almost sarcastically.

"He's straight," Tom says, referring to me.

"Tired but straight," I add.

"Alright then," the chief says. "Take it easy guys. . . And don't get into any more trouble, you," he tells Tom.

"Peace, Mick. And thanks."

Driving out of Dutch Plains, Tom sits in the passenger seat, fiddling with the radio while the girls are only semi-conscious in the back seat together.

"My kingdom for a punk station in the metro area," he grumbles before settling on WNEW. He lies back and sighs as Springsteen's "Jungleland" fills the car.

And me? I'm riding on a cloud of sweet relief. We dodged a fucking *bullet* tonight, man; nobody else I know would even believe it if I tried to tell 'em: me, goody two-shoes-Will Flaherty, a hooligan trespasser. William "Babyface" Flaherty. Tonight on *America's Most Wanted*.

"What are you smilin' about there, pally?" Tom asks.

"Me? Was I smiling?"

"From ear to ear." I smile again.

"See? You're doing it again."

"It's been an evening to remember," I say. We both take a moment to soak in the early morning stillness.

"So are we grabbin' some breakfast at Mickey D's?" he asks.

"Isn't it tradition?"

The four of us sit in the parking lot at McDonald's watching the sunrise. Shortly afterward, the place opens and we go in to eat. Tom orders just about one of everything on the breakfast menu— a meal so big, Jughead Jones would choke on it. It's almost seven-thirty by the time we finish.

"Where am I going?" I ask just as we're getting back into the car.

"May as well drop Courtney off," Tom says. "She's closest. Do you have your car at Kay's?"

"No," Kate says. "I picked him up tonight and we went back to my house." Courtney's already got her eyes closed and her head back.

"Actually, it's better that way," Tom says. "We can just drop you off after Courtney and then go straight back to Oakwood."

"You gonna be alright getting back to your house from mine?" I ask him.

"Come on, Will. We live three minutes away from each other. I think I'll manage."

We drop off Courtney, then head back to Kate's. I get out with her, holding her hand as we walk back up the driveway together. We do a little kissy-face at her door.

"I'm gonna really feel like shit in another hour," she tells me.

"You play, you pay."

"Mm. I better get a move-on." We share another kiss. "Love you."

"Love you, too."

I get back behind the wheel of George's car and drive back to Oakwood with Tom. I want to take him directly home, but he insists on going to my place.

"Are you sure you'll be alright?" I ask as I get out and Tom slides into the driver's seat. "I mean, you *were* drinkin' tonight. . ."

"I promise, Will— I won't go faster than five miles an hour."

"Five miles an hour? You swear?"

"Five miles an hour," he repeats. "On my father's grave." He slowly. . . *slowly*. . . backs out of the driveway and begins down the street. I watch him for several seconds, then begin to walk after him.

"You don't have to go *that* slow, mud brother," I say as I'm walking alongside the car.

"Five miles an hour. On my father's grave."

I stop and watch him continue on, tortoise-like, to the end of the street and turn. I chuckle to myself a moment before turning around and heading inside my house.

"Where were you all night?" my father asks me as I enter the kitchen, sounding more angry than concerned. He's at the table, his morning paper open in front of him.

"Sorry," I say. "I got arrested."

"This is serious, dammit!" the old man curses, never considering for a second that I might be telling the truth. I just laugh at him and go up to my room to collapse.

CHAPTER VIII

Meredith makes a mental note to never doubt her brother's instincts again. At least not when it comes to their mother.

George was gone, visiting his son and daughter-in-law, and Frankie and the twins had already left with their respective fathers for the weekend when Tom pulled her into his room to talk to her. He, himself, was about to go out for his usual Saturday night of debauchery with his friends, but before leaving he wanted to make sure she'd be staying home with Lisa. He told her that he found it strange, how Lisa had spent so much of the day meticulously cleaning a house that was supposed to be empty for the whole weekend. She laughed at him; told him to stop being paranoid. But he insisted that something felt wrong.

Finally, she assured him that she would stick around to keep an eye on things. And sure enough, not long after his departure, the unthinkable occurred. A guest arrived at the house.

Lou Adubato.

Yes, *that* Lou Adubato. The one she watched toss her brother around like a rag doll back in that fateful summer of 1976, when he was not yet seven years old and she was merely three. Lisa welcomed him into the house, re-introducing him to her like it was nothing. She showed him around, told a few amusing anecdotes about the family, then escorted him to the backyard.

Lisa's biggest mistake was giving him that first beer. A heartbeat later, he was on to his second and, before you knew it, he had finished off an entire six pack. That was about the time he started slamming his fists down on the table and accusing her of having turned him in to the cops all those years ago.

Now, as this stand-off goes on, Meredith finds herself wondering how she can get him out of here. She looks at her watch and wonders how much longer her brother might be. She wonders to herself what might happen if he doesn't get back soon; then wonders what might happen if he does. And she's not sure which scenario scares her more.

* * *

This whole evening has been one big bust— I'm glad we've finally decided to call it a night. Tom and I are now on our way back to Oakwood after dropping off Courtney; since Kate and I went out in her car, she just drove herself home.

"Well this has certainly been an night to remember," Tom remarks.

"At least it can't get any worse," I say.

It started with the kids at the movie theatre, who began throwing their Raisinettes and making noise the second the lights went down and the previews began. Then, coming out of the parking lot, we almost got side-swiped by this maniac in a Jeep. But the lowlight of the evening had to be sitting in the Burger King afterward, listening to Tom and Kate swapping horror stories about job hunting and the hard times their parents have been giving them since graduation. Tom had her beat when he revealed that George slips the classified section under his bedroom door every morning with various job listings circled in red pen.

"You wanna grab some coffee at my place before goin' home?" Tom asks.

"Yeah, sure."

Something's bugging Tom. He's been unusually quiet all night, like he's preoccupied with something. Maybe it's just the usual shit with George; maybe it's finally starting to wear on him.

"You okay, man?"

"Me? I'm fine. Why you ask?"

"I dunno. Seems like there's something on your mind."

We pull in the yard and the back light is already on. Then I notice Lisa and Meredith are out here, along with some guy. I look over at Tom and can see by his expression he's in shock— but only momentarily. Then, he breaks a wide smile.

"It's him," he says, almost dripping with glee.

"Who?"

"It's Lou."

Lou Adubato? The drunk who smacked Tom around? He calmly shuts the engine off, then steps out of the car. I follow suit.

"Tommy!" Meredith calls out.

"Well, well," Tom says, slamming the car door. "Look who it is. . . Luigi! See, Will— I told you that wasn't a skunk you smelled. How you been, paisan?"

"Tommy?" Lou mutters as he squints in Tom's direction. He's not what you'd call a moose, but you still get the feeling this Lou's one tough motherfucker. He's just got one of those scrunched-up, pug faces that looks like it's had a few pool cues broken across it.

"He's been making threats for the last half-hour," Meredith offers, never taking her eyes off Lou for a second. "I wanted to call the police, but. . . I was afraid to try and go back in the house. . ."

"You need to mind your own business," Louis spits out. "The two of you." Tom's eyes grow bigger.

"Mer, I think you should take Lisa upstairs," Tom says, taking a step forward. But both Meredith and Lisa stay put. I just stand motionless in the exact same spot as when I got out of the Camaro, mesmerized by what I'm seeing unfold before me.

"Tommy, stop— he won't do anything," Lisa says.

"Stay outta this!" Tom screams back at her. All of us jump at the sudden loudness of his voice.

"You know how long I've been dreaming of this day, Lou?" he continues. "Don't disappoint me, now. Do something stupid; gimme an excuse. I'm beggin' ya."

"Tell that dog to shut up," Lou says, his voice cracking a little. Tempest hasn't stopped barking since we pulled in.

"That dog'll kick your fuckin' ass," Tom says, continuing forward. "Just like the last one did."

"Go ahead and call the damn cops," Lou dares. "I haven't done anythin' wrong. Not a *thing*."

"Yeah, you're a real angel," Tom cracks. "Don't worry, Lou— the last thing I want are the cops bustin' up our fun." Lou shakes his head and sorta smirks.

"Boy, don't even think of playin' tough-guy with me. . ."

"Now before anything else," Tom calmly proceeds, ignoring his warning, "I have to ask you to get off my property. It's a formality. After you refuse, I get to kick the living shit out of you."

Nobody breathes for the next nine seconds.

"Good boy," Tom says with the biggest grin. He non-chalantly slaps Lou across the face. Hard. "Come on," he invites.

Instantly, something awakens behind Lou's eyes. He leaps forward suddenly, hitting Tom with a wild swing. But Tom never even takes a backward step. The two of them begin to wrestle, and even as Meredith lets out a screaming "no," Tom already has a hold of him and is shoving him backward, to the ground. He seems to pause a second while Lou picks himself up.

The thought suddenly occurs to me that I should be jumping in here. I look over at Meredith. Why is it that my only thought at this moment is of impressing her?

I remain paralyzed. When Lou starts forward again, Tom's waiting. His whole right arm is a blur as he smashes him full in the face. The sound of one man's fist hitting another man dead-full in the face is like nothing you hear in movies or cartoons. It's like no sound I've heard before; a sick sound. Lou's head snaps backward while the rest of his body catches up a second later, back on the ground.

"That was for my sister's nightmares," Tom informs him. He waits for him, again, to get back up. But Lou tries to get up too quickly and ends up falling right back down. So Tom steps forward, grabbing a handful of his hair. Lou grasps desperately at Tom's shirt as he pulls him up.

"And this... is for puttin' your filthy hands on my mother." Again, Tom's fist is a blur as it slams full into Lou's face. And again, Lou is on the ground. He's bleeding.

"Come on, Lou. All these years, I've been dreaming of Ali-Frazier and you're givin' me Tyson-Spinks." Tom bends down, about to drag him back to his feet yet again when Lou hits him in the stomach— with everything he's got left, apparently. Tom never even flinches. He responds with another disdainful slap across Lou's mouth that makes him go limp. Grabbing a piece of the back of his shirt in one hand and the waist of his pants in the other, Tom lifts him waist-high off the ground and throws him into the nearby trash cans. For the briefest second, he's wholly airborne.

"Uhh," Lou groans. It appears as if just lifting his head up off the ground is a monumental task. Tom calmly walks over to him and gives him a vicious kick to the ribs.

"*That*," he says, "was for my dog, cocksucker." He takes a handful of the front of his shirt and drags him up to his knees. He draws back his fist yet again.

"Tommy! Stop!" Lisa shouts, grabbing his arm. I didn't even realize she was no longer standing next to me until just now. "Tommy, please... it's enough. It's over." Meredith suddenly has her arms around him as well, trying to hold him back. I run over now, too.

Yeah, go ahead Will— it's safe.

"We better get him inside," Lisa says.

I end up helping Tom carry Lou back in the house. We dump him on the living room couch while Lisa retrieves some things from the medicine cabinet. Once she gets back, I accompany Tom and Meredith into the kitchen.

"Oh," Meredith exclaims, "your hand!" She gets some ice from the freezer and wraps it in a paper towel. "Here," she says as she sits next to him at the table, applying the ice to his right hand. "It looks a little swollen."

"Thanks, sis. At least somebody around here's concerned about me."

"You really fucked him up," Meredith says, beginning to smile a little.

"Big deal. I punked some puny, middle-aged, out-of-shape, recovering substance abuser."

They're ignoring me. I'm both relieved and offended by this, simultaneously.

"He was standing right in front of the door and wouldn't move," Meredith goes on. "I was tempted to run next door, but I was afraid of leaving Mom alone with him."

"Don't worry about it, sis— you done good."

"You want tea or anything?" she asks him.

"Yes, that would be nice, actually." She gets up to put the kettle on. Tom reaches into his pocket and takes out his car keys.

"Here you go, Robin— looks like you get to drive the Batmobile tonight." He hands the keys to me. "Just bring it back tomorrow. This whole mess should be all cleaned up by then. I hope."

"Thanks," I say with a polite smile.

"I'm sorry you had to see this tonight, Will."

"Forget about it." I know I wish I could.

He sees me to the back door, locking it behind me as I leave. I hop into the Camaro, start it up, and pull away without looking back.

The whole drive home, I'm thinking about Tom and what happened tonight; like I'll probably be doing all night, through the next few nights. Maybe even the rest of my life. A year and a half I know him, and I never saw this side of him, before. Part of me is in awe of him, now. Still another part of me is just a little bit scared of him. And then there's this tiny part of me that really. . . hates him. Hates him for revealing to Meredith, to the world, and to myself, just what a coward I really am.

* * *

"Meredith, would you mind?" Tommy asks. "I need to talk to your mother. Alone."

"Sure," she answers. After tonight, Tommy Redivo's earned a good two or three months, solid, of absolute compliance with any

156

request he makes of his sister. She quietly exits, leaving him alone in the kitchen with Lisa.

"How's the guest of honor doing?"

"Alright," Lisa answers in a low voice; turning her gaze downward, to the table. "So what did Meredith have to say?"

"She couldn't get over how stupid it was of you, inviting that piece of shit into this house." His mother says nothing. "Aren't you going to even try and defend yourself?"

She looks back up at him.

"I'm your mother," she says without much conviction. "I don't have to justify myself to you."

"That's garbage," he declares. "You owe me and Meredith, both, an explanation."

"What do you expect me to explain?"

"Well for starters, do you mind telling me what were you thinking, running out and buying a six-pack for a violent drunk?"

"I didn't run out and buy beer for him and you know it," she tells him. "He said he had changed, he said he could control it, now. I felt like if I didn't let him have any, it would be like. . . not having faith in him, or something. I couldn't say no."

"What was he even doing here in the first place, Lisa?" She twists in her chair a moment, considering her response.

"About a year ago, I got a letter from him, forwarded from our old address in Carver. He said he found God, said he understood how precious life is."

"And you believed him?"

"From his letter and from talking to him on the phone, he sounded like he really wanted forgiveness, Tommy. Like he needed it."

Tommy Redivo sits across the table from his mother, amazed.

"How could I deny him that?" she goes on. "How could I deny anyone that? So yes, I invited him over to show him that I forgive him. To show him that I believe in him and trust him."

"Please," he says, wearily. "Enough with that new age shit you think you believe in, alright?"

157

"When another human being reaches out to you like that, what do you do? Slam the door in his face? How are we ever going to make a better world if everyone did that?"

"That's all very well and good, Lees, but sometimes you have to stop and consider who it is that's reaching out to you. He pulled the same shit when he was living with us: he'd get drunk, smack you in the back of the head, sober up the next day and apologize for it. And you'd buy it. You have to learn to judge character. Or lack of character, in this case."

"You have to understand, Tommy, I was an ennabler back then— I've got to take my share of responsibility for what went on, too."

"You wanna talk about responsibility? What about your responsibility to your family? Your little experiment in redemption tonight could've gotten someone hurt. Maybe you, maybe Meredith. . . Who knows?"

"There wouldn't have been any violence tonight if you didn't start it, Tommy. I knew what I was doing; I was always in control. Can't you ever give me the benefit of the doubt?"

"Oh, Lees," he says with a smile. "You can't say *what* would've happened here tonight if I hadn't grabbed the bull by the horns."

"And neither can *you*," she goes right back at him.

"Meredith was scared to death."

"Meredith shouldn't have been here." Tommy groans, shakes his head and smiles. "Lou and I had issues, Tommy; we needed closure. He only came here because I invited him and you were wrong to attack him the way you did."

"Me, wrong?!?" he asks in shock. "I was fulfilling a sacred duty, tonight! Doing my father's work!"

"Your *father's* work?"

"Damn straight! What do you think he would've done if he were here tonight? Or if he had been around that day, seventeen years ago?"

"Tommy," she insists, "if your father had been alive, I never would've known Lou Adubato in the first place."

"Okay, forget it; I'm sorry I opened my mouth," he says. "This isn't *Fantasy*-fucking-*Island*, I should know." His voice, it sounds even more like his father's when he's angry like this. . . She shudders.

"What do you want from me? I mean, it's a closed issue at this point; we're never going to see Lou again after tonight."

"I want you to understand *why* you're wrong," he insists, pacing in front of the stove. "Since it's so obvious you don't."

She sighs. He strokes his chin, thoughtfully.

"You at all familiar with Egyptian mythology, Lees?" he asks her, sitting back down.

"Not really," she answers, softly.

"Well, the Egyptian gods were ruled by Osiris, along with his wife, Isis," he begins. "Now Osiris had this brother, Set, who really hated him. And one day, Set tricked Osiris into getting inside this box, see? And once inside, Set sealed the thing shut and threw it into the Nile, killing Osiris." He pauses a moment. "You following so far?" Lisa offers a slight nod of her head.

"Good. So anyway, some time later, the ghost of Osiris appeared before his son, Horus, and revealed all the gory details about how he was killed and ordered him to avenge his death. So Horus tracked Set down and challenged him. And the two gods had this huge brawl that lasted something like three days. Finally, in the end, Horus won. But before he had a chance to strike the killing blow, his mother Isis suddenly appeared and— much to Horus' dismay— ordered that Set be allowed to go free. So Horus, in a fit of rage, cut her head off." He puts his cup of tea to his mouth and drinks. "I think what's-his-face, Thoth, ended up giving her a cow's head as a replacement."

"And?" Lisa asks.

"*And?*" he repeats, raising his eyebrows.

"And what, Tommy? What is all of this supposed to mean? Why do you talk in riddles?"

"It's a parable, Lees." He searches her face for a glimmer of understanding, but does not find it. "Oh, forget it. Go upstairs. Get to sleep."

She pauses a moment before rising. "Tommy," she starts as she gets up from the table, "I. . ." She wants to say something maternal but can think of nothing. He looks back at her, with his father's dark eyes, and it chills her to the bone. She walks out as he remains seated at the kitchen table, staring down into the mug of tea his sister made for him.

No one understands, Tommy Redivo thinks. If his father or even his grandfather were alive, it would be different. So very different.

"Lift this burden from me, Father," he requests in a whisper. He closes his eyes, smiles, and stretches out his arms, as if waiting for some response. When he opens his eyes again, he looks at his empty hands. He sighs a modest chuckle; musing that perhaps his prayer had already been answered in his inherited flesh, his borrowed blood, his bequeathed bone... The weapons by which he smites his enemies; the one thing he has always been able to rely upon. That is enough, he tells himself. It will have to be. He finishes what's left of his tea and leaves the empty mug in the sink.

In the living room, Lou Adubato groans as he tries in vain to focus his eyes upon the shadow suddenly cast over him.

"Gllk!"

"Got your attention?" Tommy asks him. He has his knee in his chest and his hand closed tight around his throat. "Listen: come the dawn, you haul your ass up, go out in the backyard, pick up your teeth and get the fuck outta here. 'Cause if I find you still here in the morning, I'll finish what I started tonight— you got that?"

Lou says nothing, but his trembling face is answer enough. Tommy gets up and lingers over him for a moment.

"Weak," he hisses with disdain. It couldn't feel more wrong to him, just letting Lou walk away from this. He should kill him now; tear his head loose from his neck, dance on what's left of his body. He feels the itch to hit him again— *one more time*, a voice whispers from within. Hate like this can eat you alive from the inside, he knows this, yet it's so very powerful, so intoxicating, it is difficult to avoid being seduced by it. *One more time*... But he resists. He takes a few backward steps... then slowly turns and walks away.

Meredith sits waiting for him in his room, along with Tempest.

"Hey," she greets softly as he enters. "Is everything... alright?"

"As good as could be expected, I guess," he tells her as he kicks off his sneakers.

"What did Mom have to say?" she asks him.

"Ah, you know how she is. Gave me one of those flower-child speeches of hers. . ."

"Well. . . I hope you weren't *too* hard on her."

"I could've been harder." She would like to express some gratitude for what he's done tonight, but she can't seem to find the words. She watches him pull off his socks. Watches him take his wallet out of his pocket and toss it on top of the stereo cabinet. *Can't you tell I'm trying to thank you?* she wonders. *Help me out here; say something.*

"Maybe you can tell me," he begins. "What could Lisa have been thinking, letting this guy into the house?"

"I'm not sure," she answers. "I know she still carries alot of guilt over him, over what happened seventeen years ago. Maybe she's trying to face up to it somehow. Make amends, however misguided that may seem."

Tommy stops to consider his sister's analysis.

"Tell me, Mer: was I wrong for what I did tonight?"

The question surprises her. "God, Jesus, no!" she responds.

"I just don't know. When I argue with Lisa, it's like we live in two completely opposite universes, and sometimes I begin to question which of us is living in the real one."

"Trust me— you were completely in the right. There's no way that guy was just gonna yell for an hour or two, get some shit off his chest and go home. He was gonna hurt somebody if you didn't punch his lights out, first."

Tommy Redivo is well-pleased. "Thanks, sis. I guess I needed to hear that."

Meredith smiles. She feels safe here, in his room, with him. As a little girl, whenever she found herself scared by something in the middle of the night, it was her brother's room she ran to. She would have gone to her mother, but Lisa's bed would invariably be occupied by some husband, some boyfriend, some. . . whatever. So whether it was a monster under her bed or a bad nightmare or just Frankie's wailing for her four a.m. feeding, waking her unexpectedly and forcing her to face the dead-quiet darkness. . . it was always Tommy's room. Cocoa would always be there at the foot of his bed, lying on that old quilt Tommy laid out for her every night. The old dog would let out a low moan as her shadow crossed the doorway— nothing and no one ever got past Cocoa, God bless 'er— and her brother would slowly stir under the covers. When she'd ask him if it was okay to sleep in his room, he'd mumble something vaguely affirmative and roll to one side, lifting up the blanket for her. And every time, she'd slide in right beside him and fall quickly to sleep; all her fears of monsters and darkness dispelled.

She recalls those nights now and finds she doesn't want to leave. She tries to think of something else to say. And a thought occurs to her.

"Do you ever wonder what things would've been like if Mom had given you up for adoption? Y'know, like she was originally going to?"

"Oh, *constantly*," he teases. "I always dream about being taken in by this super-rich family, living in a big mansion, getting everything I want. . . with no little sisters to aggravate me." He smiles at her. "What made you think of that all of a sudden?"

"I was just wondering what the hell I woulda done here tonight, if not for you."

"You would've figured something out," he assures her.

"I think I would've ended up a very different person if I didn't have you around, growing up."

"In some superficial ways, maybe. No more."

"You think?"

"I think there's a certain foundation of character that a person is just born with; that no kind of upbringing can provide if it's not already there. And you definitely have it." He puts his hand on her shoulder and her heart bubbles over with pride.

"I thought you were Joe Existentialism; Mr. Free Will. . . Are you saying heredity is destiny, now?"

"Just the opposite: I'm saying heredity isn't destiny and upbringing isn't destiny, either. It comes down to people making the right choices, and I think you'd still make those right choices even if I wasn't around. I have faith in you, Mer."

"Thanks, bro." She rises to hug him and he reciprocates, wrapping her up in his big arms, making her feel suddenly small. And now the words come quickly; easily.

"We fight too much these days," she tells him. He laughs a hearty laugh. "Don't make fun of me," she says, letting herself laugh a little, too, "I'm serious."

"I'm not making fun, cookie. I'm just laughing 'cause you make me happy."

"I love you, stupid."

"I know. I love you too." They break away from each other.

"And if I was given up for adoption," he continues, "I would've been one those people who searches... I would've found you. Eventually."

"Oh really?" she asks, dripping with mock-cynicism.

"Hey, you ain't gettin' rid of me that easy, cookie. I'm like the biggest, baddest cockroach on the planet— you think you can just stomp on me once and finish me?"

She eyes him warily for a moment.

"Come clean now, Thomas. Weren't you just a *little* afraid, tonight?"

"Excuse me," he says with a grin, "have we met? Do you know what my name is?"

"Tommy," Meredith says knowingly, "you don't have to give me the patented name routine. You don't have to put up any front."

"Meredith," he begins, disappointed. "You've been out with me and my friends to some shows... You've seen me mix it up with some real bangers. Hell, your ninth grade boyfriend was bigger than this guy."

"Yeah, but come on— this guy's done hard time, bro." He laughs some more now.

"Mer... he's five foot-nothing, in his mid-forties and has spent the better part of twenty years abusing his body with God knows how many different drugs. I'm not quite twenty-four and in the best shape of my life— I could take ten of him at once and not even get a decent workout."

She looks at him a moment. She turns to leave, then abruptly stops at the door.

"You really weren't you scared at all? I mean, not even a little bit?"

He sighs.

"You want the truth, huh?"

"Yeah," she responds earnestly. He looks at her.

"No, Meredith," he says with a broad smile. "I was never scared. Not even a little bit."

She smiles back at him as she closes his door. Then Tommy lets himself fall back against the wall. He slides down to the floor, alongside Tempest. He pets her and wonders why all his problems can't be as simple as Lou Adubato. If only he could solve all of life's difficulties with his fists; how easy it would all be. . .

He will stay here with his dog, awake, until the dawn. Until Lou leaves. Only then will he let himself sleep.

CHAPTER IX

Tommy Redivo's stomach turns at the all-too familiar sight of flashing police sirens in his rearview mirror. He pulls over on to the shoulder and the police car pulls in right behind him. He rolls down his window as the somewhat rotund officer steps out of his car and begins walking toward him.

"Is there, anything wrong, officer?" he asks with his best choir-boy face.

"I think you already know what's wrong buddy," the cop answers. "Gimme yer license, insurance an' registration." Tommy knows the drill by now. He reaches over to the glove compartment and takes out the necessary materials.

"I'm so very, very sorry if I was speeding, officer." He hands him all that he's requested. "Honestly, I didn't realize. . ."

"Wait here. Stay in the car."

This is the last thing he needs right now. He's got a shit-paying job, a mountain of Christmas bills on top of the already sizable balance on his credit card, and no windfalls in sight. One speeding ticket is half a weeks pay, practically. He should have held on to that PBA sticker Mick gave him.

"Here," the cop says, handing him a ticket upon his return.

"Look, officer, do you think you could give me a break?" he beseeches.

"A break?" the cop asks with raised eyebrows. He stares for the longest, most tense moment. "Do you know how sick I am of seein' spoiled brat-punks like you gettin' the world served to 'em on a silver platter? And no matter how much you get, you still want more?

"You wanna know something kid?" Tommy says nothing. "I was already givin' you a break when I wrote this up— I charged you with sixty-five in a fifty-five zone, even though I clocked you at seventy-five. . . But *now*," the cop proclaims, his eyes burning with righteousness, "I'm gonna write out another ticket chargin' you with seventy-five like I shoulda done in the first place! Wait right here!"

Tommy seethes as he watches the cop waddle back to his car. He's only been ticketed once before— one of those classic speed traps where the limit sign is conveniently concealed by some bushes and the radar gun adds about twenty mph to your actual speed— but he's been pulled over many other times. Especially when he first started driving, back in Carver, where the cops are notorious for their harassment of teen drivers. Those Carver Nazis would stop him for anything; from not using his signal properly to not having his headlights on if it was the least bit overcast. It sickens him, the way these pigs get off on throwing their weight around, just because they can.

In that lively imagination of his, Tommy pictures the cop's whole life and how he got to be where he is right now. He sees him as a scrub on the football team in high school, with shitty grades, on the road to nowhere. . . getting stoned and committing date rape every weekend. Then graduating high school and sitting around the house for a year before the rest of his family grows too disgusted with his sloth to take it anymore. So Mom and Dad threaten to put him out if he doesn't find a job. And he becomes a cop, not because he cares about people or wants to serve the public, but because. . . well, because what else is a big, stupid, lazy thug like him supposed to be?

It strikes Tommy Redivo now, just how much this is against the natural order of things. How much longer will he be made to answer

166

to the ignorant? The cowardly? The weak? How unnatural it is, that this bloated, untaught fascist holds any power at all over someone young and creative and strong. In another world, a better world, a fat, bullying pig like this would bow and call him master; he would fear him and rightly so— for Tommy would be king in such a world. If this slug were to display such insolence then, why he'd be knocked to the ground with one swipe of Tommy's strong, right hand. Then he would break both his arms and legs, make him cry like a woman and beg; he'd staple his eyelids to his forehead, forcing him to watch while he took his wife, his daughter, and. . .

But of course, this is not another world. When the cop returns with the new ticket, Tommy Redivo takes it, politely apologizes, and goes quietly on his way.

* * *

I'm sitting on Tom's bed, staring at the mail left on his night table. Frankie let me in fifteen minutes ago and I've been mindlessly gawking at the envelope marked from Whitehill University the whole time I've been waiting here. I'm off work tonight, with no morning classes tomorrow, so I figured it would be a good time to hang out with Tom, maybe do some catching up. The old gang hasn't been seeing much of each other lately at all.

The last six months have not been kind to Tom. Or Keith. Or Kate, either. She's currently doing secretarial work for this news-paper publisher that puts out weeklies for different towns in Union county— she despises the work, but she's hopeful that if she sticks around for awhile, they may give her a chance to do some writing. She got the job through this friend of a friend of her father's— another reason for her to hate the job, 'cause she really doesn't get along with her Dad at all and hates feeling indebted to him. Still in all, I'd have to say she's doing the best of the three of them. Keith still works at High Notes, unable to find anything better, and Tom ended up having to take a job at that book store up at the mall. Tom even ended up graduating Cahill with degrees in both English lit *and* philosophy— since he had to go the extra semester to graduate anyway, he decided to take the two philo courses he needed to complete the major— and even that hasn't helped him land a better job.

167

Even before the book store though, all those frustrating summer months of fruitless job hunting convinced both Tom and Keith to apply to graduate school. Whitehill University was their first choice. It's kind-of a secret, Tom's applying to grad school; I guess because he doesn't wanna catch any shit from George or anybody.

Personally, I don't know about it. I mean, I just hope Tom's not doing this out of frustration. He's very insistent though, that this is what he really wants. And while it's true he's totally in his element in the academic environment (anyone who ever saw him at Cahill would tell you so), I know he was also really looking forward to paying off the debt that he rung up for tuition, books, car insurance and whatever else these past couple years. And Lord knows, if he dug himself a small hole going to Cahill as an undergrad, then going to graduate school at Whitehill— a private school, mind you— may very well bury him.

At last, Tom bursts in, eyes wild.

"Anything wrong?" I wonder. He seems to almost bite through his lower lip before answering me.

". . .Nothing."

"Rough day at the office?" I playfully ask.

"Not particularly," he responds. "Same shit, different day, basically."

"Well, I noticed some mail here that might boost your spirits. . ." He sees the Whitehill envelope. "Don't you wanna open it?"

He walks over and picks it up. He looks at it.

"Kinda thin. That's not good."

"That doesn't mean anything," I say. "Maybe they're just letting you know you're accepted, and that they'll be sending along more paperwork later." He looks back down at the envelope.

"Here goes," he says, tearing it open.

He's in. I know it. How could they not take him? I remain seated on the bed while he begins to read. When he's finished, he folds it up and stuffs it back in its envelope.

"So?" I inquire. "What's the verdict?" He stands quiet for a moment, staring straight ahead and holding the envelope in his two hands.

"I'm rejected," he reveals, ultimately.

"No," I say in disbelief.

"Yes. They 'feel they must turn down my application at this time,' unquote."

I swallow, hard. Neither one us seems to want to speak.

"I guess you don't feel like goin' out now, huh?" I try and joke. He's still not saying anything.

Damn, this is just not like him. I'm starting to get a little spook-ed, here.

"I'm sure there's something else you can do," I reassure him. "Isn't there?"

"Like what, Will?"

"I don't know. Can't you apply for non-degree courses or some-thing?"

"Whitehill doesn't offer non-degree coursework," he says som-berly.

"Well, to be honest, I never thought grad school was for you, anyway. I mean, I just don't see what you have left to learn. You're already smarter than ninety-nine percent of the professors at Cahill, right?" Again, he has nothing to offer. "Look, maybe this is an omen. Instead of grad school, why not concentrate on your writing? Maybe try and sell some of those short stories of yours, or write the next great American novel."

"I've been trying to do that for years, Will," he reveals. "You know how impossible it is to get published? Especially my brand of fiction?"

That much is true, I must concur. Tom's shared some of his short stories with me over the last year, and his style is positively. . . stark. He describes his work as Hemingway-esque, but that isn't fitting, really. Hemingway would still throw in a flowery description of the countryside here and there, while there's nothing flowery or pretty in Tom's work. His stuff reads more like an obituary column. But that's exactly what makes it good. I guess I'm not *too* surprised that there are some editors out there who fail to get it; but I also assumed there had to be at least a few who'd appreciate it.

But I guess not.

"There are rules," he says, "but no one ever explained to me what those rules are. It's pretty hard to win at the game when you don't know any of the rules."

"What are you talkin' about?"

"I mean the thing I thought would impress them most, impresses them least— the fact that I broke my fuckin' ass to pay my own way. That I'd work twenty to thirty hours a week in addition to school. . . I went out of my way to emphasize that in my application and it didn't count for a damn thing. And now look where I am— I could've qualified for this lousy job at the mall while I was still in junior-fucking-high."

"Come on, Tom. . ."

"Isn't that incredible, when you think about it? They would've been more impressed if I had a rich Daddy pay my bills for me and I had a better g.p.a. If I lived on campus, cashed a check from Mummy and Pater every month, joined a frat, got drunk every night and paid someone else to write my term papers for me, they'd have been far more impressed."

"Easy, man. Whatever the rules are, the game ain't over yet."

"I feel like I've been played for the world's biggest sucker— don't let it happen to you, Will."

"Don't let *what* happen?"

"Be aware at all times that you're being railroaded. They herd us into these cookie-cutter, no-name schools. . . I mean, Cahill's a nice school, don't get me wrong, but does anyone dream of going there? Does putting 'Cahill' on your resume open any friggin' doors? They create schools like that just to placate middle class shmoes like you and me— so we get to say we're college graduates, but we're still excluded from the real party. We have no shot of making any real progress. This is exactly where they want us and that's where they're keeping us, whether we like it or not."

"Who-they?" I ask. He gives me a look.

"Uncle Charlie."

I begin to feel slightly relieved. At least he's joking. I think.

"It just feels like it's all been planned for me," he proceeds. "Like somebody said, 'we got a middle class Italian kid from suburban New Jersey here, what are we gonna let him be? A bus driver?

A shoe salesman?' Somewhere, some soulless bureaucrat has a script that says who and what I'm allowed to be and I've got no say in it."

Now I'm stone silent along with him. I wish I knew what to say, but I don't. So I just sit here, while he stands over there, neither of us uttering a peep.

The silence is finally broken by Lisa's voice, yelling from downstairs.

"Tom? You wanna pick up the phone?"

"I didn't hear the phone ring," I say.

"She was probably already on the line," Tom tells me. "You off?" he yells.

"Yeah," I hear from downstairs.

"Hello?" Tom asks, picking up the receiver of the extension in his room. "Oh, hey Keith. Yeah, just walked in. Actually, I. . . What? Really? You. . . really?" Tom appears to go pale, just a little. I move down to the opposite end of the bed as he sits down with me.

"Yeah," he continues, "that's great. What, me? No. . . no, I'm still waiting. Yeah, I'll definitely call. Alright. Hey— congratulations, man. Take care." He hangs up the phone.

"What was that?" I ask.

"Keith got in."

"What?" I sputter. "To Whitehill, you mean?"

"Yeah."

I'm stunned.

"But how? Your g.p.a.'s are about the same, and you even scored higher than him on the GRE." Then it hits me.

"Aw, no. . ."

I can't say anything, not a word. Neither can Tom. Political correctness prevents us from even discussing it. . . Of course, we don't even know if that's what's going on here. But then again, who's to say that it's not? It just makes me sick how inevitable these questions seem; how unavoidable they are. . . Y'know, there's gonna come a day in this country when people's race will be an afterthought; when we're no longer going to concern ourselves with questions over it, either way.

I just hope I live to see it.

"God."

"I don't know," is all Tom says, his head in his hands. Jeez, I've never seen him like this.

"Tom?" It's George, from right outside the door. "You off the phone?"

"Yeah, why?" Tom asks.

"Well, can I come in?" Tom looks at me in exasperation.

"What more could go wrong?" he asks as he gets up to open the door. George gives a nod in my direction as he enters. He's carrying some papers and a pen.

"I was hoping I could talk to you," he says. "Privately." Tom looks at me, then back at George.

"Just say what you came to say," he tells him. "I'd just tell him everything later, anyway— he may as well hear it firsthand."

George appears annoyed. He sighs dramatically before continuing.

"Alright, Tommy. I wanted to talk to you about health insurance."

"Health insurance?"

"Yes. Actually, I've been trying to talk to you about this for awhile. Since you graduated school and you're over twenty-two, you haven't been covered under my regular plan. I was hopeful you'd find a job that offered health insurance benefits, but. . ."

"Who knew I was ever on your plan in the first place? I haven't been to a doctor in years."

"Look, I know you can't afford to pay for it yourself right now and I don't expect you to. Just sign these papers and I'll take care of the rest."

"Oh, I'm sure you will," Tom remarks. "Just out of curiosity, how much would this cost?"

"About $240 a month," George answers.

"Ho-lee *shit!*" Tom declares. "Forget about it. No way."

"You have to do it, Tommy; you have to be insured. It's bad enough we've put it off this long. . ."

"What would be the point? I'd never even use it! It'd be like flushing money down the toilet. I'm not signing this shit— no fucking way."

"Tommy. . . When I was younger, I had this cousin who got very sick. He was fairly young at the time; not much older than you are, now. And the family couldn't afford his hospital bills. So they put a lien on my uncle's house. . . My uncle ended up losing his house, Tommy. Is that what you want? You want us to lose this home?"

Tom's face takes on an amused expression. He says nothing.

"It doesn't even have to be that dramatic," George continues. "You've never had your appendix out— what if it happens to flare up? Do you have any idea how many thousands of dollars it would be, just for two days in the hospital?"

Now Tom is looking less and less amused. He stops and ponders a moment.

"Fuck," he sighs, snatching the papers away from George. George points out where to sign and Tom does so, quickly. Then he gives the papers to George.

"You can hold on to these," George says, handing him some papers back.

"Whatever," Tom says as he takes them.

"If it's that important to you Tom, you can pay me back later— whenever you find a decent paying job. No pressure."

"Yeah, right. At $250 a month, I'll be $1,000 in the hole in just four months. But no pressure."

"That's not what it's about and you know it."

"Just don't get too smug, George. When it's all said and done, I'm still gonna outlast you."

George smiles back at him.

"Well, I would certainly hope so."

"No," Tom tells him. "I mean I'll outlast you *here*." He points down at the floor. "In this house. In this family."

George's expression hardens; a hardness I haven't seen in him before.

"You think so?"

"I've seen alot of guys come and go with Lisa, Georgie. *Alot*. You weren't the first and you won't be the last. I'll win in the end— just wait."

"Tommy, you've been saying that for a long time now. . . and I'm still here."

The two engage in a two second staredown before George ultimately turns and leaves. Tom violently throws the insurance papers at the door as it closes. Then he turns, snorting air up through his nostrils like a mad bull. I can almost hear him in his mind, counting backward from ten. He stops and looks at the picture of his father hanging over the head of his bed. This seems to calm him, at least momentarily.

"Father, father. . . where are you when I need you?" He appears to smile a bit. It's difficult to gauge just how hard all this is hitting him.

"I know things look bad, man, but they're not. Really. It could be alot worse."

Tom just laughs— the way people do when they've gone past crying, but not so far as to jump out the window.

"I just signed away my soul to the fucking devil, Will. It doesn't get any worse." He stares at the wall, expressionless. I look down at the floor.

"I guess I should go," I say at last, standing up. I wait, hoping he'll say something. "Are you gonna be okay?"

"Sure," he insists with mock conviction. "I'll be fine."

"Alright, then. I'll see ya." I turn and hurry out the door.

I go down the back stairs, into the yard, to my car. I jump in, start the engine and wait; giving the car a chance to warm up. I slump back in the drivers seat, relieved to just be out of that house.

Christ. That was intense.

I sit for several minutes, still thinking about that look Tom had on his face. I try my best to shake it off. I remind myself that this is Tom— there's no way this will keep him down long. He'll bounce back tomorrow like this is nothing. . . I know he will. I know it.

* * *

Tommy Redivo spends the next half-hour just pacing in a circle around bedroom. Tired, frustrated, he finally stops to stare at the last picture Sam made for him, taped to the back of his door. It has a large tree in the foreground, with the sun high up in the sky, looking no bigger than a nickel. The tree's bare, dead limbs stretch painfully

174

for it, desperately wanting to grasp it, but to no avail. It will always be too far away.

He flops down on his bed. He turns off his lamp, but will make no effort to go to sleep. He just lies there, in the dark, and thinks.

It's almost midnight when he notices the voices just outside his window. Peeking through his blinds, he can see Stacy on her front porch with her new boyfriend— looks like your typical jock-type, he thinks to himself. It's freezing out, but neither of them seem to notice. He can see Stacy laughing at something jockstrap's said. Then she stops laughing. He leans in to kiss her. The obligatory goodnight kiss, Tommy supposes. She's growing up, Stacy is; no longer that skinny little girl next door anymore, but a beautiful young woman. This fact greatly disturbs him— he doesn't know why.

They spend several minutes kissing before jockstrap finally turns to leave. Stacy stays on the porch and waves goodbye as he drives off. Tommy watches out his window for a long while after she's gone inside. Then he lies back down in his bed once again, but cannot rest. Too many things race through his brain all at once: Whitehill, Keith, George, the book store, the speeding ticket, his credit card bills. . .

Courtney.

He's supposed to meet her for dinner tomorrow night and dreads it. He begins to wonder if he should call it off. . . but he can't do that. It would be wrong.

He remains awake through the dawn. And with the new day comes another day of work at the hated mall, in the despised book store. The morning is thankfully slow, with only a few rude customers to deal with before his lunch break arrives. But in front of him on line at *Nathan's* is some old man, looking older than dirt, who's upset with the restaurant's pricing policy— he demands to speak with the manager of the place about a 10% senior citizen discount that he seems certain he's entitled to. The actual difference in total that he's contesting is seventy-two cents. Still, it takes a good fifteen minutes to resolve the issue. When Tommy gets back to the book store five minutes late, he gets reamed out by his boss, of course. But he can do nothing. All he can do is stand there while she screams in his face.

Later in the afternoon, he has the misfortune of running into Kenny Drew— this spoiled rich kid he went to junior high with. Kenny comes into the store wearing this nice suit and tie, looking for some book on investing and finance. The gleeful expression on his face when he spots Tommy behind the counter is a picture Tommy Redivo will not soon forget. The two of them share a very brief conversation, consisting of the usual, meaningless banter. Then, as he's leaving, he hands Tommy his business card: "CEO of Drew Inc., Office Interiors and Furnishings" it reads. He tells Tommy if he's not happy here, he could always use a new salesman. This coming from the guy who used to beg to cheat off him every day in eighth grade math. Behind smiling lips, Tommy gnashes his teeth and shakes his hand, pretending not to be insulted.

And finally the capper. Courtney's house for dinner.

"Is that cinnamon I smell?" he asks as he steps through the front door, which she's left unlocked for him.

"Yes," she answers with pride. "I made those cinnamon cookies I know you love. But you're not allowed to have any 'til after dinner— I don't want you spoiling your appetite."

"Okay." He takes a seat on the couch in the den, right off the kitchen.

"Anything happen at work today?"

"Nothing. . . special. So where's Kim?" he asks, referring to Courtney's mother.

"Heather hasn't been feeling well, so she's over there helping out with the baby. Looks like just you and me tonight." She stops before opening the refrigerator. "*All* night."

He's sits there, watching her, when he feels something tug at his heart. There's just something about the frantic way she keeps moving between the refrigerator and the stove that reminds him of a little girl, playing house. For whatever reason, it strikes him now, just how much he loves her. *Why do I have to do this?* he thinks. *Why tonight? With so many other things going wrong in my life, can't I cling to this just a little while longer?*

No, no, no. He's put this off long enough. It's because he does love her that he must do this— and do it tonight.

"Come here," he commands softly.

176

"What? You say something, hon?"

"Come here," he repeats louder. "We need to talk."

She slowly drifts in. She looks at him and smiles. She lets herself fall into his lap.

"Courtney. . ."

"I never did give you a proper greeting, did I?" she asks as she traces her finger around his jawline. He shouldn't let himself give in, but he can't help it— being close to her like this makes him weak. Her moist lips close around his own in the sweetest, slowest kiss. . .

"Damn," he gasps as he slides out from under her. He stands up, putting a safer distance between them.

"What's the matter, love?" she asks him with a grin. "That was just getting *good*. . ."

"I need to talk to you. This is serious." She straightens her posture, but remains seated.

"Okay. What do we need to talk about, exactly?" He's slow to begin; thinking very carefully about what he wants to say.

"Do you remember the last time we were alone together like this? About two weeks ago?"

They were completely alone in his house— a rare occasion indeed. He made slow, passionate love to her over the course of hours. . . shaking her whole universe to it's very foundations, as only he can.

"I remember."

"Do you remember what you said to me?"

"I don't know— I said alot of things."

"When we were holding each other. . . afterward. You said you wished it could always be like this."

She smiles. "Yes, I remember that."

"I've been thinking about that almost constantly the last two weeks."

"You have?" she asks. "Why?"

Why? Because her voice had that far-off, Candyland quality that Tommy Redivo is all-too familiar with. It told him that her feelings were changing, deepening, and with them, her expectations.

"Courtney, you're nineteen and I'm twenty-four. You've still got a couple more years to go in college and I'm. . . I don't know where the fuck I'm going. Or where I even want to go. I just feel guilty monopolizing you like this— you should be dating other college guys, having fun. . ."

"Tom, I can't imagine having more fun with anyone else. Nobody could make me happier than you."

"You said you always wanted to be with me."

"So? Would you have felt better if I said I *didn't* want to be with you?"

"Do you ever think about the future?"

". . .Sometimes, sure."

"And do you see us together?"

"Well, of course! I love you! You expect me to picture myself with someone else?"

He shakes his head.

"Court. . . I don't think we can see each other anymore."

She looks at him in disbelief.

"You're crazy," she says, smiling. When his face does not change, she begins to worry. "Tommy, stop it. You're scaring me."

"I can't lead you on, Court. I can't keep seeing you when I know you need more than I can give. I've probably let this go on too long, as it is. . ."

"You're telling me you're breaking up with me?"

"I'm sorry," he tells her. "But I can't ask you to waste your life waiting around for something that I can't guarantee will ever happen."

"My God, it's not like I'm pressuring you to marry me or anything, Tommy! I mean, I'm totally happy with things as they are! Can't we talk about this?"

"I wish there was something to talk about. I know. . . I've just been down this road too many times before." He remembers that long car ride with Nina back from the 'Mats last gig at Grant Park in July of '91. And the steps of the Cahill school library with Simone in the fall of 1990. And in Rachel's backyard back in '89. And so many other times he only wishes he could forget.

"I love you!" she persists. "Doesn't that count for something?"

"It counts for alot. Just not enough."

BACK TO THE GARDEN

Any other man on earth would tell him he's crazy. Maybe he is. Any other man would sell his soul for one night with this girl, whom he has loved for almost two years. Two years of absolute bliss.

"But. . . it's almost Valentine's Day," she pleads. It's sinking in now, as he looks into her face, that he is robbing her of that one thing that always loved most about her: her innocence. But he must do this. He knows from experience that it will only hurt much, much worse later.

"I'm sorry," he tells her yet again. Do those words ever feel like they're enough? "I think I better just go." He begins to walk away from her as she quickly gets up and follows him.

"Tommy, wait," she says, taking hold of his arm as he's opening her front door. "Wait. . ."

Their eyes lock as he turns to face her again. She grabs on to his jacket and pulls him close to her. They share one more kiss. It is passionate; perhaps the most passionate they've ever known. She truly believes that one good kiss is all it will take to bring him back to her; pull him back upstairs to make love to her.

But it isn't.

"I love you," she tells him yet again.

"I love you too." He closes his eyes tight as he turns away from her.

"I'll call you tomorrow? Tom?"

He walks out across her front lawn, to his car.

CHAPTER X

Tommy Redivo walks along a shaded path in Memorial Park in Riverview, where he has come to think. Riverview was his home back when Lisa was married to Joe, her first husband, between 1972 and 1976. The first time a girl ever broke his heart, he returned to this place to be alone, to think. To remember simpler days and indulge in fantasy.

Some of his earliest memories, perhaps his first memories, are of this park. Originally, it was a cemetery that was closed in 1915. The place became a park in 1958, when the headstones were taken up. He knows all this because it is inscribed on a large pillar in the center of the park, along with the names of those interred here. The fact that the dead lie in the ground below him, awaiting the last day, has never bothered him. If anything, at times like this he finds the ghosts better company than the living.

It's always so quiet here; even in the warmer seasons, there's hardly ever anyone here. Especially not in the middle of the day. Often times before, when he has come here, he would fantasize that he was the sole survivor of some great disaster; the only living being left on the face of the earth. Then, he wouldn't have to worry about what anyone else was thinking or saying. He wouldn't have to concern himself with pleasing anyone else. He could take his clothes off when he danced through the barren streets and not have to fret over any prying eyes. There would be no one left for him to hurt. No one left to hurt him. He would be free.

He thinks of that girl again, that first one, as he so often does. Sheila. His first, perhaps his only, true love. When he lost her, he remembers, his whole world ended. It was as if he died and had to re-create himself, phoenix-like, from scratch. Now, the long trail of failed relationships since then have numbed him to the point of feeling almost nothing. Already, he knows how the course of events will run from here: he'll be depressed over Courtney for a month, perhaps two, but inevitably— much as he may not want to— he'll slowly begin to feel better. Then some other girl will catch his eye. And even in that moment he first sees her, he'll begin wondering again how long it will be before he's back here, regretting how he hurt her.

He loved Courtney— he still does, he believes that. But. . . how much can he really love her if he can still walk away from her like this? So many beautiful, wonderful women that he's walked away from. . . In fact, he's broken it off with every woman he's ever been with except for Sheila— she left him, the only one who did. He begins to question if he ever really got over that.

Maybe he hasn't.

Perhaps it is not numbness. Perhaps he simply did not love Courtney at all. Perhaps he has not truly loved any of the others since Sheila. Could it be he's been carrying a torch for her all this time? Is that what's kept him from loving anyone else like he loved her? Or is he losing the power to love, to feel with true passion, as he gets older?

That line from *The Breakfast Club* leaps to his mind, the line about how as you grow older, your heart slowly dies. And that's exactly what it's like. When he was sixteen, he didn't know anything about being in love or relationships. He didn't know enough to be cynical. So he let himself go, completely. And he thought of nothing and no one but that first love, all day and all night. Sheila. He lived for a mere glance from her, a moment of eye contact, an incidental brush of her hand across his arm. He worries that he may never feel that kind of passion again; that passion he felt the first time. The kind of passion that reminds you every day that you're alive.

He walks past the rusty old swing set and remembers all those times he'd sit here as a child, waiting for his mother, Lisa, to give him that gentle push in the back to get him started. He remembers how she'd cheer him on as he swung higher and higher, the chains creaking as he did so. . . He remembers the slide and sight of Lisa's beaming face, always waiting for him at the bottom of it. He remembers how every day, after leaving the park, she'd always stop at Sam's Deli and buy him a *Yoo-hoo* and a little bag of *Andy Capp's Fries*. And, if he had been really good, she'd stop by the magazine stand and buy him some comics— usually a *Spider-Man*, but sometimes a *Superman* or a *Batman*; occasionally a *Casper*, a *Hot Stuff*, a *Little Archie*. He's not sure they even publish *Casper* comics anymore.

The memories are sweet because it was the only time in his life when he was allowed to be a child. Lisa was his Mommy and Joe was his Daddy. The last and only time in his life he had a Mommy and Daddy. Because then, one day, Joe was suddenly gone and he wasn't Daddy anymore and, more so, he never was— even though he was still Meredith's Daddy. Immediately after began the long parade of "uncles," and step-fathers and "special friends," who always required so much of Mommy's attention. Suddenly, she needed him to be "Mommy's strong little guy." For her and for his sisters, she'd tell him. Like it or not, he was the man of the house. . . not only his sisters' guardian and protector, but Lisa's as well. He's spent his whole life since fighting it, just desperately trying to hold on to being a kid, to being young, to being free.

"What are you looking for?" George likes to ask him. "What do you hope to accomplish? What are you going to do with your life?" He'd like to write novels and short stories, of course, but he knows what a fruitless dream this is— nobody sells fiction for a living in this day and age. Aside from that, teaching English lit and/or philosophy at the college level could still prove quite rewarding. . . but he'd have to find some way through grad school to accomplish that.

But forget all that. He could *still* be happy, if only he could catch on with a publisher— be it books, magazines, whatever. He could start at the bottom, work his way up, become a copy editor after a year or two, then get promoted to more creative position in another couple years; end up with earning a modest living with at least *some* artistic rewards. . . There are a thousand damned publishing companies in the city— you'd think he could find an entry level position with *one* of them. But he can't. He won't. He's been trying long enough to know he won't.

What are you going to do with your life? Who the fuck does this asshole think he is, asking such a question, Tommy wonders? Does he think that because he managed to buy Lisa, that he's bought him too? Is that it— does he think him and his mother are some kind of package deal? His whole life, he's watched all these pretenders, these outsiders, these invaders, buy and bully their way into *his* family. He has always dreamed of a day when he'll no longer have to stomach such interlopers, but he begins to doubt he'll ever see it. The clock has run out.

Yes, time— it holds him tight in it's fist now, barely allowing him to breathe. He can see himself waking up one day, ten years from now, still working at that damn bookstore, still trapped there. And the picture of it in his mind paralyzes him with terror. He'll be one of those weird old geezers who wear the same pair of pants seventeen days in a row, working at a job usually reserved for part time high schoolers who are just looking to make a few extra bucks to help pay off their car insurance premiums. The ironic thing is that he won't even be able to afford a car, himself. He'll be taking the bus to work every day and collecting food stamps just to feed himself.

You keep telling yourself, "I'm not a garbage man, I'm not a mail man, I'm not a book store-flunky"; but next thing you know, you're pushing forty and it's still your job. You're a garbage man whether you want to accept it or not. Sitting behind the register on those slow days, he can't stop asking, "what turn of events, what strange twist of fate, could have led me here, could have brought me to this?" Sometimes when he's sitting there, it feels like all he's doing is sitting around waiting to die.

And this should be the most exciting of times; the beginning of life's fantastic journey. He's twenty-four, still more than six months away from his twenty-fifth birthday, and all he sees ahead of him is a bricked-off dead end. He can't even support *himself*— the idea of supporting a family someday is an outrageous fantasy.

It must be the most terrible thing in the world, he thinks, to know that you are what you once most dreaded becoming— a faceless cog in a big machine, making no real difference in the world around you. He curses the whole damn universe for constantly moving forward, for not once stopping for even a second to consider whether or not he should care for its pace. He desperately dreams of being a child again. He envies the children he sees today for having what he wants, what he can never have again. Tomorrow is a lifetime away for them. They don't have to think about living, they just live. Why can't he? Why won't the world let him?

The wind kicks up suddenly. Another heavy snow is coming. He retraces his steps past the slide, past the swings, past the pillar at the park's center, back to Vale Street, to his car. He drives in circles around Riverview for over twenty minutes. He drives past his former home. He drives past where Sam's Deli once was, where a Laundromat stands today.

He drives through Northdale, stopping at the elementary school he once attended there— the same one his father attended as a little boy. He gets out and takes a little walk around the old kickball field in the back. Then he gets back in his car and drives around some more, stopping by the church where he made his communion. And, like always when he's in town, he stops at his father's grave. As he begins to clean the headstone, he realizes there's probably not much point if there's going to be snowfall later. But he finishes cleaning it off anyway.

He gets back behind the wheel of his car, driving until he finds himself in Maple Grove. He stops by to see the old house, where he lived when Lisa and Mike were married. This is not the first time he's been back to look at the place, but it has been awhile. He remembers the little clubhouse Mike had built for him and Meredith. He sneaks into the backyard for a quick peek— and yes Tommy, it's still gone.

He drives down Madison, past the community pool— closed, obviously, for the winter. He turns onto Chrurch Avenue, goes a couple of blocks, then down Tomey Street, past the house where Pete Dunn's family once lived. Pete was a good friend from his Maple Grove days. The house looks totally different since the remodeling that took place after the fire. At times like this, he wishes there were some button he could press that could turn off his imagination— try as he might, he can't push the image of Pete's burning body out of his mind. He still resents Lisa for not taking him to the funeral.

Now, Tommy finds himself in Belltown, where he used to come and visit Johnny Baptistella, his cousin. Or second cousin. Or whatever he is.

Was.

He still can't listen to that Replacements' song, "Johnny's Gonna Die" without welling up. Poor Johnny. He never even lived to hear *Let It Be*. That whole summer of '84 he would've absolutely loved; with the 'Mats, the Minutemen's *Double Nickels on the Dime*, Husker Du's *Zen Arcade*, and the Meat Puppets' second album, too— all released that same season. Not to mention Bruce's *Born in the U.S.A.*, U2's *Unforgettable Fire*, R.E.M.'s *Reckoning*. . . He drives by that spot on the shore of the Passaic River where Johnny once threw him in. He recalls how Johnny and his buddies in the band laughed at him, and how that made him feel like crying. But instead, he pretended to laugh too.

Now he can let himself cry just a little.

Sheer inertia rolls him, inevitably, toward Carver. He walks up to the front door of his old high school, where the security guard asks him what he's doing out of class. Tommy Redivo just smiles at him. He walks around back, across the field where his old soccer class was held— the one where he first met Sheila. He stops to think about her again, for just a moment, before moving on. The wind kicks up again and the cold air stings his face. But right now it feels good to him— reminds him he's alive.

He crosses the street and enters the SubStop. There alot of students there, on their lunch break, and he finds their presence oddly troubling. Walking up to the counter, he discovers Penelope there, ready to take his order. She smiles at him as their eyes meet.

"Hi, Tommy!" she greets excitedly. He remembers the first time he saw her, the beautiful girl she was. Now, all he can see when she smiles at him are the lines in her face

"Hey, Pen. One turkey, please?"

"Be right up!" she responds, her smile growing even wider.

Jesus, he wonders, what is she so fucking happy about? She has to be thirty years old, almost, and look where she is. She started working the register here when he was a sophomore in high school— that was over nine years ago. Doesn't she want more than this?

He begins to grow angry. Enraged. He comes to a realization, finally. He exits the store quickly, knowing at long last what he must do.

CHAPTER XI

Friday, and I'm stretched out on the couch in my living room at the end of a long day and an even longer week. I wish I could relax but I can't, because try as I might, I just can't stop wondering what the hell is up with Tom.

Over a month ago, he broke up with Courtney. It came totally out of the blue, with absolutely no warning. The same night it happened, Courtney called Kate, crying hysterically, and immediately after, Kate called me. I haven't been able to really talk in-depth with Tom about it since; I've chatted with him on the phone a couple of times but haven't seen him at all. I had one small window of opportunity between blizzards to run up to the mall to try and see him, only to discover that he had recently quit his job at the book store.

My first thought when I heard about the break-up was that the guy must've just totally snapped, because it happened only one night after the big meltdown where he got rejected by Whitehill, signed George's insurance papers and all the rest of that shit. I figure that can't be coincidence, right? Kate tells me she's not so sure, though. And she's seen him go through relationships and break-ups with other girls, before I knew him, so she has a better perspective on this than I do, probably. But no one knows anything for certain, because no one's been able to get a hold of him.

I lie on the couch, eating my bowl of Honey Combs and trying to unwind, going back over all of this in my mind, when the phone rings. I get up to answer it— it's Kate.

"Hi hon, whassup?"

"Put on channel nine," she screams in my ear, "put on channel nine!"

"Why?"

"Just put it on!" Click.

I turn on channel nine and sit through a couple lame commercials before *Ricki Lake* comes on. "Mom, Dad. . . The Sixties are over! When are you going to grow up?" flashes across the screen as the audience applauds. Sitting up on stage are two teenage boys; this forty-something woman in tie-dye, headband and love beads; a college-aged girl and. . .

It's Tom.

Tommy Redivo is on *The Ricki Lake Show*.

"If you're just joining us," Ricki begins, "we're talking to people who have come here today to tell their parents that they think it's time they grew up and stopped acting like children. Joining us now is Frances— hi, Frances."

"Hi, Ricki," the girl sitting next to Tom responds. As they cut to her close-up, a graphic come up across the bottom of the screen: "Frances, 20, Florida. Wants to tell her father it's time he grew up."

"You've been having some problems with your father, true?"

"Well, yes," Frances answers, sounding slightly embarrassed.

"Why don't you tell us about it?"

"God," she sighs, "where to start? He's just always been. . . *wild,* Ricki. He loves to play his music real loud, loves to run around naked, loves to smoke grass. . ."

"*Ooooo,*" the audience moans.

"Didn't he get married recently?"

"Yes."

"Do you wanna tell us who he got married to?"

188

"He married my best friend." Again, the crowd collectively moans it's shock and titillation. "Former best friend, now."

"How old is your father?"

"He's forty-eight."

"And your former best friend?"

"She just turned twenty— same age as me."

"Fer Chrissake," I hear Tom mutter. The audience starts to laugh.

Is this real, what I'm seeing on my television screen? Or has April Fools arrived one week early this year?

"And you've got a big problem with this, huh?" Ricki continues.

"Yeah. . . I mean, even before he started going out with Allie, he was always dating young girls. I think he needs to grow up and date women his own age."

"Sounds like you're ready to talk to him!"

"Oh, yeah," Frances responds.

"Yeah, Ricki," Tom jumps in. "Wheel the old letch out here." Again, the crowd breaks up. Frances smiles at him.

"Whaddaya say gang?" Ricki asks. "You ready to meet Dad?"

"YEAH!" the audience yells.

"Come on out, Dad!" she commands.

The old letch comes out dressed up like Wavy Gravy, with the young wife in tow. The audience boos. "Bruce, 48 year old electrician, Florida. Married daughter's best friend," flashes on the screen as he sits down.

"Go ahead, Fran," Ricki starts. "Tell your Dad what you came here to tell him."

"Dad," Frances says as she turns in her chair to face her father, "I just think you need to grow up and try building a relationship with someone your own age." The audience claps.

"Dad," Ricki says, "how do you respond to your daughter?"

"I don't know," Dad answers. "We've been over this many times already, Ricki. I'm an adult, I'm her father, and I will do what I want."

"Frances is the one who needs to grow up," the young wife pipes up. "Allison, 20. Married best friend's father," comes up on the screen. "We're in love and she should just accept it like a grown-up."

189

"Look, I live with my Mom anyway," Frances says, "so it's not like it's in my face everyday, but still, I think it's disgusting."

"Of course it's disgusting!" Tom declares. The audience applauds and laughs still more.

"Okay guys, time out," Ricki pleads.

. . .And I can't sit still a moment longer.

I run back to the phone and call Tom's house but the line is busy. I try and get Kate but she comes up busy, too. I try and find Shaggy's number, then I realize I don't have Shaggy's number. I'll call Keith— I know I have his number here, somewhere. I find it on the inside cover of the spiral notebook I use for American Lit. I dial him up and he's busy, as well. Probably talking to Kate, come to think of it.

Fuck. I'm going over there.

Just over fifteen minutes later, I'm at Kate's house, letting myself in the unlocked back door. Inside, I find Kate standing in the living room, still with the phone in her ear.

". . .I got off work at 4:30 and got home just as the show was starting and when I saw Tom come out, I swear I almost fainted!" She motions hello to me. Her younger brother David is on the couch, watching the show.

"Hi Dave."

"Hmm," he grunts back in greeting, still staring at the tube. It's weird whenever he's around. Every time he looks at me, it's like *I* know that *he* knows I'm fucking his sister. . . And what am I supposed to say to him? "Thanks dude, for letting me pork your sister"?

"Alright Tam, I'll get back to you later." Kate clicks off the receiver. "Did he tell you about this?"

"Who? Tom?" I ask. "Fuck, no! I haven't even spoken to him in a couple weeks!"

"Everyone I've called is totally shocked."

"Well, I sure as hell am! Who have you talked to?"

"Keith, Greg, Tam, Barb. . ."

"Shag?"

"No, Shag wasn't home."

"I'll betcha he knew about this."

"I don't think so. Barb said he hadn't mentioned anything to her about it. You try Tom's?"

"Yeah, it was busy."

"Figures. I couldn't get through, either."

"You didn't call Courtney, did you?"

"Oh *God*, no! Are you crazy?"

"No, I mean, I didn't call, either. . . But you're closer to her than I am, so I was wondering if you might have. . ."

"No, I couldn't. I just wouldn't feel comfortable. Besides, I high-ly doubt she knew about this, anyway."

"So do you have any clue what's goin' on?"

"No. Actually, I was hoping you could tell me."

"I mean, why is he doing this? Why now?"

"I don't know. I don't know."

"In every family," Ricki begins her wrap-up as the show is drawing to its close, "there are times when a child finds he or she is embarrassed by the actions of one or both of their parents. . . What's important is that the child feels comfortable enough to discuss these feelings with their parents and that both sides always respect each other. . ."

"Remember, kids: KILL YOUR PARENTS!" Tom yells from off-camera. The audience splits its collective gut one last time.

"Thanks to all my guests," Ricki goes on with a smile, "especially Tom, the Woodstock baby, and thanks to all of you for watching. . . see you next time."

The show is over. I swear I hear Tom say "let's bust up the set," or something to that effect, as the audience begins its traditional "go Ricki" chant.

David gets up off the couch.

"Well that sure was fucked," he observes as he exits the room. Kate and I both sit down on the vacated couch. After the credits are done, Kate picks up the remote for the VCR off the coffee table and clicks on "stop."

"I wish I got the whole thing," she says as she hits rewind.

"But you saw it, right?"

"Yeah, I saw it all."

"It's a good thing you watch the show."

"I don't— David watches it."

"Yeah, right."

"I don't! Seriously, I never watch it."

"Whatever," I say with a grin.

The tape plays. First, there's that static-distortion you get when you're taping something new over an old tape. Then, when Ricki comes on, the audience is already howling and barking over something. Tom is trying to yell over them, so I assume they're worked up over something he's said. The two young guys and old hippie-lady are up in front of the audience along with Tom.

"What's going on?" I ask.

"Miss flower-child there is the mother of the two teenagers— they want her to start acting her age."

"I'm gonna be honest with you 'cause it's obvious all your friends are afraid of hurting your feelings," Tom tells the aged acid-queen. "You look like a Goddamn circus clown in that get up!"

"Jesus!" I exclaim with a laugh. Then we get to the part where I came in.

"What do you think I should've done?" letch-Dad protests. "Pretended my feelings didn't exist?"

"Hell, yeah!" Tom shouts as the crowd roars its agreement. "Try being a father and put your daughter's feelings first for a change! Keep it in your damn pants!"

Then there's a brother and a sister with deadhead parents— this part must've been on while I was on my way over here.

"You have no idea how embarrassing it is," the sister says. "Every time the Grateful Dead come to town, they *have* to get dressed up in the same stupid, old hippie-clothes and go running off to the show— all of their shows, every single one!"

"Hey grandpa— it's 1994, not 1964!" Tom tells the follicly-challenged, hippie Dad. "Don't you even care whether or not this is humiliating for your kids? You had your childhood already, now let them have theirs!"

"Go, mud brother, go!" I gleefully shout, getting caught up in it. Kate goes back into the kitchen and picks up the phone.

"Who you calling now?"

"I'm trying Meredith's line." She dials quickly but then clicks off in sudden disgust.

"What?"

"That's busy, too."

"I'm sure they've got the phone off the hook, hon. They're probably being assaulted with a million calls."

"Well I'm going stir crazy here!"

"Would it be that nuts to just go over his house?" I ask. She smiles.

"You just read my mind."

Kate jots off a quick note for her Mom and we're gone. I'm so juiced up over all of this, I run three lights on the way over to Tom's. I don't know why, but I'm surprised to find Tom at the house when we arrive. Lisa, his sisters, and Shag are here, too.

"Hey guys!" Tom greets us as we walk in the door. Frankie quickly hands us both a bottle of Yoo-hoo.

"You're just in time!" Meredith says. "We were just gonna raise a toast to my brother in honor of his most recent television appearance!"

"Are your phones off the hook?" Kate asks her. "Because we did try to call before coming over. . ."

"You know about this, Shag?" I ask.

"No, man— I just happened to catch it on the tube. I'm as floored as you!"

"Deev, how?" Kate asks. "Why?"

"I finally made up my mind, Kay. I've decided to come out of the closet."

"How'd you end up on *Ricki?*" I wonder.

"Well, the first place he tried was *Rebel,*" Meredith reveals, "but he couldn't get anyone over there to take him seriously. . ."

"After that," Tom picks up, "I tried a bunch of different places, and Ricki's producer jumped immediately— said they had the perfect show for me. We only taped it this past Monday; it was so hot, they rushed to air it today."

"And you kept mum all week? I don't believe you!"

"So what now?" Shag wants to know.

"Well, nothing big. I've got a couple interviews lined up with local papers this weekend— one with the *Oakwood Observer*, another with the *Carver Record*. The guy from Carver told me the AP might pick it up, though. From there, hopefully I'll be moving on to bigger and better things."

"I don't understand, Tom," I say. "Why? Why now?"

"It finally sank in that I had a unique opportunity here, Will. And if I squandered it, I'd be doing myself a great disservice. If I didn't take advantage of this now, while I've still got the chance, I'd regret it later."

"Well, congratulations!" Kate says.

"To my brother," Meredith toasts. "The nation's newest, brightest star!" Everyone raises their *Yoo-hoos* in the air. . . as do I. Reluctantly.

He hasn't explained anything, really. Why now? Why is now better than last year? Two years ago? Five years ago? Don't get me wrong; it was exciting as hell seeing Tom on t.v. today, and under different circumstances I'd be totally thrilled for him, but this. . . I just keep thinking about the last time I was with him here, under this roof, and how dire things seemed for him. Is this supposed to be the cure-all for all his problems, now? Is going public supposed to make it all better? That would be so. . . fake. So un-Tom-like.

I don't know. I've suddenly got a bad feeling about all this.

194

CHAPTER XII

The cruelest month.

It's April and Kurt Cobain is dead. It was just a week ago— the eighth to be exact— when his body was found in the apartment above the garage of his Seattle home, where he shot himself with a twenty-gauge shotgun.

Everything is happening so fast.

Today, Tom will be interviewed by *Rebel* magazine— Paul Hegel, the publisher and editor-in-chief, has insisted on conducting the interview, personally. Earlier this morning, the house was in an uproar in anticipation of his arrival. . . and suffice it to say, George was not pleased. Then Tom and Lisa, presenting a rare united front, told everybody else to clear out except for me and Kathy. Hegel arrived shortly afterward, along with a photographer, and he certainly lived up to his billing. He wore these beat-up blue jeans along with a jean jacket and old sneakers. What hair he had left on his graying, half-bare pate he kept tied back in a ponytail.

The word has always been that Hegel's a bit of an eccentric. He started *Rebel* as sort of a zine, before there was such a thing— basically, he took all the correspondence he was keeping with old college chums and buddies he met at Woodstock, Xeroxed multiple copies of it and re-distributed it to the whole clique. And in this correspondence, there was alot of political debate, talk of movies they had recently seen, albums heard, books read. . . get the picture? Before long, Hegel got the bright idea that he could sell all this writing as a magazine and voila: *Rebel* was born. Today of course, it's one of the top-selling pop culture mags in the country, which makes Hegel a very wealthy man, but he still insists on running around dressed like the hippie-hobo, like he never left Max Yasgur's farm a quarter-century ago.

Anyway, at this very moment, he's in the kitchen having a separate interview with Lisa (and Kathy) before talking to Tom. We can overhear just about everything they say as it echoes down the hall, into the living room. It's mainly Lisa doing the talking, but Kathy chimes in here and there with her own recollections as well. I find it funny how Lisa tells it the exact same way she once told it to me, almost word-for-word, like she's working from the same prepared script: she was in the maternity home, about a month before Tom was due, when she suddenly got cold feet about the adoption. She called Kathy, who came and picked her up. They went to the concert because Kathy had originally planned to go and they couldn't think of anything else to do or anyplace better to go. They arrived in the middle of the week and stayed at a motel for a couple of days, so they didn't experience the traffic that most everyone else did. She talks about how there were no bathrooms. About how shocked she was over the exorbitant prices— the $1 hot dogs and $1 beers. She and Kathy and Hegel all commiserate about how transcendent the whole event was, how that one weekend symbolized the solidarity of their sacred love generation. . . yada yada yada.

"You're being awfully quiet over there," I observe. Tom's been sitting on the couch, holding his can of Yoo-hoo, not breathing a word the whole time Hegel's been in that kitchen.

"I'm nervous about this," he admits.

"Nervous? You? What's to be nervous about?"

"I don't want this guy turning the interview into another one of those 'twentynothings,' what's-the-matter-with-kids-today cover stories."

"Aw, c'mon. . . you're getting a little paranoid, now."

"Just because you're paranoid doesn't mean they're not out to getcha, Will. That's why I asked you to stick around— you're my witness. You're the one who's going to be able to tell people exactly what goes on, what's said and how it's said, so there's no misinterpretation, misrepresentation or taking anything out of context."

"You over-analyze things too much. Why can't you just sit back and enjoy the ride?"

"Just my way, I guess. . ."

"This should be an exciting moment for you! Don'tcha wanna be a star?" I rib.

"There are different kinds of fame," Tom tells me, taking a swig of his Yoo-hoo. "There's the Jonas Salk, Albert Einstein, John F. Kennedy kinda fame; and then there's the McLean Stevenson and Mindy Cohn kind."

McLean Stevenson?! I bust a gut, laughing. God, I love the way he just pulls these totally obscure references out his ass like that. . . *Mindy Cohn!*

"You're too much." We get quiet again, briefly, until our silence is interrupted by the sound of footsteps in the hallway.

"Are you ready?" Hegel asks as he enters the room. Tom glances over at me as we both rise to our feet.

"Yeah," he says, "we may as well get this over with."

"Where would you like to do this?"

"Oh, it doesn't matter. Wherever you like."

"No, no— I want you to feel as relaxed and as comfortable as possible for this. Tell me where you'd like to do it."

"In that case, we may as well adjourn to my office, upstairs."

"That'll be fine, I'm sure," Hegel says. Tom leads him into the hallway. I dally slowly behind them both.

"Age before beauty," Tom jests as we come to the front hall. He steps aside to allow Hegel up the stairs. I hesitate momentarily. "Please do join us," Tom requests, motioning for me to follow him.

"Nice decor," Hegel compliments as we enter Tom's painstakingly-cleaned room. ". . .Who is this?"

"This is Soren Zeitgeist," Tom answers. "He's producing a documentary about me for Danish television."

"Hi," I say, demurely.

"Don't he speak good English? Hey pal, I always wanted to know— what do they call a cheese Danish in Denmark, anyway?" There are two folding chairs; but Tom hops on the bed, leaving one of the chairs for me. I drag my chair off to the side, tryin' to keep out of the way, while Hegel fiddles with this antique-lookin' tape recorder of his— looks like something lifted from the Thomas Edison museum.

"So how did it go with Lisa?" Tom asks.

"Very well, very well."

"Just for the record: she is *not* a real hippie, y'know. She shaves her armpit hair an' everything."

I chuckle.

"I was most impressed with your mother— she's a very strong woman. It's just a shame it's taken twenty-five years to finally meet the two of you."

"*Rebel* was the first place I went, actually, but no one was taking me seriously, so. . ."

"Yes, I'm sorry about that. It's just that we had so many fakes who tried to pass themselves off back in '89, during our first big search. . . You'll notice we hadn't been pushing to find you this anniversary year because we had basically given up all hope of locating you."

"I still haven't shown you any concrete proof, y'know. . . that I was born at Woodstock, I mean   Do you trust the fact-checkers on *Ricki Lake* so implicitly?"

"Hardly," he assures with a laugh. "We looked up the doctor who helped deliver you and he backed up your story."

"You talked to Jim?"

"I called Dr. Osterberg personally, yes. And I think it's safe to say your birth had a fairly profound effect on him— he told me that it was what inspired him to choose obstetrics as his field."

"He's a good guy. Still sends a Christmas card every year."

"Alright," Hegel says. "Are you ready to formally begin?"

"Sure," Tom answers. "Do I get a blindfold and cigarette, first?"

My heart pounds. It feels like I'm watching the living pages of a history book as they're turning. I know I may have had my doubts about it before, but at this moment, it's hard to blame Tom for grabbing at this brass ring. How many people ever get an opportunity like this? And even if Tom's right— even if this whole Woodstock thing *is* stupid— fame is still fame. However fleeting this may ultimately prove, it's damn exciting while it's going on.

"First thing's first," Hegel starts. "Why come out now?"

"I don't know," Tom shrugs. "I guess I just wasn't ready before. . . I don't know that there's any simple answer."

"What's it been like so far? How are you adjusting to it?"

"There really hasn't been any need for adjustment— there haven't been any dramatic changes in my life. At least not yet."

"So you *do* anticipate dramatic changes?"

"I'm trying not to presume too much. I guess we'll see where all this leads soon enough."

"It doesn't sound like you're terribly comfortable with your newfound fame."

"He wants to be known as the Woodstock baby like Eve Plumb wants to be known as Jan Brady," I interrupt. (See? I can be pretty quick with the cryptic pop culture references, meself.)

"Exactly," Tom says with a laugh. "I mean, I'm the guy who was born at Woodstock— what is that?"

"You attach no meaning to the Woodstock event, then?" Hegel questions, totally ignoring my gibe. "Not even symbolically?"

"To me, it was just a concert that alot of people showed up to see," Tom tells him, tossing his empty Yoo-hoo can into the wastebasket as if to accentuate his point. "Wasn't even that great of a concert, really. I mean, Jimi, Janis and the Who were good, but it could've been even better. The Stones could've been there at least— I won't even push my luck with the Velvet Underground, the Fugs, Zappa and the Mothers. . ."

"You see no unusual significance there, in the timing of your birth? None at all?"

199

"Strictly synchronicity, in my mind. The fact that I was born at Woodstock was a total accident— I mean, as far as I'm concerned, I'm the one who should be interviewing *you*. Believe me, I'm dying to hear about the whole New York underground scene of the 70s. . . Like how much do Tom Verlaine and Richard Hell really hate each other? Did you ever nail Patti Smith? Joey Ramone ever puke on your shoe, backstage at CBGBs?"

"Sounds like you're a real music aficionado. How would you categorize your musical tastes?"

"Well, I was raised on classic rock— I'd listen to what my older cousins listened to, y'know? That usually meant the standard diet of Beatles, Stones, Who, Zeppelin. . . plus your Black Sabbath, your Alice Cooper, your Elton John. Oh, and alot of Neil Young and Springsteen, too. Then, in the car with Mom, it was strictly disco era-pop. . ."

"When were you first exposed to the punk music you express such fondness for now?"

"That started when this other cousin of mine, on my mother's side, got into punk around '79. . . from there, as I entered junior high and high school, I got more and more into 80s punk and indie rock."

"What do you think of the crossover that's taken place the last few years between mainstream and indie?"

"The crossover doesn't mean much to me, personally— it's not as if I have a stake in any of these bands' mainstream success. Nor do I begrudge them that success, either."

"What do you think of Nirvana and Pearl Jam and such?"

"You mean critically speaking? I like them alot. A great deal, actually. I know there's alot of criticism from the punk side that none of these bands qualify as real 'punk' now, but I don't care about that shit. Just because I like punk doesn't mean I still can't enjoy classic rock, or disco or jazz or whatever— a band can be classic rock-influenced and still be punk, to me. Or maybe with Pearl Jam, you'd say they're more a classic rock band that's punk-influenced. . . whatever the case, I don't find it necessary for things to just neatly fit into one category."

"You wouldn't call yourself an orthodox punk then, I suppose."

"Whatever," Tom sighs. "I guess not. . . That fake elitism of the scene pisses me off that way, y'know? See, to me, 'The Replace-ments Stink!' is the best hardcore album ever— but that opinion would probably get me laughed outta most clubs."

"Why do you suppose that is?"

"Because hardcore's devolved into such standard, formulaic music. Once upon a time, you could have ironic lyrics, a hint of melody, even— God forbid— musicianship!"

"Hey, let's not get crazy, here," Hegel jokes. Tom grins. My, but this is going well, no?

"Yeah, right? But you get my point— like the Clash and the Voidoids, they probably wouldn't even be called 'punk' if they were just coming out today. . . Musically speaking, everything has to con-form to the hardcore formula, which means loud, fast and angry. That's there where all the emphasis falls, to the exclusion of crafts-manship or any different kind of message or. . . inspiration."

"So would you say the current punk influence on the mainstream signifies the anger and frustration of the new, young music buyer? Is your generation angry and resentful, generally?"

Tom's mouth drops open. He looks at me like "I-told-you-so," and I motion for him to just ignore it.

. . .Hey, it's one question, let's not jump to any conclusions.

"No," Tom answers. "I don't know that that's the case; I wouldn't presume to say."

"Since we mentioned Nirvana," Hegel continues, "how did you feel when you heard about Kurt Cobain's suicide?"

Tom stops a moment, fixing his gaze on a poster of Kurt hanging on the wall. It's a new one. . . Wonder when he had a chance to put it up?

"I dunno," he responds warily. "I know I hate it when I see people getting upset on t.v., carrying on like he owed it to the world to go on living just to entertain us. . . One thing I will say is that my heart really goes out to his daughter."

"You lost your own father, correct?"

"Yes. He had a big family, my father, and lots of friends, and they all have a million stories to share about him, but. . . There were just certain things I needed to hear from his mouth and I could. It was hard. Still is, in many ways."

"Would you mind discussing your family?" Hegel requests.

"Um. . . I guess not."

"I was just going to say, it qualifies as a sort-of post-modern, alternative family. What was it like being raised in such a family?"

"There's a broad question," Tom observes. "I've often wondered what it would've been like to be raised in a conventional family, with one mother and one father. . . the grass is always greener, right? But I can't complain, I love my family very much, as is."

"Half of the people your age have divorced parents."

"That's low-balling it, from my own experience— but yes, I think we're all familiar with the statistics."

"What is it that makes it the most difficult aspect of dealing with divorcing parents? From your experience?"

Tom takes a deep breath.

"The thing is this: when two people get divorced, it's as if they're saying that their marriage was a mistake. And if their marriage was a mistake, than their kids must be mistakes too, right? 'Cause kids are a product of their parents marriage, relationship, whatever. And how much self esteem can someone build when they know they're a mistake?"

"Does this become too much of a crutch for Generation X, though?"

Now *my* mouth drops open. I look at Tom and can tell this last question's annoyed him, too.

"No one I know of uses it as a crutch. But I do think most parents fail to recognize how painful and difficult it is for their children when they put them through it."

"But isn't it ultimately better to divorce than to live under the same roof and be at each other's throats?"

"Well obviously it's better for the parents. Then again, I guess I can't expect you baby boomers to understand since your own parents almost never divorced. That's a big part of why you're all so egotistical and narcissistic— you didn't have to wrestle with the self-doubt that comes with having divorced parents."

202

Ah! Nice zinger there, mud brother.

"Do you think baby boomers have made poor parents, then?"

"Well, as long as we're indulging in broad generalizations— then yeah, sure." Tom smiles. Hegel smiles as well.

"What would be your main complaint?"

"Mainly, I think if you want to be a good parent, you have to give up being a kid yourself, first. That's the main problem: there are no grown-ups, no adults anymore. The adult is extinct— assuming they ever existed at all."

"Would you say you're an advocate of old school morality, then?"

"What does 'old school morality' imply?"

"You know: marriage, family, God," Hegel explains. "According to alot of surveys, many twenty-somethings are becoming more involved in organized religion. . ."

"That doesn't surprise me. People always get religious when all the rational options have been exhausted. But this isn't something peculiar to just the young people of today— or any day. I think it's a pattern of human behavior that's repeated itself again and again throughout history."

"Of course, there are trends that run to the opposite extreme as well— trends toward a lack in morality, in ethics. For example, other studies have shown that today's college students are prone to cheating on tests and term papers. . ."

"I don't put very much stock in that. I don't find that conclusion either fair or accurate."

"Tell us, then: how would you describe your generation's values?"

Tom glances my way and shakes his head.

. . .Oh well. At least it was a pleasant discussion for awhile, right?

"I knew you were gonna do this," Tom declares.

"Do what?"

"Turn this into one of those 'Generation X' articles."

"What do you mean by that?" Hegel asks with a virtuous face.

"C'mon Paul— you know what I'm talking about. You're trying to turn a one-on-one interview into a study of an entire generation."

"I would have thought that by going public as you are, you would be prepared to assume a leadership role among other young people."

"I'm me," Tom informs him. "I'm Tom Redivo. I'm not part of anything bigger or smaller than that. I'm not a spokesman for anyone's generation."

"Well, the public is going to naturally assume you to be this spokesman, whether you want to accept it or not. . ."

"What do you mean 'naturally' assume?"

"Well, it's a natural assumption the media's going to put that label on you whether you like it or not."

Damn. And I thought Tom was being paranoid about this?

"What 'media'?" Tom asks. "This is your magazine, your interview— this is you. Let's not pass the buck, here, Paulie."

"That's exactly right— this is just an interview, not an article or editorial. I'm merely asking questions, which you're free to answer or not."

Tom sighs. "Go ahead— ask what you will."

"I was just asking you about your generation's value systems. . ."

"I don't believe in value systems," Tom declares, to Hegel's surprise.

"You're denouncing having values?" he questions.

"Follow me *carefully*, Paulie: I'm denouncing value *systems* because they're pre-made by someone else and ignorantly passed from generation to generation. True values can only be arrived at through personal judgment and choice. . . and the major flaw common to all these systems is that they presume a higher state of existence *has* to be possible. The truth is this: existence is hard. We waste far too much time clinging to answers that make us feel comfortable. It's time we stopped looking for quick fixes and easy solutions. All of us."

"You mention easy solutions. . . Do you think your generation concerns itself overly much with money?"

"*My* generation?" Tom's eyes nearly pop out. "Concerned with money?"

". . .Yes. Do you think young people today place too much emphasis on wealth and material possession?"

"I don't think my generation is particularly guilty of this sin," Tom defends. "Where did that question come from, anyway?"

"It goes back to the earlier point on cheating college students," Hegel enlightens. "It seems many of them are desperate to get ahead, any way they can."

"Well, though I still don't buy the premise of the question, I certainly concede that money is a concern for most people I know. For everybody I know."

"What about in your own case?" Hegel asks. "Is money a high priority for you?"

"Only in as much as I'd like my future and that of my family's to be secure."

"I hear the sponsors are already lining up around the block for your endorsement. . . Is Tom Redivo's name and face for sale?"

I raise an eyebrow.

"No, it's not," Tom fires back. "But if I did choose to do a commercial or advertisement, what would that mean? Doesn't your magazine carry advertising?"

"This interview is supposed to be about you, though," Hegel says, deflecting. "You don't feel that by signing endorsement deals you'd be selling out?"

"No one owns me, Mr. Hegel. If I decide to do a paid endorsement, that will be my business."

"And how do you justify such a position?"

"If I choose to lend my name to a product I actually use and enjoy, how would that be unethical?"

"How is it unethical? Because they'd be paying you."

"And what's wrong with that if I truly use and enjoy the product? I wouldn't be misleading anyone."

"You don't feel more responsibility toward your contemporaries? You don't feel your endorsement might carry alot of weight, and with that, a heavier responsibility?"

"I like to think a little more highly of my contemporaries than *that*. I don't really believe that any of them are going to, say, eat at McDonald's just because I told them they should in some commercial. If they eat there, it'll be because they choose to do so; not because I brainwashed them.   And on the off-chance there was actually someone dumb enough to go to McDonald's because the Woodstock baby told 'em to, well then, they're so ignorant that they're beneath sympathy."

"But don't you feel a higher responsibility, given. . ."

"Given what? That I'm the Woodstock baby? I thought we already established that was a total accident— no one should be lending any extra weight to my opinion on the basis of *that*. . . As long as I'm not deceiving the public as to my true opinions, I don't find it the least bit unethical sir— I'll do what I feel is necessary for my family's future welfare."

"I suppose the question then becomes: how much is necessary?"

"Don't get too smug, Mr. Hegel. You weren't so quick to answer about how many of those ads in your magazine are necessary, either. . . As I said, I'll do what I feel I have to do and anyone who doesn't like it can kiss my ass."

"Is it safe to say I've touched on something of a sore spot, here?" Hegel asks with a grin.

"That's safe to say, yeah," Tom says, his voice rising. "I graduate college with degrees in both philosophy and English literature and it's *my* fault I can't get a job outside the fucking service industry? You think I relish opening up my life to the whole world like this?"

"Well, you're life hasn't been too bad up to this point. . ."

"I'm not arguing that. My concern is the future."

"But I'm saying, you live in a nice house, drive a nice car. . ."

"Shit," Tom curses. "I can already see how you're going to intro this interview: 'As I'm sitting down to conduct this interview, Thomas Redivo has just arrived at his palatial estate after finishing the daily yacht race on the family's private lake. . .' "

"My point is that whatever your future may have held, there was certainly no looming tragedy on the scale of the famine in Africa or the Holocaust. . ."

Tom laughs now, almost defiantly.

"When did I ever compare my individual problems to any global crisis?" he asks rhetorically. "Or do you really expect everyone to put their personal problems on the back-burner until every last world

social ill is cured? Do you hold yourself up to such a standard?"
Hegel doesn't respond. "You talk about this house— it's not my
fucking house at all. My mother and her husband could kick me out
whenever the mood struck them. . . I am constantly aware of this fact,
believe me. And the car? You know how I got that Camaro? My
grandmother bought it for me, used, as a graduation present back in
'87— and the only reason *she* could afford it was because the car
dealer was an old friend of my father's. . . he all but *gave* it to her.
The one friggin' thing my father was able to help provide for me from
beyond the grave."

"But it's still yours," Hegel counters. "Isn't that what counts?"

"The issue is DIGNITY!" Tom shouts. "Believe me, as hard as I
work, I should be able to afford that car, myself; at least be able to
split an apartment with a friend or two without ransoming my future
away. Instead I'm stuck living at home having to listen to geezers like
you, who like to make it sound like the real reason I'm still here is that
I'm lazy; that I don't try hard enough."

"Is that how you believe yourself to be perceived? As spoiled and
lazy?"

"Am I wrong? Isn't that the 'Generation X' stereotype— that
we're all a bunch of flannel-wearing gripers who only care about
ourselves?"

"Dispel this image, then— how do you see your own generation?"
Hegel looks pleased; like this is taking the exact direction he hoped it
would.

"I don't like to put things in terms of 'generations,' " Tom tells
him. "I do so in reference to baby boomers only because you seem so
anxious to embrace that label, yourselves. But before the term 'baby
boomer,' we didn't label entire generations of people. So if it was
never done before, why should it continue after? In my mind, there is
no 'Generation X.' "

"You consider 'Generation X' what? A media creation?"

"Basically. The whole thing is more a marketing conspiracy than
anything else, as I see it."

"Then don't put it in those terms if you're uncomfortable with them; just speak from your experience. How do you and people you know contradict the stereotypes about Generation X?"

"Well. . . While I won't presume to speak for an entire generation, I will say that in my limited experience I know of no one, personally, who fits into that stereotype of sitting around, slurping lattes and reveling in their poverty and ennui. There's nothing cool about not being able to go to school because one class costs several hundred dollars and you can't afford it."

"You repudiate such images completely, I take it?" Hegel smiles. It sounds like he's kidding— I hope he is, at least.

"Of course I do!" Tom answers steadfastly. "None of my friends qualify as 'slackers,' either— another term I've really come to despise. Everyone I know breaks their ass to put themselves through college and pay their own bills. This one friend I have works in a pizza parlor and shares an apartment with his cousin and two other friends— his share of the rent is over $300 and on a good week he might bring home $130. Then he's got car payments, insurance, gas, the phone bill, groceries. . . You know what though? Even though we are overworked and under-rewarded, I see a strength in us that makes me proud. The struggle has helped make us strong, I think."

"This anger I'm hearing from you, this self-righteousness— could it be resentment toward your parents generation? Are you jealous of how far they managed to go and what you have to live up to?"

. . .The world halts as an ocean of rage strains against the dam of Tom's self-control. I know this because I can see it in his face; I can feel it.

"Maybe the reason you were able to accomplish so much is be-cause you had parents who stuck around. And stuck together." Tom's tone remains calm. The dam holds, but it's cracking in places, and you can see the water spilling out, little by little. "You were nurtured, not ignored. You accomplished more because you had more. Alot more. In fact, when you consider all the advantages you *did* have, your accomplishments don't seem like so much after all."

"So you're saying not only that baby boomers have proven to be bad parents, but that they've proven to be poor caretakers for the world as a whole."

"No, I'm not," Tom argues. "I'm just debunking the premise behind all your questions so far— which is that my generation got this perfect world handed to us on a silver platter by yours."

"What are some of the ways then, that you would say baby boomers have failed this world, this nation? What do you think you could have done better? Or hope you *will* do better?"

"I don't pretend to hold answers for the entire world. That's the mistake you keep repeating: you continue to look for one or two large scale answers for our problems as a *society* when the real issue is all the people who are lacking in *individual* character. You can pass all the laws you want to try and control people's behavior, but that doesn't change their character. We all need to look in the mirror and recognize our own individual flaws and weaknesses."

"So you see the government as pointless?"

"I see the government as not only pointless but immoral. All governments are— anarchy is the only moral society."

"Would you care to explain your reasoning?"

"Because anarchy is the only system that forces each individual to be responsible for his or her own actions. No one can say 'society made me do it' because there is no society. It's also the only system that offers complete freedom without any form of organized, institutionalized oppression. And it can't happen soon enough to please me."

"You would be pleased to live under. . . anarchy?" Hegel questions with near-amusement. "The prospect of such a thing wouldn't be at all frightening to you?"

"To make the individual uncomfortable is my task, Paul— like the man said: I haven't come to bring peace, but a sword. I'm *supposed* to be frightening you and upsetting you and confounding you and angering you. . . That's what I'm here for: to overturn the moneychangers' tables."

"Just for clarification: are you saying you would *like* to see this happen, or is this a prediction on your part of what you think *will* happen?"

"Call it my prophecy, Paulie. And whether you like it or you don't like it, learn to love it, 'cause that day is fast approaching— that day of reckoning, when the natural order will be restored. When it comes Paul, you'll be the one behind the counter of the book store while I'm running the billion dollar publishing empire."

"And what if this 'last day' should arrive and proves to be not quite as delightful as you describe?"

"Whatever it may bring, I can't imagine it being worse than life just continuing on the way it is now. . . the thought of having to struggle every day and worse— having to watch my sisters, my children, struggling right alongside me. While all the while, you, our parents, bask in luxury, getting everything you want, getting your every desire serviced. And if we want to survive, we'll have to go crawling to you; go begging to you for help just so you can feel good about yourselves. So that everything we ever have, we'll owe to you— never allowing us to accomplish anything on our own, never getting a fair shot for ourselves."

"Of course you realize," Hegel asserts, "all you're saying has done nothing to dispel the stereotype about the x-er resentment of boomers. . ."

That's it. I can see the dam bursting in Tom's head now.

"You don't think you're worthy of resentment?" he growls. "No generation before yours had ever been given more and no generation before yours has ever done less— you squandered all of it, satisfying your vulgar appetites, saddling us with the biggest debt in national history and screwing each other with such indiscriminate frequency that you turned AIDS into an epidemic and inflicted it on us."

"Well," Hegel begins vaingloriously, "Those weren't baby boomers in the White House or Senate when that debt was running up. . . I'd like to point out that it *is* a baby boomer who has begun to cut into that debt this last year or two."

Big deal. Which generation re-elected Reagan by a friggin' landslide in '84 and ran up the debt in the first place?

"You asked me before about what I might do with our 'society'? Well, you know what I'd do if I ruled the world? I'd have everyone's birthdate tattooed on their forehead the same day they're born— that way, people couldn't lie about how old they really are or disguise it with facelifts and lipo. Maybe then, people would be forced to start acting their fucking age. Then, once they got to be forty or so, we could dump 'em in the stew pot." Tom stops and smiles a moment. And even I'm momentarily taken aback by the blunt seriousness of his delivery before I realize, of course, he's kidding. "Whatsamatter P.H.? You don't care for my modest little proposal? Can't you see I just solved the social security problem *and* world hunger, all in one fell swoop?"

"Tattooed foreheads?" Hegel questions, not sounding amused. "Turning people into food? That certainly sounds like a lovely world to live in."

"That's okay. The cut worm forgives the plough."

It's tense in here. Again, his tone catches me off-guard and for the briefest moment, I'm unsure if he's for real. Then I realize better of it.

"Regardless of how serious you are. . ."

"Oh, I'm dead serious," Tom says, his smile growing.

"Regardless— it does sadden me that one generation's attempt to build a better world has led to led to such extreme resentment on the succeeding generation's part."

"Maybe that's what's really disturbing you," Tom responds. "The fact that the beast that slouched its way toward Bethel to be born twenty-five summers ago is not an aberration, not a mistake. Maybe, just maybe, I am what you and your whole fucked up generation *made* me. Is that it, Paul?"

"There is truth to that, I'll admit. I have to wonder where we went wrong; where the message got lost. . ."

This Hegel guy is too much— he's a cartoon, practically. If I wasn't hearing this with my own ears, I would never believe it.

"By all means," Tom says, "what did we miss, Mr. Hegel? What lesson should we have learned from you? From *your* Woodstock?"

Hegel hesitates a moment.

"I can only guess what this new Woodstock will be," he begins, "but I do know the first one was not about selling T-shirts. . . Viet Nam was a big part of it, like it was a big part of everything at that time. . ."

"Right. Everyone was so concerned about the young men dying over in 'Nam, that a half-million of you decided you'd get together in upstate New York for three days, listen to music and get stoned. I'm sure that saved countless lives."

"The point was that half a million people could coexist without any kind of violence and just enjoy three days of music and peace."

"Like I said: I'm sure that did the kids dying over in 'Nam alot of good."

"Well, what do you hope the '94 concert accomplishes?"

"Are you kidding?" Tom questions, sounding tickled. "I just hope it's a great show and everybody has a good time."

"You don't choose to aim any higher than that?"

"You *can't* aim any higher than that— a concert is a concert. It doesn't become a world-changing event just because you say so or wish it so."

"It will never become more than that if you don't *believe* it can be or at least *try*. . ."

"And there's the difference between us: you see a less than perfect world and immediately you have to tear it down; change it. I choose not to kid myself— I know that this world will not always be pretty, but I embrace it just the same."

"But *why?* Why is it wrong to want to make things *better?*"

"Don'tcha get it? What I'm embracing is *real*. You embrace ridiculous fantasies that can *never* be real. I affirm life, you deny it. . . The idea that some concert makes any larger social difference is ludicrous!"

"But what can you hope to accomplish with your worldview? Every great achievement begins with a dreamer, with a dream."

"Dreaming alone though, don't cut it."

"You're saying you disapprove of wanting something better than the world initially offers? Something more?"

Tom looks my way, again.

"I guess we just figured out why the boomer divorce rate is so high, huh? 'Oh well, my marriage is less than perfect, I may as well look for something *better,* elsewhere.' "

"First of all, I never said anyone was seeking perfection; second of all, there's a difference between goals in someone's personal life versus their larger goals for the world as a whole."

He's back-pedaling now. Tom's got him on the ropes.

"You talk about your Woodstock not being about T-shirt sales. . . Aren't these greedy, selfish promoters who are putting up Woodstock '94 the same ones who brought us the original? And didn't these original promoters once sue each other in court over the revenues earned by the movie and album that was released after that first concert?"

"I think it was the people in attendance that defined that original event, not the promoters."

"Pop quiz, Paulie, 'cause I'm curious: did Woodstock mark a beginning or ending in your mind?"

"As anyone familiar with my writing knows, I've often referred to it as the birth of. . ."

"Bzzzt! Trick question! The true answer is that it was both, of course. Every ending means a new beginning for something, and every beginning likewise an ending. What that first Woodstock should have been was the beginning of me and mine and the end of you and yours. Except you selfish fucks are refusing to let go."

Go, Thomas, go.

"Are you proposing that the baby boomers all lie down and die?"

"I'm proposing that you open your eyes to the truth. For thousands and thousands of years, man always exalted his children; he reveled in passing the torch, delighted in watching his children surpass him. That was the moral behind those ancient Greek myths: that the child inevitably exceeds the parent. Well, so far you've managed to swallow my brothers and sisters, but now you're lookin' at the stone you're gonna spit back up."

"I must concede, you certainly excel at literary allusions, Mr. Redivo. . ."

"Decay and death are inevitable," Tom goes on. "You and all your boomer buddies are gonna be dead someday— accept it. Deal. I know it's hard for you to imagine the world going on without you, but it will. I know this pisses you off, but don't take it out on us."

"Based on this interview, I think it's rather plain which generation is carrying the anger," Hegel responds smugly.

Tom suddenly stands up.

"The simple truth is that all those utopian dreams of yours sicken me. I can't imagine a notion more antithetical to human nature—you'd stifle every good and natural human instinct for the *illusion* of a universal peace; the *illusion* of fulfillment, as if such things were ever really possible. And all of this at the meager price of individuality. Universal peace is fake; a denial."

Forget it. He's on fire now.

"That's the difference between us, Paul: you run from life, I run *to* it. I recognize that life is defined by agony, destruction, the will to annihilation. You seek redemption from this, while I affirm it."

". . .I believe one can *accept* such things without necessarily embracing them," Hegel reasons.

"I hate everything you stand for," Tom snarls. "Your motto was 'peace,' right? 'Make love, not war'? Well if 'peace' was your motto, then make mine 'war!' You hear me?"

He thumps his chest hard with his fist, then holds it right under Hegel's nose. Hegel and I both freeze.

"I said 'war,' baby!"

. . .

"*War.*"

214

CHAPTER XIII

Finals just started this week and I've been having one hell of a time getting myself prepared. The whole semester, really, has been turned upside down because of what's happened with Tom. The same conversation just keeps repeating itself over and over with everyone I see:

Isn't it unbelievable, what's happening to Tom? Yeah. Did you already know he was born at Woodstock? Yeah. Wasn't he awesome on *Ricki Lake*? Yeah. Did you read the interview in *Rebel*? Yeah. Are you going to see him again, soon? Yeah. Isn't the whole thing unbelievable?

. . .Yeah.

Mere days ago, the *Rebel* magazine featuring Tom's interview hit the stands. Tom's grim visage, shot in glorious living color, takes up the entire cover, with "The Prodigal Son" written in red letters at the bottom. Already, countless torn-off and Xeroxed copies of it adorn various walls, trees and columns all over campus. Opening up to the interview itself, you're first treated to a black-and-white, two-page spread of Tom laying back on his living room couch. Across the top, in big letters reads the title of the piece: "I Came Upon a Child of

God. . ." I gotta say, Hegel, to his credit, published the full conversation and didn't alter a syllable of Tom's words (although he did snip out all of my own cool gibes). Of course, that still hasn't stopped just about everybody from totally misreading him anyway. Supposedly, articles in both *Time* and *Newsweek* are forthcoming.

Unreal.

I'm walking past the quad, having just finished my Statistics final, when I hear someone calling me.

"Hey Will," some guy from Latin class whose-name-I-couldn't-remember-to-save-my-life yells out. That's happened to me a couple of times this week, where people I don't even know have been calling me by name.

"Yeah, hi," I say.

"Check out what's playin' in the student lounge!"

I follow him to the student lounge where a large crowd has gathered around the television. They've got on channel five, with the *Current Affair* from last night re-playing.

"Now we all know by now about Tommy Redivo," anchor Maureen O'Boyle says, "but now we'd like to bring you the story of the *other* Woodstock baby. Carl Schulman reports."

Other Woodstock baby?

They show some old stock footage of the old hippie scene of San Francisco's Haight-Ashbury while the Beatles' "Day in the Life" serves as a musical bed. Then, you hear the inflection of this gravel-throated reporter:

"The sixties. . . History will call it an age of hope, an era of dreams. Starting with The Summer of Love in 1967— when turning on, tuning in and dropping out was all the rage. . . When flower power was all-powerful."

"Itchycoo Park" starts to play as a slew of tired 60s slogans flash across the screen against an acid-trip backdrop of melting colors: a-happening, freak out, human be-in. . .

"Many say that era came to a close with Woodstock. . . For some though, life had only just begun."

They cut to footage of this skinny brunette girl walking in a park, somewhere.

BACK TO THE GARDEN

"Star Profeta is the other Woodstock Baby," Darth Vader informs us.

"The way my mother told it," this Star-person says as they cut to an interview segment, "she originally wanted to name me 'Sun' and my father wanted to name me 'Moon.' So they compromised and called me 'Star.' "

"In November of 1969," deep throat voices over an old black and white picture of (I assume) this Star-person's parents, "just a few short months after her birth, Star's father Gerry Bifano was drafted for military service. The following year, he was killed in action in Viet Nam."

"Obviously, I didn't know my father at all," Star says sadly as the interview resumes.

"And what happened to your mother after your father died?"

"After my father died, I guess Mom kinda lost it. To be honest, it's not like either one of my parents were all that stable. . . they both had their share of problems with drugs and stuff. I haven't actually seen my Mom since I was eight years old."

"That must've been very hard on you, growing up."

"It was. . . difficult, yes. But I still had my grandparents— they're the greatest. I love them very much."

"Star graduated from college in 1992," throaty goes on over some sunny footage of a college campus, "and has since been working in a secretarial position for an insurance company in Philadelphia. . ." Cut to footage of the city of brotherly love. "Needless to say, she was shocked upon learning of the existence of another Woodstock baby."

"Is there anything you'd care to say to Tommy Redivo, if he's watching?"

"Well, um," she begins, "I guess it would be cool to meet him someday. I mean, it's nice knowing there's someone I can share this with, after all this time. . ."

"Somethin', huh?" Latin-boy asks me.

"Yeah," I say, a little numb.

I turn and walk out of the lounge. Outside, I see yet another one: that's four different people I've seen today, wearing the same bootleg Tommy T-shirt— complete with a video still of Tom, lifted from his

Ricki Lake appearance, on the front; "kill your parents," scrawled graffiti style, on the back.

Alright. It is now, officially, just a *bit* much.

"Hi. . . Will?" a female voice asks just behind me. Who the fuck is it now?

I turn around. Sweet Lordy-Lou, it's Jeanine— the hot lil' redhead from Western Civilization class that I've been secretly frothing over just about all semester. Who would've guessed she even knew I existed?

"Um, yeah, hello," I say, trying not to swallow my tongue.

"I'm Jeanine."

"From Western Civ, yeah."

"Yeah," she says, smiling. "I just saw you and I thought I could catch a word or two with you."

"Sure."

"Well, I was just wondering if it was true, about you and Tom. . . Did you really know him?" No one at school even uses his last name anymore; we all know who we're talking about. Like Madonna or Cher. . . or Charo. "Buzz is you two were good friends."

"Yeah, we're friends." Shit, I'm part of the buzz, now?

"Wow. . . how do you know him?"

"I live in Oakwood. We used to carpool to school alot. Graduated high school with his sister, too." Yeah— Meredith probably couldn't have picked me out of a police line-up back then, but we *did* go to the same high school together.

"Cool," is all she can come back with. . . Will you look at this? Someone else is actually struggling to make conversation with *me!* And not just someone, but a totally beautiful girl! If only I had a witness! Did I just say I was getting tired of this a minute ago?

"So, you on your way to an exam?" I ask.

"No, I'm through for the day, actually. I just spotted you walking and I figured I'd say 'hi.' Because, y'know, we never had the opportunity to talk in class, before."

"Yeah," I agree. "It's weird sometimes, having classes with people and you never really get to know them. But that's how it goes when you don't live on campus, I guess."

"Yeah, exactly."

She stands in front of me, desperately searching for something to say next. I recognize this only because I've been on the other end of this situation myself so many times before. It's so different being in the driver's seat for a change; so. . . awesome.

"I tell you what, blue-eyes," I say with a boldness heretofore undreamed, "buy me a cup of coffee and I'll swap life stories with you— deal?"

"I'd like that," she says with relief.

We retreat to the campus coffee shop in the basement of Bender Hall. We drink coffee and talk. She laughs at every lame joke I tell, smiles continuously, and defers to me like I'm the smartest man on earth.

I'm walking on air the rest of the afternoon.

On my way home, I stop by Tom's. "Hey, buddy!" I hail, barging in the door like I own the joint. He's in the living room, watering the plants— I can't wait to tell him about Jeanine. Frankie and the twins are on the couch, just watching him with quiet awe. . . more awe than usual, I mean.

"Hi, Will," they greet.

"Hi, girls!"

"Hey, mud brother."

"So, you're home?" I ask.

"Very good, Sherlock!"

"Well, I'm glad— it's good to see you."

Jeanine. . . Those eyes. . . That hair. . .

". . .Great to see everyone, in fact!"

"My, but you seem chipper. It's been an exceptional day, I presume?"

"Yeah," Frankie agrees, suspiciously. "I can't remember the last time I saw you looking so happy. . ."

"Uh, yeah!" I better get it together, here. "I mean, it's just been exciting, y'know? People have been comin' up to me all day— all *week*— about you, y'know?"

"Yeah?" Tom questions. "What are they saying?"

"They all wanna know when I'm gonna see you, what you're doin'. . . You know— they're all star-struck."

"God!" Tom laughs.

"So, I caught the replay of *A Current Affair* in the student lounge this afternoon. . . you see it?"

"Yeah, I saw. The show actually called me a week ago to see if I wanted to respond to anything she had to say, but I declined. Of course, that was before I knew what she looked like. . ."

"You think she's pretty?"

"Are you kidding? You mean you don't dig that whole waifish, other-worldly, elfin-type vibe she's got going? She is *totally* luscious."

"Eeee-yew!" Sam whines as she gives his shoulder a slap. "Stop talking about sex in front of your sister!"

"What about her story? Did it shock you? That there was another Woodstock baby, I mean?"

"Not really. I did find it annoying the way the whole piece juxtaposed us, y'know? Like she's the *other* Woodstock baby— the dark, sinister yin to my bright, shining yang." Tom finishes watering his last plant, then stretches out on the floor. "Not to disparage her or anything; I mean it did sound like she's been through hell and back."

I notice a couple of suitcases by George's recliner.

"Whose are those?"

"Tom's," Frankie says.

"Tommy's goin' to Hollywood," Tiffany informs me.

"You are?"

"Yup." He glances at his watch. "Shaggy should be here in less than a half-hour to pick me up and take me to the airport."

"What are you going out there for?"

"To close some deals, hopefully."

The dog barks in the kitchen as I hear a car pulling in the driveway.

"That must be George," Tom states as he stands up. "Would one of you go get Mom for me?" Frankie immediately rushes out of the room.

"Hello," George says as he walks in. "Still here, Tom?"

"No, I left ten minutes ago," Tom quips. He motions to George's chair. "Why don't you sit down— I have something to discuss with you and Mom."

George appears intrigued. He sits down as Frankie returns with Lisa in tow.

"Hello, hon," she greets George. "Hi, Will. . . What's up?"

"Grab a a seat," Tom says. She sits on the arm of George's recliner. "I wanted to talk to you guys about your future plans."

"What future plans?" George questions.

"Well, I know you'd like to sell the house, George. And you know I don't want the girls to be uprooted, nor do I want the spectre of being uprooted hanging over their heads. . ."

"Tommy," George assures, "nobody's getting uprooted. We're family— I could never sell the house out from under you and the girls."

"Of course you would never do that, George. . . but just for everyone's peace of mind, I would feel alot more comfortable about it if you would just sell the place to me, now."

"Sell it to you?" George restates.

"Don't be ridiculous!" Lisa admonishes. "How would you buy the house? With what?"

"I've already got one deal on the table right now, it's just a question of signing it when I get out there. . . and hopefully there'll be more to come by the end of the trip, if all goes according to plan."

"How much would you expect in rent?" George asks somewhat coyly.

"Why, you're *family*, George," Tom drips. "I'd never ask for rent from *family*."

"Still. . . how would we ever decide on a fair price?"

"George!" Lisa gasps.

"I'm just talking hypothetically, here!"

"We could have an appraiser come by and give us a price," Tom says. "Whatever price he or she gives is what I'll pay— no challenges from either side."

Silence. I don't really know what make of this; if George is just indulging him or what. I mean, he can't REALLY be considering

221

selling Tom the house, can he? He can't be that money-hungry, right? I can tell by Lisa's expression she's probably thinking the same thing.

"He wants to buy it for his own peace of mind, sweetheart," George coos. Lisa's face falls— as does mine.

"Mom, the price probably won't even amount to half the Pepsi money I've been offered." I raise an eyebrow. "I can afford it; trust me."

"What do you have to say about this, dear?" George asks. Lisa's eyes shoot daggers back at him, but George is totally oblivious to it— all he sees right now are dollar signs.

"You do what you think is best," she says at last. "It's up to you."

"Alright, Tommy," George concedes with a bright smile. "If all goes well for you out west, I have no problem selling you the house. If that's what you want." He holds out his hand. They shake.

"Pleasure doing business you." Lisa abruptly exits the room. George is taken aback a moment; then quickly goes after her. Tom just stands there, with this Mephistophelean grin.

"Well, Shaggy should be gettin' here any minute. . . I guess I better go get the dog."

"For what?" Sam asks.

"Whaddaya mean 'for what?' She's going with me."

"You can't take the dog, stupid!" Tiffany says.

"Sure I can. I've packed dog food and everything."

"You *can't* take Tempest with you," Frankie protests.

"Why not?"

"Because. . . you just can't!"

"Mom!" Samantha moans.

"It's not fair!" Tiffany says.

"I tell you what: we can let Tempest decide." Tom calls Tempest. She arrives quickly, and he directs her to the center of the room, where he commands her to sit.

"Alright. You guys stay over there and I'll go over in this corner, here. Now, we'll both call her and whoever she goes to is who she'll stay with. Fair enough?"

"When do we start?" Sam asks. Tom hesitates for a second.

"Go," he says calmly.

"Tempest!" the three girls all begin to yell. "C'mere girl! C'mon!" Tom just stands there, smiling, as Tempest remains sitting and staring at the girls like they're all crazy. "C'mon Temp! C'mon now! Walkies, walkies!"

Tom looks at the dog with pride. He gently pats at his thigh twice and she gets up and goes over to stand at his side.

"Awwwww!" the girls collectively whine.

"Oh, stop it," Tom chides. "I'll hardly be gone, fer cryin' out loud."

"Really?" Frankie asks.

"Of course." He hugs her. "Bad enough I have to leave all of you behind; at least let me take Temp with me for the short time I'm gone. . . okay?"

"Okay. . ." they all acquiesce. Outside, a car honks. Must be Shaggy.

"Looks like your cab's here," I say. Tom kisses his sisters, then goes over and picks up his bags.

"Tell Meredith I'll call her from out there."

"Try not to get lost out there, man," I say.

"Hey, don't worry— *I'll be bahk,*" he answers in his best Arnold voice as he leaves with Tempest right behind him.

I wish I could be as sure of that as he seems to be.

And just like that, he's gone. Damn. It's taking a little time to sink in 'cause it's all happening so very fast. . . Tom's getting interviewed by magazines, appearing on television, cutting deals with George to buy the house, flying out to California and taking Tempest with him. . . And what about me? All of a sudden, everyone on campus knows my name, I'm flirting with beautiful girls I wouldn't have had the courage to even look at a week ago. . . Everything's changing. It will never be like it was, not ever again. Not ever.

CHAPTER XIV

Mere anarchy is loosed upon the world.

"Look at me," Pig-pen screams, "I'm a hippie!"

Welcome to Woodstock '94.

It's Saturday, and I can't tell how late it is because day never had a chance to break. Joe Cocker took the stage in the early afternoon, and shortly after he finished up, night fell about six hours early. Then the rain started coming down. In buckets.

The mosh pit in front of the main stage is now the mud pit. The people have to form a human chain just to climb out— it's like quicksand, I imagine. The mud itself is a badge of honor among us. And "Pig-pen," as Kate has dubbed him, is king of the mud-people. His entire being is so caked with mud, that his ethnicity— perhaps his/it's very gender, as well— will go down in history as one of the great mysteries of western culture.

Insanity, insanity, insanity. Forgive me if I sound a bit incoherent, but you have no idea what it's *like* up here.

Some people are walking around, buck naked (unless you wanna count mud as clothing; and at this point, you almost have to). I don't know why— it's as if they're breaking rules just for the sake of breaking them. Many have told me that Woodstock is now a free concert for the second time in twenty-five years, as the crowd continues to swell. More and more of the newcomers brag about crashing the gate; that all the security has disappeared. I hear portions of 87, 32, and 9 West are all closed due to traffic problems.

It's starting to get *scary*.

Shaggy, Keith and I, we were originally going to see if we could set things up with Tom so we could stay backstage, maybe meet some of the bands. . . y'know, get the whole v.i.p. treatment— after all, Tom's only the emcee of this whole Hootenanny (along with Star Profeta), so I don't think it would've been too much trouble for him. But noooooooo. Our women collectively lost their minds; deciding they wanted the full Woodstock "experience." That meant sleeping outdoors on grass and dirt with the bugs and snakes and rats; surronded by a couple hundred thousand potential psychopaths.

We drove here in separate cars on Thursday afternoon (about a two hour drive), and while there wasn't much traffic on the way up, there were already like a thousand cars in the lot where we parked. Then a shuttle bus took us here, to the actual concert area, about two miles away. They kept us in holding pens for a while, where security— "the peace patrol"— inspected our bags while we waited to go through the metal detectors. . . And is it just me, or is there something quite Orwellian about a security force labeled "the peace patrol"? Then again, I've never even seen the movie, *1984*, let alone read the book, so what the hell do I know?

Anyway, after this security check, we were led across a bridge to the "Eco-village," where we exchanged our regular money for "Woodstock money." Then it took me four tries before I successfully pitched our tent (technically, you're not even allowed to pitch a tent, but fuck— everyone else around us has done likewise). The smaller south stage seems miles away from the main one— it's quite a trek, getting from one to the other. . . And the people here never, ever seem to stop moving. Maneuvering through the crowd just to get to the bathroom takes the better part of an hour. Kate calls it "dangerously high population density." Me, I call it just plain ridicu-lous.

DAVID SORRENTINO

And there are people here from every part of the country; from Maine to Florida to South Dakota to Utah; one couple from England, even. And I'm amazed over how many older people I'm seeing here with their little kids. . . I don't know what they came here expecting, but I think they might be in for a little surprise when they see acts like Nine Inch Nails and Metallica take the stage.

It ain't *Sesame Street On Ice*, folks.

Yesterday— before the weather turned, transforming everything to mud— it was quite a happening, man. Girls were running around with flowers in their hair, people were greeting each other with the peace sign, and we were all just generally dancing around like retards; using the word "groovy" as noun, adjective, adverb, and preposition. . . Of course, the difference between us and the last Woodstock is that we *knew* how ridiculous we were acting. Still, it was good, wholesome fun while it lasted.

It was late in the morning when Tom walked out on to the main stage and took the mic for the first time. He started off with this really bad joke: how many baby boomers does it take to screw in a light bulb? The answer: zero— boomers never screw in their own light bulbs; they hire some unemployed twenty-something with a degree in philosophy to do it for them at minimum wage.

Ba-dum-bum.

Then, much to all of our shock, somebody brought out a guitar for him. And as we watched with our mouths agape, he proceeded to launch into a blistering, thrashing rendition of "Smells Like Teen Spirit." I could not believe what I was seeing. But as if that weren't enough, after slamming down the last chord and screaming out that final "denial," he began to softly sing the first few lines of the Mats' "Unsatisfied," A Cappella— all of us in the Cahill posse went totally apeshit. And while I don't know how many others in the crowd actually recognized the song, they seemed to agree with the lyrics at least, as they showered Tom with wild applause. Then, in coolest rock star-fashion, he just dropped the guitar, letting it fall to the stage, and walked off; leaving us all screaming for more. There were alot of good acts that would go on to take the stage in the afternoon and evening, but for me, none of them proved more electrifying than

226

seeing Tommy Redivo slammin' on guitar and howling out the words of Kurt Cobain.

By nightfall, the grass and acid and mushrooms were everywhere. And it musta been some powerful shit too, because by this morning, the wildest, craziest rumors started flying. . . I mean, these people *must* be stoned out of their minds to believe this shit. We're talkin' everything from speculation of some form of Beatles reunion taking place tomorrow, to alien spaceships arriving to abduct us off to some other world as part of a government conspiracy. But the stupidest one, at least in my opinion, is the rumor of a new Woodstock baby being born. . . Now, this is 1994 folks— are you tellin' me that if a new Woodstock had been born here in the last twenty-four hours that there wouldn't be announcements plastered all over the jumbo-tron screens here? If not actual video of the kid being delivered? I mean really.

Which brings us to now. And right now, Kate is hanging on to me for dear life as the sea of people around us begins to churn. . . something is happening in the pit, up front. Shag, Bar, Keith, Tam— I don't know where they are, if they're out on a group bathroom break or on a food run or what. Wherever they are, I can't be sure if I'm even going to live to see them again. The rain is starting to fall even harder now, just when I thought it couldn't possibly get worse. But nobody here is going anywhere.

A quarter of a million Noahs, not a single ark in sight.

* * *

Tommy Redivo and Star Profeta met at a commercial shoot for Pepsi over a month ago. The attraction between them was palpable from the outset— one would have to be deaf, dumb and dead not to recognize it. He will never forget the handshake they shared when they first introduced themselves; the way she slid her thumb up from his wrist to the top of his knuckle, then down again.

"Thomas Peter Redivo," he presented himself.

"Star Profeta," she responded.

227

"What's your real name?" he asked. He couldn't shake the feeling that centuries in the future, historians would be trying to re-construct just this epochal moment.

"*'Star'* is my real name. Wanna see my birth certificate?"

"But I'm sure nobody called you 'Star' when you were growing up, right? What did they call you?" He was losing himself in those faun-eyes of hers.

"My grandparents called me 'Kristine,' after my mother. That's how most people knew me."

"Kristine," he repeated wistfully. The two of them burned dead-eye stares into one another for what felt like forever.

"I wish we'd start shooting already," she complained, finally looking away from him.

"Mmm," he murmured in agreement as his hand found it's way around her waist.

"Easy there, Ace," she playfully warned. "Cross on the green, not in-between." But her hands fell gently upon his chest, welcoming the embrace; not resisting him at all.

"Wouldn't it be something if the two of us ended up getting to-gether?" he whispered. "The two Woodstock children, together?"

"That wouldn't be too. . . predictable?" With the familiarity of an old lover, she traced her finger up and down his breast bone. They wanted each other and they both knew it— it would be insulting to one another's intelligence to try and act coy or pretend this mutual desire wasn't there.

"What are we going to do about this, Kristine?" he hissed.

Her hand found the zipper of his pants without even looking down. She tugged at it gently, pulling him forward a little. Then she suddenly stopped herself.

"No. . . not here," she told him. "Not yet." Then she just walked away.

He grinned. She was playing with him, but he didn't mind. Be-cause he already knew, beyond any doubt, that he would fuck the living Jesus out of her.

. . .Now, more than a month later, the two of them stand off the main stage at Woodstock, along with Meredith and Matt, watching as the members of Nine Inch Nails roll around in the great mud pit. They've spent countless hours together over this past month, Tommy and Star have; ironing out deals, working on various projects, and preparing for this very weekend. In that time, they've come to know each other, even love each other. And while these circumstances have often proven less than ideal for a blossoming romance, at least now— at this precise moment— they can sit back and enjoy the show. . .

BAHM-BAHM!

Trent Reznor, the mud-soaked messiah, has seized the stage at last. The entire crowd, all quarter-million of them, seem to surge forward at once.

"*Why are you doing this to me? Am I not living up to what I'm supposed to be?*"

Trent sings as if he's tied to the rack and someone is turning the wheel.

"*Why am I seething with this animosity? I think you owe me a great, big apology. . .*

"TEAR-BUL LIE!!!"

Frankie manages to wriggle her lithe, tiny body between scores of others to reach the pit. Her heart pounds in her chest as she maneuvers closer, closer to the stage.

"*. . . seems salvation comes only in our dreams. . . I feel my hatred grow all the more extreme. . . can this world really be as sad as it seems?*

"TEAR-BUL LIE!!!

"*Don't take it away from me, I need someone to hold on to. . .*"

She pogos up and down, simultaneously dodging the flying, muddy bodies. A short distance away— but miles in terms of the mass of humanity between them— Will and Kate do the same.

"*There's nothing left for me to hide. . . I lost my ignorance, security and pride. . . I'm all alone in this fucking world you must despise. . . I believed the promises, the promises and lies. . .*

"TEAR-BUL LIE!!!"

Meredith digs her nails into her boyfriend Matt's shoulder and jumps up and down, frantically. Tom and Star, in sharp contrast, stand frozen in place. Each has a hand around the other's waist, squeezing gently; lovingly.

"You made me throw it all away; my morals left to decay; how many you betray; you've taken everything!

"TEAR-BUL LIE!!!"

Meredith is spinning like a pinwheel now. Matt is shouting his approbation but no one seems able to hear him. Star rubs the top of her head, cat-like, against Tom's face. She arches back her neck and kisses his upper lip, teasingly.

"My head is filled with disease, my skin is begging you please, I'm on my hands and knees, I want so much to belieee-eeeeeeeeeeeeve!"

The audience pulses with its applause.

"You give me the reason. . . You give me control. . . I gave you my purity, my purity you stole. . ."

Suddenly, the crowd-energy knob is on nine.

"Did you think I wouldn't recognize this compromise? Am I just too stupid to realize?"

Kate whips her head violently back and forth, as if she's trying to shake loose from some invisible chain that binds her. Her wet, matted, muddy hair stings Will's naked arm.

"It comes down to this: your kiss, your fist, and your strain. . . It gets under my skin— within— take in— the extent of my sin!"

Somewhere in the massive crowd, Shaggy and Barb, Keith and Tamara, have given up looking for each other. There will be time enough to re-group later— right now, Trent has usurped everyone's attention.

"WAKE UP MOTHER FUCK-ERRRRRS!!! STEPRIGHTUP! MARCHPUSH!"

. . .And now the knob is on ten and a half.

"All the pigs are all lined up. . . I give you all that you want. . . take the skin and peel it back. . ."

Silence.

"Doesn't it make you feel better?"

. . . And the immediate return of thunder:

"SHOVEITUPINSIDESURPRISE! LIES!"

Now it is riotous. Everyone stomps their feet despite the fact the mud is already past ankle-deep.

"*I want to watch it come down. . .*"

Silence.

"*Now doesn't that make you feel better?*" The crowd howls in accord. "*The pigs have won tonight. . . Now they can all sleep soundly. . . And all of you miserable, muddy fuck-heads. . . are alright.*"

The assemblage explodes into cheers. Will and Kate collapse together in an embrace that is half-passion, half-exhaustion.

"*I still recall the taste of my tears,*" Trent begins to murmur mournfully as the crowd's consolidated emotion slows down, at least for the moment. "*My favorite dreams of you still wash ashore. . .*"

Will's open, wanting mouth meets Kate's own. It's as if some singular, outside force controls them both and they are just watching themselves from outside their bodies. Slowly, their tongues lap over one another in time to the slow beat of the song; directed by one will, one mind.

"*Everywhere I look, you're all I see— just a fading, fucking reminder of who I used to be— come on, tell me!*"

Star lets her body fall back against Tom, as his arms flow over her torso. Neither of their souls have ever felt more at peace.

"*You make this all go away, you make this all go away, you make this all go away. . .*"

As the song ends, Will and Kate end a kiss that they both wish could go on for days longer. Looking into each other's eyes, they both know that they have managed to touch that unknowable cosmic force, that invisible spark that begins and ends all life.

tat-tat-tat-tat-tat-tat-tat-tat-tat-tat-tat-tat-tat-tat-tat. . .

The gathered mass of muddy humanity lets out one piercing, collective scream as it recognizes the opening of "Closer."

"*You let me violate you. You let me desecrate you. You let me penetrate you. You let me complicate you. . .*"

Tommy holds Star tighter now. *God, I love you,* she speaks in his ear. *I love you too,* he confesses.

DAVID SORRENTINO

*"Help me— I broke apart my insides. . . Help me— I've got no
soul to sell. . . Help me— the only thing that works for me. . . Help
me get away from myself. . .*

*"I wanna fuck you like an animal. . . I wanna feel you from the
inside. . . I wanna fuck you like an animal. . . My whole existence is
flawed. . .*

"You. Get. Me closer to God."

Even the twins, back in the trailer, can feel the "eventness" of
what they are seeing on the monitor and hearing just outside. They
jump up and down on their beds like wild, jungle animals. Lisa sits
and watches, transfixed with awe, confusion, terror, and revulsion; no
longer able to recognize this world she sees on the television screen as
her own.

*"You can have my isolation, You can have the hate that it
brings. . . You can have my absence of faith. . . You can have my
everything. . .*

*"Help me— you tear down my reason. . . Help me— your sex I
can smell. . . Help me— you make me perfect. . . Help me become
somebody else. . .*

*"I wanna fuck you like an animal. . . I wanna feel you from the
inside. . . I wanna fuck you like an animal. . . My whole existence is
flawed.*

"You. Get. Me closer to God."

Now some young producer-type is shouting instructions to
Tommy and Star, directing them to where they have to be for the next
segment, but Tommy can't hear him. Won't hear him. He doesn't need
to hear him now, because after twenty-five years, Thomas Peter
Redivo's only living son is finally free. Lisa, his sisters, Star, Will,
Kate. . . they all feel their hearts stop as they see him run out on to the
stage. All of them can only watch, breathless, as he flings himself into
the crowd.

Hoisted up on a sea of hands, Tommy arches back his head and
peers up at the night sky, only to be greeted by the darkness and the
rain. The darkness bodes death— but not his own. This beautiful
darkness signals the death of decadence, of hypocrisy, of infirmity.
Only strength, honor and truth will remain. And the rain? Every drop

232

is a tear of joy, shed by his father, falling down upon him from heaven, above.

With a grinch's grin, he thrusts both fists defiantly into the air, with the crowd responding in kind. It is a portrait that will endure forever. Immortality is his. Destiny's bastard, fate's mistake, Tommy Redivo now stands lord of all he surveys. The mass of people, his subjects, roar in adulation as they pass him along a circular path atop the great mud-pit. At last, he has grabbed hold of that hand of time that once held him in its withered grasp and shattered its wrist like twine.

CHAPTER XV

I'm supposed to be taking a test right now, but in my mind I'm still there, at Woodstock. Friday, with Tom kicking it off was incredible, and from there it just grew and grew, right up until the apex Saturday night with Nine Inch Nails. After that, the crowd still managed to go crazy over Metallica, and than Aerosmith also did a cool set. . . but personally, I couldn't get into any of it. I was totally benumbed the rest of the night, once Trent left the stage.

Sunday morning came quickly, and with it another Tom-performance— this time on the smaller south stage, doing a raw and rousing rendition of Creedence's "Who'll Stop the Rain?" After that, me and Kate got together with Shag, Barb, Keith & Tam and smoked some weed for breakfast— by the afternoon, Shag and Bar were really wasted. Keith found a Reverend on the site and we almost got the two of them hitched, but the prospect of marriage managed to sober Shag up in a hurry. Shit, I still have to laugh when I think about this. Then we threw clumps of grass and mud at Green Day (the best set of the day), then watched the Chili Peppers and Peter Gabriel close out the weekend; at that point, alot of people had already left, trying to get a head start goin' home.

BACK TO THE GARDEN

We decided to stay camped out in Saugerties through Monday morning though, and it's a good thing, too— I heard later that the shuttle buses were delayed by as much as ten hours Sunday night. Driving home early that afternoon, Kate and me were still pretty worked up over the whole weekend, even by then. We were grabbin' each other's crotches nearly the whole way and almost swerved off the road a few times. Finally, we pulled over and found a cluster of trees where we tore our clothes off and fucked like a couple of horny rabbits.

It sure was one hell of a weekend.

The one thing that pissed me off was having to read all the newspaper articles and watch all the newscasts once we got back. All of them droned on and on about how all the kids there were so desperate to re-create the first Woodstock and how much we all wanted to be hippies. . . The dumb fucks don't even get that we were making *fun* of them. Christ. Are they total idiots or just completely blinded by their own love for themselves?

"Pencils down, blue books in."

I'm the last person to get to the professor's desk.

"Will there be any make-ups for this?"

He looks back at me, sternly.

"No make-ups."

I step out of Brady Hall and into the sunlight, thinking to myself about what I have to do. I took on just three classes last semester, and only four the one before 'cause I hadn't saved up enough tui-tion— it was my hope that I could make all of it up later, but now my schedule is stacked and I'm spreading myself way too thin. I'm definitely gonna have to drop a class to save my g.p.a. I guess I've known this for awhile, but was hoping another solution would somehow present itself. . . I haven't broken it to my old man yet, but I'm never gonna graduate by the spring.

I wonder about how I'm going to tell him while I make my way to the student lounge— or as I've come to call it, the "poseur lounge." Tom and Star's show is on between four and five, but they've got the channel on here 24-7 just on the off-chance Tom's name gets dropped during any of the other twenty-three hours during the day. I swear, the guy is an absolute god on this campus. . .

"I heard he flipped at the Video Awards show a couple weeks back when Roseanne pointed out her kids in the audience and said, 'those are mine, I made those, thank you.' You know how shit like that drives him nuts— parents talkin' about their kids like property an' shit."

This coming from a guy who Tom *maybe* spoke two words to in his life. Maybe.

"My parents haven't been the same since they saw those clips of him on the news; they're afraid to say two words to me, now."

Yeah, too bad. They're missing out on some really scintillating conversation, I'm sure.

"Tell me about it— I was wearing a 'kill-your-parents' shirt yesterday and I don't think my Mom said more than two words to me all day! Ha! They were probably crappin' their pants!"

Oh, sure— this guy gets it.

"You hear him on the show yesterday, though?" asks some long-haired loser in a beat-up Dokken T-shirt. "Where does he get off trashin' Metallica? Metallica blows Nirvana outta the fuckin' water, man! If he were here, I'd set him straight!"

Right. If Tom *were* here, he'd kick the livin' shit outta your heavy metal-cliché, over-moussed, hairsprayed, wannabe, *ass*, motherfucker. I swear, listening to these assholes makes me wanna hurl.

Still, I'm stickin' around anyway, in the hopes that I'll bump into Jeanine. We've been meeting here pretty regularly ever since the semester started, just to shoot the breeze; nothing heavy, just a little casual conversation. . .

Why do I feel guilty admitting this? I mean, it's not like I'm going to do anything with her— I just enjoy the attention she gives me, I guess. I'm totally committed to Kate, really, but. . . our relationship is in a very weird place right now. We finally got around to seeing *Pulp Fiction* this past weekend and it felt strange being out, just the two of us. It was just such a sedate evening; so painfully quiet. I kept wondering what Tom would say if he was there; or Courtney. I could almost hear Tom go off on one of his trademark discourses, explaining why *Fiction* was inferior to *Reservoir Dogs*. He'd be right, too.

After awhile, I give up on Jeanine. Back at home, in the hours before and after dinner, I watch one of the tapes of the Woodstock pay-per-view broadcast. There probably hasn't been a day since I got back that I haven't watched at least a little something from the tapes of that weekend. At the moment I've got Collective Soul on; recalling the feeling I had of singing along to that "whoa-oh" chorus with a quarter-million people. Reliving that moment is sweet, but I have a hard time watching the broadcast hosts, Tom and Star, practically drool on one another every time they're on camera. Just look at them— I can't help but wonder to myself how Courtney must feel when she sees this.

. . .Damn. This whole day's been a giant waste. I wish I could just roll over and go to sleep, but Tom and Star are scheduled to be on *The Tonight Show* and I can't resist staying up to see them. Eleven-thirty takes it's sweet time rolling around, but it eventually arrives. And after sitting through Jay's boring monologue and an even more boring interview with Leo Napolitano— Hollywood's flavor-of-the-month, hot young director— Tom and Star are finally out. Leo sticks around to panel with the two of them.

"I'm on t.v., therefore I am!" Tom stands up on the couch and shouts upon coming onstage.

"So tell us: what were you thinking when you jumped into that crowd?" Jay asks him, right off the bat.

"I was thinking, 'gee, I hope somebody catches me or else this is gonna be *really* embarrassing.' "

"I imagine things have been pretty hectic in the aftermath of the concert and all. Do either of you resent always having to share the spotlight together?"

"I know. It's almost as bad as being Siskel & Ebert."

"Well, in a way, your situation is even more extreme. Does it ever get to you? I mean, the two of you are in a very unique sit-uation, being the only Woodstock babies, after all."

"I don't buy into that," Tom says, sounding strangely conde-scending to my ears. "We're just two more accidental celebrities. The Woodstock-thing doesn't carry any special importance."

"We certainly can't complain, anyway," Star pontificates. "The guy I feel sorry for is the one born in the backseat at the Podunk drive-in back in '68 when the *Planet of the Apes* was playing— he can't get arrested in this town."

Tom laughs. Jay laughs. Everybody's laughing, except me.

I hate this. And I know I've flip-flopped on the issue about a million times now, but I can't help it. One minute I'm totally cool with Tom's new fame, even enjoying it— the next minute, it just feels so wrong to me that it makes me sick. As for Star, well, there's just something about her that rubs me the wrong way. I simply do not like the girl. Don't ask me why, I just. . . don't.

* * *

Tommy Redivo and Star Profeta lie together in her old bed in her grandparents house, listening to a scratchy LP of "The Best of Bread" play over and over again on her old, fold-up victrola.

"This was your Mom's old room?" Tom asks.

"Hers and mine, both."

"It's nice."

"Mmm." They both bask silently. It has been a long day.

It was only last night, they were at the NBC studios in Burbank, taping *The Tonight Show*. After the taping was through, there was a small tumult backstage when this young girl, who couldn't have been more than sixteen, was trying to get to Tom.

"Oh please," she kept begging, "if I could just touch him, touch his clothes, his shirt. . ."

"What's going on?" Tom asked after hearing the commotion.

"Nothin'," the security guy cracked. "Just got an overly enthusi-astic admirer is all."

"Let her go," Tom decreed. Much to Star's amazement, the se-curity complied.

"What's your name?" he asked her. "Where are you from?"

BACK TO THE GARDEN

"My name's Crystal, I'm from Iowa. I hitched all the way out here just to find you."

"What compelled you to come out all this way?"

"Because. . . you're the only person I ever saw on t.v. who tells the truth." She giggled a little, perhaps recognizing how crazy she sounded. ". . .Can I just please touch you?"

"Sure. It's a free country." She touched him gently, upon his chest.

"You're real," she said.

"As real as they get," he told her.

They caught the red-eye out of L.A. so they could reach Philly by morning. They stopped by the house first, where Tom was introduced to Star's grandparents. Next, it was off to the mayor's office for the obligatory photo-op. Then they swung by Star's old high school, where she gave a little speech to an assembly in the gymnasium and the school band butchered Earth, Wind & Fire's "Shining Star" in her honor.

They returned here to have dinner with Grandma and Grandpa, along with a few other select relatives. Tommy was his usual witty and enchanting self; charming the pants off the whole Profeta clan. They topped off the evening by sharing a quiet cup of coffee with just Grandma and Grandpa before retiring together. To her bedroom.

"I'm shocked, actually, that my grandparents didn't say a word about the sleeping arrangements, tonight." She gently strokes his face with the back of her hand. "Would Lisa ever let a girl sleep over with you?"

"Ah, Lisa probably wouldn't give a shit. But I'd never do it, anyway. You know, with my youngest sisters there an' all."

"You worry alot about your sisters, don't you?"

"There's no one and nothing else as important to me as them. 'Cept maybe you. . ." Acoustic guitar strings play between the pops and scratches coming through the victrola as they stare into one another's faces.

"Kiss me," she orders. He complies. They drink in the splendid deliciousness of one another's mouths; savoring it long after their lips are parted.

239

"Let's make a baby," she suggests out of the clear blue. "Gimme a baby, Tommy."

"Marry me, Kristine. Then I'll give you all the babies you want. And then some." He expects her to be totally flabbergasted by this proposition— much as he himself is— but she never even blinks.

"Gimme a baby an' I'll marry you," she counters.

"Marry me and I'll give you a baby."

"Don't you love me, Tommy?"

"Don't ask questions you already know the answer to."

"Then come on! Knock me up already!" They laugh and kiss again.

"I mean it, Kristine. Be my wife." He rolls on top of her completely now; pinning her like cat on mouse.

"I mean it too, Ace. Please— give me a baby." Her refusal only makes him love and want her all the more.

"Why won't you marry me, Kris?"

"I just know so many people who are married and miserable. Divorced and miserable, too. Marriage in this day and age means nothing, guarantees nothing, accomplishes nothing. So what's the point?"

He sighs. It is a catch-22: he could only marry someone who truly felt and understood, as he does, the terrible weight of the commitment that the institution demands. But anyone who truly does understand it will never take part in it.

"What am I going to do with you, Kristine?"

"I love that you call me 'Kristine'. . ."

"You know we were made for each other," he whispers. "Come on, baby. . . let's just elope."

"You propose to all your girlfriends like this?"

"Hardly," he responds with a short laugh.

"What about your last girlfriend?"

"I loved her alot. . . But we reached a point in our relationship where it just couldn't go any further. I realized we saw the world too differently."

"So why are you so ready to marry me?"

"You and I are cut from the same cloth. We both see things for what they really are; we don't kid ourselves. . ."

His words please her.

"Tom," she breathes.

"When I'm with you," he goes on, "it doesn't feel like there's ever been anyone else. It's like the first time again." He traces his finger around her mouth. "It's all new again with you, Kristine— like I never dreamed it could be. There are no ghosts here. . . no walls of any kind between us."

Her expression abruptly changes.

"What is it?" he asks. She sits up in the bed.

"I have to be honest with you, Tommy. There is at least one wall between us. One lie."

He remains lying back in the bed, arms folded across his chest, entirely unfazed.

"You weren't born at Woodstock," he tells her.

Stunned astonishment crashes through the floor of Star's brain, tumbling down into the pit of her stomach.

"How could you tell?"

"On a couple of the interviews we've done, I could see you getting tense— uneasy— whenever the questions got too specific."

Despite the fact they've only been together a short time, this is not the first time he has seemed to read her mind. . . Still, she is incredulous.

"God, how much longer until the rest of the world figures it out?"

"No one's ever going to know, Kris," he reassures. "The public would sooner believe I wasn't born at Woodstock."

"What makes you say that?"

"You just make a better Woodstock baby than I do. With the hippie name, all the circumstances surrounding your parents— it all cries out 'the sixties.' "

"Yeah," she somberly agrees. "Those wonderful, fun-loving sixties. . ."

"Your grandparents still haven't heard from her? Your Mom?"

"Tommy. . . my Mom died years ago. A Jane Doe on a slab in a morgue somewhere, in some backwater town. I came to grips with it a long time ago. If she was alive, we would've heard from her long before now— she would've come calling, looking to hit somebody up for money."

Her mother was a multiple drug offender. The last time she got caught, she jumped bail and split town— Star's grandparents had to take out a second mortgage on their house to pay for it. No one in the family has seen or heard from her since. Tommy has heard the story more than once before, but he's willing to listen to her tell it again if she needs to.

"My parents," she begins. "They were just so fucked up. The whole Woodstock thing started out as a joke in the family when I was little. . . Mom and Dad had taken off on one of their road trips earlier in the month, and when they got back a couple weeks later— bang, there I was. I mean, I guess it's possible I could've been born at Woodstock, how the hell could I ever be sure? My parents were probably so high at the time, I bet they didn't even realize I was being born until I was three-quarters out of the womb. It's a miracle I'm even alive today, Tommy. . ."

He reaches out and touches her shoulder as she begins to shake.

"My paternal grandparents would never even acknowledge me as their own," she breaks down and sobs. "They're right. . . God, Tommy, I can't even be sure who my real father is. . ."

"Shhhh," he hushes, pulling her in. He holds her tight, letting her warm tears stain his bare chest.

There have been many women Tommy Redivo has loved in his life, but this girl stirs something in him like no other has since Sheila. He feels what she feels and it hurts him. He wishes with all his heart he could make it go away, knowing full well that he cannot. So he will hold her for as long as she needs him to, because he loves her; loves her with an intensity that scares the hell out of him.

Never before has he been so happy to feel such fear.

CHAPTER XVI

"*I'll be along, son, with medicine supposed to, designed to make you high. . . I'll be along son, with words for a feeling and all I've discovered. . .*"

"*Old, bad eyes. . . Old, bad eyes. . .*"

"*Almighty fear. . .*"

I'm in the backseat of Tom's Camaro and I'm more than a little terrified. Why? Because Frankie is behind the wheel. She's got her learner's permit and Tom is giving her a driving lesson. They've got Live turned all the way up on the stereo while performing "Pillar of Davidson" in stichomythia fashion together, for my listening pleasure.

"*The shepherd won't leave me alone. . .he's in my face and I. . . The shepherd of my days. . . And I want you here, by my heart. . . and my head, I can't start. . . 'till I'm dead. . . Shep-heeerrrrrd!*"

"*Here I am walking home through this valley and failing to hold my head up I go back again. . .*"

Tom's been back and forth from the west coast a number of times over the last six months, but I haven't had much opportunity to really talk to him— today is proving no different.

"How am I doing?" Frankie asks.

"Great!" Tom assures, turning the volume down. "But we better head back to the house."

"I can't believe I'm behind the wheel of this car!"

"You like this car? Like how it rides?"

"Yeah! Are you kidding?"

"Would you be interested in the Camaro, Frankie?"

"You mean to have?" she asks, gushing with both shock and joy.

"Sure."

"Oh my God!" She almost goes off the road.

"Watch it!" Tom chides.

"Are you really, *really* serious?"

"Well, it's not like I have much chance to use it myself right now. And it's got too much sentimental value for me to sell it. I'd rather keep it in the family if I could."

"This is so awesome!" she squeals.

We pull into the driveway of Tom's house and Frankie immediately bolts from the car up the front porch.

"You're really giving her the car?" I ask.

"Sure, why not? See how happy she is?" Tom glances over at the handful of onlookers across the street. "Come on— let's get inside."

The whole family is gathered in the living room when we enter. The twins have their softball uniforms on and Frankie's got Lisa in a bear hug.

"Please say it's okay, Mom?" she pleads. "Please, please?"

"What's this about the Camaro?" Lisa questions.

"Hey Ace," Star greets. She slithers her arms around Tom and gives him a big, wet kiss. "I missed you."

"I've only been gone a half-hour."

"Yeah, but you know I break out in a rash whenever we're apart more than ten minutes." Only now does she appear to notice me. "Hey ya, Willie— how's it hangin'?"

Willie. I hate being called "Willie." Back in grade school they'd call me 'Chilly Willy' all the time and I could never stand it.

"I'm doin' okay," I tell her.

"Tommy?" Lisa insists. "The car?"

"What about it?"

244

"I'm not sure I'm comfortable with her driving that car. . ."

"Aw, Mom," Frankie whines. The phone rings in the kitchen and George leaves to answer it.

"What's the big deal?" Tom asks.

"It's a big responsibility, taking care of a car. I'm not sure she's ready for it."

"Neither am I," Meredith chimes in.

"Yeah," the twins agree.

"Mom!" Frankie exclaims, her face brimming with anguish. Tom laughs.

"She doesn't even have her license yet— just take awhile and think about it."

Lisa sighs. "Alright, we'll discuss it another time, then. I've got to get these two to their game, anyway."

"And we've gotta get into the city for Letterman, too," Star adds.

"Who else is on with you tonight?" Meredith asks.

"I don't know. You remember, sweetie?"

"No, I don't, actually," Tom admits. "Guess it can't be anyone good then, or I'd have remembered. . . Did I tell you about the call I got from Paul Shaffer?"

"No," Meredith responds. "What was that about?"

"This was last week. He wanted to know what song I wanted him to play when we come out tonight."

"And?"

"And I told him to play 'Unity' by Op Ivy. If he can pull it off, I'll be quite impressed."

"Lisa?" George calls from the kitchen. Lisa goes to see what he wants.

"This kid at school said he read on the internet that you were on the last Pearl Jam album," Frankie says— I heard this same rumor myself. "He said you did the voice of the little girl on that really weird last song on *Vitalogy*. He said they put your voice through a synthesizer or something. . . is it really true?"

"Trade secrets, Frank," Tom answers. "I'm afraid I can't divulge that information."

"That's a 'yes,' " Meredith adds.

"How about the guys from Live?" Frankie grills. "Have you ever met them?"

"Sure, we've met 'em," Star responds.

"Introduce me, introduce me!"

"Supposedly, they're going to be passing through here in the fall," Tom says with a smile. "I don't know if they'll be the Meadowlands or where, but I'll tell you what: when they come around, I'll take you to see them. We'll go backstage and everything."

"Aieeee!" Frankie screams.

"Take me, too!" Tiffany shouts.

"And me!" Samantha adds.

"Oh, shut up," Frankie tells them. "You don't even like Live."

"Do so!" Samantha protests.

"Um, Ace?" Star jumps in. "We don't wanna keep Letterman waiting."

"I know, I know." He kisses each of the girls and shakes my hand. "Hey Mom! I'm leaving now!"

"You are?" Lisa asks as she and George re-enter the room. "Well, take care, okay?" She hugs him.

"Who was that on the phone?"

"That was the asphalt guy," George says.

"Asphalt guy?"

"Yeah. We're gonna get the driveway touched up."

"Oh? What exactly do you mean by, 'touching up'?"

"You know— re-pave it and extend it over the lawn a little more so it's even."

"I see," Tom says in a suddenly cool tone. "Girls, why don't you wait for Mom in the car? I just remembered I have to talk to her about something. . . Kris, you may as well wait in the limo. . ."

"Alright, Ace," Star answers. "Just don't take too long, now." She walks out with the twins, both looking annoyed at being excluded from yet another conversation.

"What's the problem?" George asks once they've left.

"No problem," Tom tells him. "Just call the asphalt-guy and tell him you need to re-schedule."

"Why?" Lisa asks.

246

"Because we need to discuss this in-depth before anything gets done."

"What is there to discuss?" George questions, getting a little angry.

"First of all, you're not paving over a single inch of the lawn. My sisters play on that lawn; my dog plays on that lawn."

George is indignant. "What the hell gives you the right. . ."

"What gives me the right?" Tom interrupts. "I think you're forgetting, George: you no longer own this house— I do. And as long as you live under my roof, you'll live by my rules."

His rules? Sweet holy shit, am I ever glad I'm here to witness this!

"Well, maybe we'll just move out of *your* house, then!"

Tom smirks at this.

"That's certainly your prerogative, George. Where do you plan on going? Across the street? Over the next block?"

"I can go wherever I damn-well please!"

"Oh, I don't think so," Tom corrects him. "Is that what you want, Lees? You want to move to another town? Put the twins in a new school? Do the same to Frankie, with her senior year comin' up?"

The debate screeches to an immediate halt as we all wait on the edge of our seats for Lisa's response. She looks at George with inimical eyes.

"I better get the twins to their game," is all she says.

"Lisa," George softly appeals as she walks out; gently closing the door behind her.

"Hmm," Tom muses, looking at his watch. "Time's running out, George." He's grinning the biggest grin I've ever seen on a human being while George stands there with the vein in his forehead visibly throbbing. Then Tom's expression suddenly stiffens.

"I told you old man," he declares in a low growl. "I told you I'd win."

I take a moment to imagine myself in Tom's position with my own father. . . imagining what it would feel like, after all these long years, to finally throw back all the shit my old man has ever dumped on me, throw it all back in his face and tell him to fucking shove it. The fantasy of it alone is positively intoxicating; I can't imagine how it must feel for Tom to actually be *living* it. God, am I jealous.

Forget George. Beneath Tom's iron gaze and gravel pit voice, he melts completely; before all our eyes. He slinks out of the room, a broken man.

"Congrats, bro," Merry declares. "The king is dead; long live the king."

"Cookie, I've always been the king around here. . . it just took awhile for some of you to figure that out."

"So I'll definitely be getting the car, then?" Frankie asks. Tom laughs.

"God, I love you," he proclaims as he plants a big kiss on top of her head. "So where's my dog?"

"She's in the backyard," Meredith tells him.

"You're taking her with you?" Frankie questions.

"Hey, I left her here last time."

"Aw, c'mon. . ."

"Oh, stop— I'll be back here with her next week." A horn honks outside. "Alright, I better go. See you next week, girls. . . Sorry I didn't have more time for you, Will."

"Yeah," I say, not hiding my disappointment very well. "Hello" and "goodbye" are the only words the two of us seem to exchange these days.

Tom quickly exits, shutting the door behind him as he leaves with a modest click. Meredith slides down on the floor next to the television cabinet, alongside one of the many now-dying plants currently abundant around here.

"That was so cool!" Frankie declares.

"How about him an' Star?" Meredith asks, semi-rhetorically. "I don't think I've seen him like this with a girl since he was in high school. . . Frankie, I do believe our brother is in l-u-v, LOVE!"

"Do you think they'll get married?" Frankie asks, ecstatic.

"Shh! Don't jinx it!"

"Oooh, I'm gonna get to be in a wedding party!"

Bleh. Somebody get me an air-sickness bag, please.

"Yep. This one's definitely got a chance to stick."

"Star would be such a *totally* cool sister-in-law!"

Right. About one-zillionth as cool as Courtney, maybe.

"Well, I guess I better get going," I say. "I'm supposed to meet Kate. Can you do me a favor? Tell Tom to gimme a ring next week, if he's got the time?"

"No prob. I'll let him know."

I jog out to my car. I need to get a move on, 'cause I'm running late, though I don't think I could've stomached much more of that conversation even if I wasn't. I hop in and drive quickly home— my head still spinning from all I've seen and heard this afternoon. When I pull into my backyard, I find Kate's car occupying my usual spot.

"Kate is upstairs," the old man informs me as I pass through the kitchen. Gee, tell me something I don't know, Pop.

"Where were you?" Kate asks me as I enter my room. "You're twenty minutes late— I got off work early for you and everything."

"I was over at Tom's."

"Tom is home?" she asks with sudden excitement. "Shit! What's he doing home? Is he still here? Why didn't you tell me you were on your way over to see him?"

"I didn't know he would be there— I just thought I'd call and touch base with Lisa to see if she knew what he was up to. He picked up the phone and asked me if I wanted to tag along while he gave Frankie a little driving lesson."

"Well, what's he doing here? Is he going to stick around awhile this time?"

"No," I say, taking my jacket off and tossing it on to the bed next to hers. "He's already left. He's taping Letterman with Star between 5:30 and 6."

"Damn! I really wanted to see him!" Christ, she sounds practically wet over this. "Feels like a dog's age since I saw him in the flesh."

"You're as bad as everyone else, you know that?"

"What? What do you mean?"

"You know 'what.' You're totally star-struck."

"Oh, I am *not*. . . Don't go mental on me, Will"

"Jesus," I say. "You can't even see yourself, can you?"

"Excuse me. Tom is one of my best friends. I haven't seen him in a while and I would've enjoyed seeing him today— is that so strange?"

I'm not answering her because it's just sinking in now, the way her expression changed so dramatically at the mention of Tom's name when I first came in. Yeah. . . What the hell was that, anyway?

"Did you ever fuck Tom?"

She's completely shocked, but I can't tell if it's because I touched on something or if it's that she just finds the question so absurd she can't believe I was stupid enough to ask it.

"I think you *are* mental!" she tells me, after finally managing to compose herself.

"You still haven't answered the question." Of course, I can already tell what the answer is and whoo boy, do I ever feel like an ass for asking, but I'm too far down this road to turn back now.

"Who the hell do you think you are? You think you're only one who has the right to be his friend? The only one who's allowed to miss him? Do I need to remind you which of us has known him longer?" This line really pisses me off, for some reason.

"Just 'cause you've known him longer, doesn't mean you know him better."

"Shit, I didn't know it was a contest with you. Why are you wasting your time talking to me, then? Why don't you just ask Tom if we ever fucked, since the two of you are so tight?"

You know, that nose of hers that I once found so irresistibly sexy is becoming more and more reminiscent of the wicked witch of the west, lately.

"*I'm* making it a contest, Kate? You're the one who turns every conversation we have into a fucking debate, not me."

"Come to think of it, why the hell am I even arguing with you about this? Like it's any of your business *what* I did before we started going out."

"Alright, fuck it then, Kate. . . Whatever, okay?"

Another one of those long, tense silences follow; each of us waiting for the other to break it.

BACK TO THE GARDEN

"I think I should go," she says at last, throwing her jacket on. "I'll call you tomorrow. Maybe."

She exits in a huff while I'm standing with my hands on my hips. I know I should yell for her to stop, apologize to her, tell her how stupid I am and how embarrassed I feel about the ridiculous things I've said. But another part of me resents her for always being so fucking right all the damn time. Ultimately, I know I'm going to end up doing absolutely nothing.

Outside my bedroom window I can hear the sound of her car starting up and then pulling out, down the driveway.

. . .

Fuck me.

CHAPTER XVII

Tommy Redivo and Star Profeta are back from their meeting with the network execs.

"Kris? Honey?"

She proceeds on into the kitchen without answering him. She's still mad. The whole ride back in the limo, she didn't speak a word to him. It reminded him of that old Bugs Bunny cartoon:

Would you like to shoot him now or wait 'til you get home?

. . .'Til you get home, evidently.

"How long you plan on bein' mad?" he shouts out to her.

"I'm not mad," she insists; her voice raised but calm.

Tommy circles back around the living room couch in their luxury apartment and sits down. Tempest quietly creeps out of their bedroom, yawning and stretching as she approaches. Her tail wags as she looks up at him. He reaches down and pets her shoulders as she rests her chin on his knee.

The meeting was like nearly every other they've had in the last nine months— a disaster. The producer started off with the usual complaints over how he refuses to hype the lame-ass videos they force him to play. Tommy shot back that if they wanted him to show a little more genuine enthusiasm about the videos, they should allow him at least *some* input over what gets put in rotation. They went back and forth over this for awhile, then the movie-thing came up. Again. They still persist in badgering him for an explanation as to why he refuses to make the film— "because I read the script and I think it sucks," is not a satisfactory answer, apparently. What makes it worse is that Star has her heart set on the project, but the execs insist that they both agree to it or it's no go.

Divide and conquer. Not a bad plan. Seems to be working at the moment, anyway.

"Kris?"

". . .Yes?"

"Can you come out here? Please?" A moment later, she steps out of the kitchen, into the living room.

"I think we need to talk about why you're so upset."

"I'm not upset. What's to be upset about?"

"C'mon, sweetheart," he sighs, "this isn't us. We talk things out. Honestly. We don't play silly games like this."

"Alright," she begins. "I think you're being a short-sighted, stubborn jackass over this whole movie deal. Honest enough?"

He looks at her. "Well, I guess I asked for it, didn't I?"

She begins to feel guilty, now. She sits down next to him and takes hold of his hand.

"Come on, Tom. We're talking about a *movie*, here— haven't you ever dreamed about being in a movie?"

"I'd like to be in a good movie, Kris. And this script couldn't suck more if it had rubber lips. I refuse to make one of those shitty Pauly Shore-type movies that's in and out of the theaters in one day."

"So we get a re-write, okay? In the end, you know they'll give us what we want. . . whaddaya think, they're gonna let you and me slip through their fingers? We're the hottest thing goin'!"

"Be careful, Kristine. The shelf life of a veejay is comparable to the fruit fly, y'know."

"But we're different, Ace, we've got a hook: we're the Woodstock babies— an extremely limited commodity. They're not going to find any more of us."

253

Tommy Redivo goes quiet for a moment. They both know she wasn't really born at Woodstock; yet even here, alone together, she persists in the lie.

"The anniversary concert was last year, Kris. And the public has a notoriously short memory. We can't live off Woodstock the rest of our lives."

"Maybe not, but there's still enough blood in that rock to last us awhile, yet." He shakes his head. "Come on— let's *do* this."

"The script had singing-fucking-cockroaches in it. One simple rule I live by: if it's got singing cockroaches in it— and Kafka didn't write it— it's gotta suck. No re-write could salvage it."

"Alright, so it's not Shakespeare," she concedes. "It's a light-hearted vehicle, it's supposed to be fun."

"You know I've been talking to Leo about doin' a project. We've been e-mailing back and forth for a while; practically have a whole script written. . ."

"Tommy, you're talking about a super-low budget, limited release, art film. What we've been pitched is giant, high-profile, big budget Hollywood movie. With a big premiere night, all the stars and execs, the red carpet. . . all of it!"

"I'd rather be good than big. . ."

"And with the added promotion the network's gonna provide, this thing is gonna do *huge* box office."

"If we take our film to Sundance in January, get a distributor, we could make a nice piece of money ourselves, Kristine."

Star Profeta slumps back in her seat. She rubs her forehead and breathes out.

"Ace, I'm beginning to worry about you. . ."

"Why do you say that?"

"I think you're getting some bad advice." He laughs. "Seriously sweetie, we really need to be on the same page with these issues— present a united front. Things would run alot smoother if we had the same guy representing both of us."

"I like my agent. He takes his ten percent, keeps his mouth shut and stays out of my way."

254

"That's the whole thing. I think you need someone who's gonna push you in the right direction a little more. . ."

He looks back at her with surprise.

"I'm not exactly the type of guy who takes to being 'pushed,' Kris. If you don't recognize that about me, well. . ."

They both fall speechless. Looking away from each other, they nervously fidget for what seems an eternity.

"I hate this," Star says at last.

"I know," he agrees.

"What are we going to do about it?" He looks at her, lovingly.

"How 'bout from now on we leave business on the other side of that door, hmm?" She smiles, taking his face in her hands.

"Good idea." She draws him in and they share a sweet, slow kiss. Tempest growls at them.

"Jesus! You couldn't have left her back in Jersey last week?"

"Don't take it personally," he consoles her. "She always disapproves of my girlfriends." With one exception, of course.

"Well, she better get used to me— 'cause I'm not goin' *anywhere*." She climbs on top of him and they kiss again.

"God," he complains, "it feels like forever since I've made love to you, y'know that?"

"Yeah," she softly concurs, "we've definitely been neglecting each other. We've dwindled down to what? Twice a day, now?" He grins.

"I know," she says with a hint of mischief. "Why don't I draw us a nice, warm bath, hmmm? Put on a little Prince. . ."

"*Do me baby*," he whispers. She gets up off of him.

"Well? You care to join me?"

"In a minute. Go ahead— I'll put the stereo on."

"Don't keep me waiting, Ace."

She disappears into the bathroom. Tommy Redivo sits there and thinks to himself. Tempest looks up at him and whines.

"And what's your problem?"

"Rrrrr," she warbles back at him. He reaches down and scratches behind her ear.

"I know girl," he tells her. "I know."

CHAPTER XVIII

"There he is: Captain Woodstock. Lookatcha! Yeah, get those headphones on."

It's the Howard Stern show and Tom is on.

"Good morning, Howard," Tom greets. "Morning, Robin. Jackie. Billy. Fred. . ."

"Forget them."

". . . Jackie-puppet. . ."

"Hey, where's Star?" Howard asks. "Ta-Ta-Toothy, get in here. . . Didn't you tell me she was booked?"

"Don't get on Gary. She was supposed to come."

"Well what happened?"

"Um. . . well, let's just say she's not a morning person."

"Oh, come *on*. Are you puttin' me on?"

"Sorry, Howard. I know how disappointed you must be."

"No offense dude, but she was the one I was really lookin' forward to meeting, y'know?" Tom laughs.

"I know, I know."

"So where is she now?"

"I left her still in bed, back at the hotel."

"Still in bed. You give her a workout last night, huh pal?" Jackie offers one of his evil chuckles: *heh-heh-heh*. I can feel Tom's grin right through the radio. "Right or wrong?"

"I plead da fifth," Tom says, in his best O.J. voice.

I'm on my way to school for add-drop— it's this three day period a couple weeks before the start of the semester where you resolve scheduling conflicts for the upcoming term. It's Thursday, August 17th— Tom's birthday— and he's in town for this big birthday party Lisa's throwing for him back at the house. As far as I know, it's the first birthday party she's thrown for him since 1987.

Draw your own conclusions.

"Come on— let's call her!" Howard exhorts.

"Sure. Wake her ass up, I don't care."

Howard dials. The phone ring once. Twice.

"Hello?" a drowsy voice asks.

"Hey baby," Howard salutes.

"Hi, Howard," Star coos.

"You are one hot little minky, y'know that? What are you, still in bed?"

"Mmm, yeah."

"What are you wearin'?"

I turn off the radio in disgust. Christ— I don't wanna hear that shit. Star is already too big a phony for me to stomach without having to hear her put on some lame sex-kitten act.

I give it ten, fifteen minutes, then turn it back on. Thankfully, she's off the phone.

"So was your mom really a hippie?" Howard asks.

"I guess you could say she had a little flower child-phase, there. I wouldn't call her a hippie though— she's no Jackie Marlo."

"I bet she was into free love, huh? She ever throw any orgies?"

"Ooooooh," Fred moans in his best Jackie-voice. Billy follows suit.

"Constantly," Tom answers. "Every day, she was sending me to the store for more grapes."

Tom must be going over well, because Howard invites him to stick around and sit in on the news. Robin's first story is the O.J. trial (what else?), followed up by Dr. Kervorkian— at which point it's getting dangerously close to my appointment time and I can no longer tarry here, sitting in my car in the parking lot, listening to the radio. Getting to the basement of the student center annex, the line is already more than a hundred people deep.

"Is this the end of the line?" I ask.

"Naw, it's the front an' we're all standin' backward."

Great. A comedian. I file in behind him.

Don't let the long line give you the wrong impression— my appointment card says 10:30 and it is exactly 10:27, so I'm actually on time. This is just the way add-drop goes, unfortunately. I stand and twiddle my thumbs for a good half-hour, wishing I had brought my walkman with me, until suddenly I feel a hand on my shoulder.

"Hey, you." I turn.

"Courtney!" We hug. "Good to see you!"

"You too." I've waved at her from across campus a couple of times in the past year, but this is the first real conversation we've had since the big break-up.

"You're here to schedule, huh?" I ask like a moron.

"Yeah," she responds.

"So what time's your appointment?"

"11:15. So I guess they'll get to me by around 3, right?"

"Yeah, tell me about it."

"Well. . . As long as we don't get railroaded into one of Professor Bloom's boring seminar courses it'll be a good day, right?"

"Right! Right. . ."

God, just look at her— what a sumptuous beauty. How did Tom ever walk away from *this*? I'll just never understand it.

"So. . . you goin' to Tom's party tonight?" I can't think of anything else to ask.

"Um, no," she answers.

"Weren't you invited?"

"Sure. Meredith called me but. . . I dunno. I know it's been awhile, but it would still feel too weird, y'know?"

"Yeah. I understand." We both start looking around for something. She rubs the back of her neck; I put my hands in my pockets.

"Well, I better go," she thankfully excuses herself. "People'll start thinking I'm trying to jump the line."

"Yeah," I agree. "I guess I'll see you around."

"Yeah. Good to see you."

"You too." I watch her walk away.

Man, was that ever tense. After years of hangin' together, you'd expect us to have an easier time talking to each other than that. I turn back around and the comedian is lookin' me up and down, like he can't figure why a goddess like Courtney would be talkin' to a guy like me.

"Take a picture," I advise him, "it'll last longer."

It's 1:30 by the time I get out of the annex. When I get home, there's a message to call Kate at her house— so I do.

"How come you're not at work?" I ask, right off the bat.

"I took a personal."

"A whole day? Just for the party, tonight?"

"Like I would've gotten any work done today, anyway. . . Look, I can be there in an hour and we can go over to Tom's together."

"You wanna go over there this afternoon?"

"Sure!"

"That's crazy!"

"What's crazy about it?"

"It's two o'clock and Tom won't even be there for another five hours!"

"So we'll hang out with Meredith and Shaggy and Barb and. . ."

"No *way!*" I protest. "The whole family's getting ready for this big party and we're all gonna be hangin' out in the middle of it all, just waiting for them to trip over us? No-no-no."

I get strained quiet from the other end of the line.

"Fine," she finally concedes

"You could still come over now. We could have dinner with my folks and go over Tom's after."

"Oh, joy. That'll be fun, I'm sure."

Kate and I eat dinner with Mom and Dad; the two of us managing to stomach my mother's meatloaf along with Dad's mindless chit-chat. Around 5:30, we've finished eating and Kate is now twice as hot to

259

get over to Tom's. Somehow, I convince her to give it another hour. We pass the time in front of the television, not sharing much in the way of conversation— which isn't surprising, since lately we seem to be talking less and less.

By 6:30 I can no longer hold her back. Together, we take my car to Shepherd Terrace, only to discover the police have the street cordoned off. We end up having to park two blocks over and walk. . . Christ. It probably would've been easier forgetting the car and just walking here directly from my house.

"Toldja we should've come over this afternoon," Kate nags.

Already there's a crowd of people filling the front lawn, the driveway and what appears to be most of the backyard; a handful are scattered in the street, even. It takes us awhile to fight through the mass of humanity up the front porch and inside.

"Hey!" Tamara waves from the living room. Kate and I wriggle our way inbetween the herd of bodies to get to her. Keith, Greg, and Meredith are all here too— among others I don't recognize.

"Where've you been?" Tam asks. Kate glowers at me.

"What's with the street bein' blocked off?" I ask.

"There were so many people coming, we turned it into a block party," Meredith reveals. "Of course, that meant having to invite all the neighbors too, making the already-huge guest list immense."

"Hello," this guy next to Meredith greets as he extends a hand.

"Oh!" Meredith exclaims. "Will, Kate— this is my father, Joe, his wife, Cindy, and my baby brother, Dan."

"Good to meet you." We all shake.

"I better get used to this— looks like I'll be making introductions all night!"

"God! Where do they all these people come from?" Kate questions.

"Please," Meredith responds. "From every corner of the globe, it feels like. We pulled out all the stops planning this— we've got all his old grade school friends from Riverview and Northfield; then the ones from Maple Grove, Carver. . ."

"The place is so packed you'd think the Pope was coming," Greg cracks.

"I think the Pope answers to Tom," Keith snaps back.

"They're pulling up!" someone shrieks.

The herd converges on the front door. It takes me a good five minutes to get through. Outside, Tom and Star are just getting out of their police escorted limo. People swarm around and I battle my way over to them. He's in the midst of hugging Kate when I'm finally close enough to greet him.

"Will!" he shouts, shaking my hand over several heads that separate us. I wait until he finishes addressing the rest of the college contingent— Keith, Tam, and Greg, amid others— then try to muscle in closer.

"Hey, Pizza-boy!" It's Nina. She hugs him.

I'm about to tell Tom how good it is to see him when another girl— Simone, whose name I heard Kate drop once— grabs him from behind. After her, there's a continuing parade of delicious beauties, all heretofore unknown to me: Vanessa, Rachel, Irene, Sabrina, Kirsten. . .

"Tommy!" shouts another— this one a hot, leggy blonde with a vaguely familiar face. She grabs hold of him and gives him a healthy smooch. The twins stand behind her, smiling.

"Ronnie! How long's it been?"

"Oh, too long!"

Star clears her throat.

"Tommy?" she asks with the lilt of a jealous girlfriend.

"Oh, I'm sorry, hon— this is Veronica Hauer, the twins' older sister!"

They exchange pleasantries. Then the twins' father, Steve, steps up to shake Tom's hand. Then Frankie and her father, Mike. Tom continues ever so slowly up the driveway, into the backyard, and I try to stay with him as he makes his way through the throng.

"Gene!" Tom exclaims as he embraces this square-looking, thirty-something guy. "How'd you hear about this?"

"Kathy called me— hey, it's great to see you!"

"Has Lisa seen you? Hey, Ma!" He looks around and notices me. "Oh, Will— this is the guy who got me started playing D&D!"

"Hi," I say.

"Yeah, I was in grad school and had just started dating Lisa and it was the big, new fad. Tom picked up on the rules like that," he says, snapping his fingers. "Just by watching the rest of us. You could see the kid was a prodigy!"

Lisa barges in front of me as I'm just about to ask a question— so much for that conversation.

"Gene! I can't believe it!" She hugs him and he laughs.

"So where's the lucky guy who married you?" he asks. "You've got to introduce me!"

"Throw a dart into the crowd, Gene," Tom jests, "you're bound to hit one of 'em!"

Now that he brings it up, I notice George appears to be standing alone, on the opposite end of the yard.

"Oh, forget him," Lisa says— I don't know if she's referring to her son or her husband. "Why don't you fill me in on what you've been up to. . ."

"Hey, Tom!" someone yells. "Heard ya on Howard this morning! You were great, man!"

"Thanks!"

". . .Thomas Peter Junior!" It's Mick the cop.

"Hey! Who let in the fuzz?" Tom jokes.

The chief is followed by several other members of the Northfield High Class of 1970: Gus, Chuckie, Flash. . . I catch their names through snippets of conversation I overhear; not because Tom bothers to intriduce them to me. I continue standing back in the shadows, invisible and slowly stewing, as the procession goes on.

The Riverview friends. . .

"Tom, it's Joel! I was the kid who had every single *Planet of the Apes* doll!"

"Remember that *Action Jackson* playset?"

"Alright, I confess! I'm the one who threw your *Eagle Eye G.I. Joe* out the window!"

Northdale.

"What about the time Chet threw up in art?"

"I still can't believe you won the Pinewood Derby that year in Cub Scouts."

"Remember that big fight during the kickball game that time."

Maple Grove.

"How about that sixth grade class trip to Glen Springs?"

"Fuckin'-a, man! And the canoe tipped over!"

"How many times did we see *Return of the Jedi* together? Three? Four?"

. . .And Carver.

"Did you really tell the vice-principal to go to hell?"

"How many of Mr. C's classes did you and Shag actually *attend* that year?"

"Remember the 'Mats at Maxwell's?"

After about an hour of this, I've had enough.

I worm my way to the back door of the house and go inside. I go upstairs, up to Tom's old bedroom, and flop down on the bed. And I seethe.

Any minute now, he'll notice I'm missing— and boy, won't he feel like a jackass, then? Any minute, he'll come in looking for me, wanting to apologize for being so thoughtless and snubbing me like he has. I sit and listen to the throng mumble and laugh and generally carouse. I lie back and listen as they all sing "Happy Birthday." I listen to the ooh's and aah's of the gifts being opened.

At last, after almost two hours of lying here, I detect the sound of footsteps coming up the stairs. I sit up on the bed.

"Will?" Tom asks as he enters. "What're you doing, sitting here alone?"

"Nothing. . . Just sitting."

"Oh. . . Well, check out what Lisa and the girls got me." He shows me a framed copy of *Amazing Fantasy* #15— the first comic book appearance of Spider-Man and one of the holiest of grails for collectors. It's almost thirty-five years old and must've cost somewhere in the neighborhood of $10,000. Under different circumstances, I'd cream my pants.

"Obviously, Kristine or somebody had to advance them the money for it, 'cause Lisa and my sisters certainly could never afford it, but it was still their idea, I'm sure."

"It's nice."

"Yeah. I figured I'd leave it here; maybe put it up on this wall."
He seems to be waiting my approval of this proposal. I offer nothing.

"Is there something wrong, mud brother?" he asks, putting his gift
down and leaning on the bed frame.

"Is that what you came up here for?" I ask accusingly. "To leave
your gift here?"

"Uh. . . Yeah." I sit and burn while he offers me this smug look.
"Is there something up with you, Will?"

"So now you care all of a sudden? I guess I'm supposed to kiss
your ass now 'cause a big star like you has stooped to converse with a
peon like me?"

He's still doing it. The look.

"You know. . . Self-pity really doesn't become you, William."

"And you think that's what I'm doing? Pitying myself?"

"You're sitting up here for God knows how long, while there's a
party going on outside, just waiting for someone to find you and feel
sorry for you. . . Right or wrong?"

"Who are you to judge anybody?" I protest.

"I'm not judging you."

"You're nothin' but a Goddamn phony— I don't even know who
you really are anymore. I don't even *know* you." There's a scratch in
the vinyl of my brain and the needle is skipping. "I don't know you at
all."

"I'm sorry I couldn't give you my undivided attention tonight Will,
but there are people here I haven't seen in almost twenty years. . ."

"You think you're hot shit? You're an accidental celebrity; you're
Kato fuckin' Kaelin!"

I'm waiting for him to say something. I want him to snap back at
me; yell, scream. I need this argument. But he just keeps looking back
at me calmly, refusing to give me the satisfaction.

"Are you finished?" he asks rather indifferently.

Suddenly, I'm all out of smartass lines. I offer nothing as he turns
his back and walks out.

I spend the rest of the night in his room. I don't even come out to
say goodbye when he's leaving.

CHAPTER XIX

As dawn breaks this Sunday morning in the city of angels, Star Profeta awakens to find herself alone and afraid. It is the first day in over a year that has failed to begin in Tommy Redivo's arms. She sits up, looking left and right with no sight, no sound of him. She gets out of bed, anxiously hurries to the door. . . and is greatly relieved to discover him sitting in the living room. He's on the couch, already dressed, just finishing off his morning tea.

"You're certainly the early bird today," she notes.

The two of them have been back a few days now, and last night they shared what was perhaps the best sex they've ever had— which is to say, it was perhaps the best sex any two human beings have ever had.

"We could use a little sunlight in here, don'tcha think?" She glides over to the terrace door and begins to draw open the curtain, inadvertently tearing it.

"Shit!" she curses. "Must've gotten caught on something. . ." She glances over in his direction for some acknowledgment, but he just sits there, looking down in his cup.

"Better lose the five o' clock shadow, Ace," she says, rubbing playfully at his chin as she walks past him. "Probably gonna have to get the hair cut too, come to think of it."

"I don't think that'll be necessary," he answers with a strange tranquillity.

"What do you mean?" she asks, entering the kitchen.

"I mean I'm not going in today."

"Yeah, right!" she shouts.

"I mean it, Kris."

She steps out of the kitchen and back into the living room.

"What do you mean, you're not going in?"

"Just what I said: I'm not going in today. Or any day."

"Tommy. . . Stop kidding."

"I'm not kidding." He looks up at her at last. "I've decided to quit, Kristine."

She walks over slowly and sits down next to him.

"What are you telling me? What is this all about?"

"My deal with the network was for one year," he tells her. "They've been putting on the full press for me to re-up, but I guess I've known for awhile now that I wasn't going back. My agent just talked to Griff on Friday."

He waits for her to say something.

"And you kept this from me?"

"I didn't mean to. I really didn't. Maybe I was hoping my feelings would change, I don't know."

It is a shocking revelation. It takes several more seconds for her to fully absorb it.

"God, it'll be. . . weird working without you, I guess."

He pauses a moment, gathering himself.

"It's more than just the job. It's here; this whole place. I've. . . gotta leave. I'm going back east." Her eyes widen and her mouth drops open. "I've got a flight booked for early this afternoon."

She can't believe him. But as she looks into his eyes, she knows, incredible as it all sounds, he means it.

"You can't just walk out like this. . ." Her heart pounds as she experiences an odd kind of terror she has not known before. "This is crazy!"

"I wish there were an easier way, Kris."

"Why?" she asks, still reeling. "I mean. . . why are you doing this?"

"Alot of reasons. You know I'm not exactly a west coast-person. And the job has never been very fulfilling for me, creatively speaking. Most of all though, I just miss being with my family."

"And what about these last couple of days? You said your agent talked to Griff on Friday, I mean. . . why even make the flight back out here?"

He takes her hand in his.

"I needed these last couple of days alone with you. I'm sorry; maybe that was selfish of me, I don't know."

"Don't you love me?"

"I'm crazy in love with you," he reveals, holding her face. "More in love than I ever thought I could be, again. But our priorities have changed, I think. Or maybe they were never really the same."

"That's not true," she insists. His expression firms.

"You could always come with me. . . Would you do that? Would you come with me, Kristine?"

He already knows what the answer is. If he didn't, he would never have even started this conversation. Immediately, she knows what she wants to tell him. She begins to open her mouth.

"I. . ." is all that comes out. "I. . ."

She stops and looks down at the floor. His finger beneath her chin, he lifts her face back up.

"I. . . love you," she sputters at last; her voice cracking. It's the only thing she can say.

"I love you, too," he re-affirms, kissing her tear stained face.

He gets up and starts toward the closet door. He stops to look at her as he grasps the knob. And she at him.

The thoughts slowly begin to churn in her head: she will never see him again. She'll never touch him. Never taste those delicious morning kisses again. Time will pass, and eventually she will lose even the memory of him; leaving her with just a memory of a memory. Just a memory of a time in her life when she could precisely recall what his touch, his kiss, felt like.

Tommy Redivo calls for Tempest as he removes his overnight bag from the closet.

"I'll send for the rest of my things." He seems to hesitate a moment. "I wish you all the best, Kristine."

One thought keeps repeating itself in her mind: I can't lose him. I can't lose him. I can't lose him.

Yet she does nothing as he walks out the door.

CHAPTER XX

Okay. This is gonna sound really, really weird.

Yesterday afternoon I found a dead squirrel in my backyard. Now at first, I thought the thing just might be asleep— which is possible 'cause, I mean, they are nocturnal, right? I know hamsters and gerbils are, at least. Anyway, so I picked up this stick and poked at it, just to see. And suddenly this yellowjacket flew out of it's mouth and almost gave me a heart attack. There was no outward sign of how or why the thing was dead— not a mark, nothing. It wasn't crushed like roadkill, in case you were thinking some wiseguy might've found it in the street and tossed it over my fence as a sick joke. Nor was it torn up like it would be if a cat got it. . . It was like the thing just made up its mind to lie down and die in that particular spot.

Like I said: weird.

I'm driving home from school now, listening to Pearl Jam's "Immortality" on the car stereo and thinking about alot of different things. Like the future. School. My love life.

And of course, Tom.

Sometime around the last week in August, he bugged out like Fritz the Cat— walking away from Star, from the whole veejay gig.

With no warning, Star just appeared one afternoon in their regular time slot all by herself, introducing her stupid little videos and smiling like nothing was wrong. The rumors of his death began almost immediately, though this wasn't that unsettling at the time— after all, anytime somebody famous drops out of the public eye, black gossip like that always starts flying. It's American folklore— like that story about the Mikey-kid from the Life cereal commercials choking to death from putting too many Pop Rocks in his mouth.

Then this supermarket tabloid-rag ran an interview with this New York cab driver who claimed to have picked Tommy up this one night and dropped him off at the Brooklyn Bridge— the implication being that Tom went there for the purpose of jumping off. Now I know it's just some gossip sheet, not the *New York Times* or anything, but it's still got me freaking. I mean, there's been no real, concrete verification of the story; but at the same time, no one's really debunked it, either. And I'm just not sure what to believe. . .

Wait. Was that a black Camaro that just whizzed past?

Was that *the* black Camaro that just whizzed past?

I make a quick right into a side street to turn around. I follow the Camaro, sure enough, straight to Tom's house; pulling up right behind it. I'm shocked, however, by what I see stepping out of the driver's side door.

"Will?"

It's Frankie.

"God," I say, embarrassed. "I wasn't thinking; I just saw the car and. . ."

Waaaaaaait a minute. This isn't the Frankie I know— it's just hitting me now— the body, the legs. . . back at the party in August, she had these baggy-ass jeans on and I couldn't see it, but now she's wearing this mini-skirt and. . . whoa. And the hair— she's really let it grow out. Long, silky, jet-black hair to go along with the glowing bronze skin. . . How could I have failed to see it before now? I mean, could she really have blossomed like this overnight?

"Uh, have you gotten taller since I last saw you?"

"Probably," she laughs. "It *has* been awhile, y'know. . . So what? You thought I was Tom?"

"Yeah. Like I said, I didn't think." I rest my hands on my hips and look back and forth. "So, have you seen him?"

"Um. . . Not lately." Her hands find her jacket pockets. "Did you wanna come in?"

"Sure. That'd be great."

I follow her up the front porch, into the house. The light is on in the kitchen and I can hear the coffee pot going— someone's here.

"Hi, Will."

Meredith. And oh, is she lookin' fine. Still the champ for me, but man, is Frankie ever closin' that gap.

"Hey, Merry," I greet. Frankie leaves her pocketbook on the table and steps out.

"You timed it just right," Meredith informs me. "Coffee's just about ready. You want a cup?"

"What? No Yoo-hoo?"

"No, not since Tom's. . . gone." There's a tremor in Meredith's tone. It makes me wonder.

"Just kidding. I could really go for some coffee, actually." I sit down.

"How've you been?" she asks as she gets out a mug for me.

"Not too bad. And you?"

"I can't complain." She pours my coffee.

"How's your graduate work been going? You happy to be back in-state?"

"Oh, sure. It's alot easier; alot less running back and forth, y'know?" She takes a sip of her coffee.

"Lisa must be happy having you back at home."

"Mm. I suppose."

"How is she? And the twins?"

"They're fine— all fine."

"And George?"

She looks at me. "Frankie didn't tell you?"

"Tell me what?" I ask, intrigued.

"Lisa and George are separated. He just moved out a couple weeks ago."

"My God." And Tom's not even around to throw a party. "So where'd he go?"

"Supposedly he's moved in with his son and daughter-in-law. For the time being at least."

"Oh, man."

"Yeah, I know."

"Did you see it coming?"

"I wasn't sure," she admits. "Only because I thought Lisa might have finally sown all her oats, y'know? I mean, she was with him for long time, at least by her previous standards. I gotta give my brother credit, though— he had it called right."

"As usual," I say. I feel Sigmund rubbing up against my leg. I look down and he meows back at me. Meredith picks him up.

"Kitty misses Tempest, I think," she observes.

"Where is Tempest, anyway?"

"Wherever Tom is, Tempest is with him." I watch jealously as Sigmund cuddles up in her lap.

"And you don't know where that might be?" I question.

"No, I'm sorry to say," she responds without hesitation. "I only wish I knew."

"Were you surprised when he quit the video-thing?"

"Not really," she tells me as Frankie walks back in. She grabs the milk off the table, takes a glass from the cupboard and pours. "I mean, reading off a teleprompter, being a puppet— that's not Tom. I always figured it would be a temporary thing."

I start to feel a little bit stupid. Why couldn't I recognize this as easily as she did?

"I've gotta say, it's been strange, driving by the house, and knowing I can't just pop in and see him."

"Try living here," Frankie says, taking a swig of her milk.

"This whole year and a half has been strange, with him around, full-time," Meredith reveals. "And it's the smallest things that remind me of his absence, too— like late at night, when there's a spider in the bathtub and I go to get him and I remember he's not here."

"Yeah," Frankie concurs as she sits herself up on the counter. "Like his pancakes. I miss his pancakes."

"And the way he likes to eat his corn niblets with a spoon."

"And the way he ties his knots. He only knows how to make square ones, y'know."

"You guys are starting to sound like you don't expect to ever see him again," I say.

"When you live with someone every day," Meredith explains, "and one day they're suddenly not there, it's just. . . you just miss them."

Hmm. The way they're talking. . . I don't know if what I'm hearing in their voices is concern over Tom, or guilt over keeping something secret from me. . . But in any case, it's gotten very quiet in here. Tensely quiet.

I figure I better change the subject, so I decide to share a funny story about a recent mishap with the car, when I got this flat tire on 21 and discovered I had no spare. They, in turn, regale me with anecdotes of the twins first few weeks of junior high. The conversation continues in this more light-hearted vein another half-hour or so before I get up to leave.

"Good talking to you," Meredith says as she's walking me out.

"Alright," I say, stepping out on to the front porch. "Thanks for the coffee, Merry."

"Oh, and Will?"

"Yeah?" I ask, turning around.

"*Please* stop calling me 'Merry.' I hate that. My grandmother always calls me that and it drives me crazy."

. . .

"Oh. Okay."

I turn back around as she closes the front door. And I smile.

He got me again.

The sun is shining today and it shouldn't be because Tommy Redivo is gone. But then on second thought, a rainy, overcast day would make for far too obvious symbolism to ever suit Tom. Yes, the more I think about it, perhaps a bright, sunny day to mark his passing is more appropriate— a paradox to mark the passing of an eternal paradox, for his ending solves no mysteries about him, answers no questions. Until time's end, he will remain the enigma he was in life.

DAVID SORRENTINO

The paradox with a face, the contradiction with a name: Tommy Redivo.

Oh, I'm not saying he's dead. Or alive, either. But whatever the case may be, he's still gone. And I can't be sure I'll ever see him again.

How am I supposed to go on? Tommy's the guy who opened up the whole world to me. He taught me to rollerblade. Pushed me onstage to read that poem I wrote during open mic night at the coffee house that time. Gave me the courage to jump off that bunjee platform. He introduced me to the best fucking music on this earth; taught me what punk, hardcore, alternative, goth, power-pop, reggae, ska, and Oi! were. Dragged me to a million different clubs to hear a million different (and fantastic) no-name bands; not to mention Giants Stadium and U2, and Lollapalooza '93 with Alice In Chains and Dinosaur Jr. . . He braved the pit with me. Introduced me to underground comix. Got me drunk for the first time. He taught me about philosophy, God, the very meaning of life. . . He got me laid, fer Chrissake!

He taught me to live and then he died.

And the more I think about it, maybe he is dead. I can believe it—there's just something all-too poetic about it. I keep thinking that if this were a novel, it would have to end with his death. The first twenty chapters have been leading up to it and no place else. Makes perfect dramatic sense, right? While the rest of us fade into the pathos of old age, Tom Redivo laughs at us from the other side; never a day older, forever in the prime of life. . . I can almost see him now, hangin' out with Kurt up there, in the parking lot behind that great hardcore club in the sky.

There's this one short story Tom wrote that comes to mind— I forget what he titled it. Or if he titled it. Anyway, it was unlike most of his other stuff. . . kinda Vonnegut, actually. In it, this thirty-something guy goes out looking for this famous, old Indian medicine man on some reservation out west, somewhere. The guy's life is a real mess and he's hoping this Indian guy can offer him some life-changing words of wisdom; maybe provide some idea for a solution or two. But instead, the medicine man ends up giving the guy this magic peyote that sends him back in time— he wakes up to find himself a child again, only with all of his adult memories. And the guy finds that by re-experiencing his childhood with the adult perspective, he gains self-understanding. And with it, peace.

. . .Or something like that. It's been a while since I've read it. Anyhow, it was a very nostalgic story. All of Tom's writing is nostalgic, really, but this one was nostalgic in a sweet way; not bitter or remorseful like his other stuff. I was just thinking about it because I find myself wishing I could go back and re-live all the great times I've had these last four years. . . with Tom, with everybody. All those great times that are now lost to me forever.

Driving home in my car right now, I don't believe I've ever felt more alone.

EPILOGUE

I wasn't sure if I had lost my mind at that point, but I needed to find Tom. I needed to know what had happened to him and why; for my own peace of mind. And the only one left to talk to who might have been able to reveal his whereabouts was his grandmother. So I had decided to drive to Northdale to pay her a visit.

Going down Route 19, I was devoting half my attention to the traffic and the other half to the radio. To save my life, I couldn't find anything decent— I swear, if I had to hear that stupid Alanis song one more time, the one where she has sex in the theatre, I probably would've grabbed an axe and wiped out a small town. Alanis, Candlebox, Bush, Hootie. . . Can someone explain to me what the fuck happened, exactly? 'Cause I *still* don't get it. For one brief, shining moment there was actually *good* music on the radio— even Z-100 was listenable for about ten seconds there. Once Nirvana broke, wasn't all the crap-rock like Poison and Skid Row supposed to be banished from the face of the earth forever?

I was driving down the highway, lamenting all this, when some old, beat-up Volkswagen Rabbit blew by me with a "Kurt Cobain Lives!" bumper sticker.

Yeah. Synchronicity, Tom woulda called it.

I fished around under the driver's seat looking for a cassette. I came up with this old Replacements bootleg Tom had given me about two years before and popped it in.

"Write you a letter tomorrow. . ."

I tapped my fingers on the steering wheel in time with the music as I drove past the familiar row of middle class homes on Deo Street, many still with Halloween decorations up, until I reached the house of Tom's grandmother. As I got out of the car that Indian summer day, the sky had that purple-yet-not-really-purple glow it tends to get when it's cloudy and warm and on the verge of a massive downpour. And as I was looking up at that sky, I couldn't stop thinking about how stupid this was.

I mean, I had met Mary Redivo once, over three years before— how was she supposed to remember me? And how was I supposed to even begin to explain what I wanted from her? *Hello Mrs. Redivo, you probably don't remember me, but I'm a friend of your grandson and I was just wondering if you could tell me if you know whether he's alive or dead. Thank you so kindly for your time. Good day.*

Somehow though, I mustered the courage to begin the walk toward her front door. Then, halfway across the lawn, I wondered if I might not be better off going round back. So I turned around and started up the driveway, into the backyard. Once in back, I could hear this banging noise coming from the garage— somebody was working on something in there. And since I felt uncomfortable just knocking on the back door (because like I said, I wasn't sure his grandmother would even remember me), I figured I'd go see who was working in the garage, introduce myself, and then whoever it was could sort of re-introduce me to Mrs. Redivo.

So into the garage I went. Inside, working on the back wall, was this long-haired guy with a short beard, wearing a baseball cap along with beat up blue jeans and a dark, dingy T-shirt. He didn't see me come in. I cleared my throat before speaking to let the guy know he had company.

"Excuse me, I'm looking for Mary Redivo. . . Do you know if she's home?" The guy just looked back at me and smiled as he removed his cap. I started to take a couple steps forward, figuring he must not have heard me.

"I was just asking you if Mrs. Redivo was in."

"Sorry Will, but she's out at the moment."

It was his voice.

"Tom?"

"Have I changed that much, mud brother?"

At first, I just stood there with my mouth open. Then I threw my arms around him and hugged him. The gesture must have taken him by surprise, 'cause it took a long moment before he hugged me back. Words can't begin to capture the relief I was feeling. Before then, I don't think I had realized just how terrified I was at the prospect of never seeing him again. It was like I had been holding my breath for nearly three months and then was suddenly, finally, allowed to exhale.

"Beer for breakfast this morning, William?" he joked. I laughed.

"Have you been here all along?" It was weird, seeing him with the beard and long hair. Part of me still couldn't believe it. How could I not have recognized him?

"Yeah," he answered. "The whole time since I left the west coast, basically." Behind me, Tempest was barking.

"Temp!" I got down on my knees and hugged her, too. "How ya doin' girl?"

"Hmph. She's slowin' down. Never even heard your car pull in." I looked down in her face and noticed she appeared a little whiter around the muzzle since I last saw her.

"So what the hell have you been up to?" I asked him, unsure whether or not I shouldn't be a little more pissed off at him for hiding out so long.

"I've been keepin' myself busy around here." He showed me the nails in his left hand and the hammer in his right. "So who ratted me out— Meredith?"

"No," I answered. Then it sank in. "Wait— Meredith knew?"

"Of course," he said, putting down his tools and dusting off his hands. "The whole family knows. She really didn't tell you?"

"No. I was just playin' a hunch comin' here. . ."

"Jeez. Sorry, Will. When I asked them to keep a lid on things, I didn't think they'd keep it from you. That was never my intention." He looked around for a second, seeming lost, momentarily. "Where are my manners? Come on in the house, I'll getcha something to drink."

He led me into the basement of the house where I sat down at Nanna's table while he stepped into his father's old room to change into a fresh T-shirt. Then he grabbed the obligatory cans of Yoo-hoo from the refrigerator and sat down with me.

"Is that where you've been sleeping?" I asked, referring to his Dad's room.

"Yeah," he answered as Zappa's "King Kong" softly played in the background.

"Has it been weird?"

"Not at all. Quite the opposite, in fact— it feels like this house was made for me."

"I bet your grandmother's been glad to have you."

"I guess so. I certainly hope that's the case." He smiled.

"So you haven't been by the house in Oakwood at all?"

"Nope. I'm tryin' to keep a low profile."

"So then Lisa and girls have been coming here to see you?"

"Every other day or so, yeah. They'll either drop by here or I'll meet them somewhere, incognito."

"I never would've guessed," I said with a stroke of my chin.

"Enough about me, already. How have *you* been?" he asked, taking a deep quaff from his can of Yoo-hoo.

"Pretty good," I answered, leaning back in my chair.

"And how's school?"

"Good," I said. "I'll probably be graduating after the spring semester. My old man isn't all that thrilled about it taking me an extra year. . . but fuck 'em— I'm the one payin' for tuition anyway, right?"

"Attaboy, Will. Stick it to Uncle Charlie." Now *I* smiled. "And how's Kate?"

"She's alright." I paused momentarily, trying to be as dramatic as possible. "You know, I broke up with Kate just a couple weeks ago."

"What?!?"

I knew he would be shocked.

"Yeah, well, it seemed like we were arguing all the time, and then it started feeling like we were just staying together out of. . . I don't know. Habit, I guess."

"Whoa. So you went free-agent, huh?"

"Um, well, not exactly. There is this one girl I've kinda been seeing, Jeanine. . ."

"Will, you *dog!*" I felt myself blush a little.

"What about you and ·Star? What happened there?" Then I checked myself. "I'm sorry; maybe you don't wanna talk about it."

"No, it's alright. I mean, there isn't much to say, really. It just didn't work out." He put his empty Yoo-hoo can back down on the table. "You still see Courtney around?"

I dont know why I felt glad that he asked that question. I guess the fact that he still cared about Courtney just said something about his character; vindicated my high opinion of him, somehow.

"Yeah," I told him.

"She seeing anybody?" It sounded so casual the way he asked. The old boy was as smooth as ever.

"Uh, well. . . I heard she was sorta goin' out with that Norman-guy. . ."

Tom winced like he just took a whiff of some sour milk. "Mmmm," he moaned, Marge Simpson-like.

We both fell silent, and I took the opportunity to gather the nerve to finally say what I had been waiting months to tell him.

"Tom, I just want to tell you that I'm sorry for dumping all that shit on you back at your party. I was totally wrong."

"You have nothing to apologize for, Will," he said. "Actually, I'm quite proud of you."

"Proud? Of *me?*"

"Hell yeah, are you kidding? I probably would've harbored the same doubts in your position— at least you had the guts to tell me what you really thought. Of course I'm proud of you."

I took a moment to revel, privately.

"But look," he continued soberly, "I had to make a choice. I compromised. Now 'compromise' is normally the dirtiest word in my vocabulary, but the trade-off here was *freedom*, Will. Freedom for me *and* my family. I can be whatever I want now, and so can they."

"I'm glad for you, bro. Really— I mean it." And I did, too.

"There were times the last year and a half where it really killed me, some of those stupid commercials and shit, like I was selling my pride, my dignity." He paused, thoughtfully. "It didn't always go down easy, but. . . sometimes you gotta die a little before you can live, y'know?"

"Funny you should put it that way," I began with a chuckle. "because for a while there, I was thinking you had really checked out on us for good."

"What?" he asked, bemused. "You mean the bridge-thing?"

"Yeah. Not that the bridge-thing was true, specifically, but. . ."

"Nah, no way. I mean, I've thought about it in the same way everyone has, I guess. You know-— in that abstract, George Bailey, what-would-the-world-have-been-like-if-I-were-never-born, kind of way. And whenever I think about it, I always come back to my sisters, my mother, my grandmother. . . What would they think? Wouldn't they be asking themselves why they weren't good enough reason for me to stick around? Why they didn't make my life worth living? Even Tempest— I can imagine her wondering on some level, where I went, why I left her. I could never hurt them like that. I could never abandon them like that."

I noticed the clock on the wall. Then checked my own watch.

"Jesus," I said, standing up. "I told Jeanine I'd meet her at seven. By the time I get home and shower an' all. . ."

"Hey, I understand," he said. "You go take care of business." He and Tempest both got up to escort me out the back door.

"So what are you going to do?" I asked him.

"Well, long term I got my fingers in a couple different pies. For one, I recently signed a publishing contract. A multi-book deal."

"Alright! Congratulations!"

"Yeah. . . First, of course, they want an autobiography that they can release in 1999, in time for Woodstock's thirtieth anniversary. But after that, I'll be free to write what I like— philosophy, fiction, whatever." He held open the back door for Tempest and me.

"An autobiography? For real?"

"Well, they're looking for one of those tell-all deals where I name all the celebrity women I've bagged, but it's gonna be a little different from what they expect."

"1999," I said, clearing my throat. "That's almost *Killraven* territory, mud brother."

"Mm. *Deathlok* territory, anyway."

"Think they'll have another Wodstock concert in '99?" I wondered. Tom laughed.

"As long as there's a dollar to be made, it's a pretty safe bet!"

"Right, right," I agreed. "So you wanna get together next week, maybe? I'd love for you to meet Jeanine. . ."

"I'm afraid I can't— there's this film project I'm involved with. I'll be flying out west to work on it at the end of the week."

I swear, it was like I just got kicked in the nuts.

"I guess you'll be moving back out that way?"

"Dear God, no!" His eyes bugged. "Believe me, I tried like hell to get it done out here, but it's just not practical."

"What is it about? How'd you get involved in a movie?"

"You know the director, Leo Napolitano? Well, I met him on *The Tonight Show* over a year ago and we hit it off pretty well— we were pretty simpatico as far as our tastes an' all, in movies, books. So I pitched him this old story idea I had bouncin' around in my head, he liked it, and now we're makin' it happen!"

"Do I know it? Is it the one about the old Indian guy and the peyote?"

"No, you don't know this one— it's actually based on a story I wrote back in high school. The first real short story I ever wrote, if you don't count the homemade comics I used to make in the second grade."

"So what's the plot, already? C'mon, give it up!"

He smiled. "It's about this guy who grows up thinking his father is dead, then finds out his Mom's been lying to him and that he's really alive. So he sets out across country to find him."

"Are you just writing this, or. . ." I grinned. "What?"

"I regret to announce that I *will* be making my acting debut in this particular vehicle." He sort of shrugged and looked down at the ground.

"Ah, I always knew you were really a big ham."

"Well, the story is pretty close to my heart, and Leo tells me I've got name recognition, so. . ."

"Hey, I'm just bustin' you, man— I'm sure you'll be great."

"Thanks," he told me, still looking slightly uneasy. It was a rare sight, seeing a self-conscious Tommy Redivo. "It should be fun. Plus the story is my baby. The first of many babies to come, I hope."

"I can't wait to see it."

"Maybe you'll star in the next project." I laughed at this. "You never know— it's possible. It's all possible now. We're free, Will."

"So how long will you be out in L.A.?"

"Four, five weeks. We really can't afford to run any longer than that— it's a really low-fi, character-driven story that we'd like to wrap up and have done in time for Sundance in January."

"Sounds like you're gonna be pretty busy," I said dolefully.

"Look, I'll be back, okay?" he responded with a slap on my back. "I'll parachute in for Thanksgiving, then be back full-time before Christmas. Come April, I'll be there for the first softball game of the season. . . Don't even tell anybody in advance; I'll just show up. Then we'll throw a huge Midsummers Eve party— we'll make it an 80s theme this time around. I'll have Meredith load up the CD changer with Duran Duran, Culture Club, Cyndi Lauper. . ."

"Really Tom?" There was alot of hope in my voice. He made it sound like re-capturing some of those old times was really possible. I wanted very badly to believe him, but it just sounded too good to be true.

"William, William, William," he scolded. "Cautious cynicism is one thing; being utterly faithless is another."

I started to feel guilty. "I'm sorry," I said. "You're right."

"See you Christmas time, mud brother?" he asked, offering his hand.

"See you then."

We shook hands. Then he surprised me with a hug. Wordlessly, I turned and walked back to my car. When I started the engine, the 'Mats came blasting over the speakers.

"Jesus rides beside me!"

Quickly, I lowered the volume. Guess I had forgotten to turn the stereo off when I pulled in. Tom remained standing in front of the car, smiling at me. I just sat there a moment and looked at him. And remembered.

Remembered the guy who doted on his Nanna while imploring American youth to "kill" their parents. Remembered the guy who spoke so eloquently about God and the beauty of nature, while also gleefully prophesizing the world's imminent, violent end. I remembered the guy who sang along to cheesy disco songs with his sisters, who also merrily castrated his step-father. I remembered that gentle, nurturing soul, looking after his dog and dutifully watering his plants, who also beat Lou Adubato into mulch with his fists.

He gave me the thumbs up as I put it in reverse. I honked my horn as I backed out of the driveway.

"Lights that flash in the evening... through a hole in the drapes..."

Tempest barked and Tom waved goodbye as I started down the street.

"I'll be home when I'm sleepin'..."

I watched him in my rearview mirror as I pulled away, still waving as he fell back into the horizon...

"An' I can't hardly wait..."

COMING SOON
FROM PARADOX BOOKS

I've Got A Name
What defines a family? How do you choose between your blood and your conscience? And how much is a persons name worth? An adult adoptee finds himself still struggling with these questions even after being reunited with his biological family for ten years.
Coming in 2002

Lump
What do you call an agoraphobic, paranoid, obsessive-compulsive, manic depressive, who lives in sweat pants and whose only ambition is to lie in bed and sleep until he dies? We call him "lump."
Coming in 2005

For more information on these and other titles, contact us at:

Paradox Books
P.O. Box 1081
Maplewood, NJ 07040

Or visit us in cyberspace at:

http://members.aol.com/paradox070